also by
SCARLETT ST. CLAIR

When Stars Come Out

HADES X PERSEPHONE
A Touch of Darkness
A Game of Fate
A Touch of Ruin
A Game of Retribution
A Touch of Malice
A Game of Gods
A Touch of Chaos

ADRIAN X ISOLDE
King of Battle and Blood
Queen of Myth and Monsters

FAIRY TALE RETELLING
Mountains Made of Glass

a TOUCH of CHAOS

SCARLETT ST. CLAIR

Bloom *books*

Sourcebooks and the colophon are registered trademarks of
Sourcebooks. Bloom Books is a trademark of Sourcebooks.

The characters and events portrayed in this book are fictitious or
are used fictitiously. Any similarity to real persons, living or dead,
is purely coincidental and not intended by the author.

All brand names and product names used in this book are trademarks,
registered trademarks, or trade names of their respective holders.
Sourcebooks is not associated with any product or vendor in this book.

Published by Bloom Books, an imprint of Sourcebooks
P.O. Box 4410, Naperville, Illinois 60567-410
(630) 961-3900
sourcebooks.com

Cataloging-in-Publication data is on file with the Library of Congress.

Printed and bound in Canada.
MBP 10 9 8 7 6 5 4 3 2

All good things come to an end.

Content Warning

This book contains scenes that reference suicide and scenes that contain sexual violence including dubious consent and sexual assault.

Specific references to suicide in this novel are in chapters XXXII (Theseus) and XXXVII (Theseus).

Specific references to sexual assault are in chapters XXXII (Theseus) and XXXVII (Theseus).

The specific scene with dubious consent is in chapter XI (Theseus).

The scenes are not detailed and fade to black but please read with caution or skip these scenes to protect your mental health.

If you or someone you know is contemplating suicide, please call the National Suicide Prevention Lifeline at 1-800-273-TALK (8255) or go online to suicidepreventionlifeline.org

Are you a survivor? Need assistance or support? National Sexual Assault Hotline 1-800-656-HOPE (4673) hotline.rainn.org/

Part I

"There will be killing till the score is paid."
—HOMER, *THE ODYSSEY*

CHAPTER 1
PERSEPHONE

Persephone's ears rang, and the Underworld trembled violently beneath her feet.

She was reeling from Hecate's words.

That is the sound of Theseus releasing the Titans.

Theseus, a son of Poseidon, a man she had met in passing only once, had managed to tear her life apart in a matter of hours. It had begun with the abduction of Sybil and Harmonia and spiraled from there. Now Zofie and Demeter were dead, the Helm of Darkness was gone, and Hades was missing.

She wasn't even sure that was the right word, but the fact was that she had not seen him since she'd left him in her office at Alexandria Tower, bridled by her magic. The look on his face as he'd watched her leave still haunted her, but there had been no other option. He wouldn't have let her go, and she wasn't going to let Hades face an eternity of punishment for not granting a favor.

But something was wrong, because Hades had not come for her, and he was not here now as their realm was being torn apart.

Another tremor rocked the Underworld, and Persephone looked at Hecate, who stood opposite her, eyes dark and face drawn.

"We have to go," Hecate said.

"Go?" Persephone echoed.

"We have to stop the Titans," Hecate said. "As much as we are able."

Persephone just stared. The Goddess of Witchcraft was a Titan herself. She might be able to fight the elder gods, but Persephone had only just managed to go up against her Olympian mother.

"Hecate, I can't—" she began, shaking her head, but Hecate took her face between her hands.

"You can," she said, her eyes peering straight to her soul. "You must."

You have no choice.

Persephone heard what Hecate did not say, though she knew the goddess was right. This went beyond protecting her realm.

It was about protecting the world.

She pushed aside her doubt, growing fierce in her determination to prove she was worthy of the crown and title she had been given.

"Oh, my dear," Hecate said, dropping her hands from her face and twining her fingers with Persephone's. "It isn't a question of worth."

It was all she said before her magic flared in a powerful burst and teleported them to the Asphodel Fields. Despite the destruction Persephone had witnessed when she had faced the Olympians outside Thebes, she'd still not managed to imagine what the Titans could do to her realm, but the reality was devastating.

The mountains of Tartarus had once risen and fallen steeply like the waves of an angry sea. Despite their use and the horror they contained, they had been beautiful—a dark and jagged shadow set against the muted horizon.

Now they were nearly leveled, as if crushed beneath the feet of a giant, and the sky was split, an angry wound open to the world above.

Something had already escaped the Underworld.

The ground shook, and a massive hand shot out from the depths of Tartarus, sending an explosion of rocks flying across the land. The head of a Titan emerged from the prison, and he gave a roaring cry. The sound was deafening and just as destructive, shattering nearby peaks as if they were nothing but glass.

Persephone recalled what Hades had said about the Titans. Since they were not dead, only imprisoned, they retained all their powers.

"Iapetus," Hecate said, her voice almost a hiss. "He is Cronos's brother and God of Immortality." Hecate met her gaze. "I'll take him. You must seal the sky."

Persephone nodded, though her mind scrambled to understand exactly what that meant. She had yet to use the magic she had been granted upon marrying Hades.

Hecate teleported first and appeared in the air over Iapetus's head. Suddenly, there were three of her, all surrounding the God of Immortality, and from her hands sprang black flames that she funneled in a burning stream toward the Titan. Iapetus's roar of anger vibrated the air as her magic struck.

With him distracted, Persephone called to the darkness within her, reaching for the feelings that had fueled her destruction of the Underworld when she had stumbled upon Hades and Leuce in the Forest of Despair. Recalling that time made her feel stretched and raw. Though what she had witnessed had not been real, the emotions still shuddered through her. From that anguish, her power bloomed, a force that called to the roots of the Upperworld above her. They broke through the darkened sky like serpents twining together, sealing the open chasm.

A sense of relief flooded her, and her attention turned to Hecate, who was still engaged with Iapetus. Now Persephone could focus on trapping the Titan within his mountainous prison, but something hard struck her, and she flew through the air. When she landed, she rolled to the very edge of Asphodel where the field dropped into a valley.

Persephone drew in a deep and haggard breath, though her lungs felt frozen in her chest, and rose onto her hands and knees, coming face-to-face with a monster—a creature with three heads, those of a lion, a goat, and a snake.

The lion roared in her face, lips peeling back from sharp teeth. The goat opened its mouth and breathed a noxious fire that singed the air. The snake shot forward rapidly but was not close enough to strike with its venomous fangs.

The creature was a chimera, a haphazard mix of animals, all dangerous to some degree, and it had escaped from Tartarus.

"*Fuck.*"

The monster pounced, and Persephone scrambled back, forgetting how close she was to the edge of the valley. She fell, tumbling over the side, hitting the unyielding, grassy earth.

She teleported and managed to land on her ass at the bottom of the meadow. She glared up at the chimera, which roared at her from above, and was surprised when another roar came from behind her. Persephone turned to find another chimera looming. Two others approached, flanking the monster.

She stumbled back as a shadow passed over her head. The first chimera had jumped from the cliff and joined the fray, slowly encroaching on what little space she had left.

"Why are there so many of you?" she muttered, frustrated as her eyes slid from creature to creature, assessing.

Suddenly a large pomegranate struck the goat head protruding from the back of one of the chimeras. It whipped its head to the side, breathing fire on an angry bellow, and set the creature beside it aflame. A horrible screech escaped its mouth, and it crashed to the ground, rolling in the thick grass, but the flames only seemed to spread.

More pomegranates followed the first one, raining down on the monsters. As they turned to face their new attackers, Persephone saw that the souls had gathered in a huge crowd. The first row were women and elders with baskets of fruit. Yuri was among them, and while Persephone's heart rose at the sight of her people, her delight quickly turned to horror as the chimera stalked toward them.

She had no idea what would happen to the dead when faced with a threat in their realm, but she did not wish to find out.

As she watched, however, the second row of souls came forward—armed men and women. Ian was in the lead, and he called out orders as the chimera approached.

"Go for their necks!" he said. "Their throats are made of fire and will melt your weapons and choke them to death."

While three of the chimeras charged toward the gathered souls, one turned toward Persephone. The lion bared its teeth while the goat's eyes reddened with fire. The snake reared, readying to strike. She backed away as the creature took one predatory step after another toward her, and just as it was about to attack, the wide jaws of its three heads unhinging, she teleported. She had every intention of summoning her magic, of trapping the creature in a bramble of thorns, but as soon as she appeared behind the chimera, a massive creature barreled into it. It took Persephone a moment to realize what had attacked—a three-headed dog.

Not just any three-headed dog—Cerberus, Typhon, and Orthrus.

She had never seen them in their singular form, but Hades had spoken of it. "*Cerberus is a monster*," he'd said. "*Not an animal.*"

Sometimes Cerberus existed as one, sometimes he existed as three, and he seemed to have tripled in size, towering over her as he tossed the chimera into the air. It landed some distance away and did not move again. Cerberus turned toward Persephone, his large body wiggling at the sight of her.

"Cerberus—"

Her words were cut short when a sharp crack drew her attention to the mountainous horizon where Hecate was still battling Iapetus. The Titan's massive hands had managed to slip between the mighty roots Persephone had summoned to seal off the sky, and with one quick jerk, they tore free. A few terrified screams erupted from the souls gathered in the meadow as splintered wood rained down across the Underworld.

More of the mountains gave way beneath the impact of the falling roots. A keen and angry wail followed as seven snakelike heads emerged from the crumbling depths of Tartarus. Persephone's blood ran cold, recognizing the bulbous frame of the Hydra.

"Fuck!"

She'd only had a modicum of control over this situation before, and now she had none.

"Looks like you're in a pickle, Sephy."

She looked to her left where Hermes had manifested in all his golden glory, still dressed in armor from their encounter with the Olympians. She had lost track of him on the battlefield, but he had been one of the first to stand with her and against Zeus—he and Apollo.

The familiar scent of earthy laurel drew Persephone's attention, and she turned to see the God of Music on her right. He looked stoic and calm and offered a small smile.

"Hey, Seph," he said.

She smiled back. "Hey, Apollo."

"Rude," said Hermes. "I didn't get a greeting."

"Hi, Hermes," she said, looking back at him.

He scoffed. "It doesn't mean anything if I have to point it out."

She grinned and burst into tears at the same time, overwhelmed with gratitude by their presence.

"Don't cry, Sephy," said Hermes. "It was just a joke."

"She isn't crying over your stupid joke," Apollo snapped.

"Oh? And you know her so well?"

"He isn't wrong, Hermes," Persephone said, wiping at her eyes quickly. "I'm just…really glad you are both here."

Hermes's expression softened, but their attention was soon drawn to Tartarus again when the Hydra roared and launched itself from the peak upon which it was poised, landing in the Forest of Despair. Trees snapped beneath its massive body as if they were nothing but twigs. The monster's heads whipped about, slinging its poisonous venom. It landed across the Underworld like a deadly rain, burning and blackening whatever it touched, including a chimera whose horrid wail filled the air as the poison burned the creature to death.

At the same time, Iapetus had managed to free himself further, and now his entire head was exposed, down to his wide shoulders. His face was thin and his eyes sunken and angry, gleaming as if filled with fire. He looked wicked and unkind, and while Persephone had expected nothing different from the Titan who had been locked away for centuries, it was another thing to be faced with the sharp force of his fury.

Persephone could feel Hecate's ancient magic rush over her, as if she were drawing energy from every-thing within the Underworld. It raised the hair on her arms and the back of her neck, stole the moisture from her tongue. Then Hecate released her power in a great burst. Iapetus folded beneath its weight, his head striking the mountains, but Persephone knew it was not enough.

"We have to get them back into Tartarus," Persephone said.

"We'll work on that," said Hermes. "You worry about that massive hole in the sky."

They must have sensed her doubt because Apollo added, "You've got this, Seph. You are Queen of the Underworld."

"The one and only," said Hermes. "That we know of."

Persephone and Apollo glared.

"It's just a *joke*," Hermes whined.

Apollo sighed and took a few steps forward. His bow materialized in his hand, his quiver on his back. "Let's go, Hermes."

The God of Mischief took a step and then twisted to face Persephone. "If it helps at all," he said, "there is no one else."

She knew what he meant. No one else could trap the Titans or contain the monsters in Tartarus. No one else could mend the broken sky.

That was power granted to the King and Queen of the Underworld.

It was either Hades or it was her, and Hades was not here.

His absence made her chest ache, though she knew it was not time to agonize over what had befallen him since she'd last seen him. She had to deal with what was before her first, and the sooner she was able to contain this threat, the sooner she could find her husband.

Hermes's wings unfurled behind him, and he

launched himself into the air before bolting across the realm to the Hydra with Apollo in tow.

Persephone teleported to the edge of the Asphodel Fields. Alone, she took a moment to observe the chaos.

She had often been aware of her faults but never so much as she was at this very moment. The mountains of Tartarus were nothing more than piles of rubble, the beauty of Hades's magic was marred by patches of scorched and smoking earth from the Hydra's venom, the air smelled like burning flesh, and amid all this, the souls still fought the chimeras. Hermes wielded his golden sword against the Hydra while Apollo sent rays of blinding light to cauterize the wounds and prevent the heads from regenerating. Iapetus continued to rock the Underworld, fighting beneath Hecate's magic.

Persephone took a breath and closed her eyes. As she did, she felt the world around her go quiet. Nothing seeped into her space save her anger, her pain, her worry. Her ears rang with it, her heart pumped with it, and she used it to draw on the darker part of her magic. It was the part of her that ached, the part of her that raged, the part of her that no longer believed the world was wholly good.

"*You are my wife and my queen.*"

Hades's voice echoed in her mind. It sent chills down her spine and cradled her heart. The sound brought tears to her eyes and made her chest feel tight, stealing the air from her lungs.

"*You are everything that makes me good,*" he said. "*And I am everything that makes you terrible.*"

She swallowed the thickness that had gathered in her throat. Before, she would have balked at those words, but now she understood the power in being feared.

And she wanted to be dreaded.

"*Where are you?*" she asked, desperate for him to manifest at her side where he belonged, but the longer she remained alone, the darker her energy became.

"*Waiting to carry you through the dark if you will bring me to the light.*"

Her heart felt so heavy, a weight in her chest.

"I need you," she whispered.

"*You have me,*" he said. "*There is no part where you end or I begin. Use me, darling, as you have for your pleasure. There is power in this pain.*"

And there was *pain*.

It radiated through her, a bone-deep sorrow that had become so much a part of her that it almost seemed normal. She could not remember who she was before the hollow ache of grief had carved a spot in her heart.

"*You are more now that I am gone,*" said Lexa.

Persephone squeezed her eyes shut against her best friend's cruel words, though she knew they were true. Strange that life granted power in the face of loss, stranger yet that the person who would be most proud was not here to witness it.

"*I know your truth,*" Lexa said. "*I do not need to witness it.*"

Something cut through Persephone then, a pain so deep she could not contain it, and when her eyes opened, her vision was sharpened from the glow of her eyes. Her power waited, obedient to her will, a flame wreathing her body. For a moment, everything stilled, and she felt Hades's presence as if he had come up behind her and wrapped a possessive arm around her waist.

"*Feed it,*" he commanded, and with his warm breath on her ear, she screamed.

Her anguish became a real and living thing as her power gathered around her. It flooded the Underworld, darkening the sky. Shadows flew from the palms of her hands, turning into solid spears, impaling the chimeras and the Hydra. A cacophony of shrill screams and pained roars filled the air, and it fueled her, made her dig deeper until the earth began to tremble and the ground beneath the Hydra and the mountains of Tartarus turned dark and liquid. Thick tendrils shot out from the pool, latching onto the Hydra's large, clawed feet and what remained of its heads, dragging the monster down into its depths until its screams were suddenly silenced.

Her magic rose in dark waves over Iapetus too, aided by Hecate, whose power drove the Titan farther into his cell in the mountains, though he fought against it, arms stretched out, reaching for the still-open sky. Her darkness continued to climb, matting his hair and blinding his eyes, spilling into his open mouth. He wailed in anger until his throat was full and he could no longer speak, and when he was covered, the magic hardened, and the mountains of Tartarus shone like glistening obsidian against the dark horizon.

From the tallest peak, which was the tip of Iapetus's hand, now frozen in hard stone, her magic continued to build, mending the broken sky, and when it was finished, she dropped her hands, and her magic reeled back, ricocheting through her. She trembled but remained on her feet. She felt something wet on her face, and when she reached to touch her mouth, she found blood.

She frowned.

"Sephy, you were amazing!" Hermes said as he appeared before her. He swept her into a tight hug.

Despite the way his armor dug into her body, she welcomed his embrace.

When he set her on her feet, it was before Apollo, Hecate, and Cerberus, who was still fused into a large three-headed monster. He ambled forward and nuzzled her hand gently, all three sets of jowls dripping with saliva and blood.

She didn't care and stroked each of the heads anyway.

"Good boys," she said. "Very good boys."

In the meadow below, the souls cheered. Their enthusiasm would normally lift her heart, but instead, she felt dread.

Would her magic hold? Could she keep them safe?

Her gaze shifted to the horizon and the strange tower that now connected the mountains of Tartarus to the sky. She had no idea how she'd created it, but she knew what had fed her magic. She could still feel those emotions echoing inside her.

"I like it," said Hermes. "It's art. We'll call it… *Iapetus's reckoning.*"

Persephone thought it looked more like a scar, a blight on Hades's kingdom, but perhaps he would fix it when he came home.

Something thick gathered in the back of her throat, and she couldn't swallow. She turned to look at everyone, searching each face as if one of them might hold the answer to her greatest question.

"Where is Hades?" she asked.

CHAPTER II
HADES

The burn in his wrists woke him. The headache splitting his skull made opening his eyes nearly impossible, but he tried, groaning, his thoughts shattering like glass. He had no ability to pick at the pieces, to recall how he had gotten here, so he focused instead on the pain in his body—the metal digging into the raw skin on his wrists, the way his nails pierced his palm, the way his fingers throbbed from being curled into themselves when they should be coiled around Persephone's ring.

The ring. It was gone.

Hysteria built inside him, a fissure that had him straining against his manacles, and he finally tore open his eyes to find that he was restrained in a small, dark cell. As he dangled from the ceiling, body draped in the same heavy net that had sent him to the ground in the Minotaur's prison, he knew he was not alone.

He stared into the darkness, uneasy, aware that whatever magic existed there was his own, and yet it felt somehow foreign, likely because though he called to it, he could not summon it.

"I know you're there," Hades said. His tongue felt swollen in his mouth.

In the next second, Theseus appeared, having pulled the Helm of Darkness from his head. He cradled the weapon in his arm, smirking.

"Theseus," Hades growled, though even to him, his voice sounded weak. He was so tired and so full of pain, he could not vocalize the way he wished. Otherwise, he would rage.

"I'd hoped to make a more dramatic entrance," said the demigod, his aqua eyes gleaming. Hades hated those eyes, so like Poseidon's. "But you always were a killjoy."

Dread tightened Hades's chest, though he worked not to show a single ounce of fear. He hated that he even felt the threat of such an emotion in the presence of Theseus, but he had to know how the demigod had come into possession of his helm.

"How did you get it?"

"Your wife led me right to it," Theseus said. "I told you I only needed to borrow her."

Hades had many questions, but he asked the most pressing.

"Where is she?" he demanded.

"I must confess, I lost track of her," Theseus said airily, as if he had not been in possession of the thing Hades loved most in this world.

He jerked forward. He wanted to wrap his hands around Theseus's neck and squeeze until he felt his bones break beneath his hands, but the weight of the net made movement nearly impossible. It was as if he were suffocating instead. His chest heaved as he worked to catch his breath.

Theseus chuckled and Hades glared at him, his eyes watering from exertion. He had never felt so weak. In truth, he had never *been* this weak.

"Last time I saw her, she was fighting her mother in the Underworld. I wonder who won."

"I will kill you, Theseus," Hades said. "That is an oath."

"I have no doubt you will try, though I think you will have a difficult time given your current state."

Hades's rage ignited, burning him from the inside out, but he could do nothing—not move or summon his power.

This, he thought, *must be what it is like to be mortal.* It was terrible.

Theseus smirked and then held up the helm, studying it.

"This is an intriguing weapon," he said. "It made it entirely too easy to enter Tartarus."

"It sounds like you wish to boast, Theseus," said Hades, glaring. "So why don't you get it over with?"

"It is not boasting at all," Theseus replied. "I am paying you a courtesy."

"By breaking into my realm?"

"By letting you know that I have released your father from Tartarus."

"My father?" Hades repeated, unable to keep the surprise from his voice. He could not describe exactly how he felt, only that this news left him feeling numb. If he'd had the energy to move, it would have stopped him in his tracks.

His father, Cronos, God of Time, was free, wandering the Upperworld after nearly five millennia locked away. Cronos, the man who had envied his own father's rule and took him down with a scythe that had recently resurfaced in the black market. The man who had feared the fated uprising of his children so much that he had swallowed them whole as they were born.

It was Zeus who had freed them from that horrible and dark prison, and when they had emerged, they had been fully grown and full of wrath. Even now, Hades could recall how he'd felt, the way anger had moved through his body, the way vengeance had crowded his mind, fed every thought. After they'd succeeded in overthrowing the Titans, those feelings followed him, bleeding into every aspect of his reign and rule.

It did not seem like so long ago.

"I do not know who else managed to escape with him," Theseus said. "I must confess, I had to leave, but we are sure to find out in the coming days."

"You *imbecile*," Hades seethed, his voice quiet. "Do you know what you have done?"

It was not as if Cronos had been asleep for the last five thousand years. He'd spent all his time in Tartarus conscious and planning revenge just as Hades was doing now. He worried over what his father would do first with his freedom. His thoughts turned to his mother, Rhea.

Rhea, who had tricked Cronos into swallowing a rock so that Zeus might live to overthrow him.

It was she who would receive Cronos's wrath first. Hades was sure of it.

"Come on, Hades," said Theseus. "We both know I do not make rash decisions. I have thought about this for a while."

"And what exactly did you think? That you would release my father from Tartarus and he would be so indebted to you that he would join your cause?"

"I am under no such delusion," said Theseus. "But I will use him as I imagine he will use me."

"Use you?" Hades asked. "And what do you have to offer?"

Theseus grinned. It was an unsettling smile because it was so genuine.

"To start," he said, "I have you."

Hades stared for a moment. "So you will what? Give me as a sacrifice?"

"Well, yes," Theseus said. "Cronos will need offerings to feed his power and strength. Who better than his son and a usurper too?"

"Your father was a usurper. Will you sacrifice him?"

"If the occasion calls for it," Theseus said.

Hades was not surprised by the demigod's answer. His honesty was also likely an indication of his belief that Hades would never leave this prison.

"What happens when you both decide the other must die?" he asked.

"I suppose it is good then that I am fated to overthrow the gods," said Theseus.

Hades knew the demigod was referring to the prophecy of the ophiotaurus, a half-bull, half-serpent creature whose death assured victory against the gods.

Theseus had been the one to slay the monster, and he assumed that meant he would overthrow the Olympians, but the prophecy never specified how or whose victory would come about.

His arrogance would be his downfall, but Hades was not about to argue. Theseus could face the consequences of his hubris, as all inevitably did.

"You are not even invincible. Do you think you can win against the gods?"

Perhaps he should not have said it, but he wanted Theseus to know he knew his greatest weakness—that he could not heal like other gods. Dionysus had discovered as much when he was trapped on the island of Thrinacia. Hades wished more than anything that he could test it himself, and one day soon, he would.

Shadows darkened the lines on Theseus's face, and an evil Hades had never seen before lurked behind his eyes. The demigod dropped the helm and drew a knife. Hades barely saw the gleaming blade before Theseus plunged it into his side. For a moment, his lungs felt locked, and he could not take in breath.

Theseus tilted his head up to meet Hades's gaze, speaking between his teeth.

"Perhaps you can tell me what it's like," he said, twisting the blade before tearing it from Hades's body.

Hades gritted his teeth against the pain, which was sharp and almost electric, radiating down his side. He refused to make a sound, to let the demigod know how he hurt.

Theseus raised the knife between them, stained with his blood. Hades recognized it as his father's scythe. Part of it anyway. The end was missing, having been found in Adonis's corpse after he'd been attacked outside La Rose. He had been the first victim of Theseus's campaign against the Olympians, a sacrifice made to antagonize Aphrodite. Later, Hades would discover the Goddess of Love had been chosen as a target by Demeter for her influence over his relationship with Persephone. It was the price she'd asked for in exchange for use of her magic and relics.

"Well, look at that," said Theseus. "You bleed like I bleed." He took a step away as if to admire his work. "You would do well to remember that beneath that net, you are mortal."

Hades had never been more aware as he struggled to breathe, his chest rising and falling sharply. He felt cold, his skin damp.

"You think you can make us all mortal?"

"Yes," said Theseus. "Just as easily as I can become invincible."

The demigod did not explain what he meant, but Hades could guess. There were only a few ways to become invincible in this world. One was through Zeus who, as King of the Gods, could grant invincibility. Another was to eat a golden apple from the Garden of the Hesperides, Hera's orchard, and since the two had formed some kind of alliance, he assumed that was the avenue the demigod would take.

Theseus sheathed the bloody knife and then picked up the Helm of Darkness before reaching into his pocket to withdraw something small and silver. Hades's heart squeezed at the sight of it.

"This is a beautiful ring," Theseus said, holding it between his thumb and forefinger, twisting it so that even beneath the dim light, the gems glittered. Hades watched it, his stomach knotting with each movement. "Who would have guessed it would be your downfall?"

Theseus was wrong.

That ring was Hades's hope even if he could not hold it, even if it was in the hand of his enemy.

"Persephone will come," he said, certain. His voice was quiet, his eyes heavy.

"I know," Theseus said, his fingers closing over the ring. He spoke with a dreadful glee that made Hades sick, though perhaps he was only feeling the weight of the net and his wound.

"She will be your ruin," Hades said to the demigod, his chest tightening with the truth of those words.

"*You would burn this world for me? I will destroy it for you*," she had said right before she had torn his realm apart in the name of a love she thought she had lost.

Theseus considered their love a weakness, but he would soon discover how wrong he was.

CHAPTER III
PERSEPHONE

"Where is my husband?" Persephone asked.

Hermes and Apollo exchanged a concerned look, but no one spoke.

The longer their silence continued, the more frantic she felt.

"Hecate?" Persephone looked at the triple goddess whose troubled expression did nothing to ease her worry. She took a step toward her. "You can track him," Persephone said, her hope rising, but there was a strange look on Hecate's face, a strange and terrifying look that instantly made her feel a keen sense of dread.

Hecate shook her head. "I've tried, Persephone."

"You haven't," Persephone said. "When?"

She refused to believe it, but she knew something was wrong. She had always been able to sense Hades's magic, but even that sensation was gone, and the emptiness made her tremble.

"Persephone," Hermes started, stepping toward her.

"Don't touch me," she snapped, glaring at him, glaring at all of them.

She did not want their comfort. She did not want their pity.

Those things made this real.

Her eyes blurred with tears.

She had come to expect certain truths—that dawn would break and night would fall, that life preceded death and hope followed despair. She had come to expect that Hades would always be by her side, and his absence now made the world feel wrong.

"I want my husband," she said, and a brutal cry tore from her throat. She covered her mouth as if to contain it and then vanished, teleporting to her office at Alexandria Tower where she'd left Hades tangled in a web of her magic. The evidence of her choice remained— the buckled floor, the broken vines. She had known he would not be here. She had known that her magic was only strong enough to hold him for a short time. Still, she'd held on to a small kernel of misguided hope.

She knelt on the broken ground and touched the dark and severed vines. As she reached out her hand, she was reminded of the weight that was missing there.

A burst of Hermes's warm magic alerted her that she was no longer alone.

"Theseus took my ring," Persephone said.

"Then we can guess what happened," he said.

Hades could track the ring, and he would have used it to locate her, but where was it now, and could they trace it?

"I shouldn't have left him," she said.

She should have called to him while she'd waited

with an ailing Lexa and Harmonia at the hotel, but she had been too afraid of the consequences. Even then, would it have mattered? She had no idea at what point he'd been led astray.

"You did what was necessary," Hermes said.

"What if it wasn't?" she asked, though no matter how she reflected on it, she still felt like she'd had no other choice. There had been too many threats at play—divine justice and Sybil's well-being—except that all Persephone wondered now was if she'd assigned Hades to some other terrible fate.

"It doesn't matter," Hermes said. "What's done is done."

She knew he was right. Their only option was to move forward.

She rose to her feet and then turned to face the god who had become one of her closest friends.

"Find my husband, Hermes. Do whatever you must."

He studied her for a moment, his beautiful face somehow soft and severe at the same time. "Do you know what you are asking, Sephy?"

She took a step closer, holding his golden gaze.

"I want blood, Hermes. I will fill rivers with it until he is found."

Theseus would soon discover that he had flown too close to the sun.

Hermes grinned. "I like vengeful Sephy," he said. "She's scary."

Her gaze shifted to the reddish glow just beyond her door. She left her office and stepped into the waiting area where the view overlooked New Athens.

Light burned the horizon, and Persephone thought

26

it looked a lot like fire. She had never thought she would see the sun as a threat, but today it felt like the dawn of a new and terrible world.

The irony was that no one else would know the horror of her night.

Today, mortals would wake to see that the snow had ceased to fall, that the clouds that had burdened the sky for weeks had parted. The media would run with stories of how the wrath of the Olympians had ended and assume that the battle outside Thebes was what brought Demeter's storm to an end.

"Is it wrong to feel angry that they will not know what horror we lived through last night?"

"No," said Hermes. "But I do not think that is what makes you angry right now."

She turned her head to the side, but he was still a step or two behind her.

"What do you know about my anger?"

"You do not like when beliefs are fueled by falsehoods. You see it as an injustice," he said.

He was not wrong.

It was the reason Theseus and his organization of Impious demigods and mortals angered her so much, and Helen, her once-loyal assistant, had only helped perpetuate those lies with her news articles. And what made her stories so believable was that they were anchored in just enough truth.

"Theseus would say that is power," she said.

"It is power," he agreed. "But there is power in many things."

She was quiet and she pressed her fingers against the cool glass, tracing the edge of the New Athens skyline.

27

"They think I lied," she said.

Right before everything had taken a turn for the worst—before Sybil had gone missing and the avalanche and ensuing battle, before Theseus had traded in his favor for her compliance—Helen had decided to reveal the secret of Persephone's divinity and accused her of deceiving New Greece.

Her timing, in many ways, had been impeccable. She had known that the world had come to admire and admonish Persephone, both for writing controversial articles about the gods but also for capturing the attention of the notoriously reclusive God of the Dead.

In some ways, she'd endeared herself to a mortal public that could see themselves in her.

Now they likely felt betrayed.

"Then tell the truth," Hermes said.

She lifted her head, watching the God of Mischief in the reflection of the window.

"Will that be enough?"

"It will have to be," he said. "It is all you can give."

It felt so silly, to worry over what people thought after everything that had happened in the last twenty-four hours, but to mortals, the world was still recognizable. They would demand answers to the accusations Helen had leveled, ignorant of Persephone's agony, of Hades's absence, of Theseus's terrorism.

She was quiet for a moment and then turned to face him fully.

"Summon Ilias," she said. "We have work to do."

Before they began, however, she needed to see Sybil and Harmonia.

Persephone returned to the Underworld and found her friends in the queen's suite. Harmonia was asleep in her bed while Sybil lay beside her, wide awake and watching as if she feared her girlfriend might cease to breathe if she didn't remain alert.

Persephone knew that horror.

As she entered, Sybil looked up and whispered her name, rising and rushing to her. The oracle burst into tears as she threw her arms around Persephone's neck.

"I'm so sorry, Sybil," she said quietly, not wishing to disturb Harmonia, who lay unmoving.

Sybil pulled away just a fraction and met Persephone's gaze. Her eyes were rimmed in red, and stray tears tracked down her face.

"It wasn't your fault," she managed on a shaky breath.

But Persephone felt responsible. It was hard not to given that Theseus had targeted her because of their friendship.

Persephone took a breath. "What happened?"

Sybil swallowed, her gaze falling to Harmonia. Outwardly, she looked mostly healed. It was clear that either Sybil or Hecate had done their best to clean the dirt and dried blood from her face, though it still matted her pale hair.

"They came in the night, silent. I don't think they expected either of us to wake as soon as they appeared, but we did. I had been dreaming of death, and Harmonia felt their magic."

"So they were demigods?"

"Only two," she said. "They must have let the rest of their men into the apartment once they teleported inside."

"How many in total?" Persephone asked.

Sybil shook her head, shrugging a shoulder. "I'm not certain. Five or six."

Five or six men just to capture Sybil. Persephone had known from Theseus that they had not anticipated Harmonia's presence in the apartment, and her resistance was why she'd been hurt so badly.

"They came to wound, Persephone," Sybil said. "Not only me but you too."

Persephone knew, and it made her feel sick. It was hard to imagine that while she had walked down the aisle toward the love of her life, her friends had suffered at the hands of a deranged demigod.

"Did you see Helen?" she asked.

She asked because she wanted to know just how entwined her former friend had become with Theseus. What plans was she helping him execute, and did she feel anything as she watched them suffer?

In some ways, Persephone blamed herself. She was the one who had encouraged Helen to get close to Triad after she expressed interest in writing about the organization, though it was evident now the kind of person she was. She had no real sense of loyalty to anything, save herself.

"No," Sybil whispered.

Persephone's jaw tightened. She had only felt inclined toward vengeance a few times in her life, and this was one. With the way she felt right now—with the rage that simmered inside her—she could not say what she would do when she saw Helen again, but the reality was that Persephone had already crossed a line. She had killed her mother, even if it was not what she had intended.

Would she kill Helen if given the chance?

"She isn't healing," Sybil said after a beat of silence.

Persephone's head whipped to the side. "What do you mean?"

"Hecate said whatever she was stabbed with is preventing her from healing. When I asked her why, she said she didn't know."

Persephone's stomach turned.

Hecate always knew.

"What about you?" Persephone asked, her eyes falling to Sybil's hand, which had been heavily bandaged after two of her fingers were cut off by Theseus. The demigod had mutilated her without hesitation, which illustrated just how dangerous he was.

"I will heal," Sybil said and paused. "Hecate said she could *restore* my fingers, but I told her no."

Persephone's eyes misted and she swallowed, trying to clear the thickness from her throat.

"I'm so sorry, Sybil."

"You have nothing to apologize for, Persephone," Sybil said. "It's hard to know what evil exists in the world until it finds you."

Persephone remembered when she thought she knew evil, when her mother had convinced her that Hades's darkness was what seeped into the world from below, an influence on every terror, plague, and sin.

But evil had no effect without a master, and in the last few hours, she had learned true evil. It did not look like her husband or even her mother. It was not darkness, and it was not death.

It was the pleasure Theseus received from his cruelty, and she hated how it had invaded her life and would soon invade the world.

"We'll find a way to heal Harmonia, Sybil. I promise," she said.

Sybil smiled. "I know you will."

And though she'd said it and she'd promised it, Persephone wished she felt the same certainty.

She left them to rest, still worried. It was likely that Harmonia had been stabbed with a blade tipped with venom from the Hydra. Hades had said it slowed healing, and too many wounds could kill a god as it had killed Tyche.

Perhaps Harmonia only needed more time to recover before healing herself.

Or maybe that was only wishful thinking.

Dread pooled in Persephone's chest as she made her way to Hades's office. There was a part of her that hoped she would find him waiting, sitting behind his desk or standing near the fire, but when she opened the door, she found her friends—Hermes and Ilias, Charon and Thanatos, and Apollo and Hecate.

As much as she loved them, they were not Hades.

"Tell me of those who escaped," she said, the dread in her chest thickening.

There was a moment of heavy silence.

"There were few, my lady," said Thanatos. "But among them, Cronos."

Cronos was the God of Time, but specifically he had influence over its destructive nature. She did not know what that meant for the world above, but she would worry about that later. Right now, they had to make plans for present threats.

"And the others?" she asked.

She noted how Thanatos seemed to hesitate as he answered. "The others are my brother and Prometheus."

Persephone's brows rose at the news, though she could not say she was surprised that Hypnos had taken the opportunity to flee the Underworld. She had only recently met the God of Sleep, and he'd made it clear that he did not live in the Underworld by choice. He'd been relegated to its darkness by Hera, who blamed him for her failed attempts to overthrow Zeus.

"Everyone else who escaped Tartarus was captured," said Charon. "Many of them made it no farther than the Styx."

Persephone was not surprised. The river was not crossable except by boat. She had found out the hard way when she'd attempted to swim it upon her first venture into the Underworld. The dead who lived there had dragged her into its dark depths. If it hadn't been for Hermes, she would have drowned.

Persephone looked at Hecate, who knew the Titans best.

"What does it mean that Cronos and Prometheus have escaped?"

"Cronos is a vengeful god, but he will not act quickly," said Hecate. "He needs worshippers to be effective, and he knows this. Prometheus is harmless, mostly. The real concern is how the Olympians will react when they learn of their escape."

Persephone did not imagine they would react well. While quite a few had fought alongside her and Hades, half had stood against them, though she did not think they were all motived by the same thing. Some, like Ares, merely sought battle to satisfy their bloodlust.

Zeus, on the other hand, had wanted to put a stop to his oracle's prophecy. Pyrrha had said that Persephone's union with Hades would produce a god more powerful than Zeus himself. Though the God of the Sky had managed to foil similar prophecies, she wondered now if he had failed to understand this one. Was it Cronos who was destined to become more powerful than Zeus upon his reentry into the world, his wrath a product of his imprisonment in Tartarus?

"How much time do we have?" Persephone asked.

"If I were to guess, I think it is likely Theseus will try to use Hades to lure Cronos out of hiding," said Hecate. "The sooner we find him, the better."

Dread filled Persephone's heart. She did not want to imagine what that meant for Hades.

"Theseus has my ring," Persephone said. "Can you track it?"

"I will try," Hecate said.

Do more than try, Persephone wanted to say, but she knew Hecate was just being cautious. The goddess did not want to overpromise given that she already could not sense Hades's magic.

Persephone looked at the others.

"In the meantime, I want Theseus's men," she said. "I'll torture my way through them until one of them tells us where Hades is."

"We're on it, Seph," said Apollo.

"We will bring him home, my lady," said Ilias.

She swallowed hard, her eyes watering.

"Promise me," she said, her voice trembling.

"Hades is my king and you are my queen," said Ilias. "I will go to the ends of the earth to bring him home for you...for all of us."

"Just one question," Hermes said as he drew his

blade, a menacing expression on his face. "Do you want them dead or alive?"

"Let them choose their fate," she said. "Either way, they come to me."

Those words trickled down her spine. They were similar to ones Hades had spoken to her the night they'd met.

Darling, I win either way.

This time, she shivered.

Hermes grinned. "You got it, Queen."

Everyone left, save Hecate, who approached and took her hands. "Will you rest, my dear?" she asked.

Persephone was not sure she could. She didn't even wish to face their chamber, to face a night without Hades.

"I think…I should see my mother," she said.

"Are you certain?"

It seemed like the better alternative. If she was alone, her thoughts would play in an endless cycle, reminding her of every way she'd failed and what she should have done differently—not only to save Hades but also her mother.

She had killed Demeter.

She could not even recall how it had happened. She only remembered how she'd felt—angry and desperate to end her mother's assault on the world.

But neither thing was an excuse for *murder*.

It did not even seem real, and she was not sure yet how she was supposed to live with something so terrible, but perhaps seeing her in the Underworld would help.

"I will see her now."

Hecate gave a solemn nod, and Persephone had

a feeling she did not argue because she knew her thoughts.

She let Hecate teleport her.

Persephone had not considered where her mother might end up in the Underworld. When Tyche had died, Hades had told her gods come to him powerless, and he often gave them a role within his realm based on what challenged them in life.

Tyche had always wanted to be a mother, so she had become a caretaker in the Children's Garden. Demeter had also wanted to be a mother, but granting her a role beside Tyche seemed too much of a reward for everything she had done. Still, Persephone wasn't sure she wanted Demeter to face a sentence in Tartarus either, but perhaps that had more to do with the guilt she had in being responsible for her death.

She decided she would prepare for that, but when they appeared, it was in the golden grass of the Elysian Fields. She looked at Hecate and then out at the vast, open land, dotted with lush trees. Here, the sky was a bright blue. The souls who were scattered about the plains were dressed in white and wandered about in a near-aimless existence with no memories of the life they'd lived in the Upperworld.

"*It is necessary,*" Thanatos had said, "*to heal the soul.*"

Persephone had learned exactly what it meant when Lexa had come to the Underworld. She had been lucky to see her just as she'd crossed the Styx, and she cherished the few minutes she'd gotten with her best friend before she'd drunk from the Lethe and become someone else.

"Hecate," she whispered, her throat full of an emotion she had not anticipated. "Why are we in Elysium?"

She asked and yet she knew.

"There are some traumas a soul cannot live with," Hecate said. "Even in death, even as a god."

Tears trailed down Persephone's face. She couldn't stop them, couldn't even decide what they meant.

"What could she not live with?" Persephone asked, the taste of salt on her lips.

The version of her mother she had confronted at the Museum of Ancient Greece had no remorse for the harm she had caused. She did not care that her storm had killed hundreds, did not care that her magic was responsible for Tyche's death.

"*I will tear this world apart around you,*" she had said.

Hecate did not answer, though Persephone supposed she did not need to. What either of them had to say about the life Demeter had lived was moot. The fact was that the judges recognized that her soul had withered beneath the guilt of her decisions.

Persephone wasn't sure why, but knowing that somehow hurt worse. It showed just how lost Demeter had become.

Had her spiral begun with her rape by Poseidon? There was a part of Persephone that wished to know, that wanted vengeance for the mother she had lost and the one Demeter had become.

"It will do you no good to seek answers for how your mother lived," said Hecate.

"How do you know?" Persephone asked. She did not often question the Goddess of Witchcraft, but in this, she did.

"Because you already know all there is," Hecate replied. "As her soul heals in time, so will yours.

37

Perhaps then you will come to understand or at least accept."

"Where is she?" Persephone asked, gazing over the golden plain.

Again, Hecate did not speak, but she did not need to because Persephone had found her mother. She recognized her long, straight hair, the color of the golden grass at their feet. She looked slight and small, having lost the command of her presence.

Persephone left Hecate's side and went to her. She kept her distance, making a wide circle around her until she could see her face. It was the first time she had seen Demeter without that critical glint in her eye, without the harshness that had carved her features into a severe mask of disdain.

Demeter's gaze shifted to Persephone. Her soft lips turned upward into a gentle smile. Despite the show of warmth, none of it touched her eyes—eyes that had once turned from brown to green to gold as she moved through various stages of anger. Now they were simply a pale yellow, the color of wheat, and they possessed no recognition.

"Hello," she said softly.

Persephone tried to clear the knot at the back of her throat before she spoke, but her voice rasped anyway.

"Hi," she said.

"Are you the lady of this realm?" Demeter asked.

"I am," Persephone said. "How did you know?"

A line formed between Demeter's brows. "I don't know," she said, and then her gaze shifted—cast off across the field. When she spoke again, her voice was filled with a note of wonder. "It is peaceful here."

Perhaps selfishly, Persephone wished that she felt the same.

Abruptly, she left Elysium and found herself in the dim chamber of her and Hades's bedroom. There was no fire in the hearth to warm the air or eat away at the darkness, and in that cold room that had no life to speak of, she crumpled to the floor and sobbed.

CHAPTER IV
HADES

Hades woke to a sharp and burning sensation in his side. He roared in pain as he tore his eyes open in time to see Theseus remove two fingers from the wound he'd inflicted with Cronos's scythe.

"Good," Theseus said. "You are awake."

Hades gritted his teeth, glaring at the demigod, his eyes watering. He wanted to speak, to curse him, but his words were lodged in his throat, tight with pain.

"Forgive me," the demigod said, gaze falling to his two bloodied fingers. "But you were not roused by my calls."

It wasn't until Theseus rose to his feet that Hades realized he was in a different position than he had been when he'd fallen asleep. He was no longer hanging from chains but sitting on the floor. The massive net that had draped his body was gone, replaced by one that fit more like a shirt. Despite the difference, Hades could still feel its weight and the strange way it seemed to drain his energy—like it had teeth sinking into his very soul.

"Come, Olympian," Theseus said. "You must earn your keep."

Hades had to fight his compulsion to remain where he was. He did not like being commanded, especially by an arrogant demigod, but he could not deny that he was curious about where exactly he was and wanted any opportunity to observe and devise a plan for escape.

He rose to his feet, though his limbs trembled.

Theseus did not immediately lead him from his cell. Instead, he studied him, his critical eyes burning along his frame.

"Admiring me, Theseus?" Hades hissed, breathless.

"Yes," the demigod said and then met Hades's gaze. "Have you ever felt so weak?"

Hades scowled, and Theseus offered the barest smile before turning to open a nearly invisible door.

"Even you must admit to being impressed by our technology?" Theseus said as he passed into a narrow passage that was no brighter than Hades's cell.

Hades could feel the grit in the air, and a musty smell filled his senses, seeping into the back of his throat, making it even harder to breathe beneath the net.

"Yours?" Hades countered. "It looks like Hephaestus's work and smells like Demeter's magic."

"What is technology but the evolution of what already exists?" said Theseus.

"I didn't know you were a scholar," Hades muttered. He would have spoken louder, but the tone of his voice correlated with how badly his lungs hurt, and he preferred to save his strength.

"There is a lot you do not know about me, Uncle."

Hades cringed at the use of the familial title, though

he knew Theseus only used it to mock him. He felt no bond to the demigod, not an ounce of affection, but Hades said nothing and instead focused on his surroundings.

They were in a long corridor, and Hades could only see a few feet in front of him either way he looked. A cloudy orange light hung like mist in the air, creating pockets of darkness. The floor was sandy, and the walls were made of smooth stones, stacked high into the dark above. What he was most aware of, however, was the cold. He was familiar with the way it clung to his skin and seeped to the bone.

He was in the labyrinth where he had fought the Minotaur.

"Daedalus was a genius, no?" Theseus commented.

"He was a man who made himself useful," Hades said, following Theseus at a distance.

Certainly at the time, Daedalus was considered one of the most brilliant inventors of his age. He had been commissioned by King Minos to build this labyrinth as a prison for the Minotaur, a half-bull, half-human creature Minos's wife, Pasiphaë, had birthed. A creature that only existed because he had also built the wooden cow that allowed her to mate with a bull she had been cursed to lust after by Poseidon.

"He saw opportunity," said Theseus. "Even you must respect that."

"I do not have to respect it," Hades said.

Daedalus was a narcissist and had attempted to murder his own nephew when it was evident that his genius threatened his own.

Theseus chuckled. "Oh, Hades, I shudder to learn what you think of me."

"You know what I think of you," Hades said.

The demigod did not respond, and Hades was glad for the quiet. He hated talking anyway, but right now, it was exhausting. As he followed Theseus, he flexed his hands and realized he had movement in his arms. The net, which lay heavily against his chest, back, and stomach, did not seem to restrict his arms, and while he knew the net was impossible to escape without help, he still tried.

Theseus chuckled, though when Hades looked up, the demigod was still facing forward, moving down the corridors of the labyrinth with ease.

"You will only exhaust yourself trying to remove it," said Theseus. "Might as well save your strength. You will need it."

Hades glared at the back of Theseus's head, imagining what it would be like to smash it with a stone.

After Tyche's death, Hades had gone to Hephaestus to learn more about his creation, knowing that the net posed a great threat to the gods given its ability to immobilize and suffocate their power. Hades had asked the God of Fire to forge a weapon to cut it, but he'd not been able to obtain that weapon before he'd been captured.

It angered him that he'd fallen into such a trap. He had not had a second thought when he'd gone in search of Persephone, in search of the ring Theseus now kept in his possession. He tried to sense it, the familiar energies of the stones he'd chosen to represent her and their future together, but all he felt was the cold of the labyrinth, which became even more disorienting the longer they were within it, alternating between walking for long stretches and a series of sharp turns down shorter pathways.

Hades wondered what guided Theseus through the maze. He walked with purpose, twisting and turning through the many and varied corridors. It was possible he had memorized the route—he was certainly psychotic enough.

Finally they came to a part of the maze that was in ruins, the walls broken and crumbled from age.

"Part of the original labyrinth," said Theseus. Even in disrepair, the greatness of it was evident. "I had every intention of finishing it before you arrived, but as it is, I think it is far more fitting that you complete the prison in which you have been trapped."

Hades's gaze slid to the demigod.

"How do you propose I do that?" Hades asked.

"I have provided all the tools," Theseus said.

Hades stared. He knew the demigod was willfully ignoring the obvious—the net draped over his body made him weak.

"And you wish for me to do this, why?" Hades asked. "So you can watch?"

"What else are you going to do while you wait to be rescued?" Theseus mocked. "Pine after your wife?"

Hades ground his teeth so hard, the muscles in his neck ached. After a moment, he relaxed, tilting his head to the side.

"Give yourself more credit, Theseus. You have done enough to earn a starring role in my thoughts."

"What an honor," Theseus said and cast his eyes to the materials scattered at his feet. "You might want to get started. I've been told it takes days for mud bricks to cure." The demigod started to turn but paused. "I will pry a stone from your lover's ring each time you stop," he said. "And when there are no more, I will crush them into dust and feed them to you dry."

The demigod left, vanishing into the dark, and Hades was left alone. As much as he recognized that there were other rings Hephaestus could make, the idea of the one in Theseus's possession being destroyed by his hand felt like letting the demigod win.

That thought spurred Hades to begin.

He stared at the materials he'd been given—a trough of water, a sheaf of wheat, a bucket, a wooden box that would act as a mold for the bricks. There was nothing to cut the wheat, which meant nothing he could use as a weapon.

Everything would have to be done with his hands.

Hades recognized the futility of this work. It was not about finishing the wall at all. It was about shaming him, though Hades did not need this to feel ashamed. He had suffered with his guilt the moment Persephone had walked out the door with Theseus at Alexandria Tower.

He should have never agreed to the demigod's request for a favor, but it had been the only reward Theseus would take for the capture of Sisyphus and the return of a relic the mortal had stolen. In fairness, it was no unjust request given that Sisyphus had been using the relic to steal lives from mortals, and while Hades had thought Theseus would use the favor for nefarious purposes, he had not anticipated that he would use it to separate him from Persephone.

And to what end? He still did not completely understand what had happened in his absence, but he knew that Theseus had managed to enter the Underworld, that he now possessed the Helm of Darkness, and that he had also released Cronos from Tartarus. And while Hades did not know what that meant for the future of New Greece, he knew he could handle it all so long as Persephone was well.

I am well.

Her voice was so clear, his heart raced and he turned, thinking she would be right beside him, but found nothing save dust twisting through the hazy darkness.

It was ridiculous to expect her there, foolish to feel disappointment when she wasn't, yet he could not help how it crashed over him, a weight heavier than the net.

He ground his teeth, a wave of hot frustration settling deep in his bones. He would not be surprised to learn that Theseus had conjured some kind of illusion to distract him just so he could have the satisfaction of following through on his threat.

With the whisper of her words fresh in his mind, Hades swept the rubble from the jagged wall into the bucket Theseus had left to use in the brick mixture.

When he was finished, he lowered to the ground and dug his fingers into the sandy earth. The dirt reminded him of the fine, ashy silt in the Underworld, and as it lodged beneath his nails, he thought of how Persephone had knelt in the barren patch of earth he'd given her in his garden. She had been angry with him for snaring her into a contract, angrier when she had discovered the beauty of his realm. Even if it had not been real, the illusion only served to remind her of her inability to summon and feel her magic.

When she had risen to her feet, he had kissed her for

the first time. He remembered how she felt against him, how she tasted like wine and smelled like sweet roses. He had lost himself in her perfection just as he was losing himself in her memory now.

"What a treat to find the God of the Dead on his knees."

It was Persephone's voice, and it set Hades on edge. He knew it was a trick, conjured by Theseus to torture him. He ignored the words, the way they whispered up his spine and made his chest ache. He focused harder on his task, scooping the sand into the bucket to mix with water and wheat, when he noticed something in his peripheral—the flare of a white dress—and when he looked, he was kneeling at Persephone's feet.

He stared, his breath caught in his throat. She was more beautiful than ever with her wild, golden curls spilling over her shoulders and freckles dusting her ethereal skin. He wanted to kiss each one.

"You're not real," he said.

She laughed, her brows furrowing just a little.

"I am real," she said, taking a step closer. He could feel the air move with her. "Touch me."

He looked away, eyes falling to the ruins of the labyrinth.

Whatever this was, it was more painful than the wound at his side.

"Hades," Persephone whispered his name again, and when he looked, she was still there, though it seemed that she was in another realm. There was a brightness at her back that haloed her body, as if the sun shone behind her.

"This is cruel," he said, still kneeling, refusing to look

47

at her face. Instead, he stared at her billowing dress. The fabric was thin and white, threaded through with gold.

"Don't you want me?" she whispered.

He closed his eyes against the hurt in her voice. When he opened them again, he expected to be alone in the labyrinth, but she remained. He reached out and touched her gown, pinching the fabric between his fingers. It was soft and real.

How?

Hades looked up at her from the ground, worry etched across her sweet face.

"Persephone," he said, half in disbelief. He could no longer stop himself. He rose to his feet, his lips crashing against hers, gripping the back of her head. His other hand pressed into the small of her back, his fingers splayed, holding her to him as tightly as he could.

He released her mouth and rested his forehead against hers.

"I do not know if you are real," he said.

"Does it matter if we are together?" she asked. Her voice was quiet, and it seeped into his skin, making him shudder.

Her hands pressed flat against his chest, skin to skin, as her magic ate away at the net and his shirt. Perhaps this was more of a dream than a trick.

"Better," Persephone muttered, her hands smoothing over him. He caught her wrists and kissed her palms.

She curled her fingers.

"Let me touch you," she said. Her eyes brightened, taking on a fierceness that pierced his heart.

It wasn't that he did not want her to. It was that he already feared waking up alone.

Persephone placed her hands on either side of his face. "Live in this moment with me."

He wanted nothing else. He wanted her to take up every second of every day, to live in every part of his mind, to never leave his side. She was the dawn of his world, the warmth he carried in his heart, the light that kept him looking toward the future.

He kissed her again and dragged her up his body. He would have sighed with the weight of her in his arms, but he swept his tongue into her mouth, groaning at the way her taste made his body tighten. With her arms anchored around his neck, he gripped her hips, grinding his erection into the softness between her thighs.

Fuck, she felt so good and *real*.

She wiggled against him, and as she did, he let her slide to her feet. He was completely naked now—by the mercy of her magic, his length heavy and full between them. She touched him, her fingers teasing the veins pulsing with his blood. He felt the roar of his need in his ears.

"Will you let me please you?" she asked.

She did not need permission, but he liked the way she asked. Her voice was low and husky, her eyes gleaming with lust.

"If you wish," he said, his tone matching hers, resisting the primal urge to tangle his fingers in her hair as she knelt before him.

"I wish," she whispered, her breath on his cock.

His muscles clenched, and he grew harder as she licked him. The tip of her tongue ran along every vein and the smooth edge of his crown before she teased his head with lavish strokes. He took a few deep breaths, working through the pleasure blooming throughout his body.

Then she sucked him into her mouth, her hand working him up and down. He groaned, his chest tightening to the point that he could not take in air. He thought he would come, could feel his body reaching those great heights, just caressing the very edge of release.

He smoothed his hand into her hair, and she looked up at him as his cock slipped from her mouth, red, wet, and pulsing.

"Let me come inside you," he said.

Her eyes darkened.

"If you wish," she said.

"Oh, I wish," he growled, dragging her to her feet.

He kissed her again and let his mouth run along her jaw and down her neck, teeth grazing, pausing to suck her skin. She clung to him, her fingers digging into his shoulders. He liked the bite of her nails, which made this feel even more real. He still wasn't sure what this was, but he no longer cared.

He shoved the straps of her dress down, exposing her breasts, then her stomach and hips. He kissed down her body, his hands smoothing over her skin as he did. He spent time teasing her thighs and burying his face between her legs, licking her swollen clit until her fingers twisted in his hair. He made his way up her body before taking her into his arms again, her wet heat settling against his erection, her breasts pressed against his chest.

Trapped within this tension, their eyes held.

"I miss you," she said.

Her fingers danced along his lips before she kissed

him. He would take this distraction over the ache in his chest and carried her to what he thought was the tallest part of the labyrinth wall, but when he went to rest her against it, he found that they had fallen into a sea of black silk.

"This is a dream," he murmured.

"Then it is a good dream," she whispered.

He kissed her and made a slow descent down her body, taking time to tease and touch. She writhed, her thighs squeezing, and when he finally pressed his mouth to her heat, he found ecstasy.

CHAPTER V
PERSEPHONE

"Yes," Persephone **moaned at the press of Hades's mouth** against her. Every part of her body felt raw and open, one whole nerve exposed to the pleasure of his touch. She could barely contain her need for him. It twined through her, tightening her muscles as he worked his tongue over her clit.

She took a deep breath, the pleasure already radiating throughout her body, but then he parted her soft and swollen flesh with his fingers, and she could barely contain her relief at feeling some part of him inside her.

"Yes," she said again, looking down at him between her legs. He was staring back as he took her clit into his mouth again, sucking gently. "Fuck."

She let her head fall back against the pillow. With each stroke, she grew warmer and the pleasure that knifed through her body built in intensity.

"Please," she begged, though she was not completely sure what she was asking for. She wanted to come, to feel her whole body tense with the pleasure of release. She was addicted to it and the way Hades pushed her closer and closer to the edge.

Hades tugged gently on her clit as he released her.

"What do you want, darling?" he asked, his voice a dark whisper. It made her shiver despite the perspiration breaking out over her skin.

She was hot and damp.

"More," she said.

She needed him fast and slow, needed him to work deeper, and he did, caressing a place inside her that elicited so much sensation, she thought she would die at any moment. And then she did. Pleasure shot through her like lightning, seizing every muscle. She bent forward, body curling into itself as her orgasm crashed through her, exiting her body on a deep and guttural moan.

That was how she woke, to the sound of her release, with her hands between her legs and no sign of Hades.

A hot wave of shame fell on her, and the heat that had livened her body vanished. Cold, she drew her knees to her chest.

Gods, it had all felt so real. She'd felt his weight on her. She could taste him on her tongue, and her lips were raw from his kiss. Now that she was awake, that pleasurable ache in her core turned into something nauseating.

It felt wrong to feel aroused in his absence, even if her feelings had been ignited by his role in her dream. The worst part, though, was waking without him.

This was a nightmare.

She rose from bed and shrugged on her robe before making her way to the balcony in the darkness. Outside, the Underworld felt different. She had yet to figure out the source. Was it their union, Hades's absence, or Theseus's violation of their realm that had spurred the change? Either way, it put her on edge. She felt like, at any moment, something might explode—that the magic she'd called on to trap Iapetus might splinter and the Titan would finish tearing her world to shreds.

Because this was all she had left—this and the hope that she would find Hades before Theseus gave him over to Cronos.

She let her head fall into her hands as she braced them against the balcony rail, tears burning the back of her throat, but she refused to cry, blinking fiercely until she no longer felt the threat. Once it had passed, she lifted her head and noticed an orange glow from afar.

She stood straighter.

Strange, she thought and teleported beyond the cover of the palace gardens where she noticed a fire in the Asphodel Fields. At first, a sense of panic overwhelmed her, and she teleported again quickly to the valley below, only to notice that the souls were gathered around it, using it for light. Some bent and carved bows, others were stitching pieces of leather into armor, and some were sharpening blades.

She turned her attention to the main road at the center of Asphodel, noting that every lantern was lit, making the sky look hazy and orange. Those who were not working near the fire were making repairs to their homes from the damage done during the rupture of Tartarus.

"Lady Persephone!"

She shifted toward the sound of her name.

"Yuri!" Persephone said and went to the young soul,

drawing her into a tight hug. She had not seen her since the chimera attack and had yet to thank her for distracting the monster. "Are you well?" she asked as she pulled away, studying the soul, uncertain of what she had faced as the battle continued.

Yuri seemed puzzled by the question. "Yes, my lady," she said. "Are you?"

Persephone opened her mouth to respond, but she still had no words to describe exactly what she was feeling. Instead, she looked toward the roaring flames in the field beyond Asphodel.

"What is going on? Why are you all here?"

Souls did not really need sleep, but they tended to maintain the routines they had while living.

"We are preparing for war," Yuri said, and while Persephone could see that, she still could not quite comprehend it. "After what happened, we think it is best."

Guilt tightened her chest. She could not help thinking that they had chosen to do this in part because she had not been able to protect them.

If Hades had been here, things would have been different, though she knew she was not being completely fair to herself. She, Hecate, Hermes, and Apollo had done all they could to defend the Underworld from the threats Theseus had unleashed, and the souls had helped. They likely only wished to be better prepared for the next attack.

"The next attack," she said aloud, her voice quiet as she looked toward Tartarus.

"What happened, Persephone?" Yuri asked, but Persephone was not really prepared to answer because it meant revisiting the terror she'd faced over the last twenty-four hours.

It took her a moment to meet the soul's wide-eyed gaze. When she spoke, her voice was mournful. "I am still trying to understand that myself."

The sound of a hammer on metal suddenly echoed throughout Asphodel, and Persephone's focus shifted to Ian's outdoor forge. She had first met Ian when he had presented her with a crown, a gift from the souls. Later she would learn that he had been murdered for his skill and the favor Artemis had bestowed on him. Any weapon the man created ensured its wielder could not be defeated.

Several souls worked alongside him, some forging weapons while others hammered metal into shields and armor.

The thing about those who lived in Asphodel was that their skills matched the century in which they lived. Some had worked with wood and leather, some with iron and steel, but no matter their expertise, they shared one thing—the ability to prepare for war.

Humanity was unchanging, and it had never been more apparent to her as it was right now.

She scanned the souls gathered when her eyes snagged on a woman with a long braid.

Her brows lowered, and her heart hammered.

She took a step forward.

"Zofie?"

The woman looked up from her work and turned to face Persephone, who could not contain her tears. She had watched the Amazon die, taking a blade to the chest. She'd screamed so loud, even now she could hear the ring of it in her ears. It had all happened so quickly.

"My lady," Zofie said, a smile spreading across her face. She bowed so low, she nearly touched the ground.

"Zofie," Persephone said again and crossed the short distance toward her, hugging her close as she straightened. "Zofie, I am so sorry."

The Amazon held her shoulders as she pulled away. "Do not apologize, my queen. You have given me honor in death."

Honor.

It was the thing she'd sought as Persephone's aegis, though she still did not know what had caused the Amazon such shame among her people. In the end, though, it did not matter because Zofie had found peace in the way she needed.

Perhaps Persephone could find the same peace, though she was not sure anything would ever remedy the horror of watching her die, even seeing the Amazon so happy in death.

Persephone's eyes shifted over Zofie's shoulder to Ian, who stood with the other souls gathered behind him. In his hands, he held a blade.

"Ian," she said.

"My queen," he said and bowed. "Allow me to present you with this dagger."

She stared at the knife, which was sheathed in a scabbard inlaid with the same florals that adorned the crown he'd made for her—roses and lilies, narcissus and anemone. They climbed effortlessly over the hilt too, crowned with a piece of black obsidian atop the pommel.

As she took it into her hands, the dark gems he had set among the flowers glinted under the firelight.

"Ian," she said again, this time a whisper.

"It is a symbol of your strength," he said. "The blade is like you, unbreakable."

She met his gaze, and again her eyes burned with tears. She did not feel unbreakable, but it meant a lot that her people thought she was.

She held the blade close to her chest.

"Thank you," she said, unable to say anything else, and when she looked beyond the blacksmith and around, she noticed that more souls had gathered outside the smithy.

"All hail Queen Persephone!"

She was not sure who said it, but the souls responded by cheering, and then they knelt, and Persephone found herself at the center of their worship, completely overwhelmed.

———

Persephone spent a few more hours with the souls as they continued to prepare for battle. As much as she wished it were not needed, she felt it was necessary after what had occurred with Theseus. He had the Helm of Darkness, which meant he could return to the Underworld at any given moment unseen. Would he decide later that releasing Cronos into the mortal world was not enough? Would he seek to release more Titans or other monsters from the depths of Tartarus? Persephone had to hope that her magic would hold, that Hecate could protect the borders until Hades returned.

Pain sliced through her chest, sudden and sharp,

before it settled into a keen and constant pressure. It had accompanied her since leaving Hades at Alexandria Tower and had grown worse in the aftermath of her dream. She was tired of this feeling.

Her eyes fell to the blade Ian had given her, which sat on Hades's desk. When she had returned to the castle, she had come to his office, which felt more like a refuge than any other part of the palace. It still looked like he was here. It still smelled like him. She could pretend he was just away on business.

Hermes's magic scented the air, and the god manifested near the door. He had changed since their battle and looked far more casual in a pair of khaki slacks and a white button-down.

"Hey, Sephy," he said, his voice quiet and a little melancholy.

"Any news?" she asked.

"Not about Hades," he said.

Her heart sank, even though she had expected as much.

"I have come to extend an invitation from Hippolyta, Queen of the Amazons. She has requested your presence at Zofie's funeral."

Funeral.

It would not be the first time she attended a funeral after she had welcomed a friend to the Underworld, but she still dreaded the thought.

"When?" Persephone asked.

"She will be laid to rest tonight," said Hermes softly.

Persephone swallowed and looked away toward the windows.

"I know I am Queen of the Underworld, but I am

not yet a Goddess of Death," she said. "I do not know how to reconcile having watched Zofie die."

"You did not just watch her die, Persephone," Hermes said. "You watched her murdered."

It had happened so fast. Zofie had found them, and as soon as she entered the hotel room, Theseus buried a blade in her chest. Persephone would never forget how her eyes widened or how she had collapsed to the floor. She would never forget the way she screamed or how it had hurt her throat. She would never forget how Theseus had made her step over Zofie's body and leave her alone to die.

It did not matter that the Amazon was content. Persephone lived with the horror, and she could not help wondering who else among her friends would fall victim to Theseus.

"Will you come with me?" she asked.

"Of course," he said. "We all will, Sephy."

When Hermes left, Persephone made her way to the queen's suite, anxious for an update on Harmonia. She found Sybil sitting on the bed beside the goddess.

"How is she?" Persephone asked as she moved to the bedside.

"Hecate says she has a fever," said Sybil.

"Is that normal for a goddess?"

"She didn't say it was bad," she said and then looked at Persephone. "Perhaps her body will heal itself."

Persephone watched Harmonia's face, both pale and flushed at the same time. While she'd have liked to believe it was possible for Harmonia to heal without magic, she was not hopeful. It depended on how much Hydra venom had entered her veins.

What if Harmonia could not handle this?

Persephone tightened her jaw and pushed those thoughts away.

Losing Harmonia wasn't an option.

"Any update on Hades?" Sybil asked.

Persephone swallowed around something thick and sour in her throat.

"Nothing yet," she said.

"He will be all right, Persephone," Sybil said, her voice a quiet whisper.

"Do you know that or are you just hopeful?"

"I know what I saw before," Sybil said. "When I was Apollo's oracle."

When Persephone had first met Sybil, she had been in her final semester of college at New Athens University. At the time, she'd already caught Apollo's interest and was poised to have a promising career as the god's oracle, but he'd fired her after she'd refused his advances. It was a move Persephone had openly admonished only to face backlash from the public. Apollo, for all his faults, had endeared himself to the public, though now, needless to say, the God of Music had also endeared himself to Persephone.

"And now what do you see?" Persephone asked.

"I do not have a divine channel."

"Does that mean you do not have visions?"

"I cannot ensure accuracy without a divine channel," said Sybil.

"Would you like one?"

There was silence. Persephone looked back at Sybil, who was stunned.

"I don't know if I will ever have temples built in my

name or worshippers who seek my wisdom, but I must go to war with Helen and Theseus in the media, and I need someone I trust on my side."

Persephone had yet to seek any news, yet to see what the world was saying about her—the goddess who had masqueraded as a mortal—but she knew Hermes was right. All she could do was tell the truth, and that would start with Sybil.

"Persephone," Sybil whispered.

The goddess could not place the sound of the oracle's voice or the expression on her face. Would she say no? She had seemed to lose interest in the position entirely after her experience with Apollo.

Sybil took Persephone's hands in hers, squeezing.

"It would be an honor to be your oracle."

———

Persephone arrived at the gates of Terme with Hecate on her left, Hermes on her right, and Ilias at her back. They were all draped in white robes, the color of mourning—*a brightness that would lead souls into the dark*. At least that was the prevailing belief of the living, though Zofie needed no assistance finding the Underworld. Still, Persephone dreaded the funeral rites. In some ways, it felt like facing Zofie's death all over again.

As soon as they appeared, two guards who stood on either side of the gate knelt, bringing their spears to their breasts. Their bronze armor gleamed, ignited like the great flaming basins flanking them. Persephone could feel the heat of the fire, yet she shivered as if cold fingers were grazing her skin.

Movement within the shadowed entrance caught

her attention, and from that darkness emerged Hippolyta. She was dressed in dark robes and draped in gold—a belt that cinched her waist, cuffs on her wrists and upper arms, long earrings that cascaded over her shoulders, a crown that rested against her forehead. Her hair was pulled away from her face, though ringlets slipped free from her binds, wreathing her stern but beautiful face.

Hecate, Hermes, and Ilias knelt while Persephone remained standing. It felt strange, but it was what Hecate had instructed her to do.

"*Queens do not kneel before queens,*" she said.

"*Then what do I do?*" Persephone asked.

"*Whatever Hippolyta does,*" Hecate replied.

Persephone held the queen's heavy-lidded gaze, her eyes the color of prehnite stones.

"Persephone, Goddess of Spring, daughter of Demeter, wife of Hades," Hippolyta said, and her voice commanded attention though it was not harsh. "Welcome to Terme."

Then she bowed her head, and Persephone did the same.

"We are grateful for your invitation, Queen Hippolyta," Persephone said.

The warrior queen offered a small smile and then stepped to the side. "Walk beside me, Queen of the Dead."

As Persephone joined her, Hippolyta turned, and the gates groaned as they opened, revealing her city, cast in amber light from the torches burning in the night. Despite the dark, the lush terrain of the Amazonian fortress was evident. Thick trees dotted the landscape, sprouting between homes covered in flowering vines and gardens teeming with fragrant flora.

"I did not expect your kingdom to feel so much like home," Persephone said.

It even smelled like spring—sweet with an edge of bitterness.

Hippolyta smiled. "Even warriors can appreciate beautiful things, Lady Persephone."

Can you? she wanted to ask. *When you hold honor so high?*

But that would be an insult, and she was here for Zofie, who, despite how her own people had hurt her, believed wholly in the need for redemption. Persephone would not ruin that with her anger. Besides, it was Zofie's exile that had brought her to Persephone.

It had also brought her to death's door.

Persephone could not help the pain that blossomed in her chest as she was once more reminded that she bore witness to Zofie's murder. It had created a darkness within her, something different than what had grown in the aftermath of Lexa's death.

She feared how it made her feel, how it had changed her.

She wondered if Hades would recognize that wounded and withered part of her. If it would feel familiar because he had witnessed similar horrors.

That thought gave way to a different kind of pain, an ache she felt deep in her soul. She held her breath, hoping to suffocate every emotion that had risen inside her, and let her gaze fall to her feet. They walked along a dirt path lined with foliage, and as the leaves brushed against the hem of her robes, they seemed to grow taller and thicker.

"You are truly a Goddess of Spring," said Hippolyta. There was a note to her voice, a sense of surprise.

Reluctantly, Persephone met her gaze, hoping she had managed enough control over her emotions.

"Were you in doubt?" she asked.

"New gods are a rare thing these days," said Hippolyta.

It should have occurred to Persephone that some might be skeptical of her divinity. The world did not always take kindly to new, full-blooded gods. Such was the case when Dionysus was born. He had to fight to be counted among the Divine, and his battles had been bloody. But Persephone was not interested in proving herself—not to the world, to the Olympians, or to Hippolyta.

"It is curious that death would choose life as a bride," Hippolyta said. "It is like the sun falling in love with the moon."

"One cannot exist without the other," Persephone said. "Just as honor cannot exist without shame."

The queen gave a wry smile, and there was a tension at Persephone's back that she knew came from Hecate at her slight.

"True, Queen Persephone," Hippolyta said. "Though I suppose it is not about one or the other but what comes in between."

They continued down the path in silence when Hermes gave out a sudden, high-pitched scream. Swiftly, they were surrounded by Amazons, their weapons drawn. Persephone and Hippolyta whirled toward the god only to find his hands balled up beneath his chin and one leg off the ground.

Hecate and Ilias stared too.

It seemed to take Hermes a moment to realize what he had done, and he offered a sheepish, shy grin.

"There was a bug," he explained. "A big one."

A few of the Amazons snickered.

Hermes glowered and looked at Hecate and Ilias. "Tell me you saw it."

Both of them shook their heads in quiet amusement.

Hippolyta rolled her eyes.

"Men," she scoffed as she turned her back on the God of Trickery.

Persephone raised a brow at Hermes, who mouthed *it was huge* before swatting at another invisible bug.

They continued down the path until the city center was visible. At the site of the sunken courtyard, Persephone halted. A wooden pyre waited, and at each corner of what would become Zofie's infernal bed, there was a burning torch, the flames dancing in the muted dark.

Seeing it filled Persephone with dread. How many would burn like Zofie and Tyche?

"This is the nature of battle, Lady Persephone," said Hippolyta.

It was strange to hear the Amazon queen speak so impassively about the death of one of her subjects, even if it was one who had been exiled, though Persephone realized the greatest honor to this tribe was to die in battle, to die for a cause.

"I did not know anyone had declared war," Persephone said.

Looking back now, she realized that it had begun the moment Adonis had died.

"That is the fault of your husband," Hippolyta said. "He has been fighting since the start."

66

Persephone met her gaze, brows furrowed, but the queen did not explain.

Instead, she took a step forward. "Come."

Persephone followed the queen along a winding path to a home caged in ivy. Shoots of pink crocus, purple iris, and yellow narcissus blanketed the lawn, leading to an open door through which Persephone could see Zofie's lifeless form.

Hippolyta entered with no hesitation, but Persephone found that her steps slowed as she crossed the threshold into the house of death, which was hot and smelled like wax, likely due to the oil anointing Zofie's body.

The Amazon lay on a high table dressed in white, her hands resting on her stomach, fingers closed over the hilt of her long sword. Her dark hair was smoothed into a braid, and she was crowned with a wreath of golden leaves.

She was beautiful, her limbs glistening beneath the firelight.

"You mourn so deeply, Lady Persephone," Queen Hippolyta said. "Have you not welcomed Zofie into the Underworld?"

"I have," Persephone said with a small smile, recalling her first sighting of the aegis. "But does the promise of seeing anyone again ever ease grief?"

The queen was quiet, though Persephone did not expect her to understand, just as Hades had not understood her fear of losing Lexa. Mourning was not just about the person. It was about the world one created around them, and when they ceased to exist, so did that world.

Hecate, Hermes, and Ilias approached, each saying

goodbye in their own way—Hecate with a prayer and Hermes with a kiss on Zofie's cheek. Persephone was most surprised by Ilias, who took his time, his face inches away as he whispered words she could not hear before pressing his lips to Zofie's.

When he straightened, he met Persephone's gaze with red-rimmed eyes before stepping away, making room for her.

As Persephone neared, she looked down at Zofie's serene face, and though she was beautiful, all Persephone could see was how she'd looked in death—stunned by the pain of Theseus's blade. She touched her hair and bent over her.

"You served so honorably, Zofie," she whispered and kissed her forehead.

When she straightened, Hippolyta stood opposite her holding a wide leather belt.

"Lord Hades promised to return Zofie once she brought honor to us," said Hippolyta. "In exchange, I agreed to lend him my belt."

Persephone's brows rose in surprise. Hades had never told her how he'd met Zofie, and now she wondered why he'd asked for the belt, though it was not unusual for him to collect weapons or relics.

The Amazon queen extended her hands, the belt held flat between her palms.

"This is the Girdle of Hippolyta, a gift from my father, Ares, a symbol of my rule over the Amazons. Any mortal who wears it will be granted immortal strength."

Persephone gazed at the belt and then at Hippolyta and shook her head.

"I cannot take it," she said.

She did not understand the deal Hades had made with the queen, but it seemed wrong to accept such an item without him.

"You must," Hippolyta said. "It is not a gift. It is a symbol of the promise I made, and I do not break promises."

Persephone could not argue with that and did not wish to. She accepted the girdle, surprised by how light and soft it was. As soon as she had made the trade, Hippolyta spoke.

"It is time."

Persephone's pain flourished again as six Amazons approached. She stepped away, following Hippolyta from the home with Hecate, Hermes, and Ilias in tow. As they emerged, she found the path they'd followed was flanked by Amazons. Some carried torches while others carried weapons, and when Zofie was brought forth from the home, they began to sing a haunting melody. It followed them as Hippolyta led the procession into the courtyard where the women of Terme continued their song while they clashed their spears and swords on their shields, slammed their fists against their breasts, or tore at their clothes in grief.

They did not cease, even as Zofie came to rest on the pyre and the Amazons who carried torches threw them at its feet, not even when the flames rose and caught Zofie's dress aflame and then her flesh, filling the air with a metallic tang that lingered in the back of Persephone's throat. Her eyes began to water, and she did not know if it was from the smoke or the sorrow that weighed heavily in her limbs.

Then Hecate took her hand.

"Do not stop your tears, my dear," she said. "Let them give life."

At first, Persephone did not understand, but then she felt something brush the hem of her gown, and when she looked, there were flowers at her feet, the petals so white they glowed like moonstones.

She smiled despite her sadness as the blooming bed continued to spread, and when Hippolyta noticed, she turned toward Persephone.

"I suppose what you said is true. Death gives birth to life." Then she narrowed her eyes. "What will you birth, Persephone?"

"Rage," she answered without a second thought.

CHAPTER VI
THESEUS

The tension in the Council chamber was thick, and though Theseus could barely breathe, he did not find the sensation unpleasant. He liked what it meant, that the Olympians were at odds with one another.

He watched them from the shadows, concealed by the magic of the Helm of Darkness.

"How dare you stand against me!" Zeus was saying. "*Me*, your king!"

He stood before his great throne, large and imposing. The air around him was electric, heavy with the threat of his magic. Behind him, his golden eagle lurked, beady eyes alert but unaware of Theseus's presence.

Given Zeus's usually placid nature, it was hard to remember his power. The God of the Sky rarely intervened in matters outside his interest, and his interests extended mostly to the women he wished to bed. Now and again, he might take revenge against someone who looked at Hera too long, but mostly, he was content to watch the world and its gods do as they pleased, even if it meant going to war.

Until his reign was threatened, and then suddenly, he was a warrior.

"Someone is out there killing gods," said Hermes. "And you wish to ignore that in favor of pursuing a goddess who has done no harm."

The God of Thieves stood before his own throne, his exuberant joy suffocated beneath his anger.

"If gods are dying, they have only their weaknesses to blame," said Zeus. "I will not count myself among them, which is why my brother's lover must be eliminated."

"*Her name* is Persephone," said Apollo, who also stood, his arms crossed over his chest. "Or do you fear saying it like you fear her power?"

Zeus's eyes flashed bright like a strike of lightning on a dark horizon.

"I do not fear her," he hissed. "But I will not be dethroned."

"She did not try to overthrow you," Apollo snapped. "She *restored* Thebes, and you brought war against her."

"And when the time came to choose a side, you opposed me. That is the same thing."

An angry silence followed Zeus's words.

"Why do you defend her?" asked Artemis. The goddess was one of a few who sat on her throne, her hands curled around the arms of her chair as if at any moment, she might launch herself from it and attack. "What has she done for you?"

Apollo glared at his sister as he answered, "She is my friend."

Artemis scoffed. "You are a god. Mortals are dying to be in your presence. *They* will be your friends."

"It is not the same," he said. "But you would not know that because you have no friends."

Artemis glared at Apollo and then looked at Zeus. "I will hunt her, Father."

"You will do no such thing." It was Aphrodite who spoke this time.

"You would defend her too, my child?" Zeus asked. Unlike the anger he showed Hermes and Apollo, toward her, he was hurt.

"She took a spear for her," said Poseidon. "Or have you forgotten the way Hephaestus screamed for her?" The God of the Sea chuckled.

Aphrodite glared at her uncle before her gaze slid back to Zeus. "It is not Persephone or Hades who are dangerous, Father," she said. "It is their love. Tear them apart, and they will tear you apart."

Artemis scoffed and rolled her eyes.

"The prophecy has made the danger of their love very clear, Aphrodite," said Hera. It was the first time the Goddess of Marriage had spoken. "Together or apart, they are a continuous threat."

Zeus looked at his wife with affection, as if her defense of him was an illustration of her love, but Theseus knew otherwise—and so did everyone else in the room. Hera was just as afraid of losing her position and title, and while it was foolish for Zeus to think it meant anything more, his inability to see Hera for who she truly was worked in Theseus's favor.

So did his attention to Hades and Persephone.

But that was the danger in attempting to unravel

an oracle's words. There was no way to guess how their predictions might unfold. Indeed, Hades and Persephone's union *had* produced a god more powerful than Zeus.

But that god was Theseus.

"How many times must we pick apart a prophecy when we all know there is no avoiding Fate?" asked Athena.

"Are those supposed to be wise words?" Hera asked.

Athena narrowed her eyes and lifted her proud chin.

"You should not even be allowed a voice here," said Ares. "You and Hestia abandoned us on the battlefield. Cowards!"

"Do not pretend you participated in battle out of loyalty," Athena shot back. "You only wished to satisfy your bloodlust."

Ares pushed off his throne and took up his spear, but Aphrodite stepped in front of him, and the anger that had overtaken him seemed to vanish.

"Is she wrong, Ares?" Aphrodite asked.

Ares's jaw tightened, and his knuckles turned white around his spear, but he did not move to strike or whatever he had intended to do when he rose against Athena. Instead, he took a step back and returned to his throne.

Zeus looked at Athena and then at the gods who had opposed him.

"I have escaped Fate more times than I can count," he said. "I can assure you the last thing that will bring me to my knees is a pair of star-crossed lovers."

"You have *prolonged* Fate," said Athena. "There is a difference. Why do you think the same prophecy haunts you?"

"Worse things have haunted me, Daughter," said Zeus. "But in this moment, nothing more than your words." A heavy silence followed as Zeus assessed the gods. "Those who stood against me on the battlefield will suffer my wrath. Apollo, Hermes, Aphrodite—you are hereby stripped of your powers."

"Father—" Aphrodite said, taking a step forward.

Zeus held up his hand, silencing her.

Hermes's mouth fell open before he slammed it shut and glared at his father. Only Apollo seemed unfazed, having faced a similar punishment before.

"For one year, you will know the struggle of what it means to be mortal," Zeus continued, as if he were foretelling the future. "To those who stood with me, I offer my shield to the one who brings me the Goddess of Spring in chains. Let it serve as a symbol to be bestowed on the greatest hunter among us."

Apollo glared at Artemis, who had straightened in her throne, eager for the honor.

Hermes's aura burned with anger, a halo of gold blazing around him.

"Will Hephaestus suffer the same?" Aphrodite asked. "He was only defending me."

Theseus knew why the Goddess of Love inquired after her husband. He was the blacksmith of the gods, responsible for forging their powerful weapons—ones she would need without her powers.

"And in doing so, he has illustrated where his loyalties lie," said Zeus.

"Oh, give him a break, Brother." Poseidon chuckled. "We all know Hephaestus is limited in the ways he can please his wife."

Aphrodite's jaw ticked, but she did not speak, waiting for Zeus to make his declaration.

"If Hephaestus goes without punishment, then you must take his year."

Aphrodite swallowed but did not hesitate. "Fine."

Hermes grimaced, shaking his head.

"So be it," said Zeus, a grave edge to his tone. "You shall live two years as a mortal. Enjoy watching your fellow Olympians pursue your beloved friend while you are helpless to defend her."

"And are you prepared to face Hades's wrath?" Hermes asked.

The corner of Theseus's mouth lifted. Hermes's question was akin to a scare tactic. He knew Hades was missing and that no one could protect Persephone from what was coming for her.

"The question you should be asking," said Zeus, "is whether Hades is prepared for mine."

———

Theseus manifested outside Hera's orchard, which was known as the Garden of the Hesperides. Its walls were high and white, obscured by tall and pointed trees. Beyond the iron gates where he stood, he could see an extensive maze of low hedges and topiaries, among which colorful peacocks roamed. The orchard grew among rolling hills. Atop the tallest was a tree, more magnificent than any other. Its trunk seemed to twist from the ground, and its branches unfurled like a palm, open to the sky, fingers splayed. Each limb was heavy with dark green leaves and golden fruit.

It was the fruit Theseus sought. One bite would cure him of his one weakness: vulnerability.

He ground his teeth, and a surge of white-hot anger warmed his chest, reminding him of how he'd been injured, both by Dionysus and Persephone. He'd taken the God of Wine's thyrsus to the stomach and five black barbs to the chest from the Goddess of Spring. Both wounds had been slow to heal, but what made him most angry was that his vulnerability was no longer secret.

Hades had known, which meant Dionysus had told him, and before word spread, Theseus intended to be invincible.

He took a step toward the gates of Hera's garden but was blocked as the goddess appeared.

"The audacity of a man," she said, her expression severe. "To encroach upon my sacred space."

"The audacity comes from my divine blood," Theseus replied.

"Yet not even my husband would dare set foot here."

"Growing favorable toward him, Hera?" he asked.

She glared at him, her lip curled in disgust. "You are not entitled to my things just because we are on the same side."

"Do you wish to win or not?" he asked.

"What a ridiculous question," she snapped.

"Then allow me what I came for," he said.

"What exactly did you come for?"

Theseus tilted his head. "A golden apple from your orchard."

"You crave invincibility?"

He did not answer. The request made it obvious, but saying it aloud felt like admitting to weakness.

"It is not a tree of wishes," said Hera. "It will demand something in return."

"As all divine things," he said.

He knew this, had prepared for it. Hera just stared. After a moment, she lifted her hand, and a golden apple appeared in her grasp. "Partake of this apple," she said, "and it will take your immortality."

"That is a heavy price," Theseus said.

"An equal price," said Hera.

He knew which had more value in the present given how close they were to battle. He would worry about deification later, when the war was won and he sat on the highest throne, exalted as the one true god of the world.

"What will it be, Theseus?" she asked, extending her hand farther.

He took the apple, and as he brought it to his lips, she spoke.

"You may only eat from this tree once."

It was a warning that he could not return and make the exchange again.

Theseus took a bite.

The flesh was soft, almost slushy, as if it were close to rotting, and when he swallowed, he felt no different than before, save that his tongue was coated in a strange, sour film.

He looked at the apple, examining the juicy, white pulp, and then took another bite, gaze leveling with Hera's.

"Are you ready to make your sacrifice?"

She raised an angry brow. "And what sacrifice is that?"

"The one where you fuck your husband for the greater good."

Her eyes darkened.

"Do not pretend our sacrifices are the same," said Hera. "Yours only saved yourself."

Theseus smirked. "Are you suggesting *sex* will save the world then, Hera?"

She glared and spoke between clenched teeth. "Do your part, Theseus, so my sacrifice is not made in vain." Her eyes dropped to the apple. "You had better finish that," she said. "You wouldn't want to find out what happens if you waste a drop. Now, leave."

"At once, Your Majesty," he mocked and then vanished.

CHAPTER VII
PERSEPHONE

Persephone wore a pale pink dress with a pleated skirt.
The neckline was square and modest—*classy*, Sybil had
said as she handed her a set of pearl drop earrings to pair
with the outfit. Leuce agreed.

"Clothing is a language," she said. "It is just as
important as the words you speak."

"And what exactly is this outfit communicating?"
Persephone asked.

Sybil brushed a stray piece of her hair behind her ear
so that it blended with the elegant sweep of her curls. "It
communicates warmth, intelligence...*authenticity*," she
said. "So that when you apologize, they believe you."

"Even if I am not sorry?"

Sybil shared a glance with Leuce and sighed. "I know
it doesn't seem fair, Persephone, but Helen's article has
brought your integrity into question, and you must
rectify that."

It seemed like such a foolish thing to be concerned

with given that Harmonia was not healing and Hades was missing, but this was not just about her reputation. It was about the reputation of all gods.

Since Helen had met Theseus, she had launched a media campaign against the Olympians, calling their rule into question, and while Persephone had plenty of issues with the way some of the gods reigned, Triad was far more problematic. They were quick to demand justice when the gods did not act according to their own ideals and claimed to be able to grant what the people wanted—wellness, wealth, and immortality. They were the same desires that had mortals seeking a bargain with Hades at Nevernight, ready to sacrifice their souls in the hope of something better.

But even if Triad's demigods managed to answer prayers, all they would do was prolong their inevitable fate.

Persephone had learned that the hard way, and so would the mortals who had benefited from Triad's divine power. The question was how much influence the demigods would hold by the time the truth was discovered.

"You can do this, Persephone," said Leuce. "Just… be yourself."

The problem was that being herself meant being angry and unapologetic.

"Leuce and I are going to go check on Harmonia before we leave," Sybil said.

"Of course," said Persephone.

When she was alone, she turned from the mirror and crossed to the bar. She poured a glass of whiskey and drank it, swallowing hard against the burn in her throat before pouring another. As she downed the second, tears were already blurring her vision.

She let them overwhelm her for a moment, her shoulders shaking before she managed to compose herself. She wiped the tears from her eyes and then poured another glass, taking a deep breath before she brought it to her lips.

"Drowning your sorrows?"

Persephone turned swiftly.

"Aphrodite," she breathed. Her eyes flitted toward Hephaestus, whom she was also surprised to see. "I'm so glad you're all right."

The last time she had seen her was on the battlefield outside Thebes when Ares had launched his gold spear in her direction. Aphrodite had stepped into its path. Persephone would never forget how her back had arched at such an odd angle once pierced or how Hephaestus had bellowed his anger and pain.

The Goddess of Love offered a small smile. "Yes. I am all right."

Persephone could not help it. She drew the goddess in for a hug. Aphrodite stiffened but soon relaxed and returned the embrace. After a moment, Persephone pulled back.

"What are you doing here?"

"I have come to see my sister."

Persephone felt the color drain from her face.

"I'm so sorry, Aphrodite," she said. "I—"

"Do not apologize, Persephone," Aphrodite said. "If I had known…"

Her voice trailed away, and Persephone knew why she faltered. There was no sense in agonizing over what could have been or what they should have known. Things just were, and now they had to deal with the consequences.

Aphrodite took a breath. "You look beautiful," she said.

Persephone smoothed a hand down her stomach and glanced at her dress.

"I do not feel like myself."

"Perhaps it is because Hades is not here with you," Aphrodite said.

Persephone swallowed hard, and fear moved up her spine. What would the other gods do when they discovered Hades had been captured by Theseus?

"How did you know?"

"Hermes told me," Aphrodite said and then hesitated. "Zeus held Council today and stripped us of our powers for helping you in battle."

"What?" Persephone asked. A sudden cold numbed her entire body.

"I managed to ensure Hephaestus retained his power," Aphrodite continued, glancing back at her husband, whose fiery gaze was locked on her. Persephone could not tell if he felt gratitude or frustration, but now she understood why he had come. He'd had to use his magic to bring Aphrodite to the Underworld. "We will have weapons for the coming war at least."

When they had stood opposite Zeus outside Thebes, Persephone had not thought twice about what would happen in the aftermath of battle. She had just been grateful to have allies.

Now all she felt was guilt.

"Do not mourn for us," Aphrodite said. "It was our decision to fight for you."

Persephone shook her head. "How could he?"

"There are few instances where Zeus will illustrate his full power," said Aphrodite. "One is when he feels his throne is threatened."

"Aphrodite," Persephone whispered.

She did not know what to say. The thought of Aphrodite, Apollo, and Hermes being powerless made Persephone sick with fear. It did not matter that Hephaestus could forge powerful weapons for their defense. Theseus and his men were already targeting gods with full power. What happened when he discovered these three were powerless?

If Aphrodite was worried, she did not let it show. She continued. "The real danger is that Zeus has declared a competition—whoever can bring you to him in chains will win his aegis, his shield. It is likely that Artemis will take the bait. I cannot speak for Poseidon, though I imagine he will defer to Theseus. Ares I can…persuade."

Persephone wondered exactly what that meant, though it was evident the gods had some kind of bond. Ares, known for his lust for battle and blood, was only shaken from his reverie when he'd wounded Aphrodite.

"Does Apollo hold no sway over his sister?" Persephone asked.

"Right now, they do not seem to be on the same side," said Aphrodite. "Perhaps that will change. Until then, you must be careful."

Persephone had known there would be consequences for standing against Zeus, but his actions toward her showed just how much he feared her and the prophecy that had predicted his downfall.

"If she keeps me from Hades, I will show no mercy."

"I will not fault you," said Aphrodite. "Though you should know that Apollo does love his sister."

"Then I will give him fair warning," Persephone said. She paused, swallowing hard, and when she looked at Aphrodite again, her eyes were misty with tears. "I have to find him, Aphrodite."

The goddess offered a small smile and then placed her hand on Persephone's shoulder.

"There are few things that survive war, Persephone," she said. "Let your love be one of them."

———

Persephone looked out the windows of Alexandria Tower. On the street below, amid piles of melting snow, journalists, television crews, and mortals gathered beneath the hot sun. She should have been prepared for this given the crowds that had gathered outside the Acropolis after her relationship with Hades went public, but this was different, and it wasn't even about the number of people. It was about the energy in the air—a chaotic mix of worship and scorn. It was heady and strangely addicting, if not a little unsettling, especially given Aphrodite's news.

Even now, as she scanned the crowd and the skies, she wondered if Artemis would attack in such a public way, though it did not seem like her style. She was the Goddess of the Hunt and would likely prefer stalking her prey.

Persephone shuddered at the thought, but it also filled her with anger, and her magic ignited, an aura blazing around her. She would let it rage while she spoke, a barrier between her and the masses.

"They have been out there for hours," said Ivy. Persephone glanced at the dryad who stood beside her, nibbling anxiously at her lip. "They started lining up before it was even dawn."

She did not take their eagerness as an illustration of support. Most were curious and only wanted the chance to say they had seen her in person. Then there were the Impious, who only came to express their disdain. They were easy to pick out from the crowd, holding signs that read "Freedom and Free Will" and "Go Back to Olympus."

The latter was ironic given she had never resided there, but it illustrated how the faithless viewed all gods—as one and the same.

But this wasn't about turning the Impious to her side. It was about gaining the admiration and worship of those who were already on the side of the gods.

She needed that power right now. It would fuel her in her search for Hades.

Persephone turned from the window.

"Is it time?" she asked, looking at Sybil and Leuce.

"You have two minutes," the oracle said, checking her watch.

Persephone's stomach clenched, and she took a breath. *Just get through this*, she thought. *And then get to Hades*.

"Mekonnen and Ezio will walk out before you," Sybil said.

Persephone smiled at the two ogres who had positioned themselves in front of the doors. They usually spent their evenings handling security for Nevernight, but today, they would serve as her bodyguards in place of Zofie.

A familiar ache blossomed in her chest.

"I don't think I've ever seen you up this early, Mekonnen," she said.

The ogre smirked. "Only for you, Lady Persephone."

"Time," said Sybil, meeting Persephone's gaze. "Ready?"

She wasn't sure she'd ever been ready. Not just for this but for anything that had come her way, yet she'd survived.

She would survive this too.

Mekonnen and Ezio led the procession, taking their places at the edge of the steps just outside the doors to Alexandria Tower. Persephone followed, hit with the roar of cheers and taunting jeers as she approached the podium to speak. The sound burrowed into her ears, an ebb and flow of excitement and anger, mixing with the rapid whir and flash of cameras.

She took a moment to absorb it, to accept that this had become her reality.

"Good afternoon," she said, speaking too close to the mic, amplifying the pop and crackle of her voice, but the resulting feedback silenced the crowd with a deafening hiss. She was quiet for a moment, adjusting her stance before she continued. "By now, most of you have probably seen the article printed about me in *New Athens News* by a former colleague."

She did not wish to speak Helen's name, though Persephone knew her statement would only draw more attention to her ex-friend. She could only hope what she had to say would cast doubt on her credibility.

"First, I would like to say that it is true that I hid who I was from you." Persephone's voice quivered as she spoke, and she paused to take a breath, saying her next line with far more composure and confidence. "I am the Goddess of Spring."

There were cheers and some applause but there were also boos and angry chants—*Deceiver! Liar!*

She ignored them and continued.

"I am sure many of you were surprised to discover that Demeter had a daughter, but my mother was reluctant to share me with the world. She kept me locked in a glass house, depriving me of friends and worshippers. At eighteen, I convinced her to let me go to college. I'm still not sure why she agreed, except that I think she was comforted by the fact that I was powerless—and powerless I was. I could not even coax a flower to bloom. How could I be a goddess when I had none of the attributes that were supposed to make me divine? So when I entered the mortal world for the first time, I felt like one of you. And I loved it. I did not wish to leave it, but sometimes you are called to your purpose, and I was called to mine."

It had taken time, but Hades had been patient. He had brought her magic to life while showing her that divinity was more than power—it was kindness and compassion and fighting for the people you loved.

The thought brought tears to her eyes.

She paused to clear her throat.

"It was not my intention to cause hurt or harm, and I am sorry if you feel deceived by my actions. I know you must now think us worlds apart, but for the longest time, I truly only ever felt mortal. Even now, I am not asking for sacrifices or altars or temples built in my name. I am only asking for a chance to be your goddess, to prove I am worthy of your worship. Thank you."

Persephone stepped away from the podium as a chorus of voices shouted.

"Persephone, who is your father?"

"Show us your divine form!"

"When did Hades discover your divinity?"

"Lady Persephone will not take questions," Sybil said into the mic as Mekonnen and Ezio blocked her from view and Leuce stepped to her side.

Though the crowd was loud and most of the voices unclear, a few vicious words reached her ears—a chant that made her blood run cold.

"Death to all gods! Death to all gods! *Death to all gods!*"

CHAPTER VIII
HADES

Hades flexed his fingers around another stone, his joints stiff from mud and overuse. His back ached as he carried the heavy brick from the ancient floor to the high labyrinth wall where he added it to the final row of steps he had built. He hoped they would hold his weight long enough so that he could reach the top of the wall and get his bearings to plan his escape.

He was not sure how long he had been at this, but he was fueled by the taste of Persephone on his tongue. He did not care to think long on how she had come to be before him, but if Theseus had intended to torture him, her visage had the opposite effect.

"*I will pry a stone from your lover's ring each time you stop*," he'd threatened.

In truth, Hades had never ceased to work; he had merely chosen a different project. One would have thought Theseus would be far more careful with his words. Though it was not as if he were a man of his word.

Despite this, Hades was under no delusion. He knew the reputation of Daedalus's labyrinth. Even the famed architect could barely escape his own creation—such was the folly of man, to create the thing that destroyed him—which was why Hades had not entered the labyrinth.

It was better to observe as much from above than to get lost attempting to navigate a nearly impossible trap.

And he imagined Theseus's maze would be even more challenging.

Perhaps he had not even made it escapable.

But Hades had to try.

If only he was at his full strength…

If you were at full strength, you wouldn't be here, he snapped at himself.

It did no good to think of what he could do with magic. With this net draped around his body, he was essentially mortal.

He had never been so aware of physical pain, never so aware of the weight of anything, save Persephone.

Always Persephone.

His wife and queen.

He grew anxious thinking about her. Theseus had said the last time he had seen her, she'd faced Demeter. What had come from that confrontation? He hated that he did not know, hated that he could not sense anything beyond this prison. It would not even matter if he were free of the net. This place was made from adamant, and it suppressed his magic.

Theseus had thought of everything when he'd laid his trap, and perhaps that was what worried Hades the most, because he knew Persephone would come for him. Theseus knew that too, and Hades would never forgive himself if she ended up in this hell.

That thought renewed his determination, and he began his ascent. He'd made the steps steep, and they wobbled beneath his feet. The higher he went, the more he clung to the next stone as if it might keep him from falling. It was another thing he had never thought much about but now dreaded—the fear of falling, of feeling pain.

His muscles tightened as if anticipating his failure.

When he reached the highest step, he rose to his trembling feet, palms sliding over the coarse stone, stretching until he could reach the top of the wall. He tested his grip and lifted himself, arms shaking. When he managed to get his upper body on the top of the wall, he led with his injured side.

"Fuck!" he barked, the pain sharp and biting. He seethed between clenched teeth as he dragged the rest of his body onto the wall and collapsed.

He lay there for a moment, breathing hard and sweating before he sat up, pressing a hand to his side, slick with blood, and looked out over the labyrinth.

He'd hoped from here he might have an idea of how to escape this fucking pit, but what unfolded before him was a vast network of tunnels that stretched for miles, disappearing into the darkness. This place did not appear to have an end or beginning.

Still, it seemed better to go over the labyrinth than through it.

He was going to have to pick a route and pray to the Fates.

Gods, he was really fucking desperate.

He rose to his feet and considered his next move. He tried to guess the direction of the cells based on how far he'd walked with Theseus, but there was something disorienting about this place. Not to mention that the walls were a lesson in strategy as they varied in thickness and distance—some were narrow and close while others were wide and farther away.

He decided he would try for a straight path through—or as straight as he could manage.

Looking down at his feet, he assessed the distance between himself and the next wall.

The first jump was not so difficult as it was about the length of his stride. The second, though, looked like a chasm stretching before him, and there was nothing below but darkness.

He had always felt at home in the shadows, but not here. This was not his darkness. It was born of some other kind of evil—one he did not wish to be consumed by or let out into the world.

He jumped, landing on the very edge of the wall. He wavered for a moment before falling forward on his knees. The impact was jarring, but he was growing used to the pain. He rose to his feet again, holding his side, and prepared himself for the next jump.

There was a part of him that worried he was only fooling himself. Perhaps all he'd done by scaling these walls was provide entertainment for Theseus and his men, but even if that were true, at least he'd tried to fight this fate.

At some point, he paused to look back but found that the path behind him looked the same as the one before him.

This place was fucking maddening.

He faced forward again and then jumped, his foot sliding as he hit the wall. He fell, catching himself with one hand before he could plummet into the depths of the labyrinth, grunting as his weight jerked his arm painfully. He hung there a moment, digging his fingers into the stone before he swung his body, reaching for the edge with his other hand, but his fingers slipped.

"Fuck!"

But his curse was drowned out by a low, vibrating growl. Hades looked down into the gleaming eyes of a massive lion before it launched itself at him.

"Fuck!" he said again and dropped down into the labyrinth. As he hit the ground, his legs buckled beneath him. The lion bounced off the wall and landed behind him.

Hades scrambled to his feet, and the two circled each other.

The lion bared its white teeth and roared, its breath a sickly breeze that carried the stench of death. It turned his stomach and made him wonder what exactly it had been feeding on.

He knew this lion.

It was the Nemean lion, famous for its impenetrable hide and its silver claws, sharper than swords.

Even if Hades had weapons, they would not help him here.

The lion pounced and Hades moved, shifting out of the way at the last second. He started to run, only to feel the lion claw his back. A pained cry escaped his mouth, and he stumbled and fell to his hands and knees.

It took him a moment to realize that the net was

on the ground. The lion had managed to cut it with its claws. He ignored the burn down his back and tried to scramble to his feet, but before he could, the lion sank its teeth into his ankle. Pain roared through him, consuming him like fire as he was jerked down again.

Hades managed to roll onto his back, his leg twisting uncomfortably within the lion's mouth as he shoved his other foot into its face over and over until it released his leg from its viselike jaws.

When he was free, he got to his feet. The monstrous lion stood opposite him, and they circled each other before the lion charged again. This time, it batted at him with its large paws and long, silver claws. He managed to dodge each deadly swipe, and when the creature grew frustrated, it gave a violent roar. Hades's stomach turned at the rancid smell of its breath, but he charged at the lion, vaulting into the air and landing on its back.

Again, the lion howled and then took off at a run. Hades gripped its fur and shifted forward, hooking his arms around the lion's neck and squeezing with all his might until he shook. Beneath him, the lion slowed, its panting more of a wheeze.

Finally, the creature staggered and fell to the ground.

Hades rolled onto his back, breathing hard and covered in sweat. For a long while, he stared up at the ceiling and took stock of his injuries. His foot throbbed and his back burned, but neither of those injuries hurt as much as the wound Theseus had inflicted in his side. That one made him nauseous.

He was just lucky he still had his strength, though he could tell he wasn't at his full capacity. He would take what he could get, especially since he could not call on his magic within these prison walls.

A flash of silver caught his eye, and Hades turned his head, spotting the lion's claws. He sat up and stretched across the space between them, brushing the tip of one talon, drawing blood with barely a touch.

Claws as sharp as blades.

Hades shifted closer and started to tear strips of cloth from his shirt, wrapping them around the longest claw several times to create a buffer. When he was sure he could grip it enough not to cut his hand to pieces, he yanked it with all his might until it broke free from the monstrous paw. It was more like a sickle, slightly curved and wider at one end.

Now I have a weapon.

His eyes fell to the lion's corpse with its impenetrable fur.

And armor, he thought as his fingers closed over the blunt end of his new knife.

Hades set about skinning the lion, a tedious and bloody task. He did not enjoy it, nor did he think it was anything the monster deserved, but he was about to enter the labyrinth, and he had no idea what he would face. There were likely worse things than this creature.

He had no salt to spread over the hide so he used sand—not that it would help preserve the skin. He merely hoped it would make it less…wet. When he was finished, he wore it like a cloak, and with his claw blade in hand, Hades entered the labyrinth.

He was not sure how long he walked, but he quickly lost all sense of space and time. There was a quiet within the labyrinth he had never experienced. It was a physical thing that felt as solid as the walls around him.

The darkness was bitter and blinding.

The longer he wandered through the sinuous tunnels, the more he felt as though his whole body was winding and twisting too. His mood wavered. Sometimes he was angry that he felt so separate from the darkness, that he did not feel like himself. Other times, a strange peace descended on him, and he seemed to navigate through these passages with a cool detachment.

He recited poetry and then composed his own, attempting to convey Persephone's beauty, if only to cling to his own sanity.

"Her golden hair swept down upon him like rays of burning sun," he started and then paused. "That's fucking stupid. Besides, I hate Helios."

He tried again.

"She emerged from the dark, a sweet-voiced thing with hair that flowed like a river in spring."

That was worse.

He moved on to singing.

"Is that... 'Laurel' by Apollo?" he heard Hermes ask.

Hades glared at the god who appeared beside him as a small, chubby baby with white wings that fluttered like those of a hummingbird.

"I will murder you if you tell anyone what you have heard here."

"That is very aggressive, Daddy Death," said Hermes. "*Everyone* listens to Apollo. There's nothing to be ashamed of. He's a vibe."

Hades decided not to ask what a vibe was.

"Why do you look like that?" he asked.

"Like what?" Hermes looked down at himself.

"Like a cherub, Hermes."

The god shrugged. "Perhaps you should ask yourself that question. You're the one hallucinating."

"Trust me, I would never manifest Hermes as a child. He's annoying enough as an adult."

"Rude," Hermes said, and then he grew taller, and his feet touched the ground. He spun and faced Hades as he walked backward down the corridor.

"You know, Hades, what you need is—"

"I need out of this fucking maze," Hades said.

"I was going to say *fun*," said the god.

They were coming to another break in the wall, and with Hermes walking backward, Hades thought he would miss the turn, but he was surprised when he shifted to the right and continued down another dark passage.

"You need a hobby."

"I have hobbies," Hades said curtly.

"Drinking and fucking don't count," said the god.

"You're one to talk," Hades countered. "All *you* do is drink and fuck."

"That's not *all* I do," Hermes said. "I play bridge once a week at the library."

"What the fuck is bridge?" Hades asked.

"You own a gambling den and don't know what bridge is? Gods, you're really *old*."

"I have hobbies, Hermes. I ride horses and play cards, and I dream about how to torture you on a regular basis."

The god's brows perked. "You dream about me?"

Hades said nothing.

"And…um…how exactly do you torture me? In these dreams."

"Not pleasantly," said Hades.

"List them out, Hades," Hermes said.

There was a change in his tone, something a little more aggressive, almost as if he were giving a command.

For a moment, Hades resisted. He did not like taking orders, but if Hermes wanted to hear all the ways he'd earned his wrath, then so be it.

"I have considered castration, but I think you'd find that too pleasant," said Hades.

The god pursed his lips and then shrugged. "Fair."

"I had to nix anything that requires restraint too."

"Unfair," said the god.

"I could send you into the Forest of Despair, but it's likely your greatest fear is a life with only one sexual partner."

"A *tragedy*," Hermes said.

"Which means I'd take a different approach."

"You really have thought about this," said Hermes.

"First, I'd curse you to always appear homely to any potential lover."

Hermes gasped.

"Then, I would ensure you never find your rhythm again. That applies to dancing and sex."

"You *wouldn't*," Hermes said.

"The sight of your penis would make everyone gag."

"You beast!"

"Those aren't even my favorites," said Hades with a smirk. "My favorite is that every television series you start never finishes."

"No!" Hermes bellowed. "It is true what they say. You are a cruel god."

Hades shrugged. "You asked."

"I did," said Hermes. "I hope it helped."

Hades could hear the grin in his voice, but he didn't understand.

"What?" he asked, looking in the direction of the god, but he found he was no longer there.

Once again, Hades was alone, and while he hated the dull ache of disappointment that bloomed in his chest, he felt far more present than he had before.

With his focus renewed, he continued through the labyrinth. He had no way of knowing where exactly he was going—if he was closer to the center or farther away. He did not even know where he *should* be heading. He just knew that stopping was worse.

That was giving up.

At some point, he turned a corner and came face-to-face with a different kind of darkness. He halted at the edge of it, hesitant. He knew he had not made it to the end of the labyrinth. He suspected this was the middle—or closer to it at least.

How vast was this darkness? How endless?

He had nearly lost his mind surrounded by walls. What happened when there was *nothing*?

He let one foot slide forward and then the other, and as the dark pressed in on him from all sides, he had the thought that this was the kind of thing he would face if he was to enter the Forest of Despair—nothingness, a void.

Loneliness.

Bright lights flooded his vision, and they burned away the dark so suddenly, his eyes watered.

Theseus's laugh echoed in the space that Hades could now confirm was the center of the labyrinth, and it truly did go on for miles in each direction.

"You look ridiculous," the demigod said.

Hades blinked, adjusting to the light, and saw Theseus opposite him. Of the two, he was the one who did not look the part. He was too clean and too tidy for the madness of the labyrinth, dressed in his tailored blue suit and pressed white shirt.

"I suppose I would have been disappointed if you hadn't tried to escape."

Hades glared and held his claw blade tighter.

Theseus noticed and clicked his tongue.

"Hera will be distraught to learn you killed her pet," said Theseus.

Hades continued to say nothing.

"You know, Hades, talking to you is like talking to a brick wall."

"Then maybe you shouldn't."

Theseus smirked. "But I have *so much* to say," he said. "And so does your wife, apparently."

Hades ground his teeth. He did not know what Theseus was referring to exactly, but it sounded like Persephone had done something to piss him off.

"Perhaps you can tell me how you manage to keep her quiet," Theseus continued. "Or is it that your dick is always in her mouth?"

Hades gripped his knife tighter.

"Maybe I will have to try that," Theseus said.

Hades charged. Racing across the floor of the labyrinth, he jumped, vaulting through the air, roaring as he brandished the deadly claw.

Theseus did not move an inch as Hades barreled toward him. A sliver of unease trickled down his spine. He knew he had missed something, and then it hit him—literally.

A heavy weight sent him crashing to the floor. He landed hard, his body denting the ground. He realized quickly that he was trapped beneath another net. His fingers tightened around the lion's claw as he attempted to cut himself free, but he could not move his arm.

Still he tried to saw at the threads, breaking out in a cold sweat as Theseus approached.

The demigod crouched before him, watching Hades's struggle before he spoke.

"This would all be quite honorable if it wasn't so pathetic," he said, plucking the claw from between Hades's fingers. He studied it and then slammed it through Hades's hand and into the ground.

Hades couldn't even scream. All he managed was a pained gasp.

He glared up at Theseus, breathing hard between clenched teeth, and watched as he reached into the pocket of his jacket and pulled out a small envelope, pouring the contents into his palm.

"You've earned this," Theseus said, blowing something into Hades's face.

It was some kind of powder that invaded his nose, mouth, and eyes. He started to cough, and he couldn't stop. His eyes watered, and his chest burned. He needed water—he needed to *breathe*—but then he tasted blood on the back of his tongue.

His vision swam.

I am going to die.

CHAPTER IX
PERSEPHONE

The Underworld was different.

The air smelled like sulfur, and the sky was full of ash. When the wind blew, Persephone could feel the grit of it against her skin, rough and blistering.

There were other things too. The souls had channeled their usual merriment into preparing for war. Cerberus remained restless and three-headed, uninterested in play. All the while, the glassy obsidian mountains of Tartarus taunted Persephone, a constant reminder of what had occurred in the arsenal.

As much as she recognized she was queen of this realm and now possessed power over it, she could not bring herself to hide the changes, the slow decay. It seemed fitting given what had occurred—what was *still* occurring—and concealing it with vines and flowers felt insincere. A corpse was still a corpse, even covered in colorful flora.

There was a part of her that wondered if the

Underworld was dying, and if that was true, did it also mean Hades was dying? She pushed those thoughts away quickly. She could not bear to think like that right now. It felt like giving up, and she would *never* give up. She would fight for Hades until the world ended, and when there was nothing left, only her rage would remain.

"Have you heard anything?" Yuri asked.

Persephone met the soul's wide-eyed gaze. She frowned, realizing she had become so lost in her thoughts that she had heard nothing the girl had been saying.

"About Hades," Yuri added to clarify.

Persephone's gaze fell to her cold tea.

"No," she whispered.

Hermes and Apollo were on the hunt for Theseus's men. The challenge was finding someone close enough to the demigod who would know the answers to the questions they had, though they were finding that very few knew his plans, if any.

Hecate was continuing to trace her ring, which was proving to be far more challenging than either of them expected given that it seemed to be traveling with Theseus and revealed a rather mundane routine for someone so sinister.

Nevertheless, learning the demigod's movements was still an advantage. Perhaps they'd find someone to interrogate.

"Are the souls…" Persephone started to ask if they were afraid, but that was a ridiculous question. Of course they were afraid. It had only been two days since Theseus had released the Titans and the souls had to fight the monsters that had escaped Tartarus. They'd been brave, but there had been consequences, as she knew there would be, namely that some had not been able to withstand the trigger of battle and Thanatos had to take them to Elysium.

It had hurt everyone. It hurt now.

"Do they feel safe?" she asked instead.

"As safe as they can," Yuri replied, and she looked out her open door. "Preparing for the worst makes them feel better."

The street was busy with souls who were repairing or reinforcing their homes. Ian and Zofie continued to forge weapons, their hammers striking in an uneven rhythm.

It was almost like they did not trust her magic, though how could they when she did not even trust it herself? It was new, still foreign. It lived on the fringes of her energy, reminding her of the way Hades's magic always waited in the wings, primed to protect her no matter the cost.

Persephone's eyes burned with tears, and after a moment of quiet, Yuri whispered, her voice quivering, "I just wish everything was normal again."

Persephone hardened against those words.

It was such a natural thing to say when things felt uncertain, but the longer she lived with loss, the more the idea of normal angered her.

There was no normal. There was only the past, and it was hopeless to wish for it even at her loneliest, because nothing could return to the way it was—not in the aftermath of this.

"There is no 'normal again,' Yuri," Persephone said. "There is only new and different, and neither are always good."

The soul frowned.

"Persephone, I—"

She rose to her feet before Yuri could finish, knowing what her next words would be.

I'm so sorry.

And she could not stand to hear them either. She could not even explain why, but they were just words, empty ones people said when they had nothing else to give.

"Thank you, Yuri, for the tea."

She fled before her emotions got the best of her and teleported to the Asphodel Fields. By the time she arrived, she was already in tears. She looked out on the Underworld from where she stood, her arms crossed over her chest. The wind picked up, whipping her hair, and the asphodel around her swayed, grazing her gown.

She felt sick and lost, and she did not know where to go, because every part of this place reminded her of Hades, yet he was what she wanted most.

She closed her eyes, and cold tears spilled down her face.

"Lady Persephone."

She swallowed hard and looked over her shoulder at Thanatos. She did not care to hide her pain. He could feel it anyway.

"Can I help you?"

She knew what he was asking.

Thanatos had influence over emotion. He could ease her suffering. In the past, she'd refused. She'd wanted to feel because she felt like she deserved it, but this was different.

"*Please*," she said. The word was a plea, a broken cry.

Thanatos offered his hand, and she took it, warm and soft against her own, and suddenly peace fell over her. It was like…picnics in the meadow under the starry Underworld sky and baking cookies in a small kitchen with her best friend by her side. It felt like the fun of rock paper scissors and hide-and-seek.

It felt like…the first time she had looked at Hades and recognized her own soul.

"What are you thinking?"

She shivered at the sound of his voice, and chills pebbled her skin.

She opened her eyes.

"Hades," she whispered and touched his face, grazing the stubble on his cheek.

He felt real enough, but she had been fooled by this before and did not think she could face the pain of waking alone again.

They were lying in the grass beneath a twisted oak. She knew this place. They had been here before—they had rested and made love beneath this tree. It was at the very edge of Elysium. If she were to sit up, she would see the gray waves of the ocean cresting the horizon.

"Where are you?" she asked.

He laughed as he studied her with those dark eyes, his body pressed against hers.

"I'm right here," he said. "With you."

She shook her head, her vision blurring with tears.

She knew otherwise.

"Darling," he said, his voice a low rumble, his fingers in her hair. He leaned forward and pressed his lips to her forehead. She closed her eyes tight, focusing on the feel of his kiss, warm and heavy.

Real.

When he pulled away, he let his nose drift along hers.

"It was just a dream," he said, and she opened her eyes again.

"You speak as if you live inside my mind," she said.

Hades stared at her and frowned, his eyes drifting to her lips, and she was suddenly aware of a keen hunger tightening her stomach.

"What will it take? To prove to you this is real?"

"Nothing you do will convince me," she said. "Unless you can tell me where you are."

He was quiet, watching her.

Then he leaned closer, and the air between them felt heavier than his weight on her body.

"Lost," he answered before his mouth dropped to hers.

His kiss was like a brand that seared her skin. She opened her mouth against his, and his tongue slipped inside.

He tasted different, his mouth devoid of that smoky, sweet edge, but he smelled the same, sharp and earthy, like long shadows cast by firelight. She tried not to think about the change and what it meant.

He pulled away again, but she could still feel the brush of his lips against hers as he spoke. She kept her eyes closed as he whispered, "Live in this moment with me."

Her resistance melted away, broken by the same plea she had made before. Her mouth collided with his, and her arms went around him, hands pressing into his back, bringing his entire body flush with hers.

As they kissed, Hades moved against her and she

lifted her hips, needing to feel him where she ached the most. Each lush stroke coaxed a fire beneath her skin and stole a little more of her breath. By the time he left her mouth, she was ready for him, so aware of how empty she felt.

"Hades." She breathed his name as his lips trailed along her jaw and down her throat before he buried his face between her breasts, hands gripping. Her fingers sifted through his hair, tightening when his teeth grazed one nipple, then the other through the fabric of her dress.

Finally, he looked up.

His eyes were dark but just as brilliant as they were when he was in his true form. They possessed a fire of their own, a liveliness that only erupted when he was looking at *her*. She felt as though a void had opened in the pit of her stomach, and somehow, she became even more hollow.

"Yes?" he asked.

"Fuck me as a god," she said.

"If you wish it," he said.

"I wish it."

Hades's gaze was unwavering as he bent and pulled one of her nipples into his mouth before sitting back on his knees. She did not like the distance, but she liked watching him undress. When he was naked before her and he had dropped his glamour, she sat up and pulled her dress over her head.

His gaze on her bare skin made her feel primal and possessive. It ignited her with a will to dominate. She moved onto her knees, and Hades took her into his arms, lifting her up the incline of his thighs until she was seated against his length.

"Drop your glamour," he said, "so that I may make love to a goddess."

From this position, she was elevated slightly above him, and she used that to her advantage, teasing him as she brushed her mouth against his.

"If you wish it," she whispered.

"I wish it," he said, his tone low, almost feverish.

She let her magic go, and it fell away like a shiver down her spine.

Hades held her tighter, lifting her body higher. She knew without words what he was asking, and she answered, guiding the head of his cock to her entrance. She braced her hands against his shoulders as she seated herself on him, breathing through the pleasure as it coursed through her body, rattling her mind.

She wrapped her arms around him tighter, and as they moved together, all she could focus on was the feelings he conjured. This was a magic of its own, separate from any divine gift, and it let her live in a single moment of pure ecstasy, far from the grief and sorrow of her life.

Except for the part where it wasn't real, and suddenly her arousal was cut through with pain.

Persephone twined her fingers in Hades's hair and drew his head back, her lips colliding with his as tears streamed down her face.

"Lie down," she said as she pulled away.

Hades held her gaze but did as she asked, shifting onto his back. She adjusted her position, her palms flat on his chest.

"Tell me," he said, though his body tightened beneath hers as she began to move.

"There is nothing to say," she replied. Reaching for his hands, she brought them to her breasts.

"You always have something to say," he said, teasing her flesh with his fingers.

"A god once told me that words mean nothing," she said, growing breathless.

"Your god was a fool," he replied, his hands falling to her hips where he gripped her harder, moving faster.

"Oh?" she asked on a moan.

"Some words are not meaningless," he said.

She could no longer say anything, and he did not speak as her body seized with pleasure. It wasn't until she collapsed atop Hades that he finished, whispering the words against her temple.

"I love you, Persephone."

———

"Persephone."

She squeezed her eyes tighter, clinging to her dream a little longer, but already she could feel the weight of Hades's arms slipping away.

"Persephone."

She opened her eyes and found Hecate standing over her. It took her a moment to get her bearings, and then she realized she was in her bed. Thanatos must have taken her from the Asphodel Fields.

"Hecate," she whispered as she sat up, an ache forming between her brows. "Is everything all right?"

"I believe I have found Hades," Hecate said.

Persephone had been so desperate to hear those words for so long, she could hardly believe they were true.

"Where is he?" she asked, rising to her feet.

Hecate did not respond immediately, and Persephone's soaring hope quickly turned to dread.

"Hecate?"

"He's at Knossos," she said.

"Knossos?" Persephone asked, confused. Knossos was a city on the island of Crete. "But there is nothing there but ruins."

"Come," Hecate said, extending her hand.

Persephone could already feel Hecate's magic, ancient and electric, curling around her. Her heart rose in her throat as she took the goddess's hand and they teleported.

She half expected to appear before the ruins of Knossos but was surprised when she was brought to Hades's office at Nevernight. Hermes lay on Hades's desk while Apollo took shots of vodka from behind the bar. A mortal sat with his hands tied behind his back. He was an older man with a sharp nose, round wire glasses, and a mostly bald head.

"What's going on?" Persephone asked. "Who is this?"

"I'm Robert," said the man.

"He's Robert," Apollo and Hermes said.

They all spoke in unison. It made Persephone flinch.

"And who is Robert?" Persephone asked with more patience than she felt.

Hecate had just found Hades, and these two were… well, she wasn't sure what they were doing.

"I'm an architect," said Robert.

"He's an architect," Apollo and Hermes said.

They sounded bored.

Persephone exchanged a look with Hecate, who rolled her eyes before sending a surge of magic in both gods' directions. Hermes shot up from Hades's desk and landed on the hard marble floor, a sharp obsidian thorn in the spot where he had once lain. The vodka in Apollo's glass turned to sand just as he shot it into his mouth. He spat it out quickly, choking on the dirt.

"What the fuck?" they said.

Hermes climbed to his feet from the floor, and Apollo searched frantically for something wet, settling on an open bottle of wine to gargle.

"My husband is missing, and Hecate tells me that he is at Knossos, and instead of taking me to him, she brought me to you," Persephone said, her voice shaking with anger. "*One* of you tell me what the *fuck* is going on."

Hermes and Apollo exchanged a look.

"I'm afraid that is why I am here," said Robert.

Persephone's eyes fell to the mortal.

"And what do you have to do with my husband and Knossos?"

"I am an architect," he said.

Persephone could not keep a handle on her magic, and she didn't want to. It flared to life, heavy and dark, as black spires shot from the tips of her fingers.

The mortal's eyes widened, and he seemed to press himself farther into his chair.

She felt a hand on her arm and turned to look at Hecate.

"What the idiots are trying to say is that the ruins at Knossos are no longer ruins," Hecate said.

"Theseus has been rebuilding the labyrinth," said Apollo.

"So we thought we would find his builder," said Hermes.

"*Architect*," Robert corrected.

"But it turns out Robert here was just the *first* builder," Apollo continued.

"*Architect*," Robert said again.

"The first one?" Persephone asked.

"He hires and fires them," said Hermes. "The—"

"*Architects*," Robert and Hermes said at the same time.

"Why?" Persephone asked.

"He thinks it will add to the perplexity of his labyrinth," said Apollo.

"I told him it wasn't so," said Robert. "All he needed was a great architect, but he wanted it to be *inescapable*."

Persephone frowned, holding the mortal's gaze.

"And…why are you here again?"

"We *thought* we would get to torture him into telling us how to get through the labyrinth," said Hermes. "Turns out he's *cooperative*."

"I think you are upset about the wrong thing, Hermes," Hecate advised.

The God of Mischief crossed his arms over his chest.

"You are telling me Hades is trapped in a labyrinth?" Persephone asked.

"It is more than likely," said Robert. "I do not know much about Theseus's plans beyond the fact that he wanted a type of prison. He insisted it be constructed from adamant."

"Well, that is unfortunate," said Hecate.

Persephone looked at the goddess. "What is it?"

"It is a metal that was forged by Gaia," Hecate said. "It

means that entering the labyrinth will be like becoming a mortal. It also means we cannot teleport inside or out."

The more she learned, the more anxious Persephone became, but things were making sense. Now she knew why she could not feel Hades's magic.

"So the only way to reach him is to go through the labyrinth," Persephone said, more to herself than anyone else.

"Do you know which part of the labyrinth you built?" asked Apollo. "We could find the other architects and piece together a map."

But Robert shook his head. "It would be too hard to say which part was mine, and I imagine it would be the same for the others."

Persephone studied the mortal. "Why are you so compliant?" she asked, a little suspicious.

"Theseus never asked us what gods we served," said the man. "I have always been pious, and pious I will always be."

His sincerity rang true.

"Thank you, Robert."

He smiled. "Of course, my lady," he said with a nod. "Er…would anyone be willing to…untie my hands? They're a little numb."

Persephone turned her gaze to Apollo and Hermes. "Take him home, and one of you…grant him a favor."

Apollo and Hermes exchanged a look and then spoke in unison. "We can't."

Then Persephone remembered what Aphrodite said—that Zeus had stripped them of their powers.

"Well, how did you get him here?"

"The old-fashioned way," said Hermes.

"I think you mean the mortal way," said Apollo.

"We abducted him from outside his work," Hermes explained. "Antoni helped us."

"Did anyone see you?" Persephone asked.

"Does it matter?" asked Hermes.

"It does if Theseus's men are watching," said Persephone.

Hermes pursed his lips, and Apollo frowned.

"I doubt Theseus would waste his resources on me," said Robert. "I am one cog in his machine."

"And if one breaks, the whole thing comes down," Persephone said. "Theseus does not like loose ends." She looked at Hecate. "What can be done?" She did not wish for the man to suffer for his loyalty to the gods.

"I can cast a protection spell," Hecate said. "Though they are not infallible."

"I am grateful for anything," said Robert. "I only wish I could've helped more."

Persephone met the mortal's gaze. "You have helped enough. Thank you."

Hecate teleported with Robert and returned in seconds.

"Will he be safe?" Persephone asked.

"I'm not sure anyone is safe," said Hecate.

Her words made Persephone's stomach drop.

"You will not be able to take responsibility for every mortal who crosses paths with Theseus," said Hecate.

"No, but I would rather not see them die for helping us."

"He made his choice," Hecate said.

Persephone could not argue. There were greater things at stake.

"We have to go to Knossos," she said.

"Hold on, Seph," said Apollo. "This is clearly a trap."

"I am aware," she said, but it changed nothing.

"I know you are eager to bring Hades home," said Hecate. "But we must proceed with caution. Apollo is right. It is evident Theseus used your ring to trap Hades, and it is likely he knows we will track its energy. He wants you in that labyrinth. He is *counting* on it."

Persephone did not doubt that either. Theseus was toying with them.

"I think I know someone who can help," said Hermes. "Or at least let us know what we're up against."

"Who?" Persephone asked.

"Her name is Ariadne," he said. "Ariadne Alexiou."

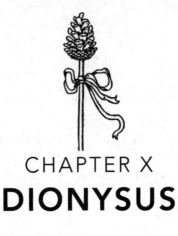

CHAPTER X
DIONYSUS

Dionysus entered the Crysos Gallery of Art and wove his way through the crowd, heading straight for the bar. The attendant must have seen him because he already had a glass of wine prepared. Dionysus snatched it with a nod and continued through the fray, observing the gathering.

He was looking for anyone he recognized, but not because he wanted to chat—it wasn't exactly a friendly crowd. It was more a matter of assessing competition for the upcoming auction. While those in attendance were making a show of observing artistic masterpieces, it was not the art up for sale tonight—it was women and young men.

Dionysus had come in search of Medusa, a gorgon who had the power to turn men to stone. She had last been seen on the shore of the Aegean. As he'd feared, Poseidon had found her, and once he'd had his way with her, he claimed to have left her alone.

"If I had known the value of her beautiful head, I'd have

cut it off where she lay," he'd said, informing Dionysus that she could only turn men to stone once her head was separated from her body. It was a cruel revelation, and it left Dionysus uncertain as to whether it was best to find her at all. But if it wasn't him, it would be someone else who valued her use over her life. Even if he did not manage to find her, he could at least extricate a few sex-trafficked victims and make note of the rest.

Eventually, the maenads would rescue them all—at least that was the goal. He hesitated to call it a plan, because he'd done this enough to understand that plans never went smoothly. Sometimes they were too late.

His chest tightened.

One day, he hoped they could put an end to this vicious cycle of abuse.

He made his way into the adjoining room, which, while more spacious, was far more crowded, likely because it featured mostly erotic art. Dionysus scanned the room, his eyes passing over portraits of Aphrodite in the hands of mortal lovers and glades full of naked nymphs, until he caught a glimpse of someone he recognized, though she was the last person he'd expected to find here, and that was because she shouldn't have been here at all.

Detective Ariadne Alexiou stood across from him, and he could not help the eruption of heat that started in his groin. His heart pumped harder, and blood rushed to every limb, making him very, very aware of the heaviness between his legs.

Motherfucker, he thought.

She was supposed to be at his club, Bakkheia, training with the maenads, yet she was here, wearing an electric blue dress that only drew more attention to her beauty.

He couldn't help thinking about how she had wrapped those long legs around his waist when he'd fucked her against a cave wall on the island of Thrinacia or how he'd twisted his fingers into that thick, dark hair just to gain better access to her mouth. She had tasted so sweet, and she'd felt so good around him.

Fuck, he ached for her.

She had yet to notice him, but as he took a step in her direction, a man handed her a glass of champagne.

What the actual fuck?

"Ari," Dionysus said as he approached. He felt almost breathless, but he knew that was his frustration.

She was in the middle of taking a drink when she spit it back into the glass, her eyes wide with surprise. Clearly she had not expected him to be here either.

"Dionysus," she said. "Hi."

"What are you doing here?" he asked.

"You know Lord Dionysus?" the man beside her asked.

Know was an understatement.

"Yes," she said. "Casually."

"Casually," Dionysus repeated. "Sure."

Her gaze seared his skin. He knew what she was saying without speaking.

Don't fuck this up for me.

He pointed to the two of them. "So what's *this*?"

The man, who was young with a swath of blond hair, hesitated and stuck out his hand. "Leander Onasis," he said.

Dionysus looked at his hand and then met his gaze. "I didn't ask who you were," he said.

The mortal blushed and dropped his arm. He started to speak, but Ariadne interrupted.

"Leander," she said and offered an apologetic smile. "Would you give us a minute?"

He hesitated, glancing at Dionysus. "Of course," he said. "I'll, uh, see you in the room?"

"Sooner," she said.

He grinned before walking away, and Dionysus glared, unable to suppress the jealousy and anger that shot up his spine.

"Really? Sooner?" he asked.

"What the fuck is wrong with you?" she asked between her teeth. "We had an agreement."

"You wanted to go back to work," he said.

"This *is* work," she snapped.

"Really? Because I happen to know your boss put you on traffic duty."

"Are you stalking me now?"

"Never stopped," he said, though it wasn't stalking, and she knew it.

They'd agreed that she could go back to her day job as a detective for the Hellenic Police Department, but she had to accept that the maenads would also watch her every move. He was going to have to have a conversation about this, however.

"Did you arrive with him?"

Her eyes were like fire, and they singed every inch of his skin.

"Is this about my job or the men I fuck?"

"I thought this was work," he shot back.

"You are such an asshole," she seethed.

She spun and stormed away. He followed, catching up to her.

"Ari—"

121

She rounded a corner and turned toward him abruptly. "Don't call me that!" she snapped.

"What? Your name?"

"That is a nickname. It denotes familiarity, a privilege I have not given you."

"I fucked you. I'd say we are pretty familiar."

"I gave you access to my body," she said. "That doesn't mean we're close."

Her words stung, and Dionysus tightened his jaw against the terrible things he wanted to say. He wasn't sure what he'd expected but he'd hoped that when they returned from the island, she'd still want him.

It turned out to be the opposite.

"Do you regret it?" he asked after a moment, unable to keep the pain from his voice.

"We're not talking about this here," she said, averting her eyes, glassy with anger.

"Now seems as good of a time as any," he said, because he knew outside this moment, she would continue to avoid him.

When she met his gaze, the full force of her fury hit.

"Every time you do this, I regret it more and more."

He searched her face desperately for any sign of a lie but found nothing.

She was telling the truth.

He took a step back, swallowing hard.

"Watch your back," he said. "You aren't among friends."

"Thanks for the advice," she said, returning to Leander, who welcomed her with a smile and a fresh drink. After a few moments, she seemed to relax around him, and Dionysus hated that she could not seem to do the same with him.

It took all his power to tear his gaze from her, but he finally left her for the main floor, returning to the bar for a second glass of wine when he was swiftly cut off by a man with a badly bruised face.

His name was Michail Calimeris, and he was the owner of Maiden House, a brothel in the pleasure district.

"Well, if it isn't Lord Dionysus," he said.

Dionysus had gone to the mortal at the start of his search for Medusa, but things had escalated quickly when Michail had recognized Ariadne as a cop. She'd ended up killing two of his men.

It was just another reason she should not be here.

"Michail," Dionysus said. "You're looking... recovered."

It was a lie, but it was also the nicest thing he could think to say to a man he loathed.

"I'm on the mend," Michail replied as if talking to an old friend.

"If you'll excuse me," Dionysus said, attempting to step around Michail, but he was stopped when the mortal stuck out his hand.

"You'll forgive me," Michail said. "But I don't think I will."

Dionysus took a step back and then glanced to his left and right. In the time he'd been with Ariadne, the gallery had been cleared of civilians, and the only people who remained were Michail's men.

They surrounded him on all sides.

Dionysus held Michail's gaze.

"To what do I owe this honor?" he asked thickly.

Michail gave a wicked smile. "I just wanted to have a friendly chat."

"You don't look particularly pleasant."

"It might have something to do with the nose job you gave me when you slammed my face into the floor."

Dionysus shrugged. "An improvement if you ask me."

"No one did," Michail said tightly.

There was a beat of silence, and then Leander walked into view with Ariadne. One of his hands was clasped tightly over her mouth, and he held a gun to her head. Dionysus's fingers curled into fists as he tried to assess how he was going to get them out of this situation.

Fuck.

He shifted his gaze from her to Michail again.

"You should have just let me have the detective," Michail said.

"She's not mine to give."

"It sure didn't look like that to me," he said.

Dionysus imagined not, given that Michail had walked in while Ariadne was grinding against his cock, but intimacy did not equal possession or ownership.

"So you've decided to take her?"

"I've decided to kill her in front of you," he said.

"You think I would let you?"

Michail chuckled. "You may be a god, Dionysus, but what power do you possess beyond filling glasses with wine and a sharp pine cone?"

Dionysus was used to people questioning his divinity. He was the God of Wine and Revelry. His influence on the world was minimal compared to the Olympians, but these mortals had not been alive during the time of his madness. They did not know what he was capable of when pushed.

And this was testing his limits. The edges of his vision were already turning red.

"You forgot one," Dionysus said. "I'm pretty skilled at breaking faces."

"But not skilled enough to realize when you've been lured into a trap."

Dionysus had to admit, that stung a little. The truth was he had not thought twice about coming tonight. He'd been to similar auctions many times; he'd taken this one for granted. Still, trapping a god was never a good idea.

Trapping Dionysus was worse.

"I am impressed," said Dionysus. There was a tremor to his voice that some might have mistaken for nerves, but it was really anger.

Michail's eyes gleamed with pride. "Thank you."

"Not with you," Dionysus said. "I'm impressed that you think you've trapped me when I have most certainly trapped you."

Dionysus summoned his thyrsus. The men in the room laughed at what they called a pine cone–tipped staff, but the fennel was a symbol of his power over nature, over hedonism and pleasure.

It was also a weapon, and his vision was red.

He hurled the staff at Michail like a spear, and it went straight through his chest, striking the wall behind him with a loud crack.

There was a moment of stunned silence.

Michail was still on his feet though there was a hole in his chest. He staggered, and blood burst from his mouth, spattering the floor.

Then he fell to the ground, dead.

Dionysus's gaze shifted to Ariadne and then to the men surrounding him.

They all looked horrified.

"I forgot to mention," he said. "My pine cone is pretty sharp."

Leander cocked his gun, and the men started to close in on Dionysus, only to freeze when a strange lurching sound escaped from somewhere deep in their throats.

They exchanged looks, both confused and fearful, before a dark liquid burst from every orifice of their bodies in a stream so powerful, they were thrown backward into the walls. When it was over, they fell to the floor like dead fish in a pool of red wine.

He'd turned their blood to wine and filled them full of it.

As he stood there, his vision started to clear, but he knew the madness was not over—this was just the start. He was about to spiral.

He had to get Ariadne out of here.

He crossed the room and plucked his thyrsus from the wall. When he faced Ariadne, he was surprised to find that she had not fled. They were both covered in blood and wine, and the smell of it thickened the air between them.

He reached for her, brushing a finger across her cheek.

"Are you afraid?" he asked.

"Yes," she said, but she did not push him away.

Dionysus held his breath, and his hand moved to the back of her neck. He stepped closer until she was forced to tilt her head back to hold his gaze and there was no space between them.

"Now you know who I really am," he said, and then they vanished, leaving the mayhem behind.

Dionysus hoped when they arrived at his house, Ariadne would put some distance between them, but she didn't, and he did not have the power to push her away.

"Ari," he whispered. His hand was still tangled in her hair, braced at the back of her neck. "I need you to leave."

He spoke the words, but he held her tighter, his body vibrating with an unfathomable lust. It was the cycle of the madness he had been cursed with, and once he was in its grip, there was only one way out.

It made him feel ashamed, that spilling blood ignited this frenzied need to fuck, and he did not want Ariadne to be the victim of his unrestrained desire, even if she thought she could handle it.

"Dionysus."

She spoke his name in a breathy whisper, and he closed his eyes as it shuddered through him. His mouth hovered over hers, and his throbbing cock pressed into the bottom of her stomach. There was no mistaking what he wanted, except that she likely could not sense the violence quaking inside him.

If they came together tonight, it would not be gentle, and neither of them would be the same.

"You do not want this version of me," he said.

His brows were furrowed, and every muscle in his body was like a bowstring pulled taut. If she said the right thing, or maybe it was the wrong thing, he would succumb to the insanity of this desire.

Ariadne brushed a few of his braids over his shoulder, and when her fingers trailed along his brow, he opened his eyes and met her gaze.

"Don't tell me what I want," she said.

"Fuck you," he said, and then he kissed her.

He bent her head back, his tongue sweeping into her mouth deeply. She could not kiss him in return, but he did not need that yet. This was not a give-and-take. It was possession.

Ariadne didn't resist, looping her arms around his neck and holding on until he eased his assault on her mouth and let her kiss him back, her tongue twining with his in a desperate dance. Then he left her mouth, kissing along her jaw and her neck, his hands moving to her breasts and then to her back, anchoring her against his arousal.

"I need this now," he said.

He pulled away enough to meet her gaze even though his vision was hazy.

"Yes," she whispered, breathless.

He groaned.

"I will not be gentle, Ariadne," he said.

"It's okay," she said, and this time, she kissed him.

His hands moved to her ass, and as he dragged her up his body, someone cleared their throat. They froze, and when Dionysus turned his head, he realized they were not alone—far from it. His living room was full of people.

"Way to go, Hecate," Hermes said. "They were just getting to the best part."

"What the actual fuck?" Dionysus snarled. His desire turned to fury instantly, his focus solely on Hermes.

"Easy now, Dionysus," said Hermes. "We had no choice."

"No choice?" Dionysus asked, releasing Ariadne and

turning to face them completely, his hands fisted. "I will tear you to *shreds*."

Hecate stepped into his line of sight, blocking him from Hermes. Her eyes were swallowed by darkness. Her energy was like shadows, reaching inside him. He heard her voice in his head.

"Be at ease, son of Zeus," she said. "Hera has no power here."

A cry erupted from his throat as he was freed from the claws of Hera's madness. He arched his back against the pain. It felt like his chest was being torn in two, and when it was done, he shook with the release. He glared back at Hecate, breathing hard.

"If you think that makes me any less violent, you are wrong." He spoke between clenched teeth. He still wanted to rip Hermes into pieces. This wouldn't be the first time he'd cockblocked him.

He was just as bad as the fucking sheep from the island.

"Perhaps not," she said. "But now you cannot blame Hera for your actions."

He glared, and the Goddess of Witchcraft stepped out of the way, and he could see Hermes, Apollo, and a female goddess he had never met. Persephone, he assumed. She looked like spring with honeyed hair and bright eyes, yet there was a darkness to her. It lived on the edges of her aura, like storm clouds haunting a bright sky.

Dionysus stared at her.

"What do you want?" he asked.

She was not fazed, and she did not hesitate.

"Hades has been captured by Theseus," she said, and

then her gaze shifted to Ariadne. "I am told you may have information about the labyrinth."

Ariadne went rigid. "Who told you that?"

"Is it true or not?" Persephone demanded, frustrated.

Dionysus took a step forward. It was a strange instinct, a wish to protect Ariadne in some way, even if it was just from words.

"If you came hoping for help, you are out of luck," said Dionysus. He felt the heat of Ariadne's gaze. "She will not stand against Theseus. Not when he has her sister, Phaedra."

She'd told them as much when Hades had asked her for information about the demigod's operations, and while it was frustrating, Dionysus knew he couldn't even begin to understand the fear she had for her sister. Ariadne had been with Theseus before he'd moved on to Phaedra, and she knew his cruelty better than most.

It was torture, watching someone so strong bow to the will of her abuser. Theseus influenced every decision she made, whether she realized it or not.

"He has your sister?" Persephone asked.

"He's married to her," Ariadne said. "He will assume any information about him was shared by me, and she will suffer for it."

Dionysus expected Persephone to be angry, to challenge Ariadne in some way, maybe even offer to save Phaedra the way he and Hades had, but she didn't.

"It doesn't matter anymore," she said, looking at Hecate, then at Hermes and Apollo. "Trap or not, I have to go."

"No, Persephone," said Hecate.

"There has to be another way, Sephy," said Hermes. "We just don't know all our options yet."

"We don't have time for options!" she seethed, her eyes watering. It was like seeing her in a new light. She was broken beneath that beauty. "Theseus has the Helm of Darkness. He has released Cronos from Tartarus. He has stripped you of your powers and placed a bounty on my head. We have *no* time. We were out of time the moment he took my ring."

"Theseus has released Cronos?" Dionysus asked.

That was news.

"We believe Theseus will use Hades as a sacrifice to gain the Titan's favor for the coming war," said Hecate. "Unless we find him in time."

No one spoke. Dionysus wanted to look at Ariadne because he wanted to see her reaction to these revelations, but he also didn't want her to feel like he was guilting her into divulging information on Theseus.

He held Persephone's gaze instead. He was about to suggest summoning his maenads, who might be able to give them other options, other ways into the labyrinth, when Ariadne spoke.

"I can help you through the labyrinth."

Dionysus's head snapped in her direction, and he could tell by the spark in her eye that she was formulating an idea.

He already didn't like it.

"No," Dionysus said, and Ariadne glared. "You would be playing right into his hands!"

He hadn't exactly figured out why, but Theseus was obsessed with Ariadne, to the point that even Poseidon knew who she was and had threatened war over her.

"We're all playing into his hands," she snapped.

He narrowed his eyes. "When Hades asked you for help, you refused. Why change your mind now?"

"Hades wanted information without a plan to rescue my sister," she said. "Theseus will want to watch our progress through the labyrinth. While he is occupied, you can rescue my sister."

"Ari—"

"It's the only chance I have to get her back!" She cut him off, her voice full of venom.

They glared at each other. Then Hecate spoke.

"You say you will lead Persephone through the labyrinth. What exactly do you know about it?"

"I know that the most dangerous part isn't getting lost," Ariadne said. "It's that you might choose to stay."

"Why would anyone choose to stay?" asked Apollo.

"Because," Ariadne said, "it will offer you what you want most."

Dionysus did not know exactly what that meant, but he instantly felt dread.

If Ariadne went through the maze, she would face the same obstacles, and they both knew what the labyrinth would offer her. Could she leave her sister behind?

He now knew he had no choice but to rescue Phaedra. Ariadne had to go into the labyrinth believing in him, believing that by the time she left, Phaedra would be safe.

"I will free your sister," said Dionysus, and Ariadne met her gaze. "If you promise not to stay in that maze."

Ariadne hesitated. He wasn't sure if it was because she was surprised by his request or if she was frustrated by what his words implied. Finally, she spoke.

"I promise."

Her voice was too quiet, too hesitant. It made him think that she did not even trust herself to face the maze, but he supposed they would all find out.

CHAPTER XI
THESEUS

Theseus stepped off the elevator on the sixtieth floor of the Acropolis. A woman at the front desk stood and greeted him with a smile.

"Good morning," she said cheerfully. "How may I help you?"

Theseus glanced at her long enough to see her smile fade before he passed her desk and continued onto the floor of *New Athens News* in search of Helen.

Behind him, the woman called out. "Sir!"

He ignored her.

He was already impatient, already annoyed. It set him on edge, and that woman did not want to know what happened when he was pushed, especially now that he had eaten the apple and ensured his own invincibility. Though depending on what Helen had to say about her plans to counter Persephone's statement, she might just find out what his true power looked like.

He scanned the maze of desks on either side of the

walkway until he caught sight of her. She was turned away from him, but he recognized her hair. He liked to bury his hand in those long locks while he fucked her from behind.

That was the only way he took her, the only way he wanted her—or any woman for that matter. He did not even wish to face his wife, whom he struggled to look in the eyes. Often, he would just bury his face in the crook of her damp neck under the guise of passion to avoid it.

Lovemaking was a taxing performance, a labor he did not find pleasing but necessary. Thank fuck Phaedra had finally moved past the stage in her pregnancy where she wanted sex every night. Now she seemed content with a few pretty words and a kiss, things he found far easier to mime than affection.

Helen didn't notice his approach. She stood with her arms crossed over her chest, her hip cocked to one side, her head tilted up toward the television where coverage streamed from Persephone's press conference.

She jumped as he grabbed her by the elbow, turning her shrewd blue eyes to him.

"What are you doing here?" she hissed.

"Move," he said, pushing her toward a wall of meeting rooms.

"Let me go," she demanded, but he ignored her, choosing the room closest to him, finding it occupied by four people—two men and two women.

"Out," he barked.

They all stared in stunned silence until one of the men finally spoke. "Call security."

Another reached for the conference phone at the

center of the table just as it exploded, pieces of plastic flying across the room.

"*Leave*," Theseus repeated. "Or I will remove you."

They scrambled out of the room, and Theseus slammed the door shut just as he was accosted by Helen, who shoved him hard.

"You fucking asshole!" she seethed.

Theseus snatched her wrists. "Fight me, Helen. You know how I like it."

She jerked free. "How dare you embarrass me!"

He narrowed his gaze, eyes darkening. "Embarrass you?"

He could think of better ways to embarrass her, and she seemed to recognize that.

Her mouth hardened.

"No," she said.

"No?" he repeated, a little surprised by her resistance, though to be truthful, it also excited him. His cock had already been hard; now it was throbbing.

He preferred fucking Helen over the others in his rotation. She did not get attached or sentimental. She wanted what he wanted—a transaction that left them both satisfied—but if she fought? Oh, if she fought, she would be the perfect vessel—the perfect fuck.

He inched closer, crowding her. She tilted her head to keep his gaze, utterly fearless, and he wondered when that light would start to die.

"This is my place of employment," she said between her teeth.

He could not decide whether to be annoyed or amused by her comment. Did she really think decorum would prevent him from taking her? She was lucky he'd chosen a room. He could have had her on the floor of *New Athens News*. He still might.

"That may be," he said, lifting his hand. He trailed a finger down her face and along her jaw, working his hand into her hair. She tensed as his fingers sank into the back of her neck. He leaned in, his lips brushing hers as he whispered, "But you work for me."

She did not react to the brush of his lips, did not try to kiss him back or give in to her hate-fueled desire. Of course, he preferred that. It told him that she was not falling for a fantasy as so many others had.

He drew back a fraction and met her gaze.

"Need I remind you?" he asked.

"I am well aware," she replied, the words slipping between clenched teeth.

In the brief silence that followed their exchange, a tension began to build. It wasn't so much sexual as it was fraught with anticipation, both preparing for the other's move.

He smirked.

"I will remind you anyway," he said as he tightened his grip. He twisted her around and pushed her to the table. She tried to dig her heels in and clawed at his arm, but she wasn't strong enough to resist. He bent her over the table, facing the television that ran the same coverage of Persephone's press conference as the one she had been watching on the floor.

He moved his hand into her hair, jerking her head back so she was forced to watch it.

"Did you know she would make a statement?"

He spoke against her ear, his body pressed against hers, his cock settling against her ass.

"How would I have known?" she snapped. "She's used to exposing everyone else's truths, not her own."

He straightened but kept his hand flat on her back.

"You should have known," he said, hiking her skirt up over her perfect, round ass. "You should have already been prepared to deliver your counterattack. *That* is how this works."

"So you will punish me for not being a fucking oracle?"

He pushed her legs apart.

"I'm punishing you because I can," he said as he unbuckled his belt and pants. "Because I want to. Because you make it *easy*."

She shoved her heeled foot into his leg and then pushed up from the table. The back of her head struck his nose and mouth, and he instantly tasted blood. He brought his fingers to his sore lip—she had split it. He ran his tongue over it, but as he did, the ruptured skin healed.

The apple had worked.

His gaze connected with hers, and that was when he saw it. The flash of fear in her eyes. She bolted for the door, and he pounced, catching her around the waist. She twisted in his grasp and hit him in the face, but her strike barely registered. He was too overwhelmed by the blood rushing to his cock and the roaring in his ears.

He pulled her back against him, trapping her hands against her sides and dragging her to the table. She fought, but he was stronger.

He'd only let her make this much progress because he'd wanted the thrill of the fight. Now he just wanted to fuck her.

He shoved her down, bending her over the table and wrenching her arms behind her back.

"Just kill me, you fucking bastard," she snarled.

He laughed.

"I'm not going to kill you when you ask for it," he said. "That would be a gift, and I am not generous."

Theseus shoved her legs apart. He licked his fingers and touched her between her thighs while fisting her hair. She did not fight as he pulled, forcing her back to arch awkwardly.

"Look at her," he ordered, commanding her to watch the television again. It gave him pleasure to know that he was responsible for the haunted expression on Persephone's face. "Remember when you promised to write for me?"

"I haven't stopped," Helen said between her teeth, and then a guttural sound tore from her throat as his finger slipped inside her. She was wet and he was ready—it was enough. He pulled free of her and drew his cock out, letting the head of it rest against her entrance.

"The longer she goes unchallenged, the more sympathy she will gain, the more worshippers will follow."

"Nothing I write will bring an end to that."

"The point, Helen," he said, gripping her hips, "is to deepen division. Have you forgotten the role of the media?"

She glared at him from over her shoulder, and he smiled wickedly.

"Now be a good girl and take my cock," he said, shoving balls deep inside her. She gasped, her head falling back. He took advantage of that angle and gripped her hair harder as he thrust inside her. The table squeaked with his movements, and his eyes fell to his hands, which were streaked with blood from her nails.

It sent a rush of pleasure to his head.

Fuck.

Helen's breaths were desperate, and her cries were loud. She pushed into him, forcing space between herself and the table so she could touch herself. There was no delusion here—it wasn't about her pleasure. If she wanted that, she'd have to find it herself. In that way, she reminded him of Ariadne, who let lust move through her, expressing it in whatever way she needed. Sometimes it was delicate, and sometimes it was rough.

That was what made his mouth water.

Helen tensed beneath him, and he gripped her harder, his fingers pressing into her skin. He imagined for a moment that it was the burnished brown of Ariadne's, and then his hand smoothed up her back, and his fingers found her throat and he squeezed until he was on the brink of ecstasy.

He released her all at once and came on her ass.

Helen collapsed to the table, her hand going to her neck as she gasped for air.

Theseus zipped his pants and adjusted his jacket. He shifted until he was in her line of sight.

"The ball's in your court," he said as he fixed his cuff links. When he met her gaze, he found she was glaring at him, hatred in her watery eyes. Perhaps he had broken her a little. He gave her a cold smile. "Don't disappoint."

———

Theseus left the Acropolis for home, teleporting to his office. He had been here less and less over the last few weeks despite Phaedra's quickly approaching due date, but he could not help the fact that his long-awaited plans were unfolding at the time of his son's birth. The reality was that opportunities could be missed, but Phaedra wasn't going anywhere.

He had not really thought long on becoming a father, because impregnating Phaedra had been a necessity—as necessary as marrying her.

Because he had to be one of *them*—just a man with a beautiful wife and a child on the way.

For a moment, he let himself think of everything he might be capable of if he did not have to play this game, but he would know soon enough.

It was part of the plan.

His eyes fell to his tidy desk, to a perfectly stacked set of papers—minus the one on top that was skewed just a hair. It was not how he had left it.

"Where have you been?"

His gaze shot up, level with Phaedra, who was standing in the doorway. She had one hand on her swollen belly.

He wasn't sure what set him off—the fact that someone had been in his office or that she had intruded so quickly, as if she'd been waiting for him, *watching* for him.

Maybe it was her tone, which hinted at her irritation.

Either way, anger curled through him like a hot knife.

"Is that blood?" she asked, taking a step forward.

"Have you looked through my things?" he asked.

Her eyes widened, and she halted. Now she had two hands on her stomach.

"What?"

He came around the desk.

"Did you look through my things?" he repeated as he advanced on her.

She backed away into the hallway.

"Theseus—" she pleaded, flinching as her back hit the wall.

He grabbed her by the hair, and she cried out.

"Answer me!"

"Please, Theseus," she begged as a guttural sob escaped her mouth. "I would never—"

Someone jerked his arm—a young girl, one of the maids. Theseus swung at her.

"Leave her alone!" Phaedra shrieked as the maid went flying, crashing into the opposite wall.

Phaedra sank to her knees, reaching toward the girl who lay across from them. She was still, her neck poised at an odd angle.

Phaedra's body shook with sobs as she repeated in a hushed voice, "Theseus. Please, please, please."

He reached for his wife and dragged her to her feet.

"Answer the fucking question, Phaedra," he snarled.

Tears streaked down her face, and snot dripped from her nose. She was disgusting, and he had never resented her more.

"I would never," she said. "I would *never*."

He released her with a push, and she flinched.

He started to pace. He wanted to rage.

"If you would *never*, then who?" he demanded.

She studied him, her gaze full of horror and shock. There was also an element of hurt, as if she could not believe she was looking into the eyes of the man she loved.

"There was a new maid," she whispered.

"A new maid?" He halted and moved toward her. "What new maid?"

She stepped away, her back now against the wall.

"What. New. Maid?"

"She arrived this morning," Phaedra explained. "I assumed you knew. You are responsible for everyone who works at this estate."

He did not miss her subtle jab.

"Fuck!" The word scratched his throat as he screamed. He swung his gaze back to his wife and pointed a finger in her face. "*Never* let anyone into this house unless I *explicitly* tell you otherwise. Do you understand?"

She nodded, and he heard a distinct trickle. He looked down, finding Phaedra standing in a puddle.

He sneered. "Go clean yourself up," he said, repulsed, but as he started to turn away, she spoke with more venom than she ever had.

"It's not piss," she said. "The baby's coming."

CHAPTER XII
PERSEPHONE

Persephone had wandered into the garden and followed the winding stone path until she reached her garden plot—the one Hades had given her when he had challenged her to create life in the Underworld. It was no longer barren but teeming with shoots of green, the leaves real and waxy.

She recalled what Hades had said when she'd first laid eyes on his realm. *"If it is a garden you wish to create, then it will truly be the only life here."*

She'd never imagined bearing witness to the truth of those words in this manner, but Hades's magic was fading around her.

The ache in her chest deepened. It felt wrong to be here, waiting for tomorrow when they knew where Hades was being held today, but they'd needed some time to plan, mostly for the rescue of Phaedra, which only added another complicated layer.

Persephone did not know what to think of Dionysus

and Ariadne. She had not expected to arrive and witness the two locked in a passionate embrace while also covered in blood.

Persephone's knowledge about Dionysus extended to his collection of wines and his club, which was known for its wild sex parties, drugs, and, of course, alcohol. She'd heard rumors about his lust-filled trek across the world, about the bloody horror of it all, and tonight she felt like she'd witnessed a fraction of it when they'd arrived at his house unannounced, though she could not really blame him. Hermes did not often have the best timing, yet they did not have the luxury of time.

Even now, she wondered if tomorrow would be too late.

"You should be resting," said Hecate. "The labyrinth will require strength."

Persephone turned to look at the goddess as she approached, cradling a fluffy black cat. Even in the moonlight, its eyes flashed a vibrant green.

"Is that a human, Hecate?" she asked, suspicious, knowing the goddess's penchant for turning mortals who irritated her into whatever she pleased.

"This is a cat," Hecate said, looking down at the animal. "Her name is Galanthis. I want you to take her into the labyrinth with you."

"Why?"

"In case there are mice," she said.

Persephone raised a brow, but she didn't ask for clarification, knowing that was the only explanation she would get. She shifted her gaze to the garden again.

"I have been thinking about what I want most," Persephone said.

She thought if she could anticipate what the labyrinth would offer, she might more easily say no. The reality was that she hadn't thought beyond what she wanted in the present, which was to rescue Hades, but she had a feeling the labyrinth would demand more than that.

"Have you decided?" Hecate asked.

"What if it isn't a choice?" Persephone asked, looking at the goddess.

"Explain," said Hecate.

"What if I'm faced with something I did not know I wanted?"

One's greatest desire seemed like something else entirely, not so much a choice but something formed around what she'd lacked all her life.

She felt Hecate's eyes on her.

"What are you afraid it will show you?" the Goddess of Witchcraft asked.

Persephone was quiet for a long moment before she spoke, a whispered fear she released into the night. "Everything Hades said he could never give me."

The silence was long and the guilt heavy.

"Are you afraid knowing will make you love Hades less?" Hecate asked.

"No, of course not," Persephone said, meeting Hecate's gaze. "But I am afraid to hurt him." She couldn't bear that. She looked away quickly. "I should not have said anything. I don't even know what I will see."

"I think you know exactly what you will see." The goddess paused and offered a small smile. "Desires change, Persephone. Tonight, you may want something you do not want tomorrow."

Persephone frowned. She didn't really wish to

entertain her fears, but she needed to say it—to speak the words so her doubt existed somewhere outside her body.

"What if I can't do this, Hecate?"

"Oh, my dear," Hecate said, taking a step closer. She brushed her cheek, and Persephone let her eyes flutter close. "You can. You will. *You have no choice.*"

———

Persephone did not sleep. She rose early in the morning before the sky brightened with Hades's muted sun and made her way to Elysium, hoping the peace of the Isle of the Blessed would seep into her bones and ease her anxiety, but even as she sat on a grassy hill looking out over the quiet landscape, dread followed.

No part of the Underworld remained untouched by Theseus's attack, and Persephone knew that would soon be the same for the entire world.

She did not know how long she sat there, her mind tumbling over everything that had happened in the last few days—not only by Theseus's hand but also Helen's.

Persephone hoped her statement regarding Helen's article quelled some of the mistrust it had inspired. It seemed so trivial to worry over public perception when so much in her world was falling apart, but the fact was that Demeter's storm had caused so much unrest and anger. Mortals were looking for any excuse to shift their worship, and the demigods—who presented as honorable advocates for the downtrodden—looked more and more appealing as the mistakes of the gods were laid bare.

Right now, that was her greatest fear, and it would only make them stronger, their power greater. Given that they had already managed to wound and kill gods, they were a true threat to the reign of the Olympians.

"*The system is broken,*" Tyche had said. "*Something new must take its place.*"

But they didn't just need something new. They needed something *right*. Otherwise, they would just trade one evil for another.

Persephone knew Zeus would not go down without a fight. The question was, would he be looking in the right direction when the attack came? Right now, he seemed to consider her a greater threat to his throne than Theseus.

Either way, she knew one thing for certain—the gods would go to war, they would face another Titanomachy, and no matter the outcome, the world would suffer.

She took a deep breath and exhaled slowly, but the tension in her chest did not ease. She had come here to escape dread, but all she'd managed was to create more.

As the sky brightened, Persephone caught movement in the distance. It was Lexa.

She straightened at the soul's approach. All the times she had come to Elysium, she had been the one to seek Lexa out. It had never been the opposite. Persephone's heart hammered in her chest the closer her friend came, wondering if something was wrong or if this was merely a sign of her improvement.

Lexa filled the empty space beside Persephone, and she turned to watch as Lexa pulled her knees to her chest, matching her pose.

"Is everything okay?" Persephone asked after they had sat in silence for a few moments.

Lexa's dark brows lowered, and then she rested

her head against her knees, angling her face toward Persephone.

She still did not meet her gaze.

"I think I have made Thanatos mad," Lexa said.

Persephone jerked her head back in surprise, which was probably an overreaction, but that was honestly the last thing she'd expected her to say.

"Why would he be mad?"

Persephone had only seen Thanatos angry a few times. She was not even sure she would call it angry so much as frustrated, but both times, it had been over Lexa.

"Because I kissed him."

"You *kissed* Thanatos?"

Persephone could not help her giddiness. It shot through her, warm and steady, a welcome distraction from the darkness of her thoughts.

Despite Persephone's excitement, Lexa was subdued. Clearly whatever had happened in the aftermath had made her feel uncertain.

"I doubt that made him mad," Persephone said gently.

"He told me it shouldn't have happened," Lexa said. "Does that sound mad enough?"

Persephone hesitated a moment, caught off guard by how much that last sentence sounded like something the old Lexa would say but also frustrated with Thanatos for being one of *those* idiots.

Everyone who was anyone knew he cared for Lexa in a way that was different from other souls. From the day she arrived in the Underworld, he had been protective of her, to the point that he had even tried to keep her from Persephone.

"Hold on," Persephone said, shifting on the grass to face Lexa. "Tell me everything."

"I…don't know where to start," Lexa said, cheeks flushed.

It was strange watching Lexa blush, because it was something the old Lexa would never have done. Just when Persephone thought she recognized her best friend, she didn't.

"Start from the beginning."

"I…don't know how it began," Lexa said.

"Where were you when you kissed?" Persephone asked instead.

"We were lying under a tree," Lexa said.

Well, that sounded intimate.

"Sometimes we sit together at night, and Thanatos tells me about his day. Usually, conversation is easy, but last night, it wasn't. I don't even know why. Nothing happened. I was just frustrated."

"So you kissed him?" Persephone asked.

"Yes," Lexa said.

Persephone tried not to smile, because Lexa was taking this so seriously. She wanted to tell her that it was likely she and Thanatos were suffering from sexual frustration, and being in each other's presence just exasperated it.

"And what did he do?"

"He kissed me too."

Persephone paused and then leaned forward a little. "How?"

"How?"

"How did he kiss you? Did he use his tongue?"

"Persephone!"

"It's a valid question!" She couldn't help it; she was grinning. Before her death, Lexa would have demanded the same details from Persephone. That Lexa no longer existed. This one was new to these feelings. "You can tell me."

"He did," Lexa finally said, bowing her head so her hair curtained her face.

"Did you like it?"

"Yes, of course," she said, straightening her legs and then lying back in the grass. "But he must not have."

Persephone twisted her body so she could hold Lexa's gaze. "I highly doubt that," she said. "He is just afraid."

"That's ridiculous. Why would he be afraid?"

"I don't know. Knowing Thanatos, he probably made up some rule that says he can't fall in love with a soul." Persephone rolled her eyes at the thought.

"If he believes that, then he won't fall in love with me," said Lexa.

"That is not true," Persephone said. "I know he cares for you."

He was probably already in love.

Lexa frowned and then looked up at the sky. "What do I do?"

"Do you like him?"

"Yes," she said. "Very much."

"Then tell him," Persephone said. "And he will likely tell you that you cannot be together, and when he does, ask why."

"And what do I do when he tells me why?"

"I think you have two options depending on what he says," she said. "You can kiss him, or you can leave him."

"Leave him?"

"Yes, leave him. *Especially* if he tells you that you cannot be together."

Lexa frowned. "Then what do I do?"

"You live," she said. "You live as if he'd told you yes."

———

Before Persephone left Elysium, she cast a quick glance across the landscape in search of her mother. When Lexa died, she had visited almost every day, even when she had not been allowed to approach her. She felt no such urge with Demeter. She wasn't even sure why she was looking for her now, save that she was curious.

She caught sight of her in the distance, recognizing the golden hue of her hair and her tall and graceful silhouette as she stared off into the gray horizon.

She was alone, which was typical of the souls who resided within the Isle of the Blessed. They came here with no memories of their former lives to heal. Eventually, most would move into Asphodel. Some would reincarnate.

Persephone did not know what would happen to her mother. Perhaps she would never leave this place.

There was a part of her that felt sad that this was Demeter's existence in the Underworld—she was just as alone here as she had been in the Upperworld. It was something Persephone had never thought long on before, but she saw it now.

"*Leave with me now, and we can forget this ever happened,*" Demeter had begged when they faced off in the arsenal, but there was no forgetting, because by the end of it, she had hurt Persephone too many times, and there was no coming back from that, no pretending it never happened.

Suddenly, her chest felt tight, and her heart ached. She hadn't had time to dwell on how everything had come to an end, and truly, she could not afford to now.

She had to focus on Hades.

That feeling in her chest grew sharper.

Hades.

She tried to imagine what it would be like to see him again after the horror Theseus had likely put him through, the extent of which she could only imagine given how the Impious and Triad had treated Adonis, Harmonia, and Tyche. The thought made her sick.

There was no way he was coming back the same, but she would love him through it, no matter how many pieces she had to hold together.

———

Persephone stopped by her suite to check on Harmonia. Aphrodite was still there, curled up beside her on the bed, asleep. Sybil sat near the fireplace working. She met Persephone's gaze over her computer as the goddess approached.

"No change?"

"No change," Sybil said.

Persephone frowned and studied her oracle for a moment. Her eyes looked dark, almost bruised.

"Have you slept?" she asked.

Sybil shook her head. "I have been working on an article for *The Advocate* about your life based on what you've told me," said Sybil. "I know this isn't your top priority, but while you work on rescuing Hades, I can work on how the public perceives you."

Persephone sank into the chair opposite her, suddenly feeling the burden of everything that had taken place over the last few days and what lay ahead.

"It seems so ridiculous, doesn't it? To care what they think…but I do."

"You care because you know the truth," Sybil said.

"My truth is not everyone's truth," said Persephone.

There were mortals and immortals alike who had experienced a different Demeter—one who had granted them favor, offered them prosperity and abundance in whatever form they'd wished.

"That does not make what you went through any less valid," said Sybil.

Persephone said nothing. Though the oracle's words eased her anxiety, their conversation had opened another angry wound. She had deserved the same kindness Demeter had shown others. No one had shown her that more than Hades and his realm. Strangers had treated her better than her mother, the woman who had claimed to want her desperately.

She could not make sense of it now, and she cast her gaze toward the bed where Harmonia and Aphrodite lay.

"What does Hecate say about her wound?" Persephone asked.

Sybil's eyes followed. "She says we may have to resort to using the Golden Fleece."

Persephone had not heard about the Golden Fleece since studying Jason and the Argonauts in college. Jason, the rightful king of Iolcos, was sent away by his uncle,

154

Pelias, to retrieve the fleece, a task he believed impossible. Successful, Jason was able to reclaim his throne, and the fleece came to represent kingship, but its real power was that it could heal.

"You are reluctant?" Persephone asked.

Sybil hesitated. "It's not using it that worries me. It's obtaining it," she said and paused. "Hecate says the fleece hangs in a tree guarded by a dragon within Ares's sacred grove."

"Ares," Persephone said. "But that should be easy. Aphrodite—"

Sybil shook her head. "Zeus has forbidden anyone from helping those who betrayed him."

Persephone wondered how Zeus would know. Was his decree bound with magic?

"We must find another way," Sybil said.

Perhaps Hades will know. Persephone thought the words but did not say them aloud. She wasn't sure why, but there was a part of her that feared her hope, because she knew what she would become if Hades was taken from her. It would be like letting the evils of Pandora's box into the world again, only she would be behind the chaos.

Before long, it was time to leave. Persephone met Hecate in the foyer of the palace. The goddess handed her Galanthis, the black cat she'd instructed her to take into the labyrinth.

"Do not worry about her. She will take care of herself *and* you," said Hecate. Then she placed her hands on either side of Persephone's face. They were cold, and she shivered beneath her touch. "Many of us have relied on magic too long to try solving problems without it, but you—you have had to live most of your life as a mortal. There is no one better suited for the labyrinth than you."

Persephone took a deep breath, trying to ease the anxiety bubbling in her chest. It didn't work, but her words were comforting.

"Thank you, Hecate," she said, her voice quiet.

The Goddess of Witchcraft smiled and dropped her hands. She might have looked like a proud mother if it wasn't for the hint of fear in her eyes.

"You can do this, Persephone."

Persephone said nothing, just held the cat tighter as she called on her magic and left the Underworld.

CHAPTER XIII
DIONYSUS

"What do you mean she's in the hospital?" Dionysus demanded.

Naia and Lilaia, two of his maenads, had just returned with news, and it wasn't at all what Dionysus had expected. Phaedra had been admitted to Asclepius Community Hospital. Given her shitty husband, he feared Theseus was responsible.

"She's in labor," said Naia.

"*Labor*," Dionysus repeated.

"She's having a baby," said Lilaia. "In case you don't know what that means."

"I *know* what it means," Dionysus glared. "But how did this happen?"

"Given how often you eye fuck Ariadne, I am surprised you don't know where babies come from, Dionysus."

"I really don't know why I put up with you," Dionysus said.

Lilaia grinned.

"Ariadne never said her sister was pregnant," Dionysus said.

Naia shrugged. "She hasn't seen Phaedra in months. It is possible she doesn't know."

"What am I supposed to do with the fucking baby?"

"What do you mean what are you supposed to do with the fucking baby?" asked Lilaia. "You bring it with you."

"That's kidnapping."

"It's not kidnapping if there is consent."

"The baby can't consent!"

There was a beat of silence, and then Naia said, "I really don't understand how you lived this long."

"That makes two of us," Dionysus snapped.

"Three," Lilaia added.

Dionysus glared at them both.

It wasn't his fault. He didn't exactly have the best parental figure. Zeus was absent completely. And Silenus taught him how to drink and encouraged him to fuck. If he had any claim to a childhood, that was it.

"Wherever Phaedra goes, the baby will go," said Naia.

Gods fucking dammit. This was going to be a nightmare.

He had known they would face retaliation if they managed to rescue Phaedra—but a baby too? He would be lucky to escape with his life and the lives of those he cared about, his maenads.

"Why the fuck did I agree to this?" Dionysus muttered.

"Because," said Lilaia, "this woman is being abused, and you know that will not change once this child is born."

"This is one life threatening hundreds," Dionysus said.

"Two lives," said Naia. "And it's worth it if we say it is."

Dionysus would not argue with that.

"What am I supposed to do?"

"You are going to shape-shift into this man," said Naia, turning her tablet around. She showed Dionysus a picture of a pale mortal with graying hair. "His name is Dr. Phanes. He is the only one allowed in Phaedra's room along with two other nurses. Lilaia will disguise herself as one. The other will be a hospital employee," Naia continued and then met Dionysus's gaze. "We figured at least one person should know what they're doing."

"I don't see your name on this plan," Dionysus said.

"I will make sure Dr. Phanes and his nurse do not make it to their posts," she said. "And when I'm done with that, I'm coming for this bumbling idiot." Naia showed another picture of a beefy man with small eyes and a permanent scowl. "His name is Tannis. Theseus has him posted at Phaedra's hospital door."

Dionysus shook his head. *What a fucking asshole.* He treated Phaedra like a prisoner.

"I'll make sure he's gone by the time we're ready to leave," Naia said. "We move as soon as Ariadne and Persephone leave for Knossos."

Dionysus stiffened, and suddenly, he felt like he couldn't take deep enough breaths. He had known this was coming, but he still didn't like it. Ariadne was essentially using herself as bait to lure Theseus away, and Theseus would go because he wanted her.

That thought turned his stomach.

He'd been surprised by her sudden change of heart.

159

She had gone from refusing to help Hades to jumping at the chance to lead Persephone through the labyrinth, but he understood now. Her participation ensured Theseus was distracted enough to extract Phaedra safely.

He didn't like it, but he would do it for her.

His only worry was what he'd do if she didn't make it out of the labyrinth.

Dionysus looked at Naia and Lilaia. "Best not tell Ariadne," he said. "She doesn't need distractions in the labyrinth."

"Tell me what?"

Dionysus whirled as Ariadne entered the room. She was dressed from head to toe in black with her hair pulled back, a duffel bag slung over her shoulder. She was followed by Persephone, who was carrying a cat.

"Nothing," Dionysus said quickly, then his eyes fell to the fluffy feline. "Why do you have a cat?"

"Hecate says to bring her to the labyrinth," said Persephone. She exchanged a look with Ariadne. "And when Hecate tells you to do something, you do not argue."

That was fair. Hecate was the Goddess of Witchcraft. Whatever she sent along with Persephone was bound to help, which meant it was also of benefit to Ariadne. Still…why a cat?

Dionysus's gaze returned to Ariadne, who dropped her heavy bag to the ground. She bent to unzip it and dug out a set of clothes before handing them to Persephone.

"Change," she said, taking the cat. "Down the hall to your left."

Persephone obeyed without hesitation, a hard edge to her pale face.

"What's in the bag?" Dionysus asked. "Other than clothes."

He didn't really care, but he wanted to keep her from pressing him about what he intended to keep from her. It was bad enough she was going to go into the labyrinth distracted by Phaedra, likely worrying over whether he was capable of rescuing her. She didn't need to worry about a baby too.

"Supplies," she said, scratching behind the cat's ear.

He didn't like that she was being so short with him, though it wasn't unusual. It seemed to happen every time they came close to fucking again. It was like, in the aftermath, she realized she had made a mistake.

He tamped down the frustration that shot through him, holding her gaze before letting his eyes drift down her body.

"Are you armed?" he asked.

"What do you think?" she countered.

"I can't imagine where you put it," he said.

The last time he'd argued with her about this, she'd showed him her ass in an elevator, and it had left him mostly speechless. He had a feeling she was going to do that again.

She raised a brow. "Can't you?"

Then she pulled the front of her jacket back to reveal a holster.

Damn, that wasn't nearly as exciting.

There was silence for a moment. He couldn't take his eyes off her.

"Are you ready for this?" he asked.

"As ready as I'm going to be," she said. "Are you?"

No, he wanted to say. *What if you don't come back?*

But he knew that wasn't what she meant.

"Our part is easy," he said.

Ariadne did not look so certain, and he wondered if her doubt came from mistrust in him. Though he didn't have the best track record with her. He had promised to help her sister before if she helped him find Medusa first. He'd believed they would need the gorgon to fight Theseus.

Persephone returned dressed similarly to Ariadne, in head-to-toe black, including a leather jacket.

"Is the jacket necessary?" Persephone asked, her cheeks flushed.

"If the labyrinth is as I remember, then yes," said Ariadne. She returned the cat to Persephone and reached for her duffel bag, swinging it over her shoulder. "Ready?"

"That's it?" Dionysus asked. "What is your plan?"

"The plan is to make it out of the labyrinth with Hades," said Ariadne.

"That's the goal, not the plan, Ari."

She glared at him. "I know what a plan is, Dionysus. I have this under control." Her eyes shifted to Naia and Lilaia. "As soon as we arrive, Theseus will know. He will come to Knossos immediately. Then you can make your move."

The women nodded.

Dionysus hated that she was talking to them and not him—as if he wasn't part of this plan.

"Let's go," Ariadne said. "The sooner we get there, the sooner this is over."

Dionysus's hands fisted, fighting the urge to touch her, even to speak, but he lost that battle.

162

"Ari," he called as she turned toward Persephone. She paused and held his gaze. "Make sure you get out so you can see your sister again."

So I can see you again, he thought.

She nodded once, and then Persephone's sweet-scented magic filled the air. He didn't take his eyes off Ariadne, staring at the spot where she had stood even after they vanished.

———

"It's time," said Lilaia, her finger resting on her earpiece as she listened to Naia give updates. They were waiting in the shadow of the adjoining parking garage, away from prying eyes and cameras. "She's in room 323."

She met Dionysus's gaze, and he nodded, quickly shifting into an identical image of the doctor Naia had shown him. His ability to change forms was more than glamour, which only gave the *appearance* of a transformation. He changed on a physical level, and it always felt wrong, like he was wearing another skin over his own.

"That is *so* unsettling," Naia said, shuddering.

"Ready?" Dionysus asked.

Lilaia secured a surgical mask over her face. "Let's get this mama somewhere safe."

He nodded, and together they left the shelter of the parking garage, crossing beneath a covered walkway and into the hospital, which was like barreling into a solid wall of sound. There was noise *everywhere*, pushing in from all sides.

It was all so loud. Dionysus felt like he could *feel* every layer of sound—from the high-pitched ring of the telephone to the shuffling of paper. It scraped against his skin, putting him more and more on edge as he made his way down the sterile hallway with Lilaia in tow.

The intercom blared, a female voice making Dionysus's ears ring.

"Dr. Phanes to room 323. Dr. Phanes to room 323."

"That's Phaedra's room," said Lilaia.

"I know," said Dionysus tightly.

They were almost to the elevators when someone slammed a hand down on his shoulder.

"Dr. Phanes!"

Dionysus whirled to face a nurse.

He had been so intent on his task, he nearly forgot who he was supposed to be impersonating.

"Y-yes?" he asked.

"Our patient in 124 just lost her mucus plug. Fetal heart rate is stable at 143, and contractions are still irregular," the nurse said. "Should we increase the Pitocin?"

What the fuck was a mucus plug, and why did the sound of it make him want to vomit?

Dionysus hesitated. "Uh…"

Lilaia kicked him from behind, and he glanced at her to see her nod.

"Yes," Dionysus said, turning back to the nurse. "Yes, increase the…"

He forgot what the nurse had said. *Pee-toe-sin?*

"Pitocin?" the nurse supplied.

"Yes, yes. The Pitocin."

"Got it."

The nurse hurried away down the hall, and Dionysus turned to face the elevators as Lilaia stabbed the top button.

"Are you sure you can do this?" she asked.

"Of course I can do this," said Dionysus as the elevator doors slid open. "How hard could it be?"

"Okay," she said in a rather singsong voice that made him think she didn't believe him at all. He glared at her back as they stepped inside the lift. They were pushed into a corner as several more people piled inside.

"You think I am not capable," Dionysus said.

"I did not say—"

"You said it with your face."

Lilaia sighed and then she looked up at Dionysus. "I don't think you're prepared. There is a difference."

"I think I can pull off an abduction," he snapped. "I have done it a million times."

Several heads in the elevator turned toward him in that moment, and Lilaia managed an awkward laugh, giving him what looked like a playful shove but was actually a hard nudge in his ribs with her bony elbow.

"I know you can pull off an *induction*," she said loudly, and then she lowered her voice and spoke through gritted teeth. "It's what comes *before* that worries me."

He started to speak, but the elevator stopped on the third floor and emptied. Dionysus followed Lilaia. To their left was a waiting area, and to their right was a locked door that led into the labor and delivery suite.

Lilaia used her badge to enter. They did not need to look at room numbers to know which room belonged to Phaedra. They could tell because only one had a guard.

He was facing them as they approached, thick arms crossed over his chest.

"You're late," the man said. "Lord Theseus isn't gonna be happy."

"Lord Theseus can suck it," said Dionysus. "His wife isn't the only patient I have in this hospital."

Dionysus was proud of that retort.

The man—Tannis, Dionysus recalled—slammed his palm against Dionysus's chest, halting him in his tracks. The god met the man's beady-eyed gaze.

"Watch your mouth, Doctor."

Dionysus pushed his hand away. "How will your boss feel when he learns you delayed me further?"

Tannis scowled at him but took a step back.

Dionysus gave him a hard look as he entered the room, only once he was inside, he very much wished he'd stayed outside.

Phaedra lay on a bed in the middle of the room. A nurse stood between her legs, pushing them back, her knees almost to her ears. Lilaia pushed past him and hurried to Phaedra's side, helping the other nurse hold her leg, as if she had done *this* a million times before.

What the fuck was happening?

He looked at Lilaia, his eyes wide. Is this what she meant by "what comes before"? An actual *live* birth?

"Dr. Phanes," said the nurse—the one who was supposed to know what she was doing. "The baby's crowning."

"C-crowning?" Dionysus repeated.

"Your gown and gloves are on the table," said the nurse.

Dionysus hesitated, and Phaedra moaned, her head rolled back, her face glistening with sweat. She looked a lot like Ariadne, and the resemblance made him uneasy for several reasons, but most of all because Lilaia and this nurse were asking him to deliver her baby.

Why did that seem like an invasion of privacy?

"Doctor! There is no time." The nurse's sharp tone brought him back to reality.

"Put the gloves on," Lilaia snapped.

He glared at his maenad. He was never going to forgive her or Naia when this was over. Why couldn't he have been the nurse? He could hold a leg.

Gods fucking dammit.

He walked over to the table and put the gloves on. They were long and powder blue. Then he turned to face Phaedra and...*oh my fucking gods.*

Suddenly, he understood crowning.

This looked like torture. It had to be something Hades had dreamed up in his demented head, because there was no way a head was coming out of *that*.

Phaedra sobbed, and Dionysus met her dark-eyed gaze, so like Ariadne's.

"I can't do this," she said, gasping for breath. "I can't." Her body shook.

"You can," said Lilaia, holding her hand tighter.

"I can't," Phaedra said.

"You're doing great," said the nurse. "Just a little while longer."

"Tell her it's going to be okay, Doctor," Lilaia said, a threatening edge to her voice.

"It isn't," said Phaedra. "You don't understand. My husband..."

Suddenly she was crying harder and breathing faster, her chest rising and falling rapidly.

For a moment, Dionysus felt panicked, but then he remembered one thing he'd learned about women in labor—and that was how they were supposed to breathe.

167

"Hee-hee-hooooo," he started. "Hee-hee-hooooo."

He kept going even when he noticed Lilaia glaring at him and the other nurse staring at him in horror, but then Phaedra joined in, following his lead.

Before long, they were all breathing in tandem, and when Phaedra was calm again, Dionysus looked down between her legs, and his breaths dissolved into a horrified scream.

"Oh my gods," he yelled.

"What? What?" Phaedra cried.

"Nothing," Lilaia said quickly. "The baby's almost out. Push!"

Phaedra bore down, and then the head was suddenly out, and Dionysus's hands were in the air.

"Guide the head!" the nurse snapped.

"How the fuck do I guide the head?" he demanded. The baby was face down. What if he hurt it by grabbing it?

"Are you insane?" the nurse snapped. "Just guide the head out!"

"If you say *guide the head* one more time," Dionysus hissed.

"Hold the head!" she yelled.

Dionysus held the head.

"Suction, Doctor! Suction!"

"Suction what?" he demanded, matching her frantic tone.

The nurse pushed toward him with some type of blue bulbous thing.

"Turn his head," she barked. "*Gently!*"

Dionysus did as she instructed, and the nurse suctioned the baby's nose and mouth.

"Push!" the nurse said.

Phaedra screamed, and suddenly the baby had shoulders, and then Dionysus was holding a whole fucking baby—a boy—in his arms.

He had him for seconds before Lilaia took him and placed him on Phaedra's chest.

Dionysus just stood there, both shocked and awed at what had just happened, but he was quickly brought back to reality when he noticed blood and fluid dripping to the floor at his feet.

He took a step back, feeling light-headed.

"Doctor, we need an Apgar," said the nurse as she and Lilaia worked to dry off the baby, rubbing its back and feet.

"He's not crying," said Phaedra. There was a note of alarm in her voice. "Why isn't he crying?"

"He's all right," said the nurse. "Sometimes babies just need a little while. They're in shock."

As if on cue, a keen wailing filled the room.

"There we go," said Lilaia.

Phaedra smiled.

"Apgar, Doctor," the nurse said again, her irritation plain.

What the fuck is an Apgar? He looked at Lilaia, who jerked her head toward the baby and mouthed something.

"*What?*" he mouthed back.

She leaned toward him, the words slipping between clenched teeth. "Use your stethoscope."

"And put it where?" he muttered.

"*Over its heart and lungs.*"

He could tell by her tone she was over him, but this was not his fault. He was not a doctor, and neither she nor Naia had told him he would be delivering a fucking baby—if that was what you wanted to call that thing in Phaedra's arms, because right now, it did not even resemble a human. It was definitely blue and covered in something…gross. That was the only way to describe it.

Hesitantly, he put the stethoscope on and placed it on the baby while the nurse wheeled over a table with something that looked like a scale.

"What is the Apgar?" she asked again as she suctioned the baby once more.

Dionysus exchanged a look with Lilaia as she mouthed a number.

"Uh…" *Fuck, he couldn't read lips.* "Ninety?"

Lilaia glared and then laughed. "You mean nine. Of course you mean *nine*."

"Yes, nine," he said and then matched her awkward laugh. "Just making sure you're paying attention."

Dionysus took a step back as Lilaia continued cleaning the baby while the nurse listened to his heart and lungs. She kept casting angry glances his way. Dionysus couldn't blame her. She was certain he was acting out of character as Dr. Phanes.

His gaze flitted across Phaedra's face. She looked so happy, blissful even, like all her previous struggles and heartache did not matter. He wondered if she even cared that her husband was not here now that everything was over.

Well, he'd thought it was over.

Until something horrifying slipped out from between Phaedra's legs.

"What the fuck is that?" Dionysus demanded.

"A placenta, Doctor," the nurse said, her tone clipped.

"A placenta. Of course," he said. He took a breath. He started to wipe a hand across his forehead but paused when he realized he was still gloved and covered in blood.

"Aren't you going to clamp it?" the nurse asked.

"No, *you* can clamp it," Dionysus said and looked at Lilaia. "Are you almost done?"

"We have to weigh the baby, Di—Doctor," she said. "And he needs another Apgar. Then we're done."

He said nothing as they finished, his mind wandering to Ariadne.

Gods, he hoped she was safe.

When Phaedra and the baby were cleaned, dressed, and warm, Dionysus met her gaze.

She smiled at him, almost dreamily.

"Thank you, Doctor."

"I do not deserve your thanks," he said, and then Phaedra's face changed, her bliss replaced by confusion as he asked, "Are you ready to see your sister?"

CHAPTER XIV
PERSEPHONE

When Persephone and Ariadne arrived at the Palace of Knossos, the light shone on the horizon, casting shadows over the scattered ruins of what must have once been a magnificent fortress. It seemed to go on for miles in all directions with only a few walls standing. Still, they were covered in vibrant frescos and beautiful murals, the colors burning brilliantly against the now all-white stone.

There was a strange peace here that Persephone found unnerving given that somewhere below all this stone was a labyrinth in which Hades was being held prisoner.

Persephone looked at Ariadne, who was rifling through the bag she'd brought.

"Where is everyone?" she asked. She had expected something akin to a guarded fortress, but instead, she found ruins, trees, and barren hills.

Ariadne rose to her feet and slung the bag over her shoulder.

"There is no one, save those who have entered the labyrinth," she said. "And they never come out."

Galanthis meowed loudly.

Ariadne smiled faintly.

"Do not worry," she said, scratching the cat behind the ears. "I imagine if anyone is the exception, it will be you."

Persephone frowned. "Do you have so little faith?"

"It isn't about faith," Ariadne said, meeting her gaze. "I know Theseus."

Persephone's stomach twisted sharply.

Ariadne turned and began navigating the scattered stone. She seemed to know exactly where she was going, and Persephone followed at a distance, Galanthis in hand. She could not help being a little suspicious of the detective, a woman she barely knew—a woman who would likely do anything to protect her sister the same way she would do anything to protect Hades.

"How long have you known Theseus?" Persephone asked.

She could not remember the first time she'd heard about the son of Poseidon, but she remembered the first time she'd met him. She'd hated the way he looked at her and refused to shake his hand, which had only amused him. Despite those initial feelings, she had not perceived him as the threat he would later become when he stood in her office with Sybil's severed finger in hand.

"A while," Ariadne said. Her foot slipped and she stumbled, catching herself before she fell.

"Why is he doing this?" Persephone asked, following Ariadne down a set of steps that led into what was now a large, square courtyard, though it was clear that it had once been the foundation for a much larger palace. "What does he want?"

"He wants to be important," Ariadne said. "He does not want anyone to look beyond him for anything they need in life. That's what he wanted from me, but when I could not be swayed, he chose my sister. He treats the world the same, only he usually executes those who do not follow where he leads."

Ariadne took a sharp turn as she passed through a narrow crack in a ruined wall and made her way down another set of steps to a darkened stone passage that was flanked with two broken columns. The air coming from inside was cold and stale. Persephone could feel it, even from where she stood at the top of the stairs, watching as Ariadne dropped the bag to the ground.

"But you have survived," Persephone said. She wasn't sure if she was asking a question or making a statement, but it didn't seem to matter to Ariadne, who paused to look up at her from where she stood, wreathed in the threatening darkness of the labyrinth.

"Because I am still useful to him," Ariadne said, her lip curling as she spoke, hinting at her disgust. She returned to her bag and withdrew something that looked like a spool, but that was not what intrigued Persephone—it was the wave of familiar magic that struck her. It made her heart drop into the pit of her stomach.

"What is that?" Persephone asked, descending the steps.

"Thread," Ariadne said as she tied an end around one of the broken columns.

"Where did you get it?" Persephone asked as she set Galanthis on the ground. The cat meowed and brushed her legs.

"I spun it," Ariadne said, holding the spool out to Persephone.

"You spun it?" Persephone echoed, staring at the silvery cord, hesitating to take it.

She had known Demeter's magic would cling to things in the Upperworld even after her death, but she had not expected to feel it so soon. She could not quite come to terms with how it was making her feel, though she knew there was really no time to process her layered feelings.

Finally, she took the spool, letting out a shuddering breath at the feel of warm sunshine resting in her palms.

"This is my mother's magic," Persephone said, her voice quiet. It even smelled like her—like golden wheat baking in the summer heat. She met Ariadne's gaze and saw she had paled. "How?"

Ariadne hesitated. "I assumed it was something Theseus had bargained for to curse me."

"You mean you did not know you had this ability?"

"One day, Theseus locked me in a room and told me to spin wool into thread," she said. "It was days before I tried—days without water or food—and when I could stand it no longer, I tried. It was...*intuitive*. As if I had done it my whole life."

Galanthis was purring loudly, rubbing against Persephone's legs.

"It's why he withholds my sister," Ariadne said. "He is hoping I will come back. Without me, he has no way to make the nets he has been using to capture gods."

Hades suspected that both Harmonia and Tyche had been subdued by a net like the one Hephaestus had made in ancient times. It was light and thin, almost imperceptible, much like the thread Ariadne had wound around this spool, but they hadn't had confirmation until now.

"Why you and not Phaedra?" Persephone asked.

"Theseus probably would have preferred her, but at the time, I think he thought he would break me. That's why I am glad it was me. I was able to leave when I saw what he was doing…but I haven't seen my sister since."

"I'm sorry," Persephone said.

"Me too," Ariadne said, looking away as if she could not handle the sympathy.

Persephone understood.

Ariadne tied a thread from a second spool around the column.

"Hold this," she said.

Persephone took the other spool in hand while Ariadne pulled on a pair of leather gloves from her bag. When she was finished, she took the thread back and looked at Persephone. "Do not let go no matter how lost you become. This is our only way out of the labyrinth."

Persephone nodded. She did not need to inquire as to the strength of the thread—it had brought down the gods. It was unbreakable.

Galanthis took the lead, disappearing into the dark while Persephone and Ariadne followed, walking side by side, unwinding their thread as they went. A flare of light caught Persephone's attention, and she looked toward Ariadne, who was holding a luminous stone. She handed one to her.

"It will last longer than the flashlight or a torch," she said.

The stone almost looked like an opal. The light cast

was minimal, not even reaching the ground, but they were no longer in complete darkness. Surprisingly, it eased Persephone's anxiety.

She did not usually mind the dark. She had come to feel at home within it, but this was different. It did not belong to Hades but to some other entity, and it pressed in on her from all sides, kept at bay by the small, ethereal light she held in her hand.

The farther they walked, the more she could feel it bearing down on her. It was such a tangible weight, she tried summoning her power only to realize she couldn't. The adamant was already oppressing her abilities.

Galanthis meowed, and Persephone took a step but there was no ground beneath her. She gave a small cry, but then her foot slammed down on a step.

"*Fuck*," she breathed, her heart racing as she held the stone out in front of her to find a set of stone stairs descending into a thick darkness. Galanthis's eye flashed as she looked back at them. It was as if she were saying *I warned you*.

Persephone looked at Ariadne, her face partially illuminated by her stone.

"How far down is the labyrinth?" Persephone asked.

"A few more flights," Ariadne said.

Persephone supposed it was silly to think that once they crossed the threshold, they would be in the labyrinth. She swallowed the panic she felt at the thought of going deeper below ground. *This is the way to Hades*, she reminded herself, wishing desperately she could feel his presence within this horrid dark, but in these adamant walls, there was nothing save a bitter cold that managed to seep through the layers of clothes Ariadne had supplied her with.

She tried to ignore it, to focus on anything else—navigating the narrow steps through the half dark, the way the thread felt in her hand, almost too thin, like a strand of her own hair—but she never stopped shivering. There was also something about being this far beneath the earth that seemed to require silence. Neither she nor Ariadne spoke. The only sound was their breathing and the scrape of their feet against the rough ground, and both seemed too loud.

Finally, they rounded a corner, and ahead, Persephone could see a strange orange light. It was no better than the stones they carried, but it seemed to illuminate a path, and she knew they'd made it to the start of the labyrinth.

Persephone pocketed the rock and took a step forward.

"Wait!" Ariadne called out, but it was too late. Vines burst from the ground, the branches creaking and groaning as they wove together, tangling the passage in a thicket of thorns.

When it was done, there was silence again, and Persephone sighed.

"As if this wasn't hard enough," she said.

"It isn't fun for him unless there are challenges," said Ariadne. She glared up into the darkness, as if she knew Theseus was watching.

"Can he hear us?" Persephone asked.

"I'm certain," Ariadne said. "He will want to hear us scream."

Hatred twisted in Persephone's stomach, and she found herself thinking of what her vengeance would look like once Hades was free. She wanted Theseus to watch as his empire unraveled, and she would ensure she was the one pulling the thread.

"Careful of the thorns," Ariadne said. "The jacket should help, but they are poisonous."

"What kind of poison?" Persephone asked.

"I don't know," said Ariadne. "I just know they sting, and the cuts are slow to heal."

Persephone didn't imagine it was possible to escape the tangle unscathed—save for Galanthis, who slipped beneath the branches as if they did not exist. Still, there was only one way to Hades, and that was forward.

Persephone chose an entry point, unraveling the thread a little before crouching and slipping between a set of serrated vines. Within the first pocket, she was able to stand fully, but as she moved into the next, she had to stay low, highly aware of the threat of the thorns, which raised the hair on her arms and the back of her neck.

When she heard a sharp inhale, she swung too quickly, narrowly missing a jab to the side of her head. Through the muted light, she could see Ariadne pressing a hand to her upper arm.

"Are you okay?" Persephone whispered.

"Yeah," Ariadne said. "*Gods*, it really does sting."

Persephone frowned and looked ahead, trying to gauge how much farther they had to go, but she could not tell. The vines were thick and the light too dim.

"What comes next?" she asked.

She hadn't started moving again. She did not trust herself to navigate the thorns and talk at the same time.

"It depends on how we leave these thorns," Ariadne said.

Persephone said nothing for a moment as she

gingerly stepped over another branch while ducking to miss another and unwound her thread.

"How did you become familiar with the labyrinth?" she asked when she could breathe again, resting in a thorn-free pocket.

"The first time Theseus introduced me, it was because he sent in a man who I had wanted to arrest for a long time. I think he thought I'd be grateful to him for dealing out the justice I had sought, but instead, I was horrified."

They were quiet after that, concentrating on making progress through the bramble path. One small mercy was that Persephone's bones were no longer shaking with cold. Now she was sweating and her back ached. She was tired of bending, tired of moving at this pace, which only made her muscles burn.

She thought that perhaps the worst thing about this was that it seemed endless.

Galanthis meowed, and when Persephone looked up, she could see the cat's eyes gleaming. She took that as a sign they were close to the end.

She tried not to rush. She'd made it this far without a scratch and did not want to fuck up now. Carefully, she turned her head to look at Ariadne, who had slowed considerably.

Persephone's heart dropped into her stomach.

"Are you okay?"

"Yeah," Ariadne said, though Persephone could tell something was wrong. She sounded weak and breathless.

"Just a little farther, Ari," she said, trying to be encouraging, but then a strange sound echoed within the narrow passage, vibrating the air.

It made Persephone's blood run cold.

"What was that?" she whispered, peering into the darkness.

Galanthis hissed.

The growl came again, deep and closer this time. It was followed by a succession of squeals and the pounding of hooves, and then there was the distinct sound of splintering wood.

All Persephone could see was a flash of white in the distance—perhaps teeth?

"Oh, fuck," Ariadne said. "It's a boar. Run!"

But running was impossible trapped within the vines. All Persephone could do was move faster and keep a hold on the thread.

At first, she tried to continue carefully, but the closer the boar drew, the less she cared about the poisonous thorns. She would take a scratch over being mauled to death by a boar, but as the thorns scraped along her arms and dug into her back, she realized how unprepared she'd been for the pain. It was sharp and biting. It made her mouth water and her stomach sour.

She wanted to vomit, but she forced the nausea down and kept going, her hands shaking as she unraveled the thread, her heart racing as the boar's cries grew louder, nearly unbearable in their terrible pitch as the creature effortlessly tore through the thicket she and Ariadne had spent so long navigating.

She cried out as she slid beneath a branch, a thorn cutting along her back, but she did not care because as she stumbled, she found that she was free—surrounded only by cold air and darkness.

"I'm out, Ari!" she cried. "I'm out—"

She turned to find Ariadne still struggling as the boar drew closer. Persephone could see it better now—a huge creature with shaggy hair and large tusks that it used to tear at the thorns.

"Go!" Ariadne yelled.

But Persephone couldn't leave her. She looked down at Galanthis, who meowed, and set the spool of thread at her feet.

"Watch this," she said and drew the knife Ian had forged and entered the tangle again.

"What are you doing?" Ariadne demanded. "I said go!"

"Just keep moving!" Persephone commanded. diving beneath and climbing over barbed branches as fast she could. All the while, Ariadne continued toward freedom.

As Persephone neared the boar, its hot breath washed over her like a furnace, smelling of rot and decay, roiling her stomach. Its large tusks tore through the wall of thorns with a strength that made them seem like glass.

She steeled herself as the swipe of its tusk came within a few inches of her and swung forward with all her might, shoving her blade into the tender flesh of the creature's nose. The boar roared and swung its head, scooping Persephone up with its tusks and tossing her through the air.

She screamed, feeling branches break across her back as she soared through the air, landing on the solid ground with the blood-soaked blade still clutched in her hand. Pain lashed through her, stealing her breath, but she knew there was no time to linger. She sat up, her head spinning.

"Persephone!" Ariadne cried, racing toward her.

Behind her, the boar roared, breaking free of the final layer of thorns.

Persephone rose, unsteady on her feet, still aching from the impact of her fall.

"Run!" Ariadne yelled.

They raced along the dim corridor with the boar on their heels. Ariadne yanked her arm, pulling her through a break in the stone wall. Persephone hoped the sudden move would put distance between them and the boar, but then there was a terrible explosion, and rocks rained down on them as the creature crashed through the labyrinth wall.

They covered their heads and continued to run, their path now scattered with debris. Persephone's foot caught on a stone.

"Persephone!" Ariadne screamed her name as she hit the ground.

The impact was jarring, the pain almost unbearable. As much as Persephone wanted to scramble to her feet, she didn't think she could manage it.

Clutching her knife, she rolled onto her back as something large and black leaped over her and crashed into the boar.

A mix of deep growls and roars erupted, booming in Persephone's ears. For a moment, she couldn't take her eyes off the large creature engaged in battle with the boar.

"Persephone, let's go!" Ariadne said, pulling her to her feet, but as they started to race away, the boar's deep growls turned into something that sounded like a high-pitched oink, and then it was suddenly silent.

Persephone slowed, and so did Ariadne as they looked

back only to find Galanthis sitting in front of the still form of the boar, licking her paw. After a moment, she looked up, her green eyes like pale lights in the distance.

"Meow," she said as if greeting them.

Then she rose and disappeared into the darkness.

Persephone took a step forward, calling after the cat…or *creature*…whatever it was. "Galanthis!"

But she soon returned with Persephone's spool clutched between her teeth, thread unwinding as she walked.

"In case there are mice, huh?" Ariadne asked.

Persephone exchanged a look with the mortal and shrugged. Then her eyes fell to Ariadne's arms, which were covered in bleeding gashes. Dark spots stained her shirt too.

"Are you all right?" Persephone asked, frowning.

Ariadne nodded, but there was a distant look in her eyes before they rolled into the back of her head. She swayed, and Persephone lunged to catch her. She managed to lower her to the ground before she started to feel *wrong* too.

Fuck.

"Ari?" Persephone said her name, though her tongue felt swollen in her mouth. It was like all the moisture in her body had been used up.

"Don't let it keep you," Ariadne said, her voice sounding far away.

"What do you mean?" Persephone asked, confused, but there was no answer.

Her head spun, and before long, she found she was lying on the ground amid the broken stones and sandy earth.

Something furry touched her leg, followed by a muted meow.

Persephone opened her bleary eyes to see a flash of bright green.

"Galanthis," she said, her voice a low slur before everything went dark.

CHAPTER XV
PERSEPHONE

"Lady Persephone."

She woke to the call of her name, but it was a distant echo, and she did not want to open her eyes.

"Lady Persephone?" the voice said again, closer now but muted.

She frowned, her brows lowered.

Just go away, she thought.

She wanted to linger in the shadows for as long as possible. It was safe here.

"Lady Persephone!"

Suddenly, it was like she had been pulled from the River Styx, surfacing from darkness. She took a deep breath as she opened her eyes and found that she was seated behind her desk in her office at Alexandria Tower. Her hands were on her keyboard, her head turned to the door, looking at a man with delicate features and a swath of brown curls. He had a youthful appearance and dreamy eyes, and she had no idea who he was.

"Late night celebrating?" he asked with a raised brow.

Celebrating?

Persephone hesitated and then frowned.

"Can I...help you?"

"Just making sure you prepare for your meeting tomorrow," he said, stepping fully into her office now.

He was dressed in a fitted button-down shirt and tight slacks, complete with a bow tie. She found herself wondering what Hermes would think of his outfit.

"Meeting?" she asked, confused.

She didn't know anything about a meeting.

The man lowered his chin, staring pointedly at her. "You have an interview with the *News*. They're doing a whole spread on how you overtook Epik Communications."

"Excuse me?"

Those were familiar things—the *News* was one of the largest national news outlets, while Epik Communications was a media conglomerate owned by Kal Stavros, a man desperate to gain a foothold in the world of the Divine. Except he'd gone about it the wrong way, and Hades had punished him severely, but that had not changed Kal's control over the media.

The man sighed. "Don't tell me you forgot."

"No one told me!" Persephone said, defensive.

She tried to think back on the last few days but recalled nothing.

"Excuse you! I sent you questions three weeks ago!"

He came around her desk and took control of her mouse, clicking around until he brought up an email that included a document detailing the structure of the interview and a list of questions. It was signed with the name Amphion. Beneath that was his title: Assistant to Lady Persephone, CEO of Key Media Company.

Key Media Company? Persephone whispered.

"See," he said smugly.

Persephone stared at the email for a moment and then looked up at the man she now suspected was Amphion.

"Could you...give me a minute?" she asked, suddenly unable to really focus. She couldn't remember anything that had happened before she'd become aware of being in her office, but it seemed like a whole host of events had come to pass, and none of it felt exactly right.

Amphion frowned. "Are you sure you're all right?"

"I'm fine. I just need a moment."

"Okay," he said, though he did not sound convinced. "Let me know if I can help." He crossed the room toward the door.

"Amphion," Persephone said. He paused to face her. "Where is Ivy?"

"Are you serious?" he asked.

"*Amphion*," she said, frustrated.

"She's at Halcyon," he said. "She's been at Halcyon since *you hired her* as the office manager."

"Right," she said, pressing her fingers to her temple. "Thanks."

Once she was alone, she turned to her computer and searched her name. One of the top headlines read:

CEO of Key Media Company Celebrates Successful Grand Opening.

The first line followed:

Persephone Rosi, owner of the largest media company in New Greece, celebrated the grand opening of Halcyon. The rehabilitation center will provide a variety of free care to mortals.

There were a lot of things about the article that stunned her. For one, it did not mention her relationship to Hades. Instead, it focused on her career and accomplishments. When she and Hades had first made their relationship public, she'd been dismayed about how the media identified her, which was usually as *Hades's lover* despite having a name and a whole identity outside that.

Except part of what surprised her *was* her title. How had she gone from *The Advocate*, a small online blog, to this? But as she started her search for answers, she came to understand—she had purchased Epik Communications. Amid articles about the merger were also articles about Kal's fall from grace, which included accusations of sexual misconduct and fraud. A picture of the man was included, his angry expression deepening the scars on his face—scars Hades had left.

Consumed in her research, she barely heard the knock at her door.

"Come in," she said, distracted.

When the door opened, she glanced to her left quickly and then back to her computer.

"Can I...?" she started but looked again, meeting a familiar pair of bright blue eyes.

"Ready for lunch?" Lexa asked.

Persephone could only describe how she felt as

189

something akin to shock. It erupted all over her body, as if all her nerve endings were on fire.

Her mouth slowly fell open.

"Lexa," Persephone whispered. She rose from her chair and approached her, drawing her into a tight hug.

She felt solid and real, but when she pulled away, Lexa looked puzzled. "Is everything okay?"

Persephone frowned. Somewhere in the back of her mind, she had thought she'd never see her again. Now she could not remember why.

"Yeah," Persephone said. "I just thought you were gone."

"You saw me this morning," Lexa said.

"Did I?" Persephone asked. "I'm sorry, Lex. I don't know what's wrong with me."

Lexa laughed. "It's okay. You've had a lot on your plate, and I doubt you slept much."

She raised a knowing brow, and while Persephone knew what she was insinuating, she also felt like she was being left out of some sort of inside joke.

She couldn't remember last night or the previous days, but she didn't care, because Lexa was here.

"So, lunch?" Lexa said after an awkward pause.

"Right. Yes," Persephone said and turned toward her desk. She was going to grab her bag when she felt Hermes's familiar magic.

"Let's eat!" he exclaimed as he appeared, blocking the doorway. "I am famished!"

"What are you wearing?" Lexa asked.

Hermes looked down at himself. "It's holographic leather."

"That sounds so hot," Persephone said.

Hermes grinned. "Thank you."

Persephone gave him a dull look. "That's not what I meant."

Lexa shook her head. "Why?"

"What do you mean why? Why not?" he asked, then he narrowed his eyes. "*I'm* fashion, Lexa!"

Persephone looked at Lexa, and they rolled their eyes together, then laughed.

Hermes glared, unamused. His shirt squeaked as he crossed his arms over his chest.

"You sound like a rubber ducky," said Lexa, still laughing.

Hermes frowned. "What's a rubber ducky?" He paused for a moment, and then his face brightened. "Is it kinky?"

"Yes," Lexa said.

Persephone raised a brow, and Lexa turned to look at her.

"What?" she asked innocently.

"Nothing," Persephone said as she bent to retrieve her purse.

"You better not be lying to me," said Hermes, suspicious.

"I would never!" Lexa said.

"Are we going to lunch?" Amphion asked, popping into the office.

Hermes looked down at him and planted his hand against the doorframe by his head. "I have something you can eat for lunch."

Lexa made a choking sound. Persephone groaned.

"Hermes, you can't say those things to my employees."

"He likes it!" Hermes said, defensive, and looked at him. "Don't you?"

Amphion's face was bright red.

"You don't have to answer, Amphion," said Persephone.

"Yes, you do," said Hermes.

"*Hermes!*" Persephone snapped.

"All right, fine," Hermes grumbled.

Persephone squeezed between the god and Amphion, leaving her office. As she did, she heard Amphion speak.

"Lunch is covered, but if you are offering dinner, I'm free."

"Oh my *gods*," Lexa whined as they piled into the elevator.

"You're just jealous because Thanatos isn't putting out," said Hermes.

"*Shut up*," Lexa hissed, elbowing Hermes in the ribs. "Ouch!"

Persephone laughed as she watched them from her place in the corner.

This is how things should have been, she thought and then frowned. Those words felt strange, and she could not figure out why they'd come to her in this moment when everything felt real and right.

This is how things are, she whispered as the doors opened on the first floor.

She was the last to step off the lift, but as she turned to follow the others out the door, her heart fell into her stomach.

"Zofie."

The Amazon stood near the front desk dressed in black. Her long braid swung as she turned her head toward Persephone and then her whole body.

"Lady Persephone," she said, bowing her head. "Ready to eat?"

Persephone took a quivering breath as a memory surfaced in her mind—one of Zofie lying on a pyre, skin white like marble, dead.

"You're...alive," she said.

"Seph," Lexa said, almost breathless. "Why would you say that?"

Persephone opened her mouth and then frowned. She shook her head. "I don't know. I..."

"Perhaps you've been having a bad dream," Zofie suggested, and her smile was so sweet, Persephone had to agree.

"Yeah," she said. "Maybe so."

They left Alexandria Tower, choosing a restaurant a few blocks over called House of Greek. Persephone noticed how her friends surrounded her as they walked— Hermes was in front, Lexa and Amphion on either side, and Zofie followed behind.

It was a formation they maintained when they arrived and made their way to their table, though it did little to obscure her from curious onlookers, even after they were seated.

Lexa twisted in her chair. "Hey! Didn't anyone ever tell you it's rude to stare!"

"Lex!" Persephone whispered.

"Well," Lexa said, turning to face Persephone. "People are..."

"Rude?" Zofie supplied.

"Yes!" Lexa said, picking up a fork and holding it in her fist.

"Whoa there," said Hermes. "It's not that serious."

She glared at him.

"They're just curious," Persephone said and then added with a bit of scorn, "*They want to see Hades's wife.*"

"Oh, they're not interested in Hades," said Amphion. "Their interest is in *you*."

"Whatever," Persephone said with a dismissive laugh.

They were always interested in Hades because they wanted what he offered.

"It's true," said Amphion. "What you did, exposing Kal Stavros...it was a big deal."

Persephone didn't know what to say, but Amphion's words made her chest feel tight. She wasn't sure why it was hard to imagine, but it just seemed that the world did not value women standing up to men.

"What are everyone's plans this weekend?" Persephone asked, wishing to change the subject.

"I hope we're all still getting hammered at Hades's surprise birthday party," said Hermes, and suddenly Persephone remembered. She'd wanted to do something to celebrate Hades given the terror of his birth. Since there had been no system to organize days at the time he was born, she decided to choose his birth date for him, November first.

"You don't think he knows, do you?" asked Lexa.

"If he did, he would never tell me," said Persephone.

He would let her have her fun, even if he dreaded its coming.

She wondered how he would react when he walked into Nevernight to find their friends had gathered to celebrate him or what he would do later when they made their descent to the Underworld where the souls waited to do the very same.

She could not imagine that he would look surprised, but she knew he would be grateful even if being the center of attention made him uncomfortable.

"Hades should challenge someone to a duel," said Zofie. "It is how we would celebrate birthdays in Terme."

Lexa looked at Persephone and then at Zofie. "I don't think…"

"It was a joke. Did you get it?" Zofie asked, and she smiled, hopeful.

"Ohh," everyone said and exchanged a look, dissolving into an awkward laughter that soon turned genuine, and by the time they left, Persephone's heart had never been so full.

———

When the day was done, Persephone returned to the Underworld. There was an element of excitement that buzzed beneath her skin. She was happy to be home and excited to see Hades, though he would not return until late in the evening, so she changed and went to Asphodel to have dinner with the souls. When she appeared at the center of their village, she faced Tartarus.

It was the first time she'd felt dread all day, and it was so acute, it stopped her in her tracks. As she faced the far-off horizon, she found that it was…warped. It was the only way to describe it—the color of the sky and the mountains seemed twisted and out of shape, like the edges of a dream.

"Persephone!"

She turned to see Yuri, who waved. She smiled at the soul but looked back toward the horizon, only this time, the mountains had regained their jagged shape, and the horizon cut along its edge like sharp steel.

Strange, she thought.

"What are you staring at?" Yuri asked, coming to stand beside Persephone.

"I thought…I saw something, but I must have been mistaken," she said, though her stomach twisted uneasily.

"The souls are waiting for you," Yuri said and took her hand, pulling her to the field beyond their village where blankets were spread across the lawn. A set of tables had been placed end to end and were laden with food and drink from different times and cultures.

They ate as if they were celebrating, which was the usual way of the souls in Asphodel. Persephone sat with them and talked and laughed, and when they brought out their instruments and began to strum, they danced.

She only stopped when she went to spin and came face-to-face with Hades—well, his chest, really. She tilted her head back to meet his dark gaze.

"Hi," she whispered breathlessly, overwhelmed as a sense of comfort washed over her.

"Hi," he said, grinning. He touched her chin with the tip of his finger and kissed her. "Did you have a good day?"

"Yes," she said when he pulled away. "And you?"

He hummed, a sound she could feel vibrating his chest before he answered. "It's better now."

It was a Hades answer, meaning it was not an answer at all. Still, she smiled.

"I interrupted your dance," he said.

"It's all right," she said. "So long as you dance with me."

He held her close, and she rested her head on his chest. They stayed like that until she grew sleepy in his arms.

"Are you ready for bed?" he asked. His voice was warm but sent a shiver down her spine.

She pulled away. "I think my mind is too busy for sleep."

"Is it?" he asked, raising a brow. He leaned closer, and she took a shuddering breath as his lips brushed her ear. "I can take your mind off things."

She turned her head, and their lips touched.

"Bold of you, God of the Dead, to assume I *want* to take my mind off things."

His lips quirked.

"Forgive me, Lady of my Fate," he said, his fingers threading through her hair. "Please advise how I might be of service."

She smiled and started to lean in when she caught movement from the corner of her eye. She turned her head and saw a cat sitting a few feet away. She was fluffy and black, and her eyes were green and bright, almost unnatural in their luminosity.

"No," she said as a sudden and deep cold overtook her body.

"What's wrong?" Hades asked.

She turned back to him, meeting his dark gaze. Concern etched his handsome face. Her heart ached when she looked at him.

Don't leave me, she wanted to beg.

"Kiss me," she said instead.

His brows lowered, but she pushed forward and slammed her lips against his, wrapping her arms around his neck. She needed him to anchor her here so she would never be lost again, but while he kissed her back, he seemed to sense something was wrong. He placed his hands on her shoulders and pulled away.

"Persephone," he said, but she wasn't looking at him. She was looking at the cat who was still sitting quietly in the grass, staring.

She turned to face it fully, angry.

"No!" she said, her eyes welling with tears.

The cat continued to stare.

"I'm not leaving," she said and pointed to the ground. "This is how everything was supposed to be!"

"Persephone," Hades said again. He reached for her, but she slipped from his grasp. The shock of his absence made her chest feel like it was split in two, but she couldn't let him touch her again, or she would really stay.

His eyes were wide, and she thought that in this moment, she'd have rather died than watch his heart break with each step she put between them.

"Tell me what's wrong," he begged.

She shook her head, tears streaming down her face.

"I can't," she said, her voice breaking. "I just...*have* to go."

She held his gaze a moment longer, his eyes so deep and ancient. They were Hades's eyes to be sure, but they were not the eyes of the Hades she loved, and she knew that in her soul.

She turned toward the cat.

Galanthis, she thought, remembering her name as she took one determined step after another toward her. The feline rose onto her feet and turned to lead her away, and as a cold darkness descended around her, Persephone could still feel the burning eyes of Hades behind her.

She hoped she hadn't made a mistake.

CHAPTER XVI
PERSEPHONE

Persephone opened her eyes to find Galanthis sitting on her chest, staring down at her.

When the cat saw she was awake, she leapt to the ground.

Persephone lay there for a moment, feeling as though she'd surfaced from some kind of nightmare, except she could still remember everything. The agony had been waking to discover she was still trapped in the labyrinth and nowhere close to Hades or the life it had shown her.

Her face felt sticky with tears, and there was a bitter taste at the back of her throat. When she sat up, her head spun, and she closed her eyes against the nausea roiling in her stomach, remnants of poison from the thorns.

When it had passed, she rose to her feet, picking up her blade, which she found on the ground beside her. Scanning her surroundings, she discovered Ariadne lying on her side. She was awake, and Galanthis sat nearby.

Somehow, the feline—or whatever it was—had pulled them from the labyrinth's snare.

Persephone crossed to Ariadne.

"We have to go," she said and took her hands, helping her up.

Ariadne did not argue, and in what muted light they had, Persephone could tell she had also been crying. Her face glistened, wet from her tears. While she wondered what Ariadne had seen, she did not ask. It was going to be hard enough to get through the labyrinth without thinking about what they'd experienced in the time they'd been out—harder still not to go back and find that place again.

If anything would take them down within these dark corridors, it would be that—the claws of a perfect world calling them home.

Persephone looked down one dark passage and then the other, uncertain of which direction they had come or which direction they should go.

She looked at Galanthis, who was licking her paw. It was as if she suddenly remembered she was a cat and not some other creature that could take down a boar and lead them from other realities.

Persephone picked up the spool of thread. "Which way to my husband?" she asked.

Galanthis finished cleaning her paw before she met Persephone's gaze. Soundless, she rose to all fours and started down the corridor. Persephone exchanged a look with Ariadne before they followed along, quiet. Though Persephone had no ability to read minds, she had a feeling they were both dwelling on the same thing—their deepest desires.

She wondered if she could retrace her steps and stumble back into that world.

Suddenly, she felt a sharp pain on her arm. She hissed and looked to her right. Ariadne had pinched her.

"I know what you are thinking," she said. "But you cannot go back."

Persephone ground her teeth. She was frustrated, both by the fact that Ariadne had known exactly what she wanted and because she felt weak.

"The danger wasn't the dream," said Ariadne. "It's the aftermath."

Persephone knew what she meant. It was the yearning. It would have them both wandering the labyrinth forever in search of their greatest desire, never to find it again.

They continued on, following Galanthis down dark passage after dark passage, each turn making Persephone dizzy and disoriented.

"Tell me a truth," Ariadne said, her voice cutting through the dark like a whip.

"What do you want to know?" Persephone asked. She couldn't really think; her mind was brimming with memories from her perfect world.

"Anything," said Ariadne. "What was your first memory?"

The question caught Persephone by surprise, and she had to think for a moment before answering. "My first memory is of me crying," she said. "I'd reached for a rose because I thought it was beautiful, not aware that the stem was full of thorns."

She'd always remembered the feel of it puncturing her skin, a sharp sting she'd felt over her whole body.

"My mother was more concerned about the rose and let me cry while she mended the petals I had shaken free."

When she had expressed her pain, Demeter had offered no comfort.

"*Let that remind you of the consequences of touching my flowers*," she'd said.

Persephone had never considered it before, but perhaps that experience was why she would later kill flowers with her touch.

Ariadne met Persephone's gaze, and there was a flash of regret in her eyes at having asked, but Persephone got the point. It took her mind off the false memories of the dream and the endlessness of the labyrinth.

"What is your favorite memory?" Persephone asked.

Ariadne took a moment to respond, and Persephone wondered how many she had to choose from. It sounded like a strange thing to compare, but Persephone could only think of a few favorite memories, and most of them had been made with Lexa or Hades.

"Probably the times I spent with my sister," said Ariadne.

"All of them?" Persephone asked when she gave no other details.

"Yes," Ariadne said, pausing a moment. "We were alone a lot growing up, and I took responsibility for her. I made sure she was dressed and ready for school. I made her lunch and her dinner. I made sure she had fun so she didn't realize what I realized, which was that our parents were too busy for us."

Suddenly, Ariadne's desperation to rescue her sister made sense.

"You can't keep taking responsibility for her, Ariadne. She makes her own decisions."

Her mouth hardened. Persephone imagined it wasn't the first time she'd heard that.

"I would have taken care of her forever," said Ariadne. "She didn't have to choose him."

"Maybe that's why," Persephone said. "Because she wanted you to be free."

Ariadne paled. Those words seemed to hit her differently than the others. After that, they were both quiet until Persephone stopped.

"Do you smell that?" she asked.

Ariadne paused and took a deep breath. "Oh gods," she whispered and exchanged a look with Persephone, confirming what she suspected—something nearby was dead and decomposing.

A terrible fear seized her heart, and for a brief moment, she let herself wonder if it was Hades.

It can't be, she told herself, even though she knew it was a possibility given that this was Theseus's domain and he could kill the gods.

They continued forward, and the smell grew worse. It was sickly sweet and pungent. It made Persephone's eyes water and her nose burn. She wanted to gag as saliva flooded the back of her throat. She wasn't sure she was going to make it without retching.

Then Ariadne began to heave, and Persephone couldn't take it any longer.

She bent over and threw up.

"This is fucking terrible," she said, placing the back of her hand to her mouth.

Now her throat was on fire, and her nose was

dripping with the same contents she'd spewed. In some ways, she did not mind because it deadened the stench of decay.

When Ariadne was finished vomiting, she hiked her shirt over her nose, and Persephone did the same. It did not help much, but it wasn't like they had a choice. Galanthis was still leading them forward, farther into the labyrinth and closer to death.

Finally, they rounded a corner, and through blurry eyes, Persephone saw the source of the smell. A large mound of flesh lay a few feet ahead.

"What the fuck is that?" Ariadne asked.

Galanthis did not seem as worried, trotting forward without a care in the world.

They followed carefully behind, approaching the corpse.

"What is it?" Ariadne asked.

Whatever it was, it was massive and *skinless*.

"I don't know," Persephone said, but as she neared its head, she thought she could guess. "I think…it was a lion," she said.

"Oh gods," Ariadne said right before she threw up again.

Persephone waited until she was finished to speak.

"What do you think happened to it?"

"This is the work of a person," said Ariadne.

"*Hades?*" Persephone asked.

"Maybe," said Ariadne.

Hope rose in her heart. Maybe they were close to finding him.

"It looks like he…" Ariadne's voice trailed away, and Persephone moved to her side to see she was looking at the lion's paws, one of which had been stripped of its middle claw.

Persephone looked at Ariadne.

"Do you think…we need to do the same?"

Before she could respond, Galanthis answered with a meow.

"You can't be serious," Ariadne said.

Persephone knelt, examining the claws.

They did not look like bone so much as steel. She reached out and touched the tip of one, surprised when it cut her so easily.

"Ouch," she hissed and drew her finger away quickly. "They're sharp…like…*knives*."

Yet she thought that these were even sharper.

"Here," said Ariadne. She pulled off her leather gloves. "Use these as a barrier."

Persephone took them and layered the gloves on one hand, hoping it would be enough to keep the claw from slicing through to her hand. She chose the middle one, and as she wrapped her gloved fingers around the sharp nail, she wondered why Hades had done this but also knew that he wouldn't unless he had a good reason.

Still, there was a wrongness to it that made Persephone's stomach turn. She grit her teeth hard as she felt around the top of the claw where it connected to bone and then used her knife to slice between them with her blade. When the claw was free, she took off the gloves and slipped the claw into the finger, storing it in the pocket of her jacket.

"Well, that was horrible," she said as she stood, retrieving her spool of thread. "Let's get out of here."

They left the lion behind and wove through the endless darkness.

"How far are we from the center?" Persephone asked.

"I…don't know," said Ariadne. "I've lost track of… everything."

Persephone had too.

"What do we do if he isn't there?" she asked, though she hated to even entertain the idea.

"Don't think that way," said Ariadne. "He'll be there, if anything because Theseus will take joy in watching you reunite and then tearing you apart."

As hard as it was to hear, Persephone appreciated Ariadne's honesty.

"What do you think will be waiting for us when we get there?"

"I have no idea," Ariadne said. "But it will be terrible."

Persephone took a breath, but she would face whatever waited for them so long as Hades was there. She would fight for him. She would reunite with him, and they would go home tonight…or tomorrow…or whenever the fuck they left this place.

Galanthis meowed, and Persephone looked to see the cat as she was swallowed by darkness.

It was different from the dark around them, deeper and colder, and there was a wrongness to it she couldn't describe.

"Ariadne," Persephone whispered. "Do you think…"

"We've made it," Ariadne said.

An involuntary shiver racked Persephone's body as they lingered at the edge of the darkness. She'd imagined this unfolding much differently in her head.

Mostly, she'd expected there to be light.

But if they were at the center of the labyrinth, then that meant Hades was near.

Persephone took a step forward and then another, but the dark remained. How was she supposed to find him here?

"Persephone!" Ariadne whispered her name in a hushed tone just as Galanthis gave a low growl and hissed.

Persephone froze as two red eyes flashed in the darkness.

"Ari," Persephone said. "What is that?"

Just as she said the words, the lights switched on. Persephone flinched at the sudden brightness, dropping her spool of thread. As her vision adjusted, a strange growl drew her attention. When she looked up, she found the source of the red eyes—an abnormally large, pure white bull with enormous horns. It appeared to be covered in bronzed armor, and it was already pawing at the ground and snorting. Thick black smoke blew from its nostrils as if somehow, it had swallowed fire.

Persephone had seen something similar from the chimera she'd fought in the Underworld. Dread pooled in her stomach.

She was certain that thing could breathe fire.

The bull's eyes were fixed on Galanthis, who stood before it, the hair down her back raised.

"Whatever you do, don't give him your back," said Ariadne.

"How are we supposed to run away then?" Persephone demanded.

"I don't know," Ariadne snapped. "Isn't your cat a fucking monster?"

"She isn't my cat!" Persephone said.

She looked behind her, wondering if they should return to the labyrinth, except that Hades was in front of them, not behind them.

The bull tossed its head and then lowered it, glaring at them with its bright red eyes. Then it charged, and Persephone watched as Galanthis transformed. She grew larger and sprouted black wings and horns, and then she launched herself at the bull.

Persephone and Ariadne didn't linger. They ran, though she cringed at the sound of the bull's strange roaring and Galanthis's howling scream.

She made the mistake of looking over her shoulder to see Galanthis being tossed into the air, and when she landed, it was on the bull's sharp horns.

"No!" Persephone screamed and came to a grinding halt.

"Come on, Persephone!" Ariadne grabbed Persephone's arm and pulled her along.

Tears stung her eyes, and her anger burned through her. It was a familiar anger that usually summoned her power, but because they were trapped in this adamant prison, it served no purpose beyond fueling her retreat.

When the ground at their feet began to tremble, she knew the bull had turned its attention to them. Persephone pulled out her blade.

Ariadne turned to face the bull as it raced toward them.

"What are you doing?" Persephone demanded.

"Go!" Ariadne ordered as she drew her gun, aiming at the bull.

"What the fuck? You've had that the whole time?"

"Bullets wouldn't work on the boar," she said, shooting several into the bull's face, but they bounced off, unable to penetrate its hide. "Fuck!"

That was usual of divine creatures—they almost always had one weakness but were otherwise invincible.

"Let's go!" Persephone snapped, pulling on Ariadne's arm.

They turned and ran again just as the creature bellowed and a searing, blustering wind slammed into them, causing Persephone to stumble. The wind was so hot, it immediately stole her breath, and she gasped for air.

As they ran, she looked at Ariadne.

"We have to split up," she yelled over the roar of the bull.

There was one bull and two of them. It couldn't charge them both at the same time.

Ariadne glared her dislike of the plan, but even she couldn't argue. They nodded at each other and then changed course, running in opposite directions.

The bull didn't hesitate.

It followed Persephone.

Fuck.

She pumped her arms and legs harder, though they burned as she raced away. She thought of what Hecate had told her about the labyrinth, that she was best equipped to handle this because she was not dependent on magic, except right now, she felt completely powerless against this creature, with or without magic.

She knew the bull was gaining ground because she could feel its hot breath all around her, and the roar of it drowned out any sound. Then she felt its head against her back, and suddenly she was flying through the air. She didn't even have time to scream as she flailed and then landed in the dirt a few feet away. Before she could rise to her feet, the bull was already charging.

Persephone dove out of the way and scrambled to her feet. The bull made a wide circle as it came to face her again. This time, she noticed that the bronze armor over its body did not cover its belly.

She went to reach for her blade in the holster at her thigh but found it was missing. Panicked, she checked each of her pockets but only found Ariadne's gloves with the claw.

Fuck. She must have dropped it.

The bull tossed its head and charged. Persephone tried to run, but she had waited too long. The armored creature barreled into her, knocking her to the ground, the impact forcing the wind right out of her lungs. As she struggled to breathe, the bull came after her with its horned head. Persephone rolled, trying to escape the brutal attack—and then suddenly, it was gone. When she looked up, she saw that Ariadne had managed to mount it, and she was hanging on to it by the horns.

The creature bucked, trying to free itself from Ariadne's weight.

Persephone rose to her feet, holding her ribs as tightly as possible. Each breath *hurt*.

She cursed herself for losing her blade. Now, her only weapon was the lion's claw. The challenge was accessing the bull's belly without getting trampled to death.

Gods, she hoped this worked.

The bull was still trying desperately to get Ariadne off its back, bucking in a haphazard circle, but when she went flying, Persephone broke into a run, sliding under the bull and shoving the claw into its exposed stomach before rolling to the side as the creature roared and bolted. It made it a few feet, blood pouring from its wound, before it staggered and fell.

Persephone's head swam, and breathing still hurt, but she got to her feet.

Ariadne approached, holding her arm to her chest.

"Is it broken?" Persephone asked.

Ariadne shook her head. "I don't think so. It just hurts. Are you okay?"

"I'm fine," she said. "Let's find Hades."

She stumbled forward, and Ariadne followed.

Crossing the center of the labyrinth was like crossing a vast ocean. There was no measure of progress because there was nothing in either direction except the sandy ground and the dark ceiling. Persephone could not decide which was worse—this or the dark corridors of the maze. What if they made it to the other side without seeing Hades at all?

But then she caught sight of something—a dark disruption in the distance—and suddenly she felt like her heart was beating in every part of her body.

"Hades," she said, breathless.

And then without realizing it, she was running. Nothing had ever seemed farther away as she raced to him. The closer she got, the more details she could make out. She could see that he was suspended from the ceiling by his wrists, that he stood on a round platform like some kind of sacrifice. His chin rested against his chest; his tangled hair curtained his face.

She didn't think twice as she scaled the platform

upon which he hung. She threw her arms around him, and there was such peace in her body as she clung to him.

"Hades," she whispered.

She drew away and touched his face.

He stirred and opened his eyes—dark, almost black.

"Hades," she said.

He frowned and lowered his brows like he was confused to see her here. "Persephone?"

"It's me," she said. "I'm here."

He swallowed, studying her. "This is a dream," he said.

"It is not a dream," she said, and she rose onto the tips of her toes and kissed him. When she pulled away, he seemed more awake.

"Persephone," he said, and he jerked his arms as if his instinct was to take her into his arms. The chains clanked, reminding them both that he was still a prisoner of the labyrinth. "How?"

"I came to rescue you," she said, stroking his face. In the time they'd been apart, his beard had grown fuller. It felt wiry beneath her hands, but she didn't care.

Hades closed his eyes and took a shuddering breath.

"I have dreamed of this," he said before gazing down at her again.

She smiled up at him, her eyes falling to his lips, and while she'd have liked to kiss him, she knew they had to get out of here. She drew back, her fingers hanging in the loops of the net draped around him. She couldn't pull it off with his hands restrained.

"It has to be cut," he said. "So far, the only success I've had is with a lion's claw."

"A lion's claw," Persephone repeated, fumbling for

the one she'd used to kill the bull. She pulled the blood-ied thing out of her pocket, and Hades offered a breath-less laugh.

"You are…perfect," he said as she sliced through the impenetrable thread Ariadne had spun. She probably cut it more than she needed, but there was a part of her that felt such anger toward the thing that had hurt so many people, including her husband.

When she was finished, she met Hades's gaze.

"I don't know how to help you out of the chains," she said, but he was already working on that.

He dug in his heels and pulled, the manacles cutting into his already raw wrists. Hades didn't seem to notice, even as his arms shook and his muscles bulged.

Finally, she heard a satisfying snap, and his hands were free and then she was in his arms and nothing else mattered.

He held her so tight, her ribs ached, but she didn't care. She clung to him, her arms locked around him, and with her head buried in the crook of his neck, she sobbed.

"Oh, darling," he said, his voice a quiet rumble, twisting his fingers into her hair. "How I hoped I would see you again."

Persephone met Hades's gaze. She wanted to say something similar—that she had dreamed of him, that every day without him had been misery, but those words were left on the tip of her tongue as Ariadne joined them on the platform.

"You might want to move a little faster," she said, out of breath. "We've got visitors."

Persephone drew away from Hades, and they turned

to see five Minotaurs approaching. They were large and had bulging muscles. Some were covered in fur; others had bare chests. Some had the head of a bull while others had more human features, but their one common trait was that their eyes were trained on their prey.

"What the fuck did Theseus do?" Hades said.

"He's been breeding them," said Ariadne.

They both looked at her.

Breeding?

Persephone's stomach turned. She didn't need details to understand what she meant, but what she wanted to know was where had the women come from, and where were they now?

That was if they'd survived the birth of such creatures.

"I asked you to help me," Hades said. "And you refused knowing that this is what he was doing?"

Ariadne glared, her features hardened. "I'm here now, aren't I?"

"That *only* matters if we survive," Hades said.

"Now is not the time," Persephone said as she looked from one to the other.

They had bigger problems—literally.

"How many bullets do you have left?" Persephone asked.

Ariadne drew her gun and checked. "Two," she said.

"Can you make those shots?"

Ariadne almost looked offended. "Yes."

"So we're responsible for three," said Persephone.

Ariadne got into position to shoot.

"Do not shoot until I say," Hades said. "Once you do it, they will rage."

"Got it," she said.

Hades looked at Persephone. "They have no great power, save for their strength," said Hades. "It makes them slow, so be fast."

She nodded, and they descended the platform.

It was a different experience being on the ground with the Minotaurs. Now she could gauge their true size and feel their approach, each of their footfalls vibrating the ground.

Hades and Persephone exchanged a look, one that promised to see each other at the end of this, and broke apart.

Persephone kept her eyes on the Minotaurs as they fanned out, two following her and two following Hades. One continued toward Ariadne. Persephone was disturbed by their very human movements—the way their eyes flashed with malice as they tracked her. One slammed its weapon—a two-headed ax—against its large palm. The other showed its teeth in a warped, wicked grin.

Though Persephone tried to keep her distance, the creatures moved fast, and as they neared, they raised their weapons to strike.

"Hades," Persephone said, her voice ringing with alarm.

"Now, Ari," Hades ordered, and two shots rang out in quick succession.

The sound made Persephone's ears ring, and every-thing following the blast seemed to happen in slow motion. The bullet struck the smiling Minotaur in the head. Its body jerked unnaturally, head whipping back from the impact as a spray of blood spattered the ground, and when the other Minotaur turned to see its companion fall dead, it roared with such rage it shook her to the core. In a matter of seconds, the creature lifted its ax and slammed it down toward Persephone.

She dodged the first blow, the blade sinking so deep into the earth, the ground cracked open at her feet, but the Minotaur was quick to pull it back and swing it at her again. Persephone could feel the power behind the weapon as it cut over her head, and she knew she didn't have a chance against this creature so long as it was armed.

That was when she spotted the dead Minotaur's weapon—a spiked club that would have been easy for a Minotaur to wield single-handedly but was far too heavy for Persephone to lift. Still, that did not mean it wasn't useful.

She just had to get to it.

Another violent cry tore from the Minotaur's throat, and Persephone bolted, screaming when she felt the ax land within a breath of her foot. Her heart pounded in her chest, but she kept going, dodging the monster's assault as she struggled to withdraw the lion's knifelike claw from her pocket. When she made it to the club, she had no time to think.

The monster swung at Persephone again, but this time, the ax lodged in the wooden club. Persephone jumped, using the leverage of the handle, and launched herself at the Minotaur. Brandishing the claw, she shoved it into the creature's neck.

Blood immediately coated her hand. It was unlike anything she'd ever seen, a strange reddish black, and it felt so *thick*. The Minotaur gave a strangled cry and fell backward. Persephone fell with it and landed on the ground beside it, but it did not move again.

Persephone scrambled to her feet and found Hades still fighting one of the two Minotaurs, his arms wrapped around its neck, squeezing. The creature had gone from clawing at his arm to hanging limp, finally collapsing to the ground. Ariadne was busy kicking her Minotaur in the face over and over again. She had a giant slash across her chest.

When she was finished, she was panting.

Persephone raised a brow. "You good?" she asked.

Ariadne nodded and shoved her hair out of her face. "I'm good."

"Are you hurt?" Hades asked.

Persephone shook her head as he approached and pressed his lips to her forehead. She closed her eyes at the feel of him, fingers twisting into the ruins of his shirt. She took a deep breath, inhaling him. He still smelled like his magic, dark and dangerous and right. This was her Hades.

"Oh my gods," said Ariadne.

"What?" Persephone said, pulse quickening as she whirled to see what she was staring at. She'd feared another monster.

"Galanthis," said Hades, a note of surprise in his voice.

"You know Galanthis?" Persephone asked.

"Yes," he said, and then he frowned, starting toward her. "She is hurt."

Hecate's creature limped along, blood spotting the ground as she walked. She had not reverted to her cat form, still sporting her large wings and horned head.

"She was injured by the bull," Persephone said, following.

"What…is she?" Ariadne asked.

"She is a eudaimon," said Hades. "A guiding spirit. They used to only be deified heroes, but then Hecate felt that pets would make better guardians. She was, of course, correct."

"Oh, Galanthis," Persephone said when they reached her, threading her fingers through her soft fur. The creature purred despite her obvious pain. "I have never had a better protector."

Hades raised a brow.

She rolled her eyes.

"We have to go," Ariadne said.

Galanthis made a sound that was something between a meow and a growl, then she knelt.

"Galanthis?" Persephone asked.

"She is offering to let us ride," said Hades.

"But…she is hurt!" Persephone argued and then looked at Galanthis. "*You* are hurt!"

Galanthis meowed, and Hades placed his hand on the small of Persephone's back.

"Come," he said, guiding her to the side of the eudaimon. Ariadne was already climbing up when a terrible screech filled the air.

Persephone turned to see what looked like a flock of giant metal birds soaring through the air straight for them.

"Oh *fuck*," Hades said. "Not again."

"What do you mean *not again*?" Persephone demanded.

"Up!" Hades commanded.

"I'm trying!" she snapped, gripping tufts of Galanthis's fur, but she was already moving, jarring them as she leapt across the center of the labyrinth toward the mouth of the maze at a speed Persephone hadn't known she was capable of.

"Grab my hand!" Ariadne shouted. Persephone climbed a little farther and then reached for the detective, but her finger slipped, and she fell. She started to scream but was caught by Hades, who was not far behind.

"I've got you," he said, his voice resonating deep inside her chest, even as her heart raced.

A series of shrill cries chilled her to her core. The birds were gaining on them, the sound of their wings beating, metal against metal, growing louder and louder. It set Persephone's teeth on edge and was just as terrible as their pursuit.

"What are they?" Persephone yelled over the grind of their wings.

"The Stymphalian birds," said Hades. "Watch out!"

Suddenly he shoved her into Galanthis's side as a strange feather-type spear whizzed past them, followed by another. Galanthis dodged them, but each movement rocked Persephone, challenging the hold she had on her fur.

Finally, she was able to climb again, and when she looked up, she found that Ariadne was facing the opposite direction, gun in hand, but she was holding it wrong—and then she threw it, aiming for the bird closest to them. When it hit the bird, it seemed stunned, and then it crashed to the ground, sending up a plume of dust.

When she was within reach, Ariadne offered her hand, and this time, Persephone did not slip as she made the final ascent to Galanthis's back. Hades followed, and once they were astride, they were consumed by the darkness of the labyrinth.

Ariadne's thread glistened, a thin rivulet Galanthis followed while the Stymphalian birds shrieked overhead, raining deadly metal on them. Galanthis did her best to evade the feathers, though at times, the arrows passed so close, she could barely react and instead slammed into the labyrinth walls, which seemed to shatter beneath her strength.

"Down!" Hades ordered as his body folded over Persephone's as he covered her head. A spray of rocks rained down on them. It was followed by the whir of several more arrows and the snap of bronzed beaks as the birds gained on them.

Galanthis covered far more ground than Ariadne and Persephone ever could on their own. Soon they were passing the corpse of the lion and the boar she'd slain, and Persephone felt her heart rise into her throat.

The only thing left was the thicket of thorns, and they would be free. Then Galanthis roared and stumbled, and they were thrown from her back.

Persephone hit the ground and rolled. When she came to a stop, she looked back to see Galanthis trying to rise, but she collapsed. Their eyes held, and then her head arched unnaturally as she was pierced through by another spear-like arrow.

"Galanthis!" Persephone screamed. She got to her feet and started to run to her, but a bronze beak closed around the eudaimon.

"Don't!" Hades jerked her around in time to see Ariadne's horrified expression. "We have to go," he said, ushering her forward.

A sob burst from Persephone's mouth. She knew he was right, but all she could think was that they'd all been *so close*.

Together, they plunged into the thicket of ruined thorns as spears rained down on them, each one hitting in an explosion of dirt and rock. They did not stop running, even when they made it to the cover of the stairs. Persephone took two at a time, her chest aching. All the while, she reached desperately for her magic. She knew they were surfacing from the adamant prison when she could feel her power on the fringes of her awareness.

"Take us home!" she screamed. Her voice grated against her throat, but instead of teleporting, the ground began to shake violently, filling the corridor with a rumble that grew into a loud roar. It made Persephone's ears ring, and she swayed, unable to stay on her feet with the ground rolling beneath them. Hades caught her around the middle and pulled her back against his chest.

"What is happening?" she asked.

"Theseus," Hades said just as a deafening crack sounded and the steps split. Overhead, pieces of stone started to fall away. The roof was about to collapse.

"Fuck. Go!"

Hades shoved Persephone, and she stumbled forward as the ceiling gave way. She whirled as the stones came crashing down, finding that a chasm had opened between her and Hades and Ariadne.

"Hades!" she screamed as he caught a large piece of falling rock and tossed it aside. Despite his efforts, Persephone knew they would soon be buried beneath the rubble.

221

His eyes met hers in the near dark, burning like embers.

"Go!" he commanded.

She glared at him, horrified and angry, but she knew at least one of them had to make it out. One of them needed magic to rescue the other.

"Just hold on…for me," she said.

Hades offered her a small smile before she turned and hurried up the remaining stairs even as they shook beneath her feet and the ceiling continued to crumble around her. She stumbled and fell, her shins hitting the stone hard. The pain was biting but she kept going, bruising her fingers and breaking her nails as she clawed her way higher and higher, knowing that she had no choice, until finally, when she reached for her magic, it was *there*.

She could have cried.

She teleported and landed on her hands and knees at the top of the labyrinth stairs where she and Ariadne had started their descent as the opening collapsed.

She rose to her feet on shaky legs. She knew she was bleeding from her fall, but she ignored the pain and summoned her magic, intending to lift the rocks, when a sudden heaviness flooded the air. It was electric and raised the hair on her arms.

She turned to see a demigod with glowing eyes and a stream of white-blue lightning surging toward her, the heat of which singed her skin even as she teleported, appearing behind her attacker, but he was already a step ahead and had turned in her direction, casting another bolt. It hit her hard in the chest, throwing her back while boiling her blood.

She landed amid the ruins of Knossos and only had time to register the pain before the demigod appeared in the sky above her and struck her again, this time with a continuous stream of lightning. Her body convulsed beneath the heat, and her senses filled with the smell of burning flesh and the sharp sizzle of electricity.

Beneath the onslaught of his magic, all she could think of was everything she had been through. But it was not just her. It was her friends too. Those she had loved most in the world. Sybil and Harmonia had been tortured, and Zofie had been murdered. The prisoners of the Underworld had torn her realm apart and retraumatized the souls. Zeus had stripped Hermes, Apollo, and Aphrodite of their powers and put a bounty on her head.

And she bore the guilt of murdering her mother.

Through all of it, she had looked forward to one thing, and that was Hades.

He was her light in the window—the glow of hope in the distance despite the deep darkness around her—and just when she had felt his familiar warmth and the safety of his embrace, he had been taken from her again.

Her fury bloomed. She could feel it in her chest, a darkness that unfurled into thorns. She screamed as they burst from her body, cutting through the white-blue light. The lightning ceased as the demigod attempted to flee, but Persephone's thorns twined around him and through him. As his blood rained down, she yanked him from the sky, and he plummeted to the earth, hitting it in an explosion of dirt and rock.

For a brief moment, Persephone lay there, expecting to feel the pain that inevitably followed her explosive magic, but she felt nothing save the hard ground at her back. It was then she realized the thorns were gone and she had healed.

She sat up and then rose to her feet, approaching the crater, finding the demigod lying at the bottom. As she looked, he opened his eyes, no longer lit with white light. She extended her hand, and vines grew around him. He struggled as they tightened, and when he began to scream, another clapped down over his mouth.

Persephone turned toward the collapsed entrance of the labyrinth and called to the stones. They were easy to find because they were made from adamant but harder to move because their energy was heavy. It made her body shake from the inside out, but she managed to shift them over the pit, locking eyes with the demigod as she dropped them on him all at once.

She caught movement from the corner of her eye and burst into tears when she saw Hades emerge from the ruins of the stairs. Ariadne was not far behind.

"Hades!"

She ran to him and threw herself into his arms, once more surrounded by his warmth and his scent. She buried her face in the crook of his neck.

"Let's go," she said, and Hades's magic erupted.

They were finally free, and Hades was home.

Part II

"And fate? No one alive has ever escaped it, neither brave man nor coward."

—HOMER, *THE ILIAD*

CHAPTER XVII
HADES

Hades could not describe how it felt to be free of the labyrinth's hold.

The only thing he had to compare it to was when he'd been thrown up by his father and released from the dark prison of his belly.

But not even this compared, because then, he'd been reborn into battle, and now, he'd been reunited with his queen, and she was all he wanted.

As they teleported, he healed what could be mended, highly aware that the wound at his side was impervious to his magic. He was already imagining what Hecate would say—how Persephone would react.

When they arrived in the Underworld, he kept Persephone close, holding her gaze as he swept a strand of hair behind her ear before tipping her head back for a better look at her face—and access to her mouth.

"Are you well?" he asked.

"Yes," she said in a hushed whisper meant only for

the dim glow of their bedroom. His hand tightened at the base of her head, desire igniting in the pit of his stomach.

"I dreamed only of you in the dark of that labyrinth," he said, resting his forehead against hers. He wanted nothing between them save this sweet tension, but Ariadne cleared her throat, and Persephone responded, breaking this hypnotic hold.

A sliver of frustration shot up his spine. It did not help that he was not particularly pleased with the mortal detective and her previous refusal to help him, especially given the horror in the labyrinth, though he had to admit, he'd like to know what finally convinced her.

"Where is Dionysus?"

"Wherever you left him," Hades replied.

"*Hades*," Persephone chided.

She pulled away, and he was frustrated by the distance.

"I answered the question to the best of my ability," he said. He did not know where the God of Wine was, and frankly, he did not care. The only thing he wanted to know was how long until he could be alone with Persephone.

"If that was your best, I feel sorry for you, Persephone," Ariadne said, her voice dripping with sarcasm.

"I am just giving you the same energy you gave me," Hades replied.

"What is wrong with you two?" Persephone demanded, looking from him to the detective.

"He's pissed because I refused to give him information on Theseus," Ariadne said, then she looked at him, eyes narrowed. "I risked Phaedra's safety once to tell you Theseus's plans, and you did nothing to help her. What makes you think I would do it again?"

Persephone met his gaze. He didn't like the way she was looking at him, like she was ready to be disappointed.

"Is that true?"

Hades crossed his arms over his chest. This was not at all how he imagined this reunion.

"I said I would help," he countered. "I never specified when."

There was a time and a place for everything, and rescuing Phaedra had, unfortunately, fallen further down the list as more and more pressing things came up—like the murder of Adonis, the attacks on Harmonia and Tyche, and the hunting and slaying of the ophiotaurus.

Not to mention, as far as Hades knew, Ariadne's sister wasn't interested in being rescued.

"Perhaps you haven't realized since Phaedra is the center of your world, but there are people who have died by Theseus's hands while she sits pretty at his side unharmed, so forgive me if she is not my priority."

Hades did not like the silence that followed or the way Persephone was looking at him, like she was stunned by his harshness, but he did not regret his words even as Ariadne's eyes reddened.

Fuck.

Maybe he did regret them.

"It's all right," Ariadne said. "Dionysus has done what you could not."

And he would pay for it too.

He bit back his reply, though he was not surprised. The God of Wine was in love with the detective and would do anything for her, consequences be damned, and while Hades could relate to that, he did not trust that Ariadne was as invested.

Hades turned away from the two. If he lingered, he was going to say something else he regretted. He crossed to the bar and poured himself a drink, surprised by how strong the amber liquid smelled. It was warm and sweet, and it burned his nose. He placed the glass to his dry lips, his mouth salivating at the thought of taking a single sip, but then he heard Persephone speak.

"I'll have Hermes—" She paused. "Never mind. I'll take you to Dionysus."

"No," said Hades. He set the glass down and turned to face them. "Hermes is more than capable of seeing her home."

Persephone's gaze was hard.

"Zeus stripped him of his powers—him, Apollo, and Aphrodite—for fighting alongside *us*," she said. "So no, he isn't."

Hades clenched his jaw. He had suspected Zeus would retaliate for what had happened outside Thebes. His rule had been challenged, and the other gods had watched as Persephone turned his magic against him and shot him from the sky.

Now Zeus had to remind everyone of his power and strength, but he could only strip his offspring of powers, not Hades or Persephone.

He wondered what the King of the Skies had planned for them.

Fuck.

He looked at Ariadne, who was covered in blood. She had scratches on every exposed part of her body and a large gash on her chest.

"I'll take her," he said. "But she must be healed first. I don't want to hear Dionysus *fret*."

"You mean the same way you fret over me?" Persephone asked, arching a brow.

He could feel her disapproval. He was definitely going to hear about this when he returned. Except that he didn't really care so long as they were alone.

Persephone turned away from him and placed her hands on Ariadne's shoulders. She was new to healing, and he wasn't aware that she had ever healed anyone but herself, so he was curious to watch her now.

When her magic ignited, it felt like the warm rays of the spring sun, and beneath it, he let go of the anger and tension that had tightened his muscles and fueled his frustration. Ariadne too seemed to relax as Persephone's power took effect, healing the gash on her chest, the scratches on her arms, and whatever unseen injuries she'd sustained while in the labyrinth.

When Persephone was finished, she dropped her hands and held the detective's gaze.

"Thank you for leading me through the labyrinth," she said. "I couldn't have done that on my own."

Ariadne offered her a small smile. "Yeah, you could have," she said, glancing darkly at Hades even as she added, "Sometimes our love forces us to do extraordinary things."

That was the first time he'd ever agreed with anything the mortal said.

Hades approached Persephone, and he was glad when she turned to him. He framed her face with his hands, threading his fingers into her hair.

"I will not be long," he said and kissed her hard and deep. His heart raced as she responded beneath him, her fingers digging into his skin. It felt dramatic to say, but he did not wish to let her go even if it was only for a few minutes.

When he released her, he was warm and aroused.

He considered teleporting Ariadne away without escort, but he knew Persephone would not approve. Besides, it was likely not the safest thing, especially in the aftermath of their escape from the labyrinth.

Or, apparently, Phaedra's rescue.

"Wait here," he said.

He did not want to have to go looking for her when he returned. He stepped away, holding her gaze as he turned toward Ariadne and reached for her with his magic. Simultaneously, he sought Dionysus and found him in his suite at Bakkheia.

Hades wasn't sure what he expected when they arrived, but it certainly wasn't Dionysus passed out in a chair wearing the skin of some old white man dressed like a doctor—except that was exactly what they found.

Ariadne's brows lowered.

"Are you sure you brought us to the right place?" she asked, looking around, but it was definitely the right place, and this was definitely the right god.

He kicked Dionysus's foot, and the god startled awake.

"What?" he snapped as he sat up in the chair, glaring at Hades, but his anger quickly melted into a strange mix of anticipation and fear. He gripped the arms of his chair and stood, pulling off the net covering his hair. He didn't seem to realize he wasn't his usual self. "Where is Ariadne?"

"She's here," Hades said, stepping aside so that the God of the Vine had a clear view of his beloved mortal.

"Ari," Dionysus breathed as he took a step toward her, but her eyes widened and she took one back.

"What's going on here?" Ariadne asked, looking from Dionysus to Hades.

For a moment, Dionysus looked confused, and then he glanced down at himself.

"Oh fuck," he said as he shifted into his true form.

Ariadne's mouth fell open.

"You didn't know?" Hades asked. "Your boyfriend here is a shape-shifter."

"Sorry," said Dionysus, rubbing the back of his neck. He seemed embarrassed. "It's been a long day."

"Where is my sister?" Ariadne asked.

Dionysus's mouth tightened. Hades guessed that this was not how Dionysus hoped their reunion would go.

"I took her to my home," Dionysus said. "I thought that would be best for her and the baby."

"*Baby*?" Ariadne said.

"*Baby*?" Hades asked.

"What baby?" Ariadne demanded.

"Your sister is pregnant," said Dionysus. "Was pregnant. She gave birth today."

Ariadne just stared at him with her mouth ajar.

Dionysus must have hated the silence because he continued, "Congratulations. Today, you became an aunt."

"You took Theseus's wife *and* his child?" Hades asked.

Fuck, this wasn't good.

"I didn't know there was a child until it was too late," said Dionysus.

"Did she give birth at your *house*?" he said.

"No—"

"Then it wasn't too late!" Hades roared.

"Don't yell at him!" Ariadne said, stepping between him and Dionysus. "He did it for me!"

Hades's eyes fell to her, and whatever she saw made her take a step back.

"You think I don't know that?" Hades seethed. "You think I don't know that everything you've ever done has been for your own selfish gain?"

"Careful, Hades," Dionysus warned.

"Theseus will come for his wife, his child, and for you, and while you *will* suffer, it will be nothing compared to those who sheltered you." Hades felt his darkness crowding the room as he spoke, but his gaze did not waver from Ariadne's stricken face. "You thought you knew pain? You thought you knew guilt? You are about to know the agony of living with the blood of innocent people on your hands." Hades straightened and looked at Dionysus, whose eyes were dark with rage. "You had better hope I am wrong," he said before he vanished.

CHAPTER XVIII
THESEUS

Theseus gathered Helen's hair into his hands as she knelt on the plush carpet of the hotel room. Even with this view, he barely registered the feel of her mouth around him, so caught up in his anger over what had happened at the labyrinth.

He had watched Ariadne and the Goddess of Spring from the moment they had arrived on the island of Knossos and made their descent into his dark prison. He'd heard every conversation, every scream and desperate cry. He'd witnessed their greatest desires come to life as the magic of the labyrinth took root in their minds, though neither surprised him.

Persephone desired identity.

Ariadne desired family.

Theseus desired to strip them of both—and he would. It was just a matter of time. What both failed to realize was that he could not be defeated. He had fulfilled the prophecy of the ophiotaurus. He was destined to overthrow the gods, and when he succeeded, they would pay for their insolence, but none so much as Ariadne.

Ariadne had betrayed him, and for that, she would suffer.

He grew harder at the thought of what he would do to her, how he would torture her, and he would start by punishing that wicked mouth.

The pressure around his cock changed, growing in intensity, and when he looked down, Ariadne was on her knees before him. A hot wave of lust tore through him, and his hold tightened in her thick hair. She paused, her dark eyes lifting to his. She straightened, bracing her hands against his thighs, knowing what was to come.

He thrust into her mouth and held her tight, shifting deeper. He could feel the back of her throat against the head of his cock as she gagged, her nails biting hard into his skin. The pain spurred him on, the pressure building until he exploded into her.

He wasn't sure if she pushed away from him or if she tore away, but when he stared down at the woman at his feet, it was no longer Ariadne but Helen. She was gasping for breath and coughing, his come dripping from her mouth to the floor. She looked up at him, her eyes watery, full of hate.

He was getting used to that expression. She'd looked at him similarly after he'd fucked her in the conference room at *New Athens News*, yet she had still come when he'd summoned her to the Diadem and knelt when he'd ordered.

She said nothing as she rose to her feet and disappeared into the bathroom. After a few seconds, he heard the shower running. He thought she might use it to muffle her cries, but instead, he could make out the distinct sound of vomiting.

He ground his teeth, disgusted, and left the room, entering the adjoining suite.

He had left Knossos shortly after Hades, Persephone, and Ariadne, not even bothering to unearth Sandros. He was likely still trapped under rubble given that it was adamant and nearly impossible for him to move on his own, but it would serve as a fitting punishment for the time being for his failure to subdue the Goddess of Spring.

Another wave of anger overtook him as he stepped into the shower, yet he knew it was futile to feel such emotion. It did not matter that the three had escaped, because he was destined to win. While he had hoped to lure Cronos into partnership by offering Hades as a sacrifice, he could do the same with Zeus.

He still had the upper hand.

Let them revel in this victory, he thought. *The higher they climb, the harder their fall.*

Theseus finished bathing, and when he returned to his room, Helen waited, a picture of perfection. Looking at her now, no one would expect that minutes ago, she had knelt before him and took his cock to the back of her throat.

As he dressed, she spoke.

"I have prepared a statement announcing the birth of your son. As requested, it states you were present upon his arrival."

The corner of his lips lifted at her disparaging tone.

"Is that contempt I hear in your voice, Helen?"

Her silence spoke volumes, but then she asked, "Do you even know his name?"

He turned to face her as he knotted his tie.

"Have you suddenly developed a moral compass?"

"I have always held certain values," she snapped.

"Oh? And what are they? Dishonesty? Treachery? Desperation?"

She glared. "You have no reason to accuse me of such things."

"Of course I do. You displayed each one when you abandoned your friends for me."

"I did not abandon anyone for *you*. I chose Triad."

"*I am Triad.*"

She glared at him, her chest rising and falling with her anger.

He scowled. "Help me with this fucking tie!"

She lifted her chin, and for a moment, he thought she would refuse, but then she rose to approach him.

"Who were you thinking about when you were fucking my face?" she asked.

Theseus did not like her question. It felt too familiar, like she was a lover demanding answers.

"Jealous, Helen?"

"She's under your skin," she said.

His muscles went rigid. She was suggesting he had a weakness. "For all you know, it was my wife," he said.

"The wife you left alone while she gave birth to your son?" she asked. "I don't think so."

He let his hands rest on her hips, fingers pressing hard into her skin.

"Know your place, Helen," he said.

"If you ever do that to me again, I will bite your dick off," she said. "I do not care about the consequences. Are we understood?"

The corner of his mouth lifted. He said nothing, and she continued as if they had never gone off topic.

"The reporters are waiting outside the hospital. When you exit the front, you will pause at the top step with Phaedra, announce your son, smile and wave, and then guide her to the waiting SUV."

She slipped the knot of his tie up, snug against his neck, causing him to cough. He knocked her hands away and turned toward the mirror, adjusting the tie so that it wouldn't choke him to death before he made it to Phaedra's room.

"I know how to charm the press," he said.

It was Phaedra they needed to worry about. This would be their first appearance together since the incident in the hall, though he suspected she would do anything to please him, clinging to the hope that if she did, he might still love her.

He did not really care what she had to tell herself, so long as she played her part. A part that was even more critical now that Ariadne had made her choice to side with Hades and Persephone.

He watched Helen cross to the bedside table to pick up her tablet and purse.

"Leaving so soon?" he asked.

"I have to work," she said, meeting his gaze in the mirror.

He turned to face her. "You work for me."

She ground her teeth, a spark of anger in her eyes.

He chuckled. She didn't like that, which made it even more satisfying.

"You are the one who told me to have a counterattack ready for Persephone," she said. "And I have a lead."

"Anything you want to share?"

"I prefer it to be a surprise," she said.

He tilted his head to the side, studying her. He waited for her to drop her gaze or fidget with her stuff—to show some kind of discomfort—but she remained poised beneath his scrutiny.

He approached, brushing his knuckles along her cheek. She stiffened as his hand came to rest against her neck.

"You wouldn't lie to me, would you, Helen?"

"No," she said.

"No?" he asked, increasing the pressure against her throat. He felt her swallow beneath his hold. "Or never?"

She did not answer, and after a moment, he dropped his hand, pleased by the way she seemed to slump when he released her. He thought he almost liked her fear more than her acquiescence.

"If you had said never, I wouldn't have believed you," he said. "And then I would have killed you."

She didn't even blink, and he could not decide if she was brave or foolish.

He had played this game for years, and he knew the kind of person she was—an opportunist, eager to please so long as it meant a ride to the top—and he was willing to indulge her until she was no longer useful, though he had no doubt she was planning to stab him in the back before then.

It was a good thing he was invincible.

Helen turned, and he watched as she retreated, speaking only as she made it to the door.

"His name is Acamas," he said, and when Helen looked back at him, he offered a warning. "I know your

240

loyalty is tied to ambition, Helen. Just remember you can't rise from the dead."

―――――

Theseus teleported to the Asclepius Community Hospital.

When he arrived, he expected Tannis to greet him in the hallway outside Phaedra's door but found it abandoned. In fact, the whole wing was quiet. His immediate reaction was not to overthink—perhaps Tannis had cleared the wing and gone inside to help Phaedra prepare for her departure.

When he entered, he found Tannis, but he was not with Phaedra. He was on his knees. Perseus stood behind him, a gun pointed at the back of his head.

Theseus closed the door.

"Tell Lord Theseus where his wife is, Tannis," Perseus said.

There was a brief pause, and then in a quiet tone, Tannis said, "I don't know."

"You don't know," Theseus repeated. He looked at Perseus and then around the room, but there was no sign of their belongings. "And what about my son?"

"I…don't know…my lord," Tannis said.

"But he was born?" Theseus's voice trembled.

"I heard his cries."

Theseus clenched his teeth. Each word only succeeded in making him angrier. He could not describe this feeling, this rage, but all he could think was that he had had a son and now he was gone. It was the only thing he could think and that…surprised him.

"*When* did you realize he was missing?"

"The doctor never left the room," Tannis answered.

Never left.

Never left.

He fixated on those words.

Never left.

Someone had certainly left, and they had taken his wife and his child.

His property and legacy.

Theseus regarded the bodyguard for a moment and then met Perseus's gaze. The demigod pulled the trigger, executing Tannis with a single bullet to the back of his head. Theseus had no more use for the man who had failed to protect his wife and child, no need to ask him any more questions. He knew who was responsible for this.

Ariadne.

"Have you located Doctor Phanes?" Theseus asked. He watched as Tannis's blood pooled on the floor.

"He is being escorted here now along with his nurse," Perseus said. "We found them in the parking garage, disoriented."

She's under your skin.

It was true. Ariadne was under his skin, and he hated her for it.

Hated her because she knew and she had used it to her advantage, to take control of this very moment. He had to admit he was surprised she had made her move, knowing he would seek revenge…knowing Phaedra would suffer too.

The door opened, and Theseus looked up to find Damian, a son of Zeus, entering with the doctor and a middle-aged woman. At first, their expressions were distant, a symptom of compulsion, but then their eyes fell to Tannis, lifeless on the floor.

The nurse screamed, and Damian covered her mouth, muffling the sound.

"Please, my lord," Doctor Phanes begged, eyes already watering. His large, sweaty forehead gleamed under the fluorescent lights. "I...I do not know what happened."

"Shh," Theseus said as he approached and pressed a finger to the man's lips. He waited until he was certain the doctor would remain quiet before pulling his hand away. "I know it was not your fault. Some things are outside your control, just like the length of your life."

Theseus took a step back, and Perseus raised his weapon.

"Please," the doctor whispered, his plea drowned by the sound of Perseus's gun firing.

The nurse screamed but she was silenced shortly after by Damian, who kept his hand over her mouth and wound his arm tightly around her neck until she slid to the floor.

In the quiet that followed, Perseus spoke.

"I will find her, my lord, and your son."

But Theseus did not need help locating them. He knew exactly where they were.

"No," he said. "You will bring me Dionysus."

CHAPTER XIX
HADES

Hades had not expected to leave Bakkheia in such a foul mood. If Persephone had heard the way he'd spoken to Ariadne, she likely wouldn't speak to him all night, but Dionysus's decision to essentially kidnap Phaedra and her son would have horrible consequences. He only hoped he could stop Theseus before the demigod saw them through, but those worries were for tomorrow.

Tonight, all he wished to concern himself with was Persephone.

Except when he returned to the Underworld, she was not alone. Hecate had joined her in his office.

"When I said wait for me, I meant alone," he grumbled, though to be fair, he was not unhappy to see the Goddess of Witchcraft.

"Shut up!" Hecate snapped as she embraced him, and though her actions surprised him, he hugged her back. "You're an idiot," she said with her face buried in his chest.

He smiled softly. "I missed you too, Hecate."

She pulled away and touched his face. He had never quite seen this look in her eyes before. It was almost like she was in *disbelief*—like maybe she had not been certain he would actually return.

That thought turned his stomach.

"You need to shave," she said.

"Noted," he replied.

"I will leave you," she said, taking a step back. "But I had to see you—both of you."

Hecate turned to Persephone and hugged her tight; then the goddess left, and they were alone.

It was the moment he had waited for, yet he did not close the distance between them. All he could do was stare at his wife, his goddess, his queen. She was so beautiful, his heart ached when he looked at her. He had spent most of his time in the labyrinth thinking only of her, conjuring her likeness from memory, and still he had not done her justice. He could never capture her truth—the unbearable beauty of her soul, the thing that called to him loudest, the thing that said they were made for each other.

Her eyes never wavered from his but seemed to burn brighter, fueled by the heat rising between them.

"We should bathe," she said. Her voice was low and shivered up his back like silk.

He wasn't going to argue. They were covered in mud and blood. Besides, he wanted to see her strip down to nothing.

"As you wish, darling," he said.

He considered carrying her through the castle to the baths as both a way to announce his return and also communicate that they were not to be disturbed, but he decided that would take too long and teleported instead.

When they arrived, he was immediately overwhelmed by the smell of eucalyptus and lavender. The humid heat stuck to his skin and warmed his sore muscles. He hadn't really paid much attention to how he was feeling other than the ache between his thighs.

They were still divided by that same distance, but it felt far more tangible than before, thick and heavy with desire.

Persephone held his gaze as she pulled off her tank top and shimmied out of her pants. She straightened and stood naked before him. He had seen her this way so many times, and he would never get enough of it.

"What are you waiting for?" she asked before she turned and entered the pool.

He watched her as she dove beneath the surface and pulled off what remained of his tattered clothes, wading into the water just as she emerged, her long hair plastered to her head.

He did the same and swam toward her. When he rose to the surface, he was inches from her.

Still, he did not take her into his arms, did not seal the space between them, save for his cock, which was so full and heavy, it pressed into her stomach.

"Everyone missed you," Persephone said.

He did not expect to feel such a strong wave of emotion at her words, but he thought maybe it had something to do with the way she was looking at him. Like something inside her had been broken in the time he had been gone and she was trying to hide it. Then he saw it. Her mouth quivered, and her eyes welled with tears, and she shook her head as if she were telling them to go away but they came anyway.

"It was horrible without you," she said.

He dragged her into his arms and held her tight, hoping that at some point, she wouldn't tremble anymore.

"I am so sorry," he said.

"I should be sorry," she said, pulling away, brushing at the tears on her face. "I should have never left—"

He reached for her, his fingers closing around her wrists. "No, Persephone," he said, shaking his head. "You knew exactly what I would do. I would have never let you leave with Theseus, never fulfilled that fucking bargain. I should have never made it in the first place."

She placed her hands on either side of his face, fingers combing through his wet beard, and after a moment, she giggled.

He liked the sound. He wanted more.

"Hecate is right. You do need to shave."

"You don't like it?" he asked. "I was thinking about keeping it."

"Hades." She was not amused.

"Do you think it makes me look older?"

She pressed her palms against his cheeks and spoke very close to his face. "I think it makes you ticklish."

"Does it?" he asked, nuzzling her neck. "Is this ticklish?"

She shivered. "*Hades.*"

This time, she breathed his name, and he wasn't sure if it was a warning or a desperate invitation, but she didn't push him away. She locked her fingers in his hair as he kissed up her neck and along her jaw.

"What about this?" he asked, teasing the lobe of her ear with his teeth.

That was when she jerked toward him and slammed her mouth against his.

Fucking finally, he thought, and his mind went blank. He pulled her flush against him and devoured her mouth, consumed by the feel of her body and the rush of blood in his veins. It made his heart pound and his cock throb.

She opened her mouth against his, and their tongues collided. He groaned at the taste of her, at the way she let him take control. He felt massive as he bent over her, his hand tangled in her hair at the base of her neck, but she clung to him and moved with him, kissing him with just as much passion as he gave.

His hands skimmed down her back to her ass, and he lifted her from the water, her legs twining around his waist. His head swam, desire roaring in his ears as her heat pressed into his aching arousal. He kissed along her jaw and down her neck as he carried her to the edge of the pool, where he let her sit while he took her breasts into his hands and mouth, licking and sucking her soft and silken skin.

"Yes," she hissed, her legs widening—inviting.

Fuck, he loved this.

"Not so ticklish anymore?" he asked, sucking on one peaked nipple.

She drew in a sharp breath between her teeth. "You are impossible," she said.

He smiled, bringing his mouth level with hers.

"But you love me," he said, letting his nose graze hers, his lips hovering over hers.

"I hope that wasn't a question," she said.

"You can answer it all the same," he said.

She wrapped her arms around his neck, drawing him close.

"Yes," she said. "Yes, I love you."

This time, she claimed his mouth, and her fingers threaded through his hair. His wound ached as she held him tighter, her heels pressing hard into his back, but he swallowed the pain.

Nothing would ruin this moment—not Theseus or his father's fucking blade.

He was frustrated that he was thinking about them at all, especially with his cock nestled so snugly between Persephone's thighs. That was what he should be focusing on, how good she would feel once he was inside her.

He kissed her harder on the mouth before making his way down to the juncture of her thighs.

"Hades, you're...bleeding!"

Persephone's voice rang with alarm, and she reacted immediately, closing her legs and jumping into the pool beside him. The water, he now noticed, was tinged with red.

Fuck.

This was exactly what he was hoping to avoid.

She reached for his hand, which he'd attempted to strategically place over the wound on his side. Her eyes widened when she saw it, and then her expression fell, and a haunted sort of look overcame her.

"You're not healing," she said and then moved back, pressing a hand to her mouth as if she wished to contain her emotions.

"Persephone, I'm fine," he said.

Her eyes flashed with anger, and she dropped her hand. "You're lying!"

"I do not want to deal with this tonight," he said, straightening to his full height. "I just spent an immeasurable amount of time away from you. I want to make love to you, and I want to sleep."

"I can't believe you didn't tell me!" she said and then paused to shake her head. "Though I shouldn't be surprised, given everything I was told while you were in the labyrinth."

Hades's brows lowered, and while he wanted to know what exactly she was referring to, engaging with it right now would get him further from what he wanted.

"Tomorrow, Persephone," he gritted out.

"No, not tomorrow," she said. "*Fuck!*"

She waded through the water to the steps, leaving the pool.

Hades turned to follow. He would beg. He wasn't above it. "Persephone—"

She paused at the top of the steps, her body glistening in the low light of the bath.

"Harmonia isn't healing either," Persephone said, her voice trembling. "*She's not waking up, Hades.*"

Suddenly he understood. She thought that would be his fate too.

He got out of the pool. "What do you mean Harmonia isn't waking up?"

Persephone reached for a towel and wrapped it around herself as she faced Hades. "Theseus stabbed her, and the wound isn't healing. She's had a fever for days."

Hades frowned at the news. It sounded like Harmonia had fallen victim to Cronos's scythe too.

Persephone pushed past him, and he followed her down the hall toward their chamber.

"I did not hide this from you," Hades said. "I forgot."

She paused and turned to glare at him.

Like the idiot you are, he heard Hecate's voice in his head.

"Are you serious?"

"I had other things on my mind, Persephone. That tends to numb pain."

"So you're in pain?"

He gave a frustrated sigh. "Yes, for fuck's sake. I was *stabbed*."

She whirled and continued to their room.

"I can't believe you kept this from me just so you could have sex!"

He didn't see the problem. It wasn't his dick that was injured.

"We," he said. "So *we* could have sex. Don't make this one-sided. You were just as eager until you found out I was injured."

"Because you're hurt!" she shouted back.

"I feel—"

She whirled on him. He felt her anger like a physical slap to the face.

"If you say you feel fine *one more time*," she threatened through clenched teeth. She didn't need to finish that sentence. He felt like he could see his life flash before him because everything she wanted to do to him was reflected in her eyes, and unsurprisingly, none of it was sexual.

When they made it to their room, she flung the door open and called for Hecate.

Hades rolled his eyes.

Great. Now he was about to be lectured by *both* of them.

He summoned a towel, not particularly eager for Hecate to see his raging erection or the amusement that would light her eyes when she found out why they were fighting.

"What is it, my dear?" Hecate asked, appearing just as he finished wrapping the towel around his waist. She was dressed in dark robes. He imagined if she had not already been out in the world above causing grief, she had been about to leave.

Persephone turned to him. "Tell her!" she commanded.

He did not like being ordered, but he disliked that he had upset Persephone more.

"Theseus stabbed me with Cronos's scythe. The wound won't heal. I was going to come to you *tomorrow*," he said pointedly. "But Persephone insisted."

Hecate pulled the hood from her head, her expression far more concerned than he expected. She crossed the room toward him and bent to study the wound, then straightened, meeting his gaze. She seemed just as irritated with him as Persephone.

"Lie down," she said, another order, and while it made him bristle, he didn't protest.

He was very aware of Hecate and Persephone watching him and ground his teeth at the sharp stab of pain that shot up his side as he sat. He held his breath as he lay back, the pain turning to a dull throb.

He hadn't thought twice about how good this would feel as he relaxed into the mattress, but after hanging from the ceiling for what felt like fucking days, this was like lying on a cloud.

"Persephone," said Hecate. "Would you be a dear and bring me towels? A lot of them."

"Of course," Persephone said, disappearing into the adjacent bathroom.

Hecate looked at Hades. "You shouldn't scare her like this," she chided.

"It wasn't my intention to *scare* her," he said. "I was going to handle it."

"Tomorrow," Hecate said, almost mockingly. "When it might be too late."

Hades averted his eyes, frustrated.

Persephone returned with a stack of towels.

"Your magic isn't reaching the wound at all," Hecate said. "I will not be able to do much beyond attempting to prevent infection."

Persephone's stare was hard, her eyes glassy.

He was frustrated that this was how he'd returned to her—far more broken than before.

Hecate placed the towels around Hades's wound, creating a barrier, and then summoned a glass pitcher. "Could you fill this with warm water, dear?" she asked.

"You know you can use your magic," Hades said when Persephone vanished into the bathroom again. "Why do you keep sending her away?"

"If I used my magic right now, the water would scald you to death," Hecate snapped. "Besides, would you prefer I berate you in front of your wife?"

"I'd rather you not berate me at all," he said.

"Then don't—"

"Be an idiot," he spoke over her. "I know. Believe it or not, I really try not to be."

"Demeter is dead, Hades."

Hades's mouth parted, but he had no words to speak.

He was usually aware of every soul that came into his realm, save for the time he'd spent in the labyrinth, and he had been too distracted upon his return to take inventory.

"How?"

"Persephone," she answered. "She needs you well and as whole as you can be—to lean on in grief but also in guilt."

Hades swallowed hard, his fingers curling into fists at his sides.

He couldn't figure out what he hated most about having been a prisoner of Theseus. Was it that he was separated from Persephone or that separately, they had gone through unimaginable things and neither had been able to be there for the other?

When Persephone returned with the pitcher of water, he couldn't help seeing her differently. The thought made his stomach turn, filling him with guilt beyond anything he'd ever felt, but knowing what she had experienced, he now felt like he could see the burden of it upon her, hardening her features.

In some ways, he recognized her on a deeper level.

Hecate got to work, cleansing his wound, which wasn't necessarily painful but definitely uncomfortable.

"Sybil said you mentioned that we may need the Golden Fleece to heal Harmonia," Persephone said.

"That is likely the only way either of you will heal now," Hecate replied.

Fucking great, Hades thought, except that Hecate and Persephone both looked at him. He must have spoken aloud. "The fleece is in Ares's territory, and in case you've forgotten, we are fighting on opposite sides. He won't give up the wool without a fight."

"Then we'll fight him," said Persephone. "He will be more than eager anyway if he thinks he can capture me. Zeus has offered his shield as a reward to anyone who brings me to him in chains."

Rage erupted inside him.

"*What?*"

"Perhaps you should have saved that piece of information for later," Hecate said, slathering a layer of something clear and sticky over his wound.

"Do not act so surprised," Persephone said as if she were unbothered. "You knew he would retaliate."

That hardly mattered, and besides, while he'd expected Zeus to retaliate, he had not exactly expected a competition between their opposing gods.

"I'll kill him," he said.

"*After* you're healed," Persephone said.

He glared. He wasn't sure he could promise that.

Hecate finished by bandaging his wound. It throbbed more now than it had before.

"Let's hope by morning, you have managed to stave off infection." She started to leave but paused, a stern look coming over her face. "*Rest*," she said. "In case you need explicit instructions, that means you probably should avoid sex for now."

"I could have gone my entire existence without ever hearing you say those words," Hades said.

When she vanished, a strange tension filled the

room, but it had nothing to do with desire. It was a clash of anger and fear, heightened on both sides. Persephone stood at the end of the bed. He wasn't sure what she was staring at or that she was really seeing at all.

"Persephone."

He called to her, and that seemed to shake her from her thoughts.

"Come, lie beside me," he said.

If he couldn't have the comfort of being inside her, he would settle for holding her close.

She didn't move, and he felt dread creep into his chest. Had he already fucked this up?

"Persephone, please," he said.

Finally, she moved, the bed dipping with her weight. He watched her crawl toward him across their sprawling bed, and when she rested against him with her head on his chest, his anxiety vanished.

"I'm sorry," he said, kissing her hair.

She did not speak, and he could feel her tears on his skin. He considered asking her to look at him so he could brush them away, but if he did, then he would have to fight the emotion welling in his throat, and he wasn't certain he was capable of facing that battle.

So he didn't.

———

Hades woke to Persephone's kiss.

He groaned and pressed one hand into her back. The other sought her breast, first through her robe and then sliding beneath it. He twisted her nipple between his fingers, pleased with her breathless groan.

He released her for a moment and tore the tie of

her robe free. He rolled on top of her and buried his face between her breasts, kissing her there before lavishing each one with his tongue, licking and sucking her while she writhed beneath him and slid her foot along his engorged cock.

"Fuck," he breathed as he brought his mouth to hers.

She pulled him down and he took the chance to dig his feet into the bed, grinding into her, flesh against flesh. He could barely think, it felt so good.

He moved to the side, and his hand swept lower, over her stomach to the apex of her thighs, where he circled her clit and let his fingers slide along her slick entrance.

"*So fucking wet,*" he hummed against her skin, kissing down her neck. He withdrew his fingers, coating her clit with that liquid heat until it grew hard beneath his touch, shifting over her again. He had every intention of kissing down her body and fucking her with his tongue when her fingers dug into his skin, halting him.

"*Hades,*" she said. He knew by the tone of her voice that she had surfaced from the haze of her desire.

Don't say stop, he pleaded, but it seemed wrong to say those words aloud.

"Just let me taste you," he groaned.

She sat up, which forced him to sit back on his knees.

"You're bleeding," she said.

He looked down at the bandaged wound, stained with crimson.

"I was probably bleeding before this," he said, though those words likely didn't help his case.

Persephone's lips flattened, and she pulled her robe closed. "I'm sorry, Hades. I shouldn't—I didn't mean—"

"*Never* apologize for that," he said.

They stared at each other, and he knew she felt terrible. She crawled to the other side of the bed.

He sighed, frustrated, and flopped onto his back.

His cock mocked him, pointing straight into the air. He lay there, silent for a few moments, before he wrapped his fingers around his erection. He couldn't believe he was going to have to jerk off while his wife lay beside him, wet as fuck.

"What about 'no sex' is so hard for you to get?" Persephone asked.

"My fucking dick, Persephone," he snapped. "That's what's *hard*."

Silence followed his angry outburst. He let go of himself, placing both his hands beneath his head. In the quiet, he felt ridiculous for being so frustrated.

"I'm sorry," he said. "I just…imagined all this very differently."

After a few moments, Persephone whispered, "Me too."

He felt her move, and then she was beside him, shedding her robe.

"What can I do?" she asked.

"Anything," he answered. Excitement shot straight to the end of his cock.

She gave him a wry look. "That won't hurt you."

He pretended to consider her question, but he had a list of answers.

"Sit on my face," he said.

Her gaze slid to his cock and back to his face. "I don't think that will ease your…*affliction*."

"I beg to differ," he said. He saw her doubt and pushed forward, explaining, "Pleasing you pleases me. If you're worried about hurting me, this is the best option. You have control. You're the one who moves. I'll just hold you."

And fuck you with my mouth, he thought.

He could tell she was considering it, and then she rose onto her knees and guided her leg over him, straddling him with her slick heat. He brought his hands down on her thighs, feeling triumph for the first time.

"Are you sure this is okay?" she asked. Her palms were pressed flat against his chest, her breasts swollen between her arms.

"What are you worried about?" he asked, holding her glittering gaze in the dim light of their room.

"Hurting you," she said and then added sheepishly, "suffocating you."

"If this is how I suffocate, I would gladly drown in your heat."

"*Hades.*"

"Put your weight on your knees, darling. I'll do the rest," he said. "Come."

She relented and shifted up his body. His muscles tightened with excitement as her knees came to rest on either side of his face. She looked down at him, holding his gaze as he placed his hands on her legs and guided her down, his tongue running along her slick flesh. He was instantly consumed, overwhelmed by her pleasurable scent and the way he was able to watch her from between her legs. She let out an audible gasp, her hands slamming down on the headboard, and he buried his tongue in her heat, delighted when she began to move her hips.

"Ride, darling," he said. "Like you are on my cock."

He was eager to show her how good this could be for her.

She was tentative at first, but she quickly found a rhythm, and as she moved, he gripped her ass and spread her wider, taking her deeper. When she grew tired and was still, he would change his approach, kissing and licking and sucking her, rubbing her clit until her body began to shudder, and when he felt her climbing toward release, he climbed too. His muscles locked, and his hips shot off the bed, heels digging into the mattress as he held Persephone hard against his mouth.

She came with a sharp cry, her thighs pressing in on either side of his head. It was all he needed to release the pressure that had been building inside him. His orgasm tore through him, twisting every part of his body.

Fuck, he would ache tomorrow, but he didn't care because as he came down from his high, his mind was finally quiet.

CHAPTER XX
DIONYSUS

Hades's words had ignited a primal urge within Dionysus to protect Ariadne.

Unfortunately, that primal urge was directly linked to his madness, and it took everything within his power to quell the tremors shaking his spine, to shove down his anger, to stay rooted to the spot and not go after the God of the Dead and tear him limb from limb.

You would never win, he told himself. Even with frenzied strength, he was no match for one of the three most powerful Olympians.

"Gods, he is the *worst*," Ariadne said.

It took him a few more breaths before his heart stopped racing, and then he met her gaze.

"He isn't the worst, believe it or not," said Dionysus. "But Theseus certainly is."

"What are you saying?"

"I'm saying he isn't wrong about Theseus," said

Dionysus. "If Phaedra doesn't go back to him, he will come for her. He'll come for you."

"We knew that going in," she said. "Are you saying you regret it?"

"I'll only regret it if anyone gets hurt," he said.

He could tell she didn't like his response by the way her lips flattened.

"Take me to her," she said and paused. "Please."

His eyes lowered to her bloodied clothes. "I think you might want to shower first."

She looked down at herself as if she'd forgotten she'd just come from the labyrinth.

"I don't have clothes," she said.

"I'll find you some."

He thought she would leave then to go downstairs, but she hesitated.

"The baby," she said. "Is he healthy?"

"Yes," said Dionysus.

"And...who does he look like?"

"You mean other than an alien?"

She rolled her eyes. "I should have known better than to ask." She turned and headed for the door.

"I think he has your nose," Dionysus called after her. She paused, and when she turned to look at him, he added, "And your eyes."

"You can't know that," she said. "He's just a baby."

"I would know your eyes anywhere," he said.

She pressed her lips together, as if she were trying not to smile, and left his suite.

When he was alone, he blew out a frustrated breath. *Gods.*

What the *fuck* was he thinking?

He should never have gone down this path with her. He didn't know how he'd managed to come this far or how he'd gotten so involved in this battle between the Olympians and the demigods, but here he was, delivering babies and kidnapping wives. He might as well have painted a target on his back, because he'd just invited a fucking sociopath into his territory.

And it was all because of Ariadne.

Fucking feelings, he thought as he left his suite and headed to the basement.

As he stepped off the elevator, he found the maenads scattered around the living area. Some were knitting, some cleaning weapons, some reading. A group of them were gathered in front of one of several television screens watching the finale of *Titans After Dark*...or whatever it was called.

As he crossed the room, he caught a glimpse of Oceanus on screen, his face stricken with horror as he looked at Gaia, who wailed beside him. They were watching the world burn, ignited by Zeus's lightning in the aftermath of the death of Typhon, who, in a previous episode, had laid siege to Mount Olympus.

Not that Dionysus was invested or anything. It just unnerved him. He felt like he was about to watch the same scene unfold around him in the mortal world.

Dionysus made his way down one of several darkened hallways that branched off the main room in search of Naia, who would likely have clothes for Ariadne.

The door to her room was ajar, but he knocked anyway, not wishing to intrude. She answered quickly, a book in her hand.

"You okay?" she asked, her eyes alight with amusement.

Clearly Lilaia had told her about what had transpired in the delivery room. He narrowed his eyes.

"How much do you know?" he asked.

"Oh, *everything*," she said.

"And how many of the maenads know?"

"Oh, *everyone*," she assured him.

Dionysus sighed, rubbing the back of his neck. "Great."

"If it helps, I expected you to faint," she said.

"It doesn't," Dionysus said dryly.

She snickered.

"I came to see if you have any clothes I could borrow," he said.

"We're not really the same size, Dionysus."

"For *Ariadne*," he said. "She's out of the labyrinth."

Naia's amusement withered. "Is she okay?"

"I think so," he said. "She yells at me like she is."

Naia frowned. "Did you ask her if she was okay?"

"No," he said. "I didn't exactly have a chance."

He decided not to tell her about how Hades had also yelled at them.

Naia pursed her lips but said nothing. She disappeared into her room and came back with a bundle of clothes.

"She's not all right, Dionysus," said Naia.

"Then I guess she'll tell her sister," he said.

Naia leveled a hard look at him. "You care about her?"

"Do you really have to ask?"

"Then make sure she's okay," she said, shoving the bundle into his chest.

"Fine, I'll ask," he said. "But you know what she's going to say? Just take me to my sister."

"The point is, Dionysus, that you cared enough to ask."

He was still thinking about Naia's words as he wandered down the hall to Ariadne's room. He knocked on the door, but there was no answer. He tried the handle, and it turned, but he hesitated to enter. Was this an invasion of privacy? She had to know he was coming to deliver her clothes, right?

The sheer amount of anxiety this gave him was absolutely absurd, yet he didn't want to give Ariadne any more reason to be irritated with him.

He cracked the door.

"Ari," he called into the room.

Again, there was no answer, and he assumed that meant she was still in the shower and it was safe to enter.

He slipped inside.

Her room was sparse, having only a small bed and desk. She hadn't tried to make this a home, though Dionysus was not all that surprised. She hadn't exactly come here willingly and had spent her early days trying to escape. She stayed now because she was in danger— because Theseus wanted her, though that did not seem to scare her as much as it should. She was willing to risk herself for others, even if they did not wish to be saved.

Her sister was a prime example. He wasn't sure he'd ever tell her the truth of Phaedra's rescue, which was that she had begged to stay.

"*It will be worse for everyone if I leave,*" she'd said.

"*We will keep you safe,*" Dionysus had said, but he knew what had convinced her to leave with them, and

265

that was the promise of seeing Ariadne. It was a testament to the love they had for each other, but Dionysus knew Phaedra's fear of Theseus was stronger. She would return to her husband. The only question was how much destruction Theseus would have to cause before she left.

And would her return even stop his chaos?

Dionysus approached Ariadne's bed with the intention of leaving her clothes there, but as he did, he noticed a picture pinned to the wall. It was creased and stained, yet that did not dull the bright smiles of a young Ariadne and Phaedra staring back. It made him wonder what led them to where they were now, but he thought he could guess the answer. It was a predator named Theseus.

His eyes lowered to her bed, and as he set the clothes down, he noticed something sticking out from under it. He bent to pick it up and found it was a leather-bound journal.

"What are you doing?"

Dionysus whirled to find Ariadne in the doorway of her bathroom. She stood, wrapped in a white towel, her dark hair plastered to her head. He knew she'd asked him a question, but he couldn't think beyond her and the water dripping off her body, which led to other thoughts like the fact that she was naked under that towel and how she'd felt against him and around him in the cave.

Fuck. He was aroused, and she wasn't even naked.

Ariadne's eyes fell to the journal in his hands. At first, she looked horrified, and then she looked pissed.

Say something, you idiot! he thought, but he couldn't unstick his tongue from the top of his mouth.

She crossed to him and yanked the journal away, simultaneously dropping her towel.

Suddenly, she was naked, and Dionysus continued to be speechless, but he did manage to retrieve her towel—or at least he tried, but Ariadne moved at the same time. Their heads knocked together hard, and while Dionysus barely felt anything, the impact sent Ariadne to the ground. It did not help that she landed in what was probably the most erotic position ever—on her back with her legs splayed.

Fuck me, he thought.

She lifted herself up onto her elbows and rubbed her head.

"Gods, I hate you," she whined.

Those words shook him, and he realized he was still holding her towel.

He shoved it out to her and then offered his hand, helping her to her feet. He held up the journal she'd dropped too. She took it and hugged it to her chest along with the towel.

"I didn't read it," he said quickly. "I just saw it on the floor and picked it up." Though now he had to admit he was even more curious about what was inside. "I… uh…" he said, swallowing. "I brought you some clothes. They're from Naia."

Gods, he was embarrassing.

"Thank you," she said.

They stared at each other, and then he lifted his hand, calling on his magic to heal the blossoming redness across her forehead. Her eyes fluttered closed beneath his touch, and his fingers lingered, tracing along her cheekbone to the corner of her mouth.

He wanted to kiss her there, but instead, he dropped his hand.

She opened her eyes.

"Are you okay?" he asked. He hoped she knew he was asking about more than just her head.

"I will be," she said. "Once I see my sister."

It was the answer he had expected, but he understood.

"I'll let you get dressed," he said.

When he stepped outside her room, he ran his hands over his braids, hooking them behind his neck.

"You are a fucking idiot," he muttered to himself and proceeded to pace until she emerged a few minutes later. "Ready?" he asked.

He knew the answer, but he felt like he needed to ask before teleporting.

She nodded, taking a breath. She seemed nervous, and he wondered why. From what he could tell, she and Phaedra had a good relationship, though it was possible Theseus had poisoned the connection between them.

"I'm ready," she said.

He offered his hand. He didn't need to touch her to teleport, but he thought it might be comforting. She didn't hesitate, and when his fingers closed around hers, they vanished, appearing in the living room of his home.

When they arrived, she immediately released his hand.

"Where is she?"

"In your room," he said and then corrected himself. "Well, not *your* room, exactly. The guest room."

He had never seen her eyes so bright or her excitement so high, and truthfully, it made him sad. It was the first time he realized what all this had really done to her.

She started toward the door but paused.

"Thank you, Dionysus," she said. "You don't know how much this means to me."

He hoped it meant the world, because that was exactly what it would cost.

She did not wait for a reaction. She turned and raced to the door, knocking quietly.

There was a pause, and then it opened, at first only a crack and then wider, and there was Phaedra, ghostly pale, illuminated from behind by a warm amber light.

"Ariadne," she whispered.

Ariadne nodded, her mouth quivering, but it was Phaedra who burst into tears first, and then she threw her arms around Ariadne's neck and sobbed.

Dionysus left the sisters then. It felt intrusive to linger.

He headed down the hall to his room and showered. When he was done, he climbed into bed. For a while, he just lay on his back and stared at the ceiling. His mind felt so full of words and emotions, he could not even begin to process what had taken place over the last twenty-four hours. He just hoped that when Theseus came, he was powerful enough to protect his people.

———

It was late when Dionysus woke to Ariadne entering his room. He didn't remember falling asleep and wasn't sure how long he'd been out. He rose onto his elbow.

"Ari?" he asked, feeling groggy and a little disoriented. He spoke as he yawned. "Is everything okay?"

"Yes," she whispered. "I didn't mean to wake you."

He might be half-asleep, but he thought that was strange. "What exactly did you mean to do?"

She stared at him from the end of the bed, and then it dipped with her weight, and he watched in disbelief as she crawled to him.

Suddenly, he was very much awake.

"Ari," he said.

"Dionysus," she replied, her voice a heady whisper.

"What are you doing?" he asked as she guided him to his back with a hand on his chest.

"What does it look like?" she asked as she straddled his already-hard cock.

This has to be a fucking dream, he thought.

He let his hands rest on her thighs.

"I think you should explain it," he said. "In detail."

Her eyes glittered in the darkness, and she rolled her hips against him lightly, as if testing how he felt against her.

He let out an audible breath.

"I wanted to thank you again," she said. "For rescuing my sister."

He raised a brow. "By having sex with me?" he asked.

"Are you saying you don't want to?" she asked, planting her hands against his chest, grinding harder against him.

Fuck, she was making this difficult. It wasn't that he didn't want her. He didn't want the feelings that would inevitably come with it.

His fingers pressed into her thighs.

"I'm saying I don't want you to fuck me because you feel obligated," he said.

"I don't feel obligated," she said.

She bent and pressed a kiss to his chest and then another.

"Ari."

But at the sound of her name, she ran her tongue over his nipple, then her teeth, and he decided he didn't really care why she'd come to his bed, only that she was here and touching him.

She kissed down his stomach, tugging the blankets away until her mouth hovered over his cock.

This is really happening, he thought as she met his gaze.

"You don't have to do this," he said, except he was really hoping she would.

She didn't say anything, just took him into her hand and licked him from root to tip. He thought he was going to die, except he couldn't, because then he would miss this whole thing, and he *really* didn't want to miss this.

He was also really glad she couldn't hear his thoughts, because that would be embarrassing.

"Fuck yes, Ari," he hissed as her warm and wet mouth closed over his cock, her tongue swirling in dizzying circles.

He reached for her hair, raking it to the side so he could see her better, watching as her head bobbed and her mouth stroked. When she released him, it was with an audible pop and a delicious groan.

Then she met his gaze and smiled, licking the come that had beaded at the tip of his cock. He wasn't sure what was more arousing, the feel of her mouth or the fact that she was having fun doing this.

"Fucking tease," he said, inhaling between his teeth as she ran her tongue lightly over the pulsing veins of his shaft, all the way to his balls, which she lavished with her tongue.

When she started to move back to his dick, he sat up and she followed. Their mouths collided, and Dionysus gripped her ass, pulling her forward so her knees were on either side of him and his cock rested between her thighs. His hands dipped beneath her shirt, smoothing up her sides to her breasts. He squeezed them and teased them. All the while, she rocked against him.

His head felt so hot he thought it was going to explode.

They parted long enough for Ariadne to pull her shirt over her head, and then Dionysus buried his face between her breasts and took each of them into his mouth, tasting her sweet skin. He liked the way she arched against him, the way she pulled his hair.

"I want you inside me," she said as she kissed him.

He said nothing because he couldn't. His mind was blank, filled to the brim with nothing but sensation and need.

He wanted inside her too.

She shifted away, pulling off her shorts before rising onto her knees and straddling his lap. He pulled her closer, and he ran the tip of his cock through her wet heat, pushing deeper when he knew he was in the right spot. Then Ariadne slid down, and her legs locked around his waist. Every part of them was aligned, including their eyes. It was intimate in a different way, beyond just being inside her.

"You are so fucking beautiful," he said.

A small smile curved her lips, and she leaned forward, her mouth moving over his as she teased. "And you didn't want me."

"I always want you," he said. "Even when you don't want me."

Then he kissed her hard, and Ariadne pressed against him, hugging him tighter. He was so deep inside her, his balls rested against her ass, and he could feel her clit scrape against the hair on his lower stomach.

She used him for her pleasure, and he grew harder inside her. There was a primal part of him that could not help moving, aching to thrust into her.

Finally he lay back, bringing her with him, and rolled. He did not think she could get any more beautiful, but she stared up at him with hooded eyes and a swath of dark hair fanning out over her head, touching and squeezing her full and swollen breasts as he drove into her.

His body felt like it was on fire as he watched her writhe beneath him, and he knew she was close when she reached between them and rubbed her clit. Soon after, she dug in her heels and lifted her hips, and he felt her whole body tighten around him.

He bore down when he felt it, grinding into her as she gripped him tight, and then his orgasm hit, shuddering through him so violently, his arms and legs went numb.

Light-headed, he lowered his body, and though he could barely breathe, he kissed her deeply.

This time wasn't like the last when he hadn't known how to handle her after sex. Then, he'd doubted she wanted anything more from him once they had finished, but this time, he gave it no thought. He did what he felt guided to do and was pleased when she kissed him back.

"Are you okay?" he asked.

"Yes," she whispered. "Thank you."

He frowned. He couldn't tell what she was thanking him for, but if it was the sex, he wished she wouldn't. He rolled onto his back and then sat up.

"If you want to freshen up, you can use my bathroom," he said.

"Thank you," she said again.

The words made him grind his teeth. He wasn't sure why they put him on edge so much, but each time she said them, he felt like they were strangers.

She rose from bed and went into the bathroom. The light blinded him for a brief moment until she shut the door. While she cleaned up, he gathered her clothes, expecting that she would want to dress and leave quickly, but when she returned, she lingered at the end of the bed.

"Can I stay? Just...for a little while."

Her question sent a thrill through him, though he thought it was odd that she was so bold when it came to sex, but in this, she seemed shy.

"Of course," he said.

He pulled the blankets down for her as she crawled into bed next to him. He held her close, one arm beneath her head, the other wrapped around her waist. Their bare bodies felt seamless and warm. It was murder on his cock, which was already hard against her ass, but he refused to give in to his desire until she was ready.

They were quiet, and soon, Dionysus's eyes grew heavy, but before he succumbed to sleep, he needed to ask her one question.

"Did you see Theseus?" he asked. "In the labyrinth?"

It took her a moment to answer, but when she did, he could tell her voice was thick with tears.

"I didn't see him, no," she said. "Just the horror he was capable of."

CHAPTER XXI
HADES

Hades focused on the softness of the bed beneath him, the cold caress of the sheets against his skin, and the warmth of Persephone against his chest.

He counted her breaths and her sighs and each time she moved.

The labyrinth was the first time in a long while he'd been deprived of any luxury, and he wondered if being trapped in its dark depths was the Fates' way of saying he'd grown too bold—that he deserved to fear an end to his blessings.

Except that he had never stopped fearing for Persephone.

Even now as they lay in the quiet of their room, blanketed by peace and solitude, he knew that beyond these walls, turmoil was brewing. He could feel it beneath his skin. The souls whose threads marred his body were restless.

It was a dreadful omen, but he knew from where it stemmed—from the magic of an old and angry god.

His father, Cronos.

Since the moment Theseus had told him the God of Time was freed from Tartarus, Hades had felt an unimaginable sense of dread, and now that he was home, that feeling had only grown worse.

He knew his father would come for him. He would come for Zeus and Poseidon too.

But before that, he would go after their mother.

Hades rose from bed and dressed, and with a final look at Persephone's sleeping form, he called up his magic and vanished.

———

Hades manifested at the Edge of the World. It was an open-air circular temple made of white marble columns. It was so tall, it touched the clouds, which billowed like blue and silver waves in the night. From here, one could look upon the Divine and witness Atlas straining beneath the weight of the Earth or Nyx casting her veil over the world, tangled within Erebus's dark embrace.

It was the temple of divine direction, and it was here where Rhea sat staring off toward the east.

From where he stood, she was only a shadow, the edges of her body illuminated by starlight, but as his eyes adjusted, he could see that she wore robes the color of the sunset, cast in orange and red hues. Her long, black hair cascaded down her back like the fringes of night, and a turret crown gleamed like the rising sun atop her head. On either side of her lay her two loyal lions.

It would have been a breathtaking scene had it not been for the fact that the lions were dead and a river of blood was running from them and Rhea, over the mosaic floor, to his feet.

He was too late.

As he approached, he could hear her ragged breathing. His heart beat in tandem, breaking with every step. He rounded on her and saw a great spear embedded in her breast. She turned her head and looked at him, and he recognized the shadow in her eyes.

It was death.

"Have you come to take me away, my son?"

"It seems I must," he said. Hades knelt beside his mother. "When did he come?"

He did not wish to say Cronos's name for fear that his father might hear.

"I do not know," she said. "Time is different when he is near." She turned her head away and looked east again. "I knew when he had entered the world again." She spoke in a whisper. "I could feel it in my heart."

"Why did you not hide?"

She smiled a little. She smiled like him.

"Perhaps…this is what I deserve," she said.

"For what?" Hades demanded.

"For not protecting you," she said. "For saving the one child who would become nothing more than a cruel and wicked king."

He wanted to say something, to ease her guilt, but he had to admit that he had wondered often why she had chosen to save Zeus when she could have tricked Cronos from the start.

"I am here to watch the dawn," she said. "Do you think Eos will open her gilded doors for me?"

"If she does not, I will knock on them for you,"

he said, following her gaze to the gates behind which the morning sun was trapped, its crimson rays reaching beyond their great height, bleeding into the night. "Are you afraid?" Hades asked as the light grew more golden minute by minute.

"Yes," she said, and he took her hand. "Will I remember you?"

"In time," he said.

She turned her earthly gaze back to him. "Do you promise?"

"I promise," he said.

She made a small sound, like a satisfied sigh, and golden light warmed her face. Just then, Eos cast open her great doors and stood in saffron-colored robes, wreathed in the blinding rays of the dawn.

And in that brilliant light, Hades held his mother's hand until she was cold.

———

Later, after Hades had brought Rhea to the Underworld, he stood on the balcony at the front of his palace, ignoring the stabbing pain in his side. It was radiating like heat across his stomach. He knew that wasn't a good sign and he'd have to tell Hecate soon, but for now, he watched his realm slowly brighten beneath his muted sun.

Normally, he would watch his world wake, but it seemed it had never slept—not the souls who hammered steel in Asphodel or Cerberus, who patrolled the borders of the Underworld.

He knew they were restless because they were afraid.

Theseus had brought battle upon them in a life where they were only supposed to know peace. Hades felt angry that his people had suffered, guilty that he had not been here to prevent the chaos Theseus had unleashed.

None of this would have happened if you had been here, he thought bitterly, but those words felt wrong. Mostly, they minimized what Persephone had gone through to protect their realm, and the last thing he wanted was for her to think she had not done enough—that she had not *been* enough.

"What are you doing out here?"

He stiffened, straightening at the sound of Persephone's voice. He turned to see her standing just inside the threshold of the balcony doors. She looked beautiful and sleepy, illuminated by the morning glow of the Underworld and wearing nothing but black silk.

He felt like an idiot for not returning to her side.

"Just...observing," he said in answer to her question.

She paled, and her eyes shifted from him to the dark horizon where the mountains of Tartarus gleamed like black glass.

"That is Iapetus," she said, though he already knew.

She took a breath and shivered violently, which only deepened his anger and his guilt. He wished he had been here to protect her from this horror.

She left the threshold and came to stand beside him, her eyes locked on the monstrous mountain.

"I tried to hold him with my magic alone, but it was not as strong as yours," she said.

"There is no difference in our magic, Persephone."

As soon as he said the words, he realized how frustrated he sounded. It had not been his intention to reprimand her. It had to be overwhelming, to have only just grown comfortable with her own power and suddenly have access to his, but one was not more than the other.

He tried again, gentler this time.

"Some things work, and others don't. It is that simple."

She glanced at him and then away toward Tartarus, tapping her fingers against the stone railing, anxious.

"I thought maybe you could change it back...to the way it was before," she said, almost as if she were suggesting a new addition to the castle or a plot in the garden.

"Why would I change it?" he asked.

The thought had not even occurred to him.

"Because of what it represents," she said.

He frowned, brows lowering. "What do you think it represents?"

"Terror," she said.

"Is that because you were afraid you couldn't contain him?" he asked.

Her jaw tightened, and she did not speak.

He stepped up behind her, grinding his teeth against the pain that radiated down his leg as he caged her against the balcony. She felt rigid against him, and he willed her to relax to no avail.

"You have not seen how the souls look upon them," she said, hands fisting beneath his. "As if they do not trust they will hold."

"It isn't unusual to fear something happening again, Persephone. It is not your magic they doubt."

He could feel her shudder against him as she took a breath.

"So the mountains will hold?"

"Yes," he whispered, his lips brushing her ear. "But if they are too much for you, I will change them."

She was quiet, and after a moment, she turned in his arms, tilting her head back to hold his gaze, and his eyes fell to her mouth. She was so beautiful and so haunted, all he wanted to do was bring her comfort. He leaned forward, brushing his lips against hers, and though the kiss was gentle, they held each other tighter.

"I'm sorry," he said when he pulled away, smoothing his thumb over her jaw. "I did not mean for you to wake alone."

She watched him, eyes seeking something in his expression, and he grew anxious, thinking she was not finding what she was looking for.

"I know you left the Underworld," she said. "Where did you go?"

He tried not to look surprised, but he could safely say he had not expected her to ask or to know that he had left at all, and while she likely knew that, she did not seem angry, only curious and concerned.

His gaze fell as he sought her hands, which were twisted into his robes.

"I went to say goodbye to my mother."

Persephone's brows lowered. "What do you mean goodbye?"

He could tell by the way she asked that she knew what he meant, so he said nothing.

"Oh, Hades," she said and took his face between her hands before sliding her arms around his neck and pulling him to her. "'I'm so sorry," she whispered into his neck.

He wrapped his arms around her and swallowed

hard, trying to loosen the sharp knot in his throat, fighting each wave of emotion as it welled in his chest. The irony that he would mourn his mother was not lost on him. It was indeed some sort of divine vengeance given that he had been so cold toward Persephone when Lexa died.

"*I don't see why death matters,*" he'd told her. "*You come to the Underworld every day. You would have seen Lexa again.*"

"*Because it's not the same,*" she'd said, and at the time, he hadn't understood, but suddenly he did. It didn't matter that he could see her here—*in another life*. It was the simple fact that she had died out there. It was that she had been alone when Cronos had come for her. That he had killed her prized lions before he'd slammed his spear into her chest. It was that all she'd wanted was to see the sun rise a final time. It was that he would never forget looking upon her face as the veil of death descended to see a single tear on her cheek.

It was not the same because nothing would stop him from remembering everything that had preceded her existence within his realm.

"He killed her," Hades said.

Persephone drew back. "Who?"

"Cronos," he said and looked away, staring off toward Tartarus, and while Persephone had feared that her mountains would not hold Iapetus, she had forgotten that his had failed to contain his father. "I think I am next."

"Don't say that," she said.

He didn't want to scare her. It was just the truth.

"How do we stop him?" she asked.

"I don't know."

He had been thinking about it since Theseus had taunted him with the news of his father's release in the labyrinth. They had succeeded before because the Olympians had been united against the Titans and because Zeus had his lightning bolt, Poseidon, his trident, and Hades, the Helm of Darkness.

Now, the Olympians were divided. Some did not even have magic, and the Helm of Darkness was in Theseus's possession.

Not that Cronos would fall for those tactics again. They would have to think of something different and soon, but he also knew that he could not face his father with this wound. If he was being honest, it hurt, worse even than it had the day before, and he knew it would get to the point where he could not ignore it any longer. It was impacting his ability to plan.

Persephone turned on her heels.

"Persephone?" he called.

She did not stop.

"Persephone, where are you going?" he asked, catching up with her in the hall. She did not slow her quick stride.

"To get ready," she said.

"For?"

"If we are going to defeat Cronos, we need the Golden Fleece," she said.

"And do you have a plan to retrieve it?" he asked, though he did not disagree with her. He would need to be at full strength if he was going to face his father in battle.

"I already told you my plan," she said.

He paused for a moment at the top of the steps while she continued down, practically sailing.

Already told me?

It took him a moment to recall their brief conversation from yesterday. Gods, he hated how much his wound was affecting him. He closed his eyes for a moment, and then he remembered—Zeus had offered his shield in exchange for her.

He teleported to the base of the steps, just as she reached the bottom.

"Get out of my way, Hades," she said as she tried to sidestep him, but he planted his hands on her waist. "We don't have time for this!"

"You will not trade yourself for the Golden Fleece!" Hades snapped.

"I'm not going to trade myself," she said, glaring up at him. "I'm going to bargain."

"Not with your fucking *life*."

Suddenly, they were interrupted by a loud crunch, and when he looked over his shoulder, he found Hermes standing in the middle of the hallway, hugging a large bowl of popcorn, wearing only a pair of small floral boxers and a sheer pink robe lined with feathers.

"Is that…my robe?" Persephone asked.

Hermes was reaching back into the bowl as he looked down at his ensemble.

"Oh yeah," he said. "I borrowed it. I didn't think you'd mind."

"When?" Persephone asked, a demanding edge to her voice.

"When I got here."

285

"And *when* did you get here, Hermes?" Hades asked, impatience threading through his voice.

Hermes tilted his head, stroking his chin as he thought—or pretended to at least. "You know, I can't really remember. Since I lost my powers, everything is just so.…*fuzzy.*" He paused, and then his face brightened. "Like this robe." He lifted a feathery sleeve.

"You slept here?" Hades asked.

"Sure did," Hermes said as he scratched his lower back and then stretched loudly, one arm lifting into the air as the other clutched the bucket of popcorn. "And let me just say, you really need to wash the sheets in your guest rooms and invest in Wi-Fi. I couldn't even watch the finale of *Titans After Dark.*"

"I am not interested in making your stay more comfortable."

Hermes's mouth fell open as he scoffed. "But I am a guest!"

"There are no guests in the Underworld, Hermes. Only unwanted visitors."

Hades tried to turn back to Persephone, but Hermes continued.

"Now that's just rude," he said. "Do you know how hard it was to get here? I had to climb down a *mountain*, and I *hate* walking. I was *exhausted*, and then when I finally made it to your ugly palace and found a room, all I wanted to do was *sleep*, except I couldn't because as soon as I lay down on your dusty bed, I heard *you.*" Hermes turned his face toward the ceiling, arched his back, and threw out his arms, moaning loudly. Several kernels of popcorn went flying. "That's it! Ride like you are on my cock, darling!"

Hades raised a brow at the god's exaggerated display, though he supposed that answered his earlier question about when the god arrived.

Hermes straightened and popped another piece of popcorn into his mouth. "And I couldn't sleep because I couldn't stop wondering—what is she riding if she isn't on his cock?"

"My face, Hermes," Hades said. "She was riding my face."

"Oh my gods," Persephone whispered.

Hermes's shoulders dropped in disappointment. "Well, that's not very creative."

Maybe not, but it was the first time with Persephone in far too long, and it had felt fucking great, even as the wound on Hades's side continued to weep blood.

"Might I suggest—" Hermes began.

"*No.*" Hades and Persephone spoke in unison.

"You don't even know what I was going to say!"

"That's the point, Hermes," said Hades.

"I don't even know why we're friends," Hermes huffed.

Sometimes, Hades wasn't sure either.

Persephone took that opportunity to slide past him on the bottom stair.

"Persephone—"

He reached for her again, but she turned to face him, her eyes bright and determined.

"I'm going to Ares's island today," she said. "We have to have the fleece. Harmonia is getting worse... and so are you." Persephone looked pointedly at his side.

Hades stiffened, surprised that she knew. His reaction

seemed to confirm her suspicions though, and despite her frustration, he also saw her hurt.

Fuck. He didn't want to worry her, but he'd kept too much from her already.

He started to speak, but Hermes interrupted.

"Too bad you can't just trap Ares in a bronze jar again. He was gone for a whole year, imprisoned by giants, and only escaped because *I* rescued him." He paused to pick some popcorn from between his teeth. "He still owes me for that."

Hades and Persephone both stared.

"What?" he asked.

"Ares owes you a favor?" Persephone asked.

"Yeah, like, from *ancient* times," Hermes said, still oblivious to what Hades and Persephone were thinking.

"Hermes," Persephone said, taking a step forward. "I need you to use your favor with Ares to get the Golden Fleece."

"What?" he asked. "No."

"Hermes, please," Persephone said. "I will grant you favor in return. I will—"

"It isn't *about* the favor. It's about Ares. His island is one giant booby trap!" He paused and chuckled. "I've always wanted to use those words."

"I am glad you still have your sense of humor in the face of Harmonia dying," said Hades, barely biting back his anger.

"The point is, Hades, I am very much mortal right now, and because it is my favor, I have to go. What if *I* die?"

"I'll protect you," Hades said.

288

Hermes's lips parted. "I've waited my whole life to hear those words," he said, shivering.

"And you can wear the Girdle of Hippolyta," said Persephone.

Hades looked at her, surprised that she had it. She noticed his gaze.

"Hippolyta gave it to me at Zofie's funeral," she explained. "She said something about an agreement you made for it."

He could hear the accusation in her voice, clearly unhappy with the way she'd discovered that bit of information. He had never really expected her to find out about the girdle...or Theseus for that matter, but he was suddenly realizing that he might have protected her too much.

She turned back to Hermes. "At least you'll have immortal strength."

"What the fuck is a girdle, and why does it sound ugly?" Hermes asked.

"Think of it as a corset," Persephone said.

"Hmm," the god said. "I am intrigued. Give it to me."

"Not until we leave," Persephone said. She turned and headed down the hall toward their bedroom, calling out as she went, "Be ready in an hour!"

"I like Queen Sephy," said Hermes. "She's like...old Sephy but angrier."

She was angry—the result of watching those she loved hurt. In some ways, Hades mourned the fact that she had to witness any of this, but they both knew it was her anger that fueled her power.

And it was her anger that would save them.

Hermes's chewing drew Hades's attention again, and he looked at the God of Mischief.

"Popcorn?" he offered.

Hades reached into the bowl and took some. He held Hermes's gaze as he popped it into his mouth. The popcorn was buttery and melted on his tongue.

"Hmm, not bad," he said, then licked his fingers.

Hermes looked a little dazed, and he swallowed. "Now you're just being mean," he said.

Hades chuckled and headed down the hall. "One hour, Hermes."

CHAPTER XXII
PERSEPHONE

Persephone was just buttoning her jeans when Hades entered the room. She was trying hard to breathe through her frustration, knowing that only a few hours earlier, he'd brought his mother to the Underworld, but it was difficult, because if he'd had the choice, he wouldn't have admitted that his wound had worsened. After all they'd been through, he was still keeping the truth from her.

"You're upset," Hades said.

For some reason, that made her even angrier. She gritted her teeth and refused to look at him.

"Persephone," he said as she reached for the shirt that she'd tossed on the bed.

"I don't want to talk about it," she said, sliding the tank over her head.

"I didn't tell you how I was feeling because I didn't want you to worry," he said.

She froze and looked at him and let her anger blossom. She had warned him.

"You didn't want to worry me?" she asked. "Did you think the worry just stops and starts on your command?"

He was still and expressionless, but Persephone got the sense that he realized how stupid he sounded.

"You *never* tell the truth," she said.

His expression darkened. His anger slammed into her, a quick and violent thing.

"I haven't lied to you," he said.

"You don't have to lie to not tell the truth," she said and then shook her head. She almost felt unable to communicate how this had made her feel, but she needed to say it all the same. "I recognized it when I found out about Theseus's favor," she said, noting how Hades's body seemed to grow rigid. "And in the moment, it was shocking but nothing compared to what followed, so I didn't think long on it. But then there was Zofie and the belt. Zofie who worked as my aegis. Zofie was my companion, and I knew nothing about how she came to be in your care, but I told myself to honor her privacy. Then I watched you argue with Ariadne, which made me realize that you have been involved in this fight with Theseus far longer than I ever knew. And now you pretend you aren't in pain from a wound that has become infected overnight. If you were concerned about my feelings at all, you would have told me. Everything. Because this…finding out like this, hurts worse than any of those things would have."

Once the words were out, she felt less burdened. She had not realized how heavily they had been sitting on her heart until now, just building while she tried to survive. She was supposed to be his equal, his queen, but

instead, he coddled her. And he didn't seem to understand that his choices left her vulnerable.

Hades looked…haunted.

The silence between them was loud, almost unbearable. She felt as if a chasm separated them, and it was full
of all his secrets, which honestly felt like lies, and Hades
had to cross it or they would not survive.

"The wound hurts like a motherfucker," he said at
last. "And I haven't looked at it because I don't want to
know the truth."

Persephone just stared.

"I don't know why I didn't tell you any of those
things," he said. "Maybe I thought none of this would
bleed into your life, that I could prevent it before it
became *our* life, and then you would never have to know
the horror of what is coming."

Persephone took a step toward him. "When I chose
you, I chose everything, Hades—your people, your
realm, your enemies," she said. "The only thing I fear is
not having you at my side."

Hades took her face between his hands and leaned
closer.

"I am at your side," he said. "I will never leave again."

"Is that a promise?" she whispered. She knew it
couldn't be, not really, yet she wanted him to say it all
the same.

"It is an oath," he said and brought his lips to hers.

————

Before they left for Ares's island, Persephone visited
Harmonia. As soon as she walked into the room, she
knew something was wrong. The air was stifling, thick

293

with sickness, and she was immediately reminded of visits to Lexa in the hospital.

It reminded her of death.

Dread built in the back of her throat, and then she saw Harmonia and went cold.

The goddess was pale, her lips colorless, and she was covered in a thin sheen of sweat.

Sybil lay beside her, and Aphrodite sat on the other side, while Opal was whimpering at her feet. They were both crying.

Hecate stood near, her expression sorrowful.

"No," Persephone whispered.

"She is not yet gone," said Hecate. "But it won't be long. I have done everything I can."

"We'll get the fleece in time," Persephone said.

I promise, she wanted to add but could not bring herself to speak the words aloud.

Aphrodite shifted to face her, vigorously wiping tears from her swollen face.

"Be careful, Persephone," she said. "Ares is a cruel god."

Any hope Persephone had had that she might sway Ares with Aphrodite's suffering suddenly vanished at her warning.

"I thought he was your friend," she said.

Aphrodite's gaze shifted to Harmonia as she answered in a whisper.

"Perhaps he isn't anymore."

Hecate approached. "It is true that Ares is cruel, but he is also a coward. If you wound him, he will run."

"I thought he was the God of Courage," Persephone said.

Hecate smiled. "He is, but he is also the god of its opposite."

Persephone left the suite. Once she stepped into the hallway, she felt like she could breathe again. The air was cool and cleansing, yet it did not ease her anxiety.

Harmonia had taken a turn for the worse and quickly.

Now she worried that Hades would too.

She continued down the hall and found her husband waiting in the foyer, and though she had expected him, she was surprised by the way he was dressed. He wore a pair of dark tactical pants and a gray shirt that only seemed to draw attention to his chest and shoulders. His hair was wet and pulled into a bun at the back of his head. It seemed ridiculous to say, but she found this version of Hades incredibly attractive.

She had expected him to show up in a suit, no matter how impractical.

"What is it?" Hades asked, suddenly concerned.

"What?" she asked, surfacing from her thoughts.

"You're staring. Is it the shirt?" he asked, pulling at the fabric. "Hermes said this would be appropriate."

"It isn't the shirt, Hades," Persephone said, laughing.

"She thinks you're hot, you idiot," said Hermes as he approached. "For someone who gets laid so often, you are really fucking oblivious."

He was wearing skintight biker shorts and a bright green shirt. Hippolyta's belt was cinched tight around his waist.

"Gods, you're like a fucking beacon," said Hades. "Ares is going to see you coming from the shore."

Hermes crossed his arms over his chest. "I didn't realize we were conducting a sneak attack."

"Why are you wearing a fanny pack?" Persephone asked, noticing the small pouch hanging low on his waist.

"It's for my snacks," he said.

They both stared.

"Judge all you want, but when you get hungry, I'm not sharing."

"I hope we're not there long enough to *be* hungry," Persephone said.

"How is that even possible? I am always hungry."

Hades sighed as if he was already annoyed.

"When we arrive at the island, we will take every precaution. No killing, no teleporting. I do not wish to anger Ares any more than we already will just by being in his territory."

"Would he risk divine punishment by denying a favor?" Persephone asked.

"I am more concerned that he will see you as a prize. I'd rather approach hospitably. Perhaps he will extend the same to us."

"Yeah, right," said Hermes. "Ares doesn't know the meaning of hospitality."

"Let's just get this over with," Hades said.

Persephone felt Hades's magic rise and wrap around her, familiar and dark, an electric energy that brought her comfort despite the dread she felt as they vanished.

———

"This is it?" Hermes asked.

They stood ankle-deep in the ocean, staring at Ares's island, which was far smaller than Persephone expected. It reminded her of a hill that had grown out of the ocean.

A shore scattered with rocks and clamshells led into a thicket of trees and beyond that, higher ground where all she could see was patchy earth.

"If he is using this place to try to impress people, no wonder he's single, because it is *dis-a-point-ouch*!"

Hermes jerked beside her, his hand clamping down on his shoulder.

"What the fuck?" he said as he plucked what looked like a dart from his arm. A perfect line of blood dripped down his golden skin.

"Is that a feather?" Persephone asked.

Hermes's face twisted into a look of disgust. He met Persephone's gaze and then jerked again as another feather-like dart struck his opposite shoulder.

"Seriously?" Hermes demanded.

"Fuck," Hades said. "Not again."

At first she was confused and then she noticed movement from the trees as a bird shot from the leafy canopy. It moved quickly, soaring like a spear launched by a god. It was followed by a second bird and then another, and suddenly, there were hundreds, and with them came a spray of thin, feathered darts.

"Wanna take back that rule about not killing anything, Hades?" Hermes asked.

"Run," said Hades, grabbing Persephone's hand.

They took off across the shore toward a cluster of large rocks. Hades tried to shield her from the onslaught of needlelike barbs, but they were too numerous. She gritted her teeth as each one hit, pulling handfuls of feathery darts from her arms and legs as she ran, only finding relief when they managed to scramble behind the rocks, which the birds flew past in a dizzying blur of white.

Hades held her against him, his hands placed protectively over her head. For a few brief moments, all she could hear was the sound of the birds' violent cries and the whirring of their wings.

Then everything went quiet—except for her heart, which felt like it was going to beat out of her chest. Hades's, she noted, was unsurprisingly steady.

"Are you hurt?" he asked as Persephone reluctantly peeled herself away from him.

"No," she said, wincing as he plucked a feather she had missed from her shoulder. "Thanks."

"Did you say *not again*?" Hermes demanded. "How many times have you been chased by assassin birds?"

"Three," Hades replied. "If you count this one. Though these are relatively harmless comparatively."

"Harmless? *Harmless*?" Hermes's face was turning pink. "Look at my ass, Hades. Does this look harmless?"

He turned to show his backside, which was covered in feathery darts. He looked like a peacock or maybe a porcupine, she couldn't decide, but it took everything in her to keep from giggling. She pressed her lips together and, when that didn't work, covered her mouth to hide it.

Hades didn't even try. He just laughed, a deep sound that made her stomach flutter as she realized how much she had missed it.

"Laugh all you want," said Hermes. "But you're going to heal this."

It took Persephone a moment to regain her composure, and while she felt bad for Hermes, she couldn't deny that it had actually felt good to laugh—deeply, fully.

It had been a long time.

"Hermes, let me help," she said, taking a step toward him just as a feather struck the sand near her foot.

"Oh no," she said and looked up to see a horde of birds speeding toward them.

She covered her head, and Hermes screamed. It was shrill and sharp, worse than the sound he'd made at Zofie's funeral. It twisted through her whole body, grated against every bone. She was so focused on the sound, it took her a moment to realize the birds hadn't attacked, and when she looked up, she saw they had begun to swarm, darting in every direction as if the sound of Hermes's scream had made them go mad.

His wail slowly subsided.

"Wh-what's happening?" he asked.

"It appears Ares's birds find you just as annoying as I do," Hades said.

Hermes glared. "I think what you meant was 'Thank you, Hermes. I had no idea you would be so helpful when I forced you to come to this island that is inhabited by deadly assassin birds, *and* by the way, *I've been chased by them twice before.*'"

Hades opened his mouth to respond, but Persephone spoke over him, knowing whatever was on the tip of her husband's tongue would not be helpful. "That's exactly what he meant, Hermes," she said, glaring at Hades as she spoke. "Thank you."

"At least someone appreciates my help," Hermes said.

"Fucking Fates," Hades muttered, rolling his eyes. "Let's get out of here before those birds regroup."

They crossed what remained of the shore, heading for the thicket of trees ahead.

"No, no, nope," Hermes said as they neared. "I am not going in there."

"Scared, Hermes?" Persephone asked.

"I just ruined my vocal cords to save us from those fucking birds, and you want to wander through their home!"

"The birds don't live in the trees, Hermes," said Hades, who had not stopped walking.

Hermes's frustration vanished suddenly. "Oh," he said and paused. "Well, where do they live then?"

"In the cliff side," Hades replied.

"Oh."

Hermes started to walk again, and Persephone fell into step beside him as they crossed the tree line.

"When did he become such an expert on birds?" Hermes muttered.

Persephone smiled. "I thought you were a warrior, Hermes," she teased.

"Nature is a different kind of battlefield, Sephy."

They were not beneath the cover of the trees long when they came to a sheer wall of rock. At first, she thought they were going to have to climb it, but then she noticed a narrow path worn into the side at a slow incline.

Seeing it brought about a deep sense of dread. It seemed too easy, like an invitation to something far more terrible, but she said nothing as they made their way up the cliff, which took them high above the trees, giving them a view of the endless ocean. From here, the world looked so beautiful, and she mourned that it was ruled by someone so terrible.

When they came to the top of the cliff, any feelings

she had of admiration vanished, replaced by a sense of unease. It trickled down her spine and made her hair stand on end. She tried to keep from shivering but failed. The wind was colder here too.

Before them, a field stretched for miles. It was barren save for golden spikes sticking out of the ground. They looked like wheat. Far in the distance, on the opposite side of the island, was a great oak, and there, glimmering even in the grayish light, hung the Golden Fleece.

Persephone's heart rose into her throat. The urge to teleport across the field overwhelmed her. She curled her fingers into fists to keep herself from giving in.

"I know you're all about this hospitality thing," said Hermes. "But you could have at least arrived on *that* side of the island."

Hades did not respond. He was looking at the ground.

"What is it?" Persephone asked.

"Earthbound warriors," Hades said.

"You mean the wheat?" she asked.

"That isn't wheat," he said. "It is the tip of a spear."

The tip of a spear, and there were *hundreds*.

"You mean...they are buried beneath this field?"

"They were sown," he said. "With dragon's teeth. They are called Spartoi, the earth-born."

"Well, how threatening can they be underground?" Hermes asked. He started to bend and touch one of the spears.

"Don't," Hades snapped, and Hermes snatched his hand back, holding it to his chest as if he'd been slapped. "If you touch them, you will awaken them and find out just how much of a threat they can be."

"You could have led with that lifesaving information," Hermes said, rising to his feet.

"Watch your feet," Hades said, taking the first step into the field.

Persephone followed. It would have been easier had the warriors been sown in straight lines. Instead, they were staggered, which made crossing far more tedious.

"This is like hopscotch," Hermes said.

Persephone paused to look at the god, who was jumping from space to space on one leg, then the other.

"Except if you lose, you are speared to death," said Hades.

The delight that had lit Hermes's face vanished.

"You ruin everything," he said.

"Just reminding you of your mortality," Hades said.

Persephone caught sight of his smirk before he turned his attention back to the field. She also continued, looking up now and then to gauge how long they had until they reached the oak and growing more and more disappointed when it did not seem to be any closer.

"Gods, this is taking forever," she muttered, and then her stomach rumbled.

"I told you to bring a snack," said Hermes.

She looked at the god, who was already munching on some kind of granola bar. He reached into his pouch and pulled out a second.

"Here, catch!"

Before she could say anything, the bar was already flying through the air. It hit her chest, and she tried to catch it, but it fell to the ground—right beside one of the golden spears.

"Oh, fuck," Hermes said. "Did it touch?"

"I don't know, Hermes," Persephone snapped. "Why didn't you just wait?"

"Well, excuse me for sharing!" he said. "I thought you were hungry."

They were all still and silent for a few minutes, waiting to see what would happen. When nothing did, Persephone finally let herself breathe, but the sound of Hades's voice put her on edge.

"Persephone," he said. "Come to me."

She met his gaze. His expression was dark, and his body was turned fully toward her, his hand outstretched like he was ready to pull her into his arms.

She took one step before a hand shot out of the dirt and clamped down around her ankle, jerking her to the ground. She screamed as terror took root in her body. If she fell, she would be impaled. She teleported out of the creature's grasp to Hades's side.

All around them, warriors sprang from the ground, breaking free of their slumber and the earth, fully armored and armed.

Persephone looked at Hades.

"I think I'm over hospitality," she said.

Just like the warriors who had sprung from the ground, so did her magic. Vines erupted like snakes, slithering around the bodies of the soldiers and their weapons, dragging them back to the earth. Some broke free but were quickly restrained again. The more they struggled, the faster the vines moved until the entire plain was covered in thick, leafy greenery. The spears stuck out of the ground haphazardly.

Hades looked at her, and there was a gleam of pride in his eyes that she loved.

"Nice save, Sephy," Hermes said as he approached, pulling out another bar from his pack. He started to open it when she snatched it away. "Hey! It's my last one."

"I think," Hades said, "what you meant to say was 'Thank you for saving my life, Persephone. If it wasn't for my idiocy, we wouldn't even have been in that situation to begin with. As a token of my appreciation, here is a snack.'"

Hermes slammed his lips together and crossed his arms over his chest. "You're never on my side," he said.

Persephone tried not to laugh, but Hades sighed and started across the field, arming himself with a spear as he went. Persephone followed. The ground was now springy under her feet, making it a little harder to walk on. When her stomach growled again, she broke the bar and offered Hermes half.

"Thanks, Sephy," he said, and then he hesitated. "I am thankful you saved us from my idiocy."

"I know, Hermes," she said and smiled at the god.

"You're a really great friend, Sephy," he said. "Sometimes I don't think I deserve—"

His words faltered, and so did Persephone's steps as the ground began to shift beneath them. There were several crisp snaps as warrior after warrior broke free from her bindings, and before they could flee, they were surrounded.

"Maybe stronger vines next time, Sephy," said Hermes.

She was already trying to plan her next move when Hades materialized beside them and flung out his hand. Beneath his magic, the warriors turned to dust.

Persephone tilted her head back and looked up at Hades, who was peering down at her.

"Fuck hospitality," he said, and then they teleported and came to stand before the oak tree where the Golden Fleece hung.

She had known from a distance that the tree would be grand, but nothing could have prepared her for its greatness. The oak was massive, with thick, long-reaching limbs that wound and spiraled, some so heavy they had bowed beneath their own weight and now touched the ground.

But what stunned Persephone was the dragon-like creature whose body was coiled around the base of the tree like a serpent. It was covered in shimmering scales that gleamed like fire. Its eyes were open and unblinking, ever watchful.

Nearby, beneath the fern-covered boughs of the tree, stood Ares.

He was large and imposing, his horns only adding to his dreadful appearance. They were long and sharp, curving behind his head. He wore armor that burned gold and a helm that matched. There was no kindness in his face, only malice.

"You killed my warriors," said Ares.

"They will be reborn," said Hades.

Ares's mouth hardened. "You come to my island uninvited to steal from me," said the God of War. "And you insult me by harming what is mine."

"We have not come to steal," Persephone said, angered by his accusation, though she regretted drawing his furious attention.

"So you have come to ask for a favor? Even worse, traitor goddess."

"We are not here for ourselves," Persephone said. "We are here for Harmonia. Aphrodite's sister is dying."

305

At her words, a little bit of Ares's composure slipped, his angry eyes flashing with concern before he recovered and seemed to dig further into his aggression.

"You lie," he said, looking at Hades. "I can smell the blood."

"I did not lie," Persephone said between her teeth. "Harmonia is dying. The Golden Fleece is the only thing that will save her!"

"And your lover, it seems," said Ares. "Tell me, why should I help you?"

"Because you have no choice, Ares," said Hermes. "I have come to collect my favor, one of many, might I add, that you owe me from all the times I saved your ass."

"As helpful as that would be, I am not inclined to grant it."

"You would risk divine retribution?" Persephone asked.

"Currently, Hermes is mortal, and by divine law, I am not obligated to uphold a promise made to a traitor."

Persephone looked at Hades for confirmation of his words, but he wasn't looking at her. He was staring darkly at Ares.

"Now you are just being an ass," said Hermes.

"I have no wish to make the King of the Gods angry and no desire to lose my power," Ares said.

"Even if it means hurting Aphrodite?" Persephone asked.

Ares was still, and she noticed his throat constrict as he swallowed.

"If you think I won't tell her you refused, you're wrong," Persephone said. "She will hate you forever."

Ares was quiet, and then he shifted his spear into his other hand.

"Who said you were going back?" Ares asked. Summoning his shield, he teleported.

Hades shifted, knocking Persephone to the ground as Ares appeared before them, stabbing his spear toward Hades's face.

"Sephy!" Hermes raced toward her, pulling her away from the embroiled gods as she scrambled to her feet.

Hades summoned his bident, thrusting his weapon at Ares, who blocked the blow with his shield. The sound of the weapons meeting was like a lightning strike, and it seemed to rouse the dragon-like creature from its strange, open-eyed slumber. It growled and then rose, slithering higher up the tree, smoke rising from its nostrils and mouth.

Neither Hades nor Ares seemed to notice as they fought. It was hard to track them, they moved so fast, each stab more furious than the last, and while Persephone understood the source of Hades's rage, she did not understand why Ares had chosen to fight them over aiding Aphrodite and her sister—the one goddess he was said to be closest to, the one who had shown him kindness in the face of the Olympians' resentment.

Was he seeking the approval of his father? The esteem of other Olympians? Or had he merely been born like this, furious and bloodthirsty, always choosing battle over peace?

As the two fought, Persephone's attention was drawn to the Golden Fleece and the dragon guarding it. Its eyes were fixed on Hades and Ares, its throat glowing brighter the longer the two struck at each other. It seemed to be biding its time, and Persephone did not want to find out for what.

She summoned her magic, calling to the twisted limbs of the oak the dragon was cradled within. They lengthened and crawled, winding slowly around the slithering serpent until, all at once, the branches closed around it, coiling tight around its deadly mouth. Still it managed a muffled roar as it lurched violently beneath the bindings, its neck now bright white with fire.

Persephone looked at Hermes.

"Get the fleece!" she ordered just as Ares appeared before her, striking her with the face of his shield. The blow made her feel like her entire body had been snapped in two and sent her flying. When she hit the ground, she ceased to breathe, landing in the field, striking the golden spears left behind as she rolled. When she came to a stop, she inhaled violently, healing her broken body as she got to her feet, pain still lancing through her.

Ares came for her again, but this time, his blow was stopped by Hades with a shield that seemed to be made of shadow, only it was solid. The impact of Ares's attack sent Hades sliding back a few feet. Their weapons clashed again, and Persephone's vines shot from the ground, gripping Ares's arms and his spear, but they snapped under his great strength.

"I got it, Sephy! Let's go!" Hermes yelled.

Her head whipped to the side to see Hermes running with the fleece, and then Ares teleported. Hades and Persephone followed but Ares arrived faster, striking Hermes as he appeared and sending him flying across the island. Hades attacked from above with the intention of slamming his shield down on Ares, but the god teleported behind Hades and drove his spear into his back. Another jerk, and it went through his chest.

Persephone screamed as Hades fell to his knees.

Ares shoved his foot against him, pulling out his spear as Hades hit the ground, following with a kick to the side that sent him onto his back, finishing with a final blow to his existing wound.

It had all happened so fast, Persephone had no time to act—to help her husband. Now she stood opposite them, watching as Ares released his spear, leaving Hades pinned to the ground. Then he turned and picked up Hades's bident.

"There is nothing more victorious than taking up the weapon of the god you have defeated," the God of War said, twisting the weapon in his hand.

Persephone's heart raced, but so did her rage. Her gaze darted to Hades, whose head was turned toward her. His eyes usually held some kind of light—a hint of the life that burned within him—but it was gone.

Her gaze returned to Ares.

"You are despicable," Persephone spat. The ground beneath her feet began to quake.

If Ares noticed, he did not seem to care. "This is war, little goddess," he said. "Now, let's see how you fight."

Little goddess.

That name only made her more furious.

He took a few steps and then came toward her at a run, thrusting Hades's bident at her only to drop it and his shield as a branch from his elm stabbed through his back and out of his chest.

Persephone flinched as blood from Ares's mouth

sprayed her face, but she held his gaze, his eyes wide with shock. The only sounds were his choked breathing and the steady spill of his blood as it pooled on the ground.

She considered saying something, but she felt like this all spoke for itself. Ares had become overconfident, and that had made him reckless.

She bent and picked up Hades's bident. It was heavy, a grounding weight. With a final, hate-filled look at Ares, she went to her husband.

"Hades!" She hurried to his side, dropping the bident and pulling Ares's spear free before falling to her knees beside him. Tears welled in her eyes and her throat went dry when he didn't respond. "Hades," she said again, taking his face between her hands.

His lashes fluttered, and then he opened his eyes. When he saw her, he smiled and she wept, suddenly overwhelmed. She bent and pressed her forehead to his and then her lips, pulling back to meet his gaze, but his eyes were closed again.

"Hades," Persephone said. "Hades!"

She yanked up his shirt. The wound to his chest had not healed, and the one on his side was far worse, oozing blood and pus.

"No."

She placed her hands over each, trying to mend them with her own magic, but nothing happened.

Something was wrong. Was the infection preventing him from healing?

"Fuck!" she screamed. She had to find Hermes, but just as she got to her feet, she caught sight of him in the distance. He was running as fast as he could, arms and legs pumping, his cheeks puffing as he breathed, the Golden Fleece gleaming in his hands.

"I got it, Sephy! I'm coming—ah!"

She watched as the god lost his footing and tripped, falling face-first on the ground.

She teleported to him.

"Come on, Hermes," she said, and when he took her offered hand, she returned to Hades's side.

"Oh fuck," said Hermes. "What happened?"

"He isn't healing at all now," she said, spreading the fleece over Hades. "Is this how it works?"

"I think so," Hermes said. "That is how I was able to heal when Ares tossed me across the island. Thank fuck it landed with me."

They waited and Persephone smoothed her hands over the fleece, her gaze falling on Hades's face. Her eyes welled with thick tears once more.

"Hades," she whispered. "Please." When he didn't move, she chose anger. "You said you wouldn't leave my side. You swore an *oath*." And then she begged, burying her face in the crook of his neck. "Please, I will do anything. Just don't leave me."

She felt him move, and then his fingers tangled in her hair.

"Careful with your offer, darling," he said. "I might just ask for anything."

She started to cry harder and then lifted her head and kissed him, reveling in the feel of his breath on her lips.

Then she sat back and dragged the Golden Fleece off him, revealing his perfectly healed wounds.

Hades sat up, his gaze shifting to the still-bloodied

tree Persephone had used as a weapon against Ares. The God of War had fled just as Hecate had predicted.

"Let's heal Harmonia," Persephone said.

This time, it was her magic that surrounded them and carried them home to the Underworld.

CHAPTER XXIII
HADES

Hades followed Persephone into the queen's suite where Harmonia lay near death, clinging to life by a frayed thread. He had sensed the change in her before they left but hoped the Fates would let her live for as long as possible. They did not like when their chosen allotment and destiny were disrupted, which was likely why she'd held on this long, but even they would not stop a thread from snapping if the soul decided it was time.

It was the only mercy they ever granted.

He did not approach the bed with Persephone, choosing to stand apart from the others, watching as Sybil, Leuce, and Aphrodite shooed Opal off the bed and pulled the blankets back, allowing Persephone to lay the Golden Fleece over Harmonia. They all silently waited for its power to take effect.

Hades had been able to feel it, a warmth that seeped deep into his skin. In truth, he felt better than he ever had, even before his imprisonment in the labyrinth. He hoped the same would be true for Harmonia.

"She's taking deeper breaths," Sybil said, voice rising with hope. She leaned over her, smoothing her hair. "Harmonia, we love you. So much."

The color returned to Harmonia's face and lips, and then she stirred, and suddenly, everyone burst into tears.

When Harmonia opened her eyes, she frowned. "Why is everyone crying?"

Her question was followed by a round of harder tears and laughter and Opal yipping and chasing her tail.

Hades's gaze shifted to Hecate as the goddess approached.

"The fleece was not easy to obtain, was it?" she asked.

"I did not expect it to be easy," said Hades. "But I have to admit, I thought Ares would be more moved by Aphrodite's plight."

"Few among the gods have any love for Ares and his violence," said Hecate. "He likely saw an opportunity to gain his father's favor."

And in the process, he'd sacrificed the friendship of the only goddess who had ever offered him kindness.

"I do not know how he will retaliate," said Hades. "It was Persephone who ended his bloodlust."

"He will likely wait for the battlefield," said Hecate. "He will want her distracted, given that he has lost to her one-on-one."

Though he had already targeted her during battle before.

"Aphrodite will be devastated," Hades said in a low voice.

"She will," said Hecate. "But it will give way to her

rage, and that is the level of power we need right now."
They exchanged a look. "It will not be long now," she
said. "Once the first blow is struck before mankind, the
war for dominion over Earth begins."

That was what Zeus and his loyalists failed to understand. This was not just another attempt to overthrow
the King of the Gods. It had become more than a fight
for a single throne. It was a fight for every throne on
Olympus, a fight for worship from a population that had
been shown the neglect of the gods, and Hades feared
that by the time they realized it, it would be too late.

"Enjoy tonight," said Hecate. "It may be the last you
have alone for quite some time."

She left his side, and Persephone approached, her
eyes swallowed by darkness. Her face was flushed, and
he could feel that same warmth in the pit of his stomach.

They left, teleporting to their chamber.

Their gazes held, and so did the distance between
them.

Hades could feel the tension building. It tightened
every muscle in his body and thickened his cock.

"I have no intention to rest, no desire to sleep," he
said. "I want to spend every second making up for each
day I was absent from you."

His words were met with a pleasing shiver. It made
her nipples hard beneath her shirt.

"Then why are you wasting precious time talking?"

His lips twitched.

Spoken like a true queen.

And then there was suddenly no space between them
as they came together, their mouths colliding. Hades
drove her back into the post of the bed, gripping her

hard as he ground into her, the friction sending a dizzy-ing thrill straight to his head.

He smoothed his hands over her ass and then dragged her up his body, and as she twined her legs around his waist, he carried her to bed where he kissed her harder and deeper, until his lungs burned from drowning in her.

Only then did he move on, trailing his lips along her jaw and neck, pulling up her shirt for access to her breasts, which he lavished with his tongue while she raked her fingers through his hair until it was free from its tie.

As he made his way down her stomach, Persephone started to shimmy out of her jeans, and Hades chuckled.

"Always eager," he muttered as he helped, stripping the jeans from her legs.

He took a moment to appreciate the way she looked before him—body flushed and open, her sex already wet, soon to be full of his come.

"Hades," Persephone whispered his name, a note of worry in her tone.

He met her gaze, and he thought that she had never looked more beautiful—more *his*. The vibrant green of her eyes was swallowed by the darkness of her pupils, filled with a desire for him. Her lips were swollen from their kiss, her skin marked by his mouth.

"I want you to feel me inside you for weeks after this night," he said. "When you are on the battlefield, this is what you will fight for, the pleasure of being beneath me again."

Her eyes narrowed. He could not tell if she liked his words, but then she sat up and her mouth was level with his cock, which pressed, thick and heavy, against the rough material of his pants.

"And what will you fight for, King of the Underworld?" she asked.

Despite the layer between them, he could feel the warmth of her breath on him, and it made him regret that he was still clothed.

He stared down at her, trying to imagine how he must look right now. He felt rigid, and his energy was angry and a little violent, a storm that made the air between them crackle.

She unbuttoned his pants and took out his cock, handling it as if it belonged to her—though he supposed it did.

She shifted forward on the bed, jerking her hand up and down his shaft.

"Will you fight for this?" she asked as she licked him from root to tip, ensuring her eyes met his as she collected the come that had beaded at the top.

He filled his lungs with air and let it out slowly, fisting his hand in her hair as her mouth closed around him.

"Fuck." He cursed under his breath, throwing back his head for a moment as he focused on the warmth of her mouth, the pressure of her tongue, the feel of her hand wrapped around his flesh. Somehow, though she only held this one part of him, she managed to invade his entire being.

His fingers tightened in her hair, and she let him slide from her mouth between the firm hold of her lips, gazing up at him with those eyes, clouded with things he recognized—grief and anger and violence—and he wondered if they would ever have taken root in her soul if they had never met.

"I like your mouth, my queen, especially when it is

around my cock," he said, brushing his thumb over the swell of her bottom lip.

"I am waiting for your answer, my king," she said.

What will you fight for on the battlefield?

He studied her, very much aware that his heavy cock remained between them, wet from her mouth and aching.

"Do you ask because you do not know or because you wish to hear me say it?"

"It does not matter," she said. "I gave you a command."

"Oh, it matters, my love," he said. His hand slipped to her neck, and she tilted her head back farther. "If the first, I shall have to remind you of my devotion, but I warn you, it will not be kind."

He did not have that sort of control within him tonight, but she knew that. She could feel it just as much as he could feel the violent storm of her emotions.

"I did not ask for kindness, my king," she said. "You promised to fuck me."

He would have laughed, not at her but in disbelief that any of this was real, had her words not made his ears ring and the blood rush right to the head of his cock.

His mouth came down on hers, and he guided her to her back, kissing her with his teeth and tongue, ruthlessly claiming her mouth. His hand was still wrapped around her throat as he thrust his cock against her naked flesh. The friction felt so fucking good, but it did little to relieve the ache of his need for her, especially with the way she writhed beneath him.

He released her and slipped off the bed to remove his clothes. He liked the way she rose onto her elbows to watch him, her breasts heavy, her nipples peaked and rosy, her legs open.

He looped his arms under her knees and jerked her toward the side of the bed. He bent over her and took her mouth, kissed between her breasts and her stomach, and then knelt between her thighs, where his lips and tongue caressed that sensitive skin, retreating when he came too close to her sex, enjoying the way her color deepened and her clit swelled beneath the teasing.

"Hades," Persephone gritted out, digging her heels into his shoulders.

He chuckled, dragging his nose along the inner part of her thigh. Her frustration was palpable, her body wound so tight, he wondered if she would explode the moment his mouth touched her.

She glared at him, and he held her gaze, his mouth hovering over her heated flesh.

"I did not promise kindness," he reminded.

He noticed how her skin pebbled at the feel of his breath.

"No," she said. "But I will hardly remember the feel of your teasing on the battlefield."

He didn't recognize the laugh that came out of his mouth.

"Oh, darling, I will never let you forget it."

His hold tightened as his mouth came down on her.

At the first touch of his tongue, she sighed. The sound went straight through him to the head of his cock, which brushed against the cool silk draped over the bed. It made the roar in his head louder and his desire burn hotter.

Fuck.

Despite her eagerness, he started slow. Even if she did not realize it, he was at her command. Each deep moan, each choked breath guided him to continue with the pressure and pace of his tongue.

When he took her clit into his mouth, circling and sucking, he slipped his fingers inside her.

Fuck. She was so wet, she felt like silk.

He couldn't wait to feel this all around his aching cock.

He curled his fingers inside her and kept his mouth on her clit, setting a ruthless pace. She squirmed beneath him and seemed torn between grinding into his face and retreating altogether, both desperate and overwhelmed by the pleasure. Still, he held her there, tightening his grip. He could feel her rising toward release, tensing and easing until her muscles finally locked and her orgasm descended.

He kept the pressure on her clit, each pass of his tongue eliciting a harsh cry from her open mouth. When she finally relaxed, he released her and rose to his feet, climbing into bed and sliding between her legs.

He stroked the head of his engorged flesh through her slick heat.

"Hades, please," she moaned, trying to shift closer.

"Do you remember what I said?" he asked.

"That you would not be kind," she said, and then she reached and wrapped her fingers around his wrist—the same hand that held his cock at her entrance—and whispered, "I can handle you."

Those words were enough, and he slid inside her with a single hard thrust.

Persephone gasped, and he bent to take her

mouth against his, setting a pace that had her rocking beneath him.

"Yes," she moaned, wrapping her legs around his waist, her fingers digging into his back as she anchored herself against the onslaught.

She took him like a queen, like she was fucking made for him. He moved his hand to her neck and kissed her again, their mouths colliding in a jarring kiss before he sat back. His hand remained on her throat while he slipped the other beneath her knee. He did not cease moving inside her, pounding into her warm flesh, but he did increase the pressure on either side of her neck.

"Oh, fuck," Persephone breathed, and her hands came down on his arm. Each word she spoke was punctuated by the slam of his hips against her. "It feels so good."

Her fingers bit into his arm, and the sounds that came from her throat grew louder, a keen cry that made the bottom of his stomach burn.

Fuck, she was perfect.

"Look at me," Hades commanded, and she opened her eyes, beautiful and green, clouded with lust and love.

He released her neck and bent over her, planting his hands on either side of her face. Their breaths were heavy, their bodies warm and slick, and Hades's cock throbbed inside her, but he had to say this.

"You asked me what I would fight for on the battle-field," he said. "It is this. It is to have you look at me with these eyes. You worship me with these eyes."

A smile curved Persephone's lips. "You are a romantic, my king," she said.

"I am in love," he said. "There is a difference."

Persephone's smile widened, and Hades lowered to kiss her, slipping an arm behind her neck. This time when he started to move, it was slow and deep. He was aware of everything that was her—the way her nipples scraped against his chest, the way her knees pressed in at his sides, the way her fingers dug into his biceps.

She held his gaze until she couldn't, and her head rolled back over his arm. Her body was tightening, growing taut beneath him. She was close to release. He felt the burn of his own in the bottom of his stomach, the pressure building at the base of his cock.

He bent and kissed her neck, licking and sucking the skin before burying his face in the hollow of her shoulder. His knees dug into the bed on either side of her ass as he moved a little faster, a little harder, a little deeper.

One of Persephone's hands twisted into his hair, clamping down on his neck as her cries filled the room, one for each new thrust, and then her grasp on him tightened all at once from the inside out, even her breath held, and she began to shudder beneath him as her orgasm hit.

He plowed through it, rocking into each wave until he could no longer contain the pressure building in his own body. He came in a blinding rush, aware only that his body was trembling and his arms and legs were numb. When it passed, he realized that he had collapsed against Persephone and that her fingers were sifting through his hair.

He lifted himself a little, shifting his weight so he wasn't suffocating her, though she did not seem to mind.

"Are you well?" he asked.

He loved staring at her, but especially after sex. He

liked knowing that he was the reason for the flush on her cheeks and the swell of her lips.

She smiled, her gaze heavy-lidded.

"Yes," she whispered. "And you?"

"I am more than well," he said.

Neither of them moved, content to lie in the aftermath of their lovemaking.

"I missed this," Persephone said, and Hades noticed that her eyes were welling with tears as she brought her hands up to cover her face.

Hades frowned and bent to kiss her fingers. "You do not have to hide from me," he said. "I want all of you, even your pain."

He waited for her, and after a few deep breaths, she dropped her hands. Her eyes were still watering, and tears spilled down the side of her face.

"I do not know why I am crying," she said, taking a trembling breath.

"You do not need a reason," he said, though he would argue that everything she had been through in the last month was reason enough. This was likely the first time she'd had the space to let her body stop fighting, and the reality of the world was crashing down on her all at once.

Hades shifted onto his back, bringing Persephone with him, and he held her as she cried until she was silent and sleeping in his arms.

————

Hades woke a short time later to Persephone grinding against his cock.

She was already wet and her hands were flat against his chest as she moved. He groaned, his fingers splayed across her waist, digging into her heated skin. She lowered and kissed him. Her mouth was hot, and her breasts brushed against him just as maddeningly as her slick sex. He took them into his hands, squeezing them together, twisting her hard nipples before he took them into his mouth.

As he devoured her, he felt her hand slip between her thighs. She straightened, riding her fingers as she straddled him, using her thumb to rub her clit. With her other hand, she touched her breasts. She kept her eyes closed, her head rolling from side to side, her breaths setting a pleasing rhythm as she moved back and forth and up and down, chasing some kind of feeling building inside her.

His chest felt so heavy under the weight of his desire, he could barely breathe as he watched her. There was a part of him that wanted to join and a part of him that was content to watch this escalate, to feed the fire of his need for her until he was at his absolute breaking point.

He would see the fucking stars when he was finally inside her, but for now, fuck, she was beautiful, and she was his for an *eternity*.

Her hand fell from her breast to her clit as she worked herself harder and faster, and then she went rigid and fell forward on his chest, her back curling as her orgasm tore through her.

She lay there a moment, breathing hard, before she moved her hand from between her legs and brought her fingers to his mouth. He sucked them hard before releasing each slowly, and then their mouths collided in a wet kiss. Hades bent his knees, which brought his length firmly against her ass, his hands already digging into that soft flesh and spreading her wide.

She seemed to understand what he wanted and sat back, reaching behind to run her palm over the head of his cock before she rose and slid down him with a moan.

Hades took a deep, audible breath, and Persephone smiled at the sound, rocking back until he was fully and completely encased in her warmth. She leaned forward and pressed a kiss to his chest, then let her tongue slide over each of his nipples. She moved as if she were about to put her mouth on his, only she didn't.

Instead, she rose until he was barely inside her before coming down hard. Then she did it again and again, and slowly her pace began to increase until the sounds of their flesh slamming together filled the room. He loved it, wanted more of it. His hands tightened on her waist, and when she grew tired, he took over, thrusting into her. He couldn't decide what he liked most: the way her breasts bounced as he took her or the look of ecstasy on her face. Both filled him with an insatiable lust.

He shifted, framing her face with his hands, holding her in place. The instructions were clear—*look at me*.

She did.

Her hands flexed over his shoulders, her knees pressed in on his sides, and her mouth hovered over his, her breath hot on his lips. His eyes fell there, and then he kissed her and rolled, bringing her beneath him. He ground into her a few times as their tongues clashed before rising to his knees. He gripped her thighs and pulled her closer until he could feel her ass against his balls, and then he drove his hips into hers, his muscles tightening with each arch of her back and twist of her fingers into the sheets.

Then she started to move, and he was completely

lost, unaware of anything save her. His fingers spread across her skin as he gripped her hips harder. He knew she was close when she reached for his thighs, when she ground into him to ensure he stayed in one spot, so he trapped her clit between his fingers, sliding up and down. As her climax swelled, so did her clit, and the urge to take it into his mouth was too overwhelming to pass up.

He withdrew from her to the shock of Persephone, whose cry of frustration was silenced by a deep moan as his mouth closed over the swollen bud, sucking and licking until the first wave of her orgasm hit. As she writhed, he kept pressure on her clit with his fingers and slammed into her again, letting her muscles contract around him and coax him to release.

He groaned as the first stream of come burst from him. The second made his arms shake, and after the third, he collapsed against Persephone's slick skin. He rested his head against her breasts as her fingers shifted through his hair. He was so content and his eyes so heavy, he could have fallen asleep, but then Persephone spoke.

Her voice was almost jarring after they'd spent so long in silence, save for their ragged breaths, though sometimes Hades felt like their bodies said more than words could manage.

"How do I know if my mother was fated to die?"

That *is what you're thinking about right now?*

It was what he wanted to ask because he'd much rather know that she was thinking about him and how he'd just fucked her utterly and completely mindless.

Except that, apparently, he hadn't.

He'd have to try again.

Except he knew why she was asking this question. She was trying to find a way through the guilt, to lessen the blame.

He lifted his head and met her gaze. "Do you think knowing will make accepting your role in her death easier?"

Her breaths grew heavier, and he knew she was about to cry. He shifted higher up her body so their faces were aligned.

"I don't know how to live with this," she said, her body quaking beneath him.

He shifted to his side, pulling her back to his chest, curling himself around her as she sobbed. It was all he could offer. He had nothing else.

CHAPTER XXIV
THESEUS

Theseus waited by the door of Zeus's office wearing the Helm of Darkness. Hypnos, God of Sleep, whom Theseus had plucked from the Underworld during his attack, had taken the form of a colorful bird and was chained to a perch nearby.

Across the room, Hera stood before a row of tall windows overlooking the vast estate she shared with the God of the Sky on Mount Olympus. She was dressed in a silk robe, cinched tight around the waist. She had anointed herself with oils that smelled both sharp and sweet, and when she moved, her skin glistened. She was sure to be an inviting treat for Zeus, who would not see that she was too proud to be beautiful and too severe for seduction, because despite his wandering eye and raging cock, he loved her.

"What is taking so long?" Theseus demanded in frustration.

He checked his watch.

They had been waiting for over an hour, and he was growing impatient. This was only the start of his plan, but its success would determine how the rest of the day—and those following—unfolded.

"You expect Zeus to be mindful of my time?"

"Any man would be mindful of time when sex is on the table," he said. "Unless, of course, he is not motivated by the promise of your body."

Theseus noted how the goddess stiffened and glared in his direction, though she could not see him.

"I *asked* for a meeting," she said.

"So you thought to lure him with the promise of what? Talk?"

She ignored him, and there was silence in the room.

"Are you certain you can seduce him?"

"Do not mistake my disgust for an inability to execute this plan," she snapped and returned her gaze to the window. "He is probably off seducing some lowly mortal."

Her words rang with bitterness, and Theseus found that he did not understand her jealousy. If she did not love her husband, why should she care who he fucked? It was not as if she did not benefit from his power and title, but he did not often understand human emotion, and gods seemed to be more human than even mortals.

It was an attribute Theseus did not possess. The closest thing he had ever felt to passion was violence.

He liked violence, preferred it, and his future would be full of it.

Suddenly, the air in the room felt charged with electricity, and Zeus appeared as quick as a lightning strike, his presence just as thunderous. Though Theseus had a lot of contempt for the God of the Sky, the truth was that his very presence commanded attention. Even Hera could not deny it as she whirled to face him, though she would likely claim she was only playing a role.

"My king," Hera greeted.

"Hera," Zeus said, his voice a low rumble. His eyes glittered darkly as they trailed down her robed body, lustful despite the loss of his balls at the hands of the goddess Hecate. "You have not dressed for the day."

"I have not dressed at all," she said and let the silk slip from her shoulders, pooling at her feet.

The air in the room became thick and heavy with Zeus's desire but also his suspicion.

"Why did you summon me?"

"Is it not obvious?" she asked.

He narrowed his eyes. "It is not usual."

Hera let her eyes drop for a moment, and she took a step forward before meeting his gaze again, almost shyly. "I hoped we might put our differences aside."

Zeus also stepped closer.

"We have many, Hera," he said, though his voice had grown quiet—the tone of a lover and not a king. Perhaps that was Zeus's greatest downfall. At heart, he wished to be a romantic and not a ruler.

"Have we not always overcome?" Hera asked. Now she was so near to Zeus, her breasts brushed his chest.

"This is a trick," he said.

Hera's eyes flashed. "Can I not desire my husband?" she asked, her tone hinting at the fury boiling in her blood.

Theseus wondered if her anger would sway him or if it would ruin this moment.

Zeus studied her for a long moment, his eyes falling to her lips.

"I have dreamed of it," he admitted quietly. "But I can hardly believe it is true."

"Then touch me," she said. "And know that I am real."

Hera reached for his hand and guided it to her breast, where Zeus's eyes stayed as he squeezed her, pinching her nipple between his fingers. Hera's breath caught, and she closed her eyes. Her mouth was tight, and her arms went to her sides, fists clenched. They were signs that could be interpreted as desire, and they seemed to satisfy Zeus, who bent his head closer to Hera's.

"I cannot please you the way I wish," Zeus said, and she opened her eyes to hold his gaze. "But I can bring you pleasure all the same."

It took Hera a moment to speak, to gain control over her voice as she managed to lie.

"All that matters is that it is you."

Zeus kissed her, and his hands sank into her skin as he brought her slick body to his.

When he broke away, he spoke, his mouth close to hers. "You know it has only ever been you," he said, impassioned. "I have only ever loved you."

"Shh," Hera implored. "Do not speak. Love me instead."

Zeus's eager mouth closed over hers again before he kissed along her jaw and down her neck. Her fingers tangled into his graying hair as he made his way to her breasts, lapping at the oil coating her skin.

"You taste so good," he said with a growl.

Like sleep, Theseus hoped, annoyed that this was

taking *so long*. He glanced at Hypnos, who remained on his perch, eyes averted from Hera and Zeus's painful display of affection.

Had Hypnos given Hera a fake potion? It would be one way to enact revenge.

If something did not happen soon, Theseus would snare Zeus and Hera together. What torture it would be for the Goddess of Marriage to be trapped beneath her husband, who would then know her seduction had only been a scam.

There was a part of him that wanted to witness that aftermath.

Zeus continued his descent, and as he lowered to his knees, Hera turned her head to the ceiling.

"How long does it take?" she asked.

Zeus chuckled, assuming her frustration was borne from ignorance.

"Patience, my pearl," he said. Hera's gaze dropped to his, and his expression grew very serious, his eyes shining with a strange light. "I will kneel for no one but you."

Hera let her hands thread and twist into his hair as he pressed kisses to each of her thighs, his mouth inching closer to her sex.

He groaned, and then his head fell heavily against her legs.

"Zeus?" she asked and then took a step back.

He swayed and then fell to the ground with a hard smack.

"By the gods, that took long enough," Hera said, snatching her robe from the ground and securing the tie firmly around her waist. "I shall have to bathe in acid to scrub the memory of his touch from my skin."

She shuddered visibly.

Theseus removed the Helm of Darkness while Hypnos transformed from a chained bird to a chained god.

"If you had used the potion the way I instructed, you would not have had to endure such…torture," said Hypnos haughtily. "It was meant to be consumed, not licked from your body."

"I *told* you," Hera snapped. "Zeus will not accept food or drink from me."

"Could it be because the last time you offered him a draught, he woke up in chains?"

"Perhaps he should not wake up at all," said Hera, glaring down at her sleeping husband.

"As much as I would like to indulge you," said Theseus, "we need him."

"*You* need him," Hera countered. "I am not trying to win Cronos's favor."

"But you are trying to win a war," said Theseus.

"Yes," Hera hissed. "And you released the one Titan who has had endless time to dream of all the ways he will take his revenge against the Olympians."

"Perhaps you should cease considering yourself an Olympian."

"Do you think that will matter? Cronos does not forget transgressors."

"A trait you seem to have inherited from him," said Theseus.

"And *you* inherited your father's arrogance," she countered.

"I did," he said. "But at least mine is not unfounded."

He had killed the ophiotaurus and eaten the golden

apple. He was now destined to overthrow the gods, and he was invincible.

"Well?" Hypnos snapped. "What now?"

Theseus summoned the net with his magic and laid it on Zeus as if it were a blanket, covering his entire body. It was so finely made and so light, it was hard to believe the mesh could restrain a god.

"He will hang in the sky as he hung me," said Hera. "Let the Olympians bear witness to his shame."

For a brief moment, Theseus wondered why he hadn't considered trapping her and Zeus. He was under no grand illusion. He knew the goddess had only allied with him in the hope of overthrowing Zeus and taking the throne for herself.

What she failed to understand was that the future of the world did not include Olympians.

"Only Olympians?" Theseus questioned.

Hera stiffened. "The mortal public cannot know. They will question our power."

"They already question your power," said Theseus. "And now they will know you can be defeated."

Hera's mouth tightened, but Theseus held her gaze.

"The lightning bolt, Hera," Theseus said. "Bring it."

She did not move.

As he stared at her, four of his men entered the study, all demigods of varying parentage. Two dragged Zeus away, and two dragged Hypnos forward.

"Release me!" Hypnos snapped, struggling in their grasp, but Damian and Sandros, the sons of Thetis and Zeus, maintained their hold.

The god glared at Theseus.

"What are you going to do?" he asked.

"Use you," said Theseus as a blade materialized in his hand. He jabbed it into the god's neck. Blood gushed from the wound, bathing Theseus in a spray of crimson. Hypnos's eyes went wide, and he gave a few gurgling breaths as he fell to his knees, his white wings spread wide before he tipped forward and landed on his front.

He did not move again.

Theseus looked at Hera.

The goddess had yet to witness the effects of the Hydra's venom or the power of his weapons firsthand.

He was satisfied with the fear in her expression.

"The lightning bolt, Hera," he said again.

This time, she did not hesitate.

CHAPTER XXV
DIONYSUS

Dionysus woke many hours later to Ariadne in his arms, and he immediately stiffened.

Unfortunately, it wasn't just his dick that was surprised, but his brain too.

He'd expected her to be gone by morning, even though she'd asked to stay a little longer last night. He'd told himself not to get too excited about that request, just like he'd decided he didn't care about her reasons for wanting to have sex with him. She'd been through some pretty traumatic things in the last twenty-four hours. Fuck, her whole life was a tragedy.

She was just seeking comfort.

And he was fucked up enough to give it.

He repeated that to himself over and over, hoping that if he thought it enough times, it would stop his heart from racing when he looked at her and keep it from breaking when she decided he was her biggest mistake.

"Ari?" He shook her gently to rouse her.

"Hmm?"

"I think you… I mean, I'm not sure…but your sister might be worried."

There was a pause, and while he couldn't see her face, he imagined the reality of last night was settling in. He even leaned back a little so she wouldn't hit him in the face when she jerked up and jumped from his bed in complete shame.

Except that she didn't do that at all.

She rolled over to face him, looking sleepy and content. She even smiled. This had been part of his dreams for a while, and now that it was real, he hated the alarm going off in his head that told him to be cautious.

"Hi," she said.

He took a moment to overcome the urge to narrow his eyes and ask her what was wrong, which would inevitably lead to some kind of fight. Then he would have only himself to blame for ruining the best morning of his life.

He swallowed the suspicion.

"Hi," he said. "How did you sleep?"

"Fine," she said. "You?"

He nodded.

She frowned. "Are you sure?"

"I *said* yes."

"You didn't *say* anything," she said. "You just nodded."

"I realize I'm not well-versed in mortal customs, but I believe that means *yes*."

She narrowed her eyes. "Why don't you just admit something's wrong?"

"Nothing is fucking wrong, Ari," Dionysus said. "Just leave it alone, gods-dammit."

Fuck, he should have just led with his initial question.

"So there *is* something wrong—"

"Why did you sleep with me?"

If she was going to insist, he might as well ask.

She blinked, surprised, and closed her mouth before answering, "Because I wanted to. Why do you think I slept with you?"

He didn't answer.

"*Dionysus.*" She spoke his name like a command.

"You said you wanted to thank me."

"Because I am grateful for what you did," she said.

"I'm not sure I like when you say that," he said.

Her brows lowered. "What?"

He averted his eyes. "I'm not sure I like when you kiss me or fuck me and tell me you're grateful."

"You don't like it…but you fucked me anyway?"

Her tone set him on edge. It was full of rage, but that was okay, because he could match it.

"I fucked you because I wanted you," he said. "I fucked you because I *like* you. Because I'd like to fall in love with you, but I don't fucking trust you, and it has nothing to do with Theseus and everything to do with the fact that you regret me every time you have me."

A strained silence followed his words. Now that they were out, he wasn't sure why he had said them at all.

Beside him, Ariadne was still. She wasn't looking at him either. She'd turned her face away and was staring straight ahead. After a few seconds, she threw off the blankets and scrambled out of bed.

"Ari—" Dionysus said, doing the same.

She was at the door when she whirled to face him.

"You think I regret you?" she asked.

"You *said* so!" He inched toward her. "And even if you hadn't, I would know."

"You would know? Can you read minds? Is that another power you failed to tell me about?"

Dionysus ground his teeth. "Every time we have sex, you distance yourself."

"We've had sex *twice*!" she seethed.

"And when we came back from the island, you ran."

"I didn't run. I'm here, aren't I?"

He swallowed, and when he didn't say anything, Ariadne shook her head, lifting her arms in a frustrated shrug. She turned to the door.

"So you're going to run now?"

She froze. His heart beat hard in his chest as he waited for her to decide, and finally, she turned to face him with such fire in her eyes, it ignited the one smoldering in the pit of his stomach.

"Fuck you."

He thought she would leave then, but instead, she closed the distance between them, and then her mouth was on his and her arms around his neck. Dionysus drove her back into the door and lifted her into his arms. His arousal pressed into her naked flesh, and then he was inside her again. He paused for a moment, unmoving, his forehead resting against hers.

There was a part of him that questioned what they were doing and if it was right. Was this just some challenge Ariadne wished to win?

He felt her hand splay across his chest, and his words built up in his throat as she whispered, "I don't know what you want from me."

He swallowed hard and then drew back to look into her eyes as he answered, "I just want more of you."

Once the words were spoken, he couldn't take them back, and the only reason he would want to was that it had just now occurred to him that maybe she had nothing more to give at this very moment. If that was the case, he would accept anything, take anything.

What she offered was her lips and her tongue as she kissed him again. It sparked some kind of frenzy inside him, a thing he could not take control of. His hands bit into her skin as he held her pinned against the door. Each thrust seemed to steal the breath from her lungs, yet he could not get deep enough.

He peeled her away from the wall and tumbled into bed, hips grinding and thrusting, and she took it all, her nails scraping along his back and digging into his ass, pulling him closer, pushing him harder. Just when the pressure began to build inside him, his door opened, and it felt like everything happened at once.

Phaedra stood there looking horrified, and he froze.

"Oh my gods," she said. "I am so sorry!"

"Phaedra!" Ariadne called, pushing against Dionysus's chest. "Fuck."

She didn't even look at him as she pulled away and hurried after her sister.

———

A half hour later, Dionysus was dressed, but he hesitated to leave his room.

It was ridiculous given that this was his house, yet he could not help feeling anxious about what he would find once he left, and it had nothing to do with Phaedra walking in on them. Today, he would have to face the reality of everything that had happened and plan for Theseus's inevitable retaliation.

The demigod was not stupid. He did not need evidence to connect Ariadne to Phaedra's disappearance. He did not need evidence to know that Dionysus had helped her, which meant everyone associated with him was now in danger. The only thing working in his favor was that the refuge and the tunnels that led there were secret.

Finally, Dionysus left his room.

He was hoping that Ariadne would be in the living room so he could speak to her about today's plan, but she was not there. He did find the television on and the baby sleeping in a bassinet that the maenads had brought the day before along with a fuck ton of other items.

Dionysus inched closer to the crib, peering down at the child who was swaddled tightly, his head covered with a cap. He looked different from yesterday. Less alien.

"For someone so small, you breathe really loud," Dionysus said in a hushed tone. He leaned closer. "At least you are cute."

He heard a sharp intake of breath, and his head snapped to the left. Phaedra had returned to the room. Dionysus straightened.

"My Lord," she said, bowing her head.

The title felt strange. He did not hear it often, as it was mostly reserved for Olympians.

"I'm sorry," he said. "I didn't mean to startle you."

"You didn't," she said.

An awkward silence followed. Dionysus did not know what to say. His introduction to Phaedra was an abduction, and this morning, she'd caught him fucking her sister. He had a feeling it would take a while for them to become friends.

"Is Ari—" He started to speak when Phaedra did.

"Do you pay my sister for sex?" she asked.

Dionysus's mouth fell open, shocked by her question. "What?"

"Do you pay my sister for sex?" she asked again, her gaze unwavering. He wanted to ask if everyone in her family had that same piercing stare. Gods, it was unnerving.

"No," he said, and when she continued to stare, he added, "Is it that hard to believe she chose me?"

Finally, Phaedra dropped her gaze and approached slowly. "It's what Theseus told me," she said. "That Ariadne had turned to prostitution. She showed me pictures of you with her in the pleasure district."

"That is *not* what we were doing in the pleasure district."

Mostly.

Phaedra was quiet, her gaze focused on her son.

"I'm not sure what makes me feel worse," she said. "That my husband lied to me…or that I believed him."

"Do not feel guilty for what he made you believe," said Dionysus.

Phaedra was quiet, but after a moment, she spoke in a voice so low, Dionysus did not think her words were meant for him.

"I just don't understand," she said.

He could relate, in a way. He had often tried to understand Hera's hatred toward him, but more than that, he had witnessed other women attempt to make sense of the very thing Phaedra was now.

"You do not have to understand today," he said.

It was likely she never would, but he also wasn't going to say that today either.

Then he caught something from the corner of his eye, and his gaze shifted to Theseus on television.

"What the fuck?"

Dionysus snatched the remote from the coffee table and turned up the volume. Phaedra turned, and her hand clamped down over her mouth at the sight of her husband on the screen. A red banner at the bottom announced the reason for his emergency press conference: WIFE AND SON ABDUCTED FROM HOSPITAL.

"Today I had hoped to stand here beside my beautiful and loving wife, Phaedra, and announce the birth of my son, but instead of celebrating our happy news, I am here to plead with you. My wife and our son were taken from Asclepius Community Hospital by a god."

He paused, and Dionysus clenched his teeth. He had to admit, the demigod had mastered the role of tortured husband and father. He looked absolutely devastated.

"Many of you know the battle I have led in opposition to the Olympians. I believe this is a cruel attempt at revenge and likely the most extreme example of why we can no longer kneel to the archaic rule of the gods. Today I am here to plead for the return of my wife and child but also for the lives of every mortal on this earth. We do not deserve this treatment. Let us remind the gods of our power and cease our worship...today."

He paused and took a shuddering breath, looking directly into the camera.

"And to the god who stole my family, I am coming for you."

It took Dionysus a moment to get his thoughts in order. They were racing to a million things at once. While he'd expected Theseus to retaliate, he had not quite expected the demigod to essentially declare war against the gods, and that fact had worried him to a degree he could not even put into words.

What did Theseus have planned that had given him such confidence?

The door to Ariadne's room opened, and she stepped out, freshly showered and dressed. When she saw them, she halted, hesitating.

"What's going on?"

He started to speak when there was a knock at his door, and Ariadne stood just feet away from it. She met Dionysus's gaze.

He spoke quietly and quickly.

"Downstairs, there is a cellar with wine stored in rounded alcoves. Once you enter, count until you reach the seventh. Touch the plaque on the wall. It will reveal the entrance to a tunnel. Get inside, close the fucking door, and don't look back. It will take you all the way to Bakkheia. Got it?"

She nodded, and then the doorbell rang, and his heart froze in his chest as the baby began to cry.

Fuck.

"Go," he ordered.

Phaedra picked up the child and started toward the stairs, but Ariadne hesitated. Dionysus summoned his thyrsus.

"I said go!"

He didn't like the way she was looking at him, like it was the last time they might see each other, but she went, disappearing down the hallway just as he felt the ground tremble, and he realized too late that his attention should not have been on the door but the windows.

They exploded with a power that knocked Dionysus to the ground. He was immediately aware of how badly he hurt, and he knew his body was riddled with glass and pieces of debris.

He groaned as he got to his feet, wincing as he put pressure on his left arm, which was impaled with a large splinter of wood.

Double fuck.

Dionysus tried to pull the fragment free, but before he could, he felt a new pain—a sharp stab to his back. He screamed and then whirled to face his attacker, lifting his weapon, only to discover no one was there.

They must have teleported, he thought, except that if that were the case, he would have sensed it. The pain from the wound on his back pulsed throughout his entire body. He was not used to feeling this kind of aftershock. He typically healed without thought, except right now, he didn't seem to be healing even *with* thought.

Dionysus breathed heavily through the pain, his teeth clenched, glaring at the burning and smoky remains of his living room. He tightened the hold on his thyrsus, and then he felt it—a subtle change in the air—and he raised his thyrsus to block the attack, surprised when he felt the impact of a blade against it.

His eyes widened as he realized his opponent was invisible.

A second blow came, and he felt the blade sink into his stomach and then a little farther before his attacker shoved him down. Years of healing had prevented him from ever feeling this kind of pain.

He felt so hot and could barely breathe as he watched a man appear before him, having removed Hades's Helm of Darkness. He was a demigod, young with curly hair. If Dionysus had to guess, he would say a son of Zeus.

Dionysus could not speak, and the man smirked.

"I thought you should know the face of the man who took your life."

Dionysus took two great breaths, hoping he might clear his mind enough to summon his magic, but then the demigod stiffened as something struck the side of his head. He crumpled to reveal Ariadne. She was holding a bronze statue, which she slammed down on the man's head again before leaving it and coming to his side.

"You have to get up," she said, her eyes gleaming with just as much determination as the command in her voice.

He nodded and gritted his teeth hard as he sat up and got shakily to his feet. Ariadne anchored one of her arms around his waist. They staggered down the hall and stairs, into the basement, where he collapsed despite Ariadne's attempts to keep him on his feet.

She fell with him but quickly got up and began pulling on his arm. "You have to get up! Dionysus! Get up!"

"Ari," he said, his voice barely audible.

Her eyes began to water.

"I can get help! Just tell me what to do!"

But they were interrupted by pounding on the steps, and when Dionysus turned his head, he saw that the demigod had risen, his face covered in blood but healed. Instead of running, Ariadne turned fully toward him, intent on fighting, but despite her capabilities, there was no way she could win.

That thought brought with it a sense of hysteria, a stirring in the pit of his stomach that rang of madness. He latched on to that, fueled it as his magic roared to life, and with it, he reached for Ariadne and Phaedra and the baby and teleported. In the process, everything went dark.

CHAPTER XXVI
PERSEPHONE

Persephone woke with a start.

She did not know what had roused her, but a deep sense of unease clung to her. She pushed up from where she lay against Hades, a hand on his chest, eyes scanning the room, but nothing was there. Still, the feeling did not ebb. She sat up farther, and she was followed by Hades, his face etched with concern.

"What is that?" she asked.

She could not really describe the feeling except to say that it felt like the air within their realm had become a physical weight, composed of nothing but sorrow. As they breathed, it filled their lungs.

"It's Thanatos," Hades said. He threw off the blankets and left the bed.

Persephone followed, pulling on her robe, when she noticed Hades hesitate. She knew exactly what he wanted to say—*stay here*. His eyes were already pleading with her, but the words never left his mouth. Instead, he called on his magic, clothing himself in dark robes, and held his hand out.

The frustration that had been building inside her turned into a dizzying warmth. She had been ready to argue, had already thought of the things she would say to explain why she was coming with him, but suddenly, she did not need any of those words, and it felt like maybe he was finally starting to understand that there was a time and place for his protectiveness.

Besides, there was nothing he could say that would keep her in this room—not after what she had already faced within their realm.

They teleported and found Thanatos on the bank of the River Styx. He was sobbing and on his knees, clutching the hem of Hypnos's robes.

Charon was only a few steps away, his boat docked at the pier behind him. He was holding his oar like a staff. He stared at Thanatos and his brother, his expression almost blank, as if he could not quite comprehend the scene in front of him.

Persephone was not even sure what she was witnessing.

"Oh great," said Hypnos as they arrived. "Now we have an audience. Don't you have any respect for the dead and those who mourn them?"

The dead?

"This cannot be," said Thanatos.

"Do not mourn for me, Brother," Hypnos said. "This changes very little for me. I was already a prisoner of this hellhole. Now I am just a dead one."

Hypnos helped Thanatos to his feet.

It was almost disconcerting to see Thanatos so

349

aggrieved, but she could not blame him. The last thing the God of Death had ever expected was that he would one day welcome his own immortal brother to his realm as a soul in the afterlife.

"I could scarce believe it myself when he arrived at my dock," said Charon.

"What happened?" asked Persephone.

"I died," Hypnos responded. His voice dripped with sarcasm. Clearly he hadn't lost his sense of humor—or lack thereof.

"Why don't you try answering that question again?" Hades suggested, his tone dark.

She could feel his frustration—he was not in the mood for games. Hypnos might be able to make light of his death, but the rest of them couldn't, not when so many had come before him and had the potential to follow.

Hypnos's mouth tightened.

"You want to know what happened? Theseus happened," he said. "He brought me before Hera, who threatened to kill my wife if I did not provide her with a sleeping potion for Zeus. So I did."

It would not be the first time Hera had required the use of Hypnos's powers to lull Zeus into slumber. She'd done it twice before with the intention of overthrowing her husband.

But Persephone was surprised at the extent to which the leader of Triad had aligned himself with the Queen of the Gods. Though he had once claimed an alliance with Hera, Persephone was skeptical of the depth of the connection.

"Theseus brought you before Hera?" Persephone

asked. What was the possible benefit of the demigod working with Hera?

"That is what I said."

Persephone's gaze shifted to Hades. "Did you know about the extent of this alliance?" Hades opened his mouth, but Persephone already knew the answer before he spoke. She looked away quickly, returning her attention to Hypnos. "You said Hera wanted a sleeping potion for Zeus. Is he…"

"He's sufficiently comatose."

Strangely, Persephone had no feelings one way or the other about Zeus. He deserved to be deposed and so much worse, but the end of his rule would be useless if someone even more terrible took his place.

"But they killed you and not him. Why?"

"For the same reason Theseus kept me alive," said Hades. "He still hopes to convince Cronos to join his side—at least until he has conquered the world."

"Does Theseus really believe he can take on a Titan?" Persephone asked.

"Theseus believes he is undefeatable," said Hades.

Persephone wanted to ask why. Was it just his arrogance or something else? But then Hypnos spoke.

"I imagine he feels pretty invincible at the moment given that he is now in possession of the lightning bolt."

"What?" Persephone asked, shocked by his words. Beside her, Hades went rigid.

Hypnos looked annoyed. "*I said…*"

"I know what you said," Persephone snapped, but she did not wish to believe it. Theseus was now in possession of the Helm of Darkness and Zeus's lightning bolt, and he likely had access to Poseidon's trident, being that he was his son. Those were the three weapons that had aided the Olympians in overthrowing the Titans.

"Did he say anything else?" Hades asked.

"Nothing of his plans," said Hypnos.

Persephone looked at Hades, who returned her stare. She wanted to say something, but everything seemed obvious. They had to stop Theseus. They had to make a plan. They had to do it quickly.

"Thank you, Hypnos," said Hades. "I am sorry it had to end this way."

Persephone expected the god to give some kind of biting reply, but he didn't. Instead, he asked another question as he looked from Hades to Thanatos.

"Who will tell my wife?"

It was then Persephone understood what Hypnos truly mourned about his death.

"I think it would be best if she heard it from your brother," said Hades.

Thanatos did not disagree.

They left the Styx and returned to the palace, no longer suffocating beneath the weight of Thanatos's shock and sadness.

"We have to do something," Persephone said when they appeared in their room.

Hades did not speak and turned away, which only made her more frustrated.

"We cannot just keep letting Theseus get away with these murders," she said.

Hades halted and faced her. "Is that what you think I have been doing? *Letting* him get away?"

That was not what she meant to insinuate, but she was still working through the frustration she'd felt since she discovered everything he had kept from her, and it appeared those secrets were still coming out.

"Apparently I know nothing about what you've been doing," she said. "Hera and Theseus are close allies?"

He looked away, glaring at the wall, but after a moment, he took a breath, and she felt the anger in the air between them lessen.

"Around the time you lost Lexa, Hera asked me to help her overthrow Zeus," he said. "When I refused, she found someone else to help her execute her plan. She chose Theseus because she believed he was capable, but she also thought he would be easy to dispose of. I think she learned otherwise today."

And now it was too late. He was dangerously armed, both with the weapons of the most powerful Olympians but also weapons that could kill gods.

"There is much more to that story," he said. "But given what we have learned, I think we should summon our allies."

As curious as she was, she agreed. Silence fell between them for a moment. She didn't like the feel of it, like something angry still lingered between them, so she spoke, needing to be sure he knew how she felt.

"I…did not mean to suggest you haven't tried to stop Theseus," she said. "And I know there are still things you are working on telling me. I think I am just afraid of what I don't know."

Hades moved closer and took her face between his hands. "I am no less afraid even with all I know," he said. "But I can promise you that I will never leave you in the dark again."

She tipped her head back farther, holding his burning

gaze. The corners of her lips lifted just a little as she brushed a strand of his hair away from his face.

"I want your darkness," she said. "But I want your secrets too."

"Darling," he said. "Give me time, and I will give you everything."

"I just want to know that we have time." She spoke quietly, unable to keep the fear from entering her voice. "I want to know that we have forever."

Hades studied her, slipping one hand around her waist. He kept the other on her face, his thumb caressing her cheek.

"Then perhaps we should dream about it," he said. "So that we can think about it when we are on the battlefield."

She raised a brow. "Did you not say that I am to think about the pleasure of being beneath you?"

"Well," he said with a small smile. "That is one part of our forever I look forward to."

He leaned close, his lips brushing hers, but instead of deepening the kiss, she felt him freeze, and she knew something was wrong. Instantly, her heart started to beat faster. Then a scream tore through the quiet.

"Somebody help! Please!"

"Is that...Ariadne?" Persephone asked. She exchanged a look with Hades before they both raced from their chamber, following her desperate screams until they found her in the foyer, bent over Dionysus's bloodied body. Another woman—Phaedra, Persephone realized—stood nearby, holding her screaming baby and looking terrified.

"Help him, help him, please," Ariadne sobbed as

they approached. She was also covered in blood, but it was hard to tell if it was hers or Dionysus's.

"Fucking Fates," Hades muttered.

"He's not healing," Persephone whispered.

She was about to hurry down the hall to the queen's suite for the fleece when Hades spoke.

"Hecate, the fleece!"

The goddess appeared. When she saw Dionysus, her eyes widened, and she moved to place the golden wool over him. There was no silence as they waited for the god to heal between Ariadne's sniffling and the baby's frustrated cries, which only seemed to grow louder the longer Phaedra tried to comfort him.

Persephone drew nearer to Hades as they watched Dionysus. She wondered if there were limitations to the fleece. Was there a point when even it could not heal?

Dionysus's breaths deepened, and then his eyes fluttered and opened. For a brief moment, he seemed confused, but that was quickly eased when his gaze found Ariadne's. He whispered her name and pressed his palm to her cheek. The detective smiled, though her mouth still quivered, and she covered his hand with her own.

"I'm so sorry," Phaedra said, still unable to calm her newborn, whose cries seemed to move an octave higher.

"Do not apologize," Persephone said. "He cannot help it, and you are doing your best, especially given these...harrowing circumstances."

She could not be sure exactly what they had witnessed, but seeing Dionysus in this state was enough, especially since Phaedra had just given birth.

"Come," said Hecate, nearing. "I will show you to the library so that you may ease your little one."

"I will come with you," Ariadne said, rising to her feet, letting Dionysus's hand slip from hers.

"I think it is best you stay," said Hecate. She looked past her to Hades and Persephone. "Lord Hades and Lady Persephone have questions, and I think it is likely you are the only one who can answer them."

Persephone noted Ariadne's curled fists, though she did not think it was frustration. The detective likely felt anxiety without eyes on her sister. Persephone knew that feeling because it lived in her heart every day. It was the fear that one day, she would wake up in a new world, one where Hades no longer lived, just like the day she arose without Lexa.

"Anyone want to explain what happened?" Hades asked.

Dionysus sat up, his hand going to his head.

"Are you all right?" Persephone asked, frowning.

"Yes, just dizzy," he said. "I…I have never felt anything like that."

"You mean pain?" Hades asked.

"Exactly," Dionysus said, rising to his feet. "I am usually able to heal, but whatever I was struck with…"

His voice trailed off, but they did not need any more of an explanation.

"Who attacked you?"

"I am certain it was one of Theseus's men," said Dionysus. He was looking at the floor as he recalled what happened before he arrived in the Underworld. "I did not see him until it was too late. He had your helm, Hades."

Dionysus met Hades's gaze as he spoke the last words, and Persephone felt Hades's anger rising, a wave of energy that heated her own skin.

"His name is Perseus," said Ariadne. "He is a skilled warrior and an excellent tracker."

"Perseus," Hades repeated. "A son of Zeus?"

Ariadne nodded. "Of all the demigods, I would say he is the closest to Theseus."

There was silence, and then Dionysus spoke. "I thought you might rejoice, Hades. You were right. Theseus did come."

"I take no pleasure in your pain, Dionysus," Hades said. "And if that is what you think, then you misunderstood my words."

The silence that followed was strained, though something in Dionysus's demeanor shifted. For a moment, Persephone thought he might apologize for his comment, but Hades was quick to dismiss them.

"We were just about to summon our allies to hear council on how we should proceed with Theseus," he said. "At least now I do not have to go looking for you. Go. Bathe and be ready in an hour." Hades looked down at Persephone. "Brief Aphrodite, Harmonia, and Sybil. I will return with Ilias, Hephaestus, and Apollo."

"What about Her—"

Hades pressed a finger to her lips.

"Do not speak his name," said Hades, dropping his hand.

Persephone drew her brows together. "Is…there something else I should know about?"

"Unless you want to hear another monologue about the faults of our hospitality and how loud you moan when I fuck you, then I suggest waiting until the last possible second to summon the God of Glitter."

357

Persephone arched her brow. "As I recall, his monologue included an impression of *you*, not me."

"That was before our most recent interlude," he said.

She narrowed her eyes. "You know he doesn't have any magic, right?"

"He doesn't need magic to be summoned. At this point, it is a sixth sense. He's just selective when he decides to use it." Hades tilted her head back a little farther. "I will see you in an hour."

She smiled as he kissed her, ignoring the dread that seeped into her stomach when he vanished, unable to keep from worrying that he might not return. The thought frustrated her, but she knew it would be a long time before that fear ever went away, given the horror of the labyrinth.

Persephone left the foyer in search of Aphrodite, Harmonia, and Sybil. When she did not find them in the queen's suite, she wandered outside. As she stepped into the light, there were no signs of the decay that had plagued her realm during Hades's absence. The air smelled like spring, earthy and floral, and everything seemed brighter and fuller. While it should feel normal, Persephone thought it seemed almost overdone, almost as if Hades thought he could make everyone forget what had happened during his absence.

She wondered if she had made a mistake when she'd allowed the Underworld to wither. In that moment, it had seemed like the right thing to do. She did not know if she would have been capable of summoning anything beautiful and lively with how she had felt, and what would she have done had he not returned? She thought of how Hades had described the start of his reign in the

Underworld, how he'd lived a colorless and desolate life. Would she have subjected her people to that existence again?

The thought scared her.

She did not wish to be that kind of queen.

"Persephone!"

She looked up at the sound of her name and saw Sybil, who had risen to her feet at the sight of her. Persephone had been so lost in thought, she had nearly walked past her, Aphrodite, and Harmonia. They sat on a marble bench among the palace gardens, looking ethereal beneath the glow of the sun.

She smiled, feeling a genuine burst of happiness warm her chest, her anxiety momentarily forgotten as she crossed the green to them, embracing Sybil, then Aphrodite, then Harmonia. She held on to her longest before pulling away, holding the goddess's clear-eyed gaze.

"I am so glad you are well," Persephone said.

"I am well because of you," said Harmonia. "Thank you, Persephone."

"I do not deserve your thanks," said Persephone. "You would have never found yourself in such a position if it wasn't for me."

"Do not shoulder the guilt of what happened to us," said Harmonia. "You could not have known Theseus would be so evil."

It was true that Persephone had not understood the extent of his malice until it was too late. Perhaps that would not have been the case had Hades been honest about his own dealings with the demigod.

All of a sudden, she felt an incredible rush of anger. It was like lightning in her veins, burning her body. As quickly as it shot through her, it was gone, leaving her cold and shaken. It was the first time she understood how she really felt about the entire thing, and it scared her.

"As much as I wish to give you more time for peace, I'm afraid I have come with bad news," she said. "Hypnos arrived at the gates of the Underworld, slain by Theseus's hand."

Aphrodite looked pale, and Harmonia pressed a hand to her mouth. She decided she would wait until the meeting to tell them about Zeus and the lightning bolt.

"We are summoning our allies to discuss how we will move forward in our war against Theseus. I would like for the three of you to be present. Hades has already left to call on Hephaestus and Apollo. We will meet in Hades's office within the hour," Persephone said.

There was silence for a moment. Persephone's attention was drawn to Aphrodite as the goddess shook her head.

"We act as if we are not gods," she said. "We should have killed this man years ago."

"We may be gods," Persephone said. "But we are ruled by a power greater than us."

"You mean the Fates?" Aphrodite sneered. "There is no greater betrayal than their golden threads, weaving pain and suffering while they sit idly in their mirrored halls. Perhaps it is they who should—"

"Aphrodite!" Harmonia snapped, her tone full of warning. "You sound like *them*."

Like the Impious. Like Triad.

Except in some ways, Persephone agreed. The Fates

were not directed by a sense of justice. They measured, wove, and cut to control under the guise of maintaining balance. When Hades took or gave life, they demanded an exchange. When Demeter had begged for a child, they had given her a daughter but entangled her fate with one of her greatest rivals.

It had been a punishment for Demeter and a gift to Hades and Persephone, but even now, they knew not to take it for granted, always aware that at any moment, the Fates might unravel their destiny. While Hades had always sworn to find his way back to her, deep down, she knew that while the three lived, it would be impossible.

Persephone could not help wondering what they had prepared for the future of the world.

"Do you think the Fates will really allow Theseus to overthrow the Olympians?" she asked.

"If they wish to punish us," said Aphrodite.

"Even if Theseus intends to kill them?"

"The Moirai cannot see their end," said Sybil. "It is the price they pay for weaving the fate of the world. It is likely they do not expect to die any time soon, especially at the hand of a demigod."

Zeus had assumed the same, and now he lay tangled within the bonds of eternal sleep, weaponless and vulnerable, but perhaps that was the end they had woven for their father. It was impossible to know, and the sisters certainly wouldn't tell.

It left Persephone wondering if, in some ways, Theseus was right. Should their battle begin with the end of the Fates?

CHAPTER XXVII
HADES

Hades manifested in a dark room within his palace where Hermes had taken up residence. He was immediately hit with the sound of the god's guttural snoring. It was so loud, it vibrated the air around him, and he wondered if Hermes was actually breathing.

Hades summoned light in the fireplace and the sconces on the walls, but Hermes didn't even flinch.

"Hermes!" Hades's voice thundered in the small room, but the god did not startle.

He probably cannot hear me over the sound of his own snoring, Hades thought.

He approached the bed on which Hermes lay starfished on his stomach.

"Hermes!" he said again.

Then he grasped the coverlet and pulled it off.

"Fucking Fates," he muttered.

Hermes was naked.

Of course he was naked.

Hades summoned a splash of ice-cold water. As it hit his bare back, Hermes screamed. It was the same high-pitched tone he'd managed while on Ares's island. He rolled onto his back and somehow managed to jump to his feet. He looked as if he were ready for a fight.

Hades tossed him the blanket, and Hermes grabbed it, hugging it to his front.

"What the fuck, Hades," he snapped. "A gentle shake would have sufficed."

"I am not interested in being gentle with you."

"Oh, come on," he groaned. "Now you're just fucking with me."

"I am not fucking with you."

"Yes, you are," he hissed. "Don't you know how sexual that sounds?"

"No," Hades said.

"Liar," Hermes said and then collapsed to the bed. "I am assuming you are not here to ravish me, so what do you want? I was sleeping so well."

"It certainly didn't sound that way."

"What do you mean?"

"I could hear you snoring from my chambers."

"*I do not snore!*"

"Oh, you most certainly do. Loudly. It shook the very ground beneath my feet."

Hermes glared. "I hate you."

Hades chuckled.

"If I am snoring, it's your fault. This bed is like a fucking rock. Sephy's going to have back problems if she sleeps here."

"The bed is perfectly comfortable," Hades said. "And you are overly concerned for my wife."

"Of course I am. She has to deal with you."

Hades rolled his eyes.

"I need you to summon Ilias and Apollo within the hour."

"No," Hermes said.

Hades lifted a brow. "No?"

"What about *I have no powers* don't you understand?"

"You have no power, but you are a divine messenger and part of this war."

"Why can't *you* summon them?"

"I have other matters to attend to," he said.

"I hope it's trimming that gods-awful beard."

That was exactly the matter at hand. He also wanted to bathe. There were just some things glamour couldn't replace.

"Even if that is the case—and it should be the case—you can summon Ilias and Apollo and shave faster than I can leave the Underworld."

There was a brief moment of silence, and then Hades spoke. "Fine. I suppose I can just...*send an email.*"

Hermes gasped. "You wouldn't."

Hades shrugged. "You have given me no choice."

"After all I've done," Hermes said, throwing off his blanket. He jumped from the bed and started searching the floor for something. Hades hoped it was clothes.

"If you are still referring to Ares's island—"

"I'm talking about being your best friend!" Hermes said. "But best friends don't use their archenemy, do they? No. You know what's so fucking stupid about email? There are faster ways to communicate! Phones! You could just text! But you are so old, you don't even know that!"

Hades blinked slowly. "Are you finished?"

Hermes was still red in the face and breathing hard. "No," he snapped, crossing his arms over his chest, but he said nothing.

"I am well aware that cell phones exist. I have one, yet who have I always relied on to deliver my messages? You."

"Don't make me feel guilty. I am powerless!"

Hades narrowed his eyes. "There is more to being a god than power, Hermes."

"That is easy for you to say. When were you last without power?"

"In the labyrinth," Hades replied.

Hermes's face fell, and he paled. "Hades, I'm sorry. I—" He paused and then scrubbed his face with both hands. "Fine, I'll summon Ilias and Apollo, but can you at least teleport me? I have no interest in trekking across the Underworld again."

"Of course," Hades said, his magic rising to meet the god's demand.

"Wait! Let me get dress—"

But before Hermes could finish speaking, he vanished.

Hades had sent him to the mortal world completely naked.

Perhaps, Hades thought, it would give the media something else to talk about in the midst of the scandal Dionysus had caused.

Hades sighed.

Suddenly, his head *hurt*.

Hermes was fucking exhausting.

Hades returned to his chambers where he showered and shaved. Once he was dressed, he waited in his office for his allies to arrive. He had even poured a glass of whiskey, though it sat on his desk, untouched. While he might look like himself, he had never felt more different. It was hard to say exactly how he had changed. He only knew that in the coming days, weeks, and months, he would come to understand the full impact of his imprisonment, the same way he had when he'd been freed from his father.

He dreaded how it would manifest and mostly how it would affect Persephone, who was already dealing with her own trauma from her experiences with Theseus and Demeter. Now she was going to have to deal with what had happened in the labyrinth too.

He knew she was not well.

He could see it in her face and feel it in her energy, but mostly, he knew because of the things she'd said when she'd dissolved into tears in his arms. As he held her, he was acutely aware of how he had not managed to chase away her grief, how he'd left her vulnerable, how he had failed her.

He had brought her into this world, and he had not prepared her, believing that he could protect her from every evil thing, but in the end, he had saved her from nothing.

In the end, *she* had saved *him* from everything.

As he worried over what he had done, the mistakes he had made, he looked down at the glass on his desk, noticing a ripple in the amber liquid.

He frowned and then looked up just as the door burst open.

Ilias stood there, wide-eyed and wheezing. He had been running. When he saw Hades, he froze for a moment and then let out an odd, breathy laugh.

"You're back."

Hades hesitated. He did not know how to respond. He had not expected Ilias to seem so...relieved by his return. It made his chest feel tight.

Hades's smile was brief and sincere.

"I am," he said with a small nod. "What news?"

"Nothing good," said Ilias. "Theseus made a public appeal for mortals to withdraw worship. He claims a god is responsible for the abduction of his wife and child."

Ilias spoke as if he did not believe the demigod.

"Did he release the name?" Hades asked.

"What?" Ilias asked, surprised by his question. "You don't really think..."

Hades just stared, and Ilias's eyes widened as reality set in.

"He did not," the satyr confirmed. "Hades, you didn't—"

"No," he said. "Dionysus."

Ilias curled his fingers into fists. Hades understood the frustration. Dionysus's actions did not just affect him and his territory. They affected all gods.

"Still, he must have a death wish to invoke the wrath of the gods."

"On the contrary," Hades said, looking out the windows. From where he stood, all that was visible was a swath of green trees shrouded in mist. "Theseus is feeling pretty invincible at the moment. He has managed to lull Zeus into eternal sleep and steal his lightning bolt."

"Why didn't you tell me Zeus was asleep?" Hermes demanded.

Hades turned to see that the god had arrived with Apollo.

"I guess he has to die before we get our powers back," said Apollo as Aphrodite, Harmonia, and Sybil entered the room. "Fuck!"

"At this rate, you may get your wish," said Hades. "We know Theseus intends to sacrifice Zeus to Cronos."

"Unless we rescue him," said Harmonia.

"Now let's not get too crazy," said Hermes, glancing around the room. "I mean, does anyone actually want to see Zeus *free*?"

"I did not say to wake him from slumber," said Harmonia. "But is it right to leave him with our enemy?"

"I think what Harmonia means is that we should capture and imprison Zeus ourselves," said Aphrodite, her eyes darting to the corner of the room where Hephaestus had manifested, his smoldering eyes holding hers. "Then at least he cannot be used by Theseus."

Hades had not considered rescuing Zeus. He had come to accept that his youngest brother would die at the hands of their father, and he had no wish to stop it even if it meant Cronos aligning with Theseus.

It was still possible that one of the two remaining Hecatoncheires would free Zeus as their brother Briareus had done before—unless, of course, Hera also had them murdered.

After this meeting, Hades would have to send Ilias to warn the hundred-handed ones.

"It is nice to know the meeting has started without us,"

said Dionysus, entering with Ariadne. They had clearly come straight from the baths. The ends of Dionysus's hair dripped water on the floor while Ariadne's was plastered to her head.

"Maybe you would've been on time if you hadn't been fucking," said Hermes.

"I believe Dionysus and Ariadne are right on time," said Persephone as she entered the room.

Hades straightened, his eyes locked with hers as she approached. "Forgive me," he said. Taking her hand, he brushed his lips across her knuckles. "Our conversation got out of hand."

She smiled at him. "You are forgiven," she said and turned her attention to the group. "Did I hear right? Are we discussing rescuing Zeus?"

"Rescuing Zeus does not neutralize the threat of Cronos," said Hades. "Theseus has other bargaining chips, among them the lightning bolt and my helm."

There was a heavy pause as the news settled on those who had not yet heard that two of the greatest Olympian weapons were now in the hands of their enemy.

Hades continued. "For now, I suggest we focus on Theseus. He has the most power, and he has weapons that can kill us. He must be stopped first."

"I'm just going to throw this out there," said Apollo. "But what if...we assassinate him?"

"If it were so easy, we would have already done so," Hades snapped. "Theseus has endeared himself to the public, and as of today, they see him as a victim. If he goes down at the height of his popularity, Triad and the Impious will ensure the gods are blamed."

"If Theseus has the world believing his wife and

child were abducted by a god, then can't his wife simply tell the world otherwise?" asked Ilias.

"No," Ariadne said sharply. "Unless Theseus is subdued or dead, you cannot ask that of her. It is too dangerous."

"Do you not trust us to protect her?" Aphrodite asked.

"Forgive me, but you all pointed out how Theseus is just as much of a threat to you as he is to everyone," Ariadne said. "So no."

"Yet you have no trouble leeching off our kindness and accepting our protection."

"Aphrodite," Dionysus warned as Hephaestus loomed behind the Goddess of Love.

"I don't recall you having anything to do with this," Ariadne returned.

"Stop," Persephone commanded. Her voice was like a whip and struck them all silent. "If Theseus does not kill us first, then infighting will. Kindness and protection should not have to be repaid. If Phaedra wishes to make a statement, she can, but it should be her decision and no one else's."

Persephone's eyes grew brighter as she spoke, and she glared at Aphrodite and then Ariadne. Hades straightened, his slacks suddenly too tight.

Fuck, his wife was hot.

"There are other ways to discredit Theseus," said Hades. "We must choose something that will force him to show his true nature publicly."

"I can investigate his background," Sybil suggested. "Perhaps there is something in his past that will—"

"You won't find anything," said Ariadne.

370

"No man is without secrets," Aphrodite countered.

"Do you not think I have tried to dig up dirt on this man?" Ariadne snapped.

"I imagine you have put in the effort, but you are only a mortal after all."

"I might be mortal, but I know this man," she said. "If he has secrets, they die with the people he told."

"You're still alive," Aphrodite countered.

"I'm alive because I can weave his fucking nets."

"*You* wove the nets?" Dionysus asked, just as surprised as everyone else—except Persephone, apparently, because when Hades looked at her to gauge her reaction, her face had turned rosy with guilt.

"Why do you think he wants me so badly?" Ariadne asked.

There was a beat of silence.

"I could hold funeral games," said Aphrodite. "For Adonis, Tyche, Hypnos, and those who died during the attack at Talaria Stadium. It would force the world to see and acknowledge what the Impious and Triad have done and take a side."

Funeral games were almost always held in the aftermath of great loss and were a series of athletic competitions. While they were meant to distract from grief, these would likely only encourage a deeper divide between the Faithful and the Impious.

At the mention of the stadium, Persephone placed a hand over her shoulder. She had been shot during the scuffle, and while she had healed, Hades would never forget the sight of her blood.

"No," Hephaestus said immediately.

There was a finality to his tone that told Hades there

would likely be consequences to contradicting him. He was about to suggest that he could host when Aphrodite turned to glare at her husband.

"You are only saying that because I mentioned Adonis."

Hephaestus did not flinch. His large arms were crossed over his chest.

"You have already been targeted by Triad," said Hephaestus. "If you host the games, you will only draw more attention to yourself, and you are powerless."

"The point is to force them to act publicly," said Aphrodite. "They wanted my attention, and now they have it."

"You will not," he said. "I will not let you."

"*You will not let me*?" Aphrodite repeated. "Since *when* have I required your permission for anything?"

"This isn't up for discussion," he said.

"What is this? Some feeble attempt to act like my husband? You let me out of those obligations a long time ago, remember?"

Hephaestus towered over her, narrowing his eyes. "Do not act as if you were not eager to be free of me."

"You call this free?"

"Why don't you both just fuck and get it over with?" asked Hermes.

Aphrodite whirled on Hermes. "I will *murder* you!"

"Point and case," said the god.

"It's case *in* point, Hermes," said Sybil.

"If we hold funeral games for Tyche and Hypnos," said Apollo, "we communicate to the entire world that Theseus has found a way to murder us all."

"That is better than letting Theseus do it," said

Sybil. "At least then you have control over the narrative."

"And what narrative is that?" Apollo asked. "That Theseus is more powerful than the Olympians?"

"That Theseus murdered innocent gods," Sybil replied.

"If that is true, then has he fulfilled the prophecy of the ophiotaurus?" asked Dionysus.

"We will know come nightfall," said Hades.

If the prophecy had been satisfied, then the ophiotaurus would return to the sky as a constellation, but Hades was not hopeful.

"Holding funeral games may help our favor with mortals, but it does not solve the problem of Theseus," said Dionysus.

"Unless he dies during the games," said Apollo.

"That would be a violation of the rules," said Harmonia.

Which was true. It was traditional for warring sides to declare a cease-fire. The games were supposed to be a time to celebrate life, not encourage more violence.

"Given the circumstances, the last thing I would concern myself with are rules," said Hades.

"I thought you were worried about public perception," said Sybil. "If you kill Theseus during a cease-fire, you will only prove him right."

"Do not make the mistake of thinking Theseus will fight fair," Hades said.

"Can we be sure he will even attend the games?" Persephone asked.

"He will attend," said Ariadne. "He will want to defend himself against Aphrodite's accusations."

Hades could feel Hephaestus's anger spike. That was exactly what the god feared.

A tense silence followed.

"So this is your plan?" asked Dionysus. "Execute Theseus publicly and then what? He has an army of demigods with weapons that can kill us."

"Then we attend armed and assume the games will end in battle."

No one spoke, not in favor or opposition, but Hades knew they had to do something. Theseus's plans were already in motion. They had been from the moment he'd requested a favor from Hades in exchange for Sisyphus. That favor was his access to the Underworld—to his helm and to Hypnos. Zeus's slumber was just another phase, and now that Theseus was in possession of the lightning bolt, Hades dreaded discovering what came next.

He hoped he didn't have to find out.

"Make the announcement, Aphrodite," he said.

The Goddess of Love cast an angry gaze at her husband before departing. Harmonia followed, and so did Sybil. Slowly, the others left, save Hephaestus, who lingered, his eyes trained on Hades.

"I will leave you," Persephone said.

Hades hated to lose her warmth, but he did not argue.

Once she was gone and the door was closed, Hephaestus spoke.

"You would have never let your wife risk herself in such a way," said the god. "Why let mine?"

"What I know about our wives is that they will do what they want despite our wishes," said Hades, though

374

it had taken him too long to realize that. "I'd rather walk in Persephone's shadow, ready to save her at the first sign of a threat, than have her keep secrets. I know you feel the same."

Hephaestus's jaw ticked, and he looked away.

"If Aphrodite could become the sun, she would, just to be rid of my shadow," said the god.

"That is not true," Hades said.

Hephaestus met Hades's gaze. "We will agree to disagree," he said with a small, sad smile. "Come to Lemnos tomorrow. I will arm the gods."

With that, Hephaestus vanished.

CHAPTER XXVIII
DIONYSUS

Dionysus returned to Bakkheia with Ariadne, Phaedra, and the baby.

He chose to manifest underground, in the tunnels beneath his club, aware of the possibility that it too might be targeted by Theseus.

When they arrived, they found that the maenads had convened in the common area. They were dressed in black tactile bodysuits and armed to the teeth.

Naia was speaking, and Dionysus recognized the tone.

She was preparing for a fight.

"Earlier today, Dionysus's home was subject to an attack. Upon arrival, several of our own were found dead with no sign of Dionysus, Ariadne, her sister, or her child. We believe this attack was orchestrated by Theseus, though footage pulled from the premises shows some sort of invisible force—"

As Naia spoke, she scanned the room, and when her

gaze fell on him, she ceased to speak. Slowly, the other maenads turned to look at them. Naia cut through the crowd and threw her arms around Dionysus.

"It's nice to know I am missed," he said, hugging her back.

Naia pulled away and hit his shoulder; her eyes were watering. "I...we didn't know what happened! Your home. It's..."

"Destroyed. I know," he said, and then his eyes shifted to the other maenads. "The demigod who attacked is named Perseus. He was wearing the Helm of Darkness and carrying a weapon laced with venom from the Hydra. It proved to be a deadly combination. I...almost didn't make it."

The assassins exchanged uneasy glances. "The Helm of Darkness?" Lilaia asked. "How do we fight an invisible assailant?"

"I don't have an answer," Dionysus said. "I was lucky. Ariadne came back for me." She met his gaze, her eyes wide with surprise before melting into a warmer expression, one that made him want to take her into his arms and kiss her, but instead, he forced his attention back to the maenads. "But I think we all know Theseus will strike again."

"No, please," said Phaedra. She pushed forward into the open space before them, holding her baby tightly. "I am worth none of this—"

"Phaedra!" Ariadne sounded both shocked and angry.

"I can end this, Ari," Phaedra said, and the hard part about her words was that Dionysus knew she was wrong.

"You can't end this," he said. "Even if you return to

Theseus, he will still come for us, and there is no guessing what he might do to punish you."

There was a moment of quiet, and then Naia spoke. "You are not responsible for Theseus's actions."

"I left. I—"

"Fled," said Ariadne. "You fled an *abuser*, Phaedra."

"He wasn't—" She started to protest but glanced at Dionysus, swallowing her words. "How do you know Theseus was responsible for the attack on your house?"

"Phaedra!" Ariadne gasped, "Perseus *works* for Theseus."

"You do not know that Theseus sent him," Phaedra argued. "Perhaps Perseus acted on his own. It would make sense. Theseus would never threaten the life of his son."

Her words did not even anger Dionysus, because he had expected them.

"Theseus would do anything to gain public favor. *He wants to be a god!*"

"He does not want to be a god," she said. "He wants freedom and fairness—"

"If you really believe that, then you are a fool," Ariadne snapped.

Phaedra paled. She looked just as stricken as Ariadne sounded. Then she glanced from side to side, seeming to remember they had an audience, and she fled.

For a few moments, Ariadne just stood there, stunned.

Dionysus thought about putting his hand on her shoulder, or maybe he should draw her close. He was not sure what would be appropriate, but before he could decide, Ariadne left, calling after her sister.

"I only hope he's dead before she manages to flee," said Lilaia.

It was a harsh statement, but Dionysus agreed.

"We must prepare for anything," he said. "Fortify the tunnels. I want all entrances monitored twenty-four hours a day. If you see something strange—if for any reason you sense something is wrong—raise the alarm." The maenads nodded as he added, "Sleep with your weapons nearby. The Olympians are going to war."

With their orders given, the maenads dispersed, save Naia, who pulled Dionysus aside.

"I have news for you," she said.

"All right," he said, dread seeping into the pit of his stomach.

"Hebe sent word this morning. She knows what happened to Medusa."

Hebe was one of the maenads tasked with locating the gorgon, and the way Naia spoke now made Dionysus think the worst. He straightened. "What happened?"

"She was kidnapped by Tyrrhenian pirates," Naia said. "They are holding her for ransom."

While that was not the worst thing imaginable—the worst being death—it was a close second. He had a long history with the Tyrrhenian pirates that stretched back to ancient times, which meant that it did not matter if he could meet their ransom demand. They would not do business with him.

"*Fuck.*" He smoothed his hand over his head. "When was the ransom announced?"

"Just this morning," she said.

"How do we know it is really her?"

There were few descriptions of the woman beyond

the fact that she was beautiful and that she could turn men to stone with a glance. As it turned out, her head had to be separated from her body for that power to work.

Now he feared the actual worst—that she was, in fact, dead.

Naia hesitated. "Well, we don't actually know," she admitted. "But I do not think we can ignore the possibility that they are telling the truth. She was last seen on the shore of the Aegean."

That was true. Even Poseidon—terrible bastard that he was—confirmed it.

I fucked her and left her, he had said. *If I had known the value of her beautiful head, I'd have cut it off where she lay.*

Dionysus's hands curled at the thought.

The God of the Sea was almost as great an enemy to him as Hera. Indeed, they had been rivals since ancient times. It had begun with Beroe, a nymph they had both loved, and now Ariadne, a woman Poseidon and his son Theseus seemed to be obsessed with.

"I have an idea," said Naia.

"What is it?" Dionysus asked, turning to face her.

"Perhaps...it is time to consult your oracle," she said.

"I do not have time to unravel a silly rhyme," Dionysus said, immediately dismissing her suggestion. "And in case you've forgotten, my oracle is supposed to speak for *me*, not the other way around."

"She is your oracle. She offers you prophecies as well!" Naia argued.

"Prophecy. Prediction. *Not certainty*, which is what we need right now."

"Well, you have nothing right now, so which will it be?"

Dionysus ground his teeth.

"Do not be a child," Naia said. "Just because you used to date—"

"We did not date," Dionysus snapped.

"Oh, sorry. *Fucked*."

He glared.

"Dionysus," Naia said, her gaze both hard and pleading. "Think about what happens if Theseus gets his hands on Medusa."

He didn't want to think about what would happen. He already knew. Theseus would decapitate her, and not only would another innocent woman die at his hands, but the demigod would also have another powerful weapon.

He scrubbed his face, "Fuck," he said again under his breath before dropping his hands. "You will be okay?"

She knew what he was really asking. Was everything going to be okay?

"We'll be all right," she said, smiling a little. "You have to do this. You have no choice."

He swallowed, nodding.

"I'm…uh…going to tell Ariadne," he said.

She would want to know where he was going—not for his sake but because their partnership had begun over their quest to locate the gorgon.

"Of course," she said, but as Dionysus turned to go, she called after him. "Might I advise you not to take too long with your goodbyes."

Dionysus held up his middle finger as he disappeared down the hall in search of Ariadne. He did not have to look long, finding her sitting on the floor outside her room, her knees drawn up to her chest.

She was crying.

He knelt in front of her. "Hey," he said. "Are you all right?"

"No," she said, her voice thick with tears. "I feel awful. I should have never said those things to Phaedra."

"You were not wrong," he said.

"There is a time and a place," she said. "And I chose wrong."

"Come," Dionysus said, rising to his feet. He held out his hand and helped her up, a rush of warmth spreading through his chest when she did not try to pull free of his hold. He led her to a modest bedroom at the end of the hall. "This is where I stay," he said. "If you wish to give your sister some space, you can sleep here."

When he met her gaze, he found her staring back.

"Thank you," she whispered.

He lifted his hand to her cheek.

"I hate seeing this pain in your eyes," he said.

"I do not know myself without it," she said.

Dionysus didn't know what to say, but her words made it hard for him to breathe.

"If I could take it away…"

"You would have to be death himself," she said.

"Do not speak of such things," he said.

"No? Even when I was the one who had to watch you nearly die?"

He stared at her for a moment and then asked, "Why did you come back?"

He had told her to go—ordered her to take her sister into the tunnels and not look back.

"I had to," she said.

"You didn't. You could have done as I said. You could have escaped in the tunnels."

"No, I couldn't," she argued. "You risked everything to save my sister. You risked everything for me. Who would I be if I just left you?"

"Smart," he said. "Really fucking smart."

Then he pulled her close and kissed her, and while he would have liked to continue, he knew he had no time.

When he pulled away, he held her tightly in his grip.

"I must go," he said. "We have word on Medusa's location."

Ariadne's eyes widened. "Let me come with you."

Dionysus felt his gaze soften at her request. He was surprised she'd made it, given that it meant leaving her sister.

"As much as I would like that," he said, brushing her hair from her face, "Phaedra needs you."

"She might need me," Ariadne said. "But she does not want me."

"That's the truth for tonight," he said. "That will not be true tomorrow."

"You intend to be gone long?"

"There is no intention behind it," he said. "I will return as soon as I am able."

He did not even know if his rescue mission would be successful. The pirates had announced Medusa's ransom on the black market, which meant that everyone who had been looking for her before would be after her now, and many of them—himself included—had no intention of actually paying their price.

Ariadne's gaze fell to his chest, her fingers twisting into his shirt.

"Please be safe," she said, and he heard what she was really saying—*please don't leave me.*

He tilted her head back. "If you are here waiting for me, I will always come back."

He kissed her again, harder this time, ignoring how it felt less like saying goodbye and more like the end.

———

Dionysus had temples all over New Greece, but the one he found himself standing before was located within the citadel of Perperikon in Thrace. Like the little city it overlooked, the temple was carved into the mountainside. Twenty-five steps led to a covered porch that was supported by a set of identical columns crowned with scroll-like patterns. The pediment was carved with an image of him surrounded by his frenzied followers, and it mimicked the merriment taking place in real time.

The porch was crowded with people, their bodies bathed in firelight as they danced, drank, and fucked, caught in the throes of holy ecstasy. The smell made him dizzy. It was a vibrant blend of perfumes, both musky and powdery, and the putrid mix of alcohol and drugs, particularly Evangeline, which had the distinct, pungent odor of ammonia.

It was a far cry from other places of worship, where devotees would come in quiet peace to pray, leave offerings, and hear the word of the reigning oracle. Perhaps the hardest part for Dionysus was that this particular brand of worship was a result of Hera's madness, and despite being "cured," his body still trembled at the sight.

He hated that he held on to the memory of that volatile time, hated that he felt dread at the doors of his own temple where the priestesses within worshipped him. In truth, he feared slipping back into the chaos, losing control, and never surfacing again, and it made him feel as though he would never truly know freedom from the horror of Hera's magic.

He was not sure how long he waited at the base of those steps, but eventually he felt stable enough to make his way inside. Unfortunately, there was no relief from the jostling crowd, which spilled out of the temple doors. His frustration mounted. He considered transforming into a jaguar or a lion and leaping over their heads, but he would likely only cause a fatal stampede.

Finally, he came to the altar where a statue of his likeness was raised, and it was there beneath its shadow that he found his oracle.

She was a beautiful woman. Tall and willowy, she rose to stand from where she had been reclined at his feet, surrounded by attendants who fed her grapes and offered wine.

"Erigone," he said in acknowledgment.

She tilted her head, her arms braced behind her. It was a stance that pushed her chest forward, and because she was draped in sheer, shimmering robes, he could see every part of her.

He remained intently focused on her dark eyes, which were bright with amusement.

"Dionysus," she said. "It has been a long time."

"I fear I have not required your talents."

"Or desired my counsel," she said, accepting a golden

chalice from one of the attendants. "Until now, it seems. You must be desperate."

There was a beat of silence following her comment, and it was filled with fury.

"I am," he said. He knew humility would go a long way with his oracle, especially since he usually avoided her, even if it was hard to say aloud.

She sighed. "What do you want, Dionysus?"

She sipped her wine, which had already stained her lips a deep burgundy.

"I require assistance locating a woman," he said.

"Does she wish to be found?"

"She likely didn't," he said. "But she has since been kidnapped by pirates. Now they are holding her for ransom."

Erigone studied him for a moment, her gaze hard and unwavering. Despite their history, she would not deny a woman in danger.

She handed off her cup and then gathered her shimmering robes into her hands.

"Come," she said, and he followed her into the darkness of an adjoining room.

A few torches burned low, illuminating piles of glittering gold and shining silver, offerings brought by worshippers across lifetimes. She wound her way through the treasure until they came to the center of the room where there was a small table and a tray of incense.

"This woman," said Erigone, lighting one of the slender sticks in the torchlight. "Is she a lover?"

"Would that matter?" Dionysus asked.

"No," she said, turning back to him. "But she must be important to bring you here."

Dionysus said nothing, and Erigone narrowed her eyes as she blew out the flame. Ribbons of smoke danced around her, smelling of spice and resin.

"Do you recall how I would prophecize for you, Dionysus?"

He shifted on his feet, uncomfortable. "Must we revisit the past?" he asked.

"I am not asking to revisit," she said. "I am asking if you remember."

He stared, frustration making his teeth clench. "I remember," he said.

"On your knees," she said. "Between my thighs."

"That was a long time ago, Erigone," he said. "We are both beyond that."

"Perhaps you are," she said. "But I still want you on your knees."

He stared at her for a few slow seconds and then spoke. "You are my oracle."

"And like anything that has belonged to you, I have been abandoned," she said. "Does this woman know? The one who has you so chivalrously holding my gaze and shifting with discomfort in my presence, that your loyalty is as flimsy as a spider's web in the wind?"

"Give me the prophecy, Erigone," Dionysus said.

"You are a pathetic god," she said, her eyes gleaming. "The only reason you still have followers is because everyone likes to drink and fuck."

His fists tightened; his anger felt molten in his veins, and for a few brief seconds, he wanted to kill her. Those were the claws of his madness digging deep.

Erigone gave him a shrewd smile, and for a moment, he thought that perhaps that was what she wanted too, but then she threw her head back and spread her arms wide. The smoke from the incense became a straight column rising into the darkness. She said things, but they were not words he could understand and were more like a song, spoken in a low and lyrical cadence.

It was unnerving but mesmerizing to witness, and there was a part of him that wanted to crawl inside her, to see what she was seeing for himself, but that was the magic of Erigone. She was a seductress as much as she was an oracle, and she gave prophecy like she fucked, with reckless abandon.

Dionysus's nails sank into his palms. It was that sweet sting that kept him grounded, that ensured he did not descend into the strange madness of her fortune-telling, and when she emerged from her trance, she looked upon him in dazed disappointment.

He did not move, too afraid to break the spell.

"You have neglected a sacred duty. You have left the dead unburied," she said.

Before the oracle was finished with her foretelling, Dionysus knew what he had to do—bury the ophiotaurus, which he had left to rot on the island of Thrinacia after Theseus murdered him.

Fuck.

"Correct this offense," Erigone continued. "And all will be revealed."

He should have listened to Ariadne the moment she'd begged to return to the island and complete the task, but at the time, her request had seemed rash given the danger.

"You know what you must do," the oracle said.

"I do," he said.

They were silent for a few moments, and then Erigone spoke again.

"Death marks your path, Dionysus. Be careful where you tread."

With the echo of her words on his heels, he left the small room.

He could have teleported then, but instead, he returned to the crowd and waded through their revelry, knowing he would need their worship to carry him through the coming days. Even as their energy washed over him, he could not shake the keen awareness that they were all coming to the end of their days. Soon, this warmth that surrounded him would no longer come from their bodies but from their ashes.

———

Dionysus needed a way to reach the island of Thrinacia since he could not teleport directly, given it was Poseidon's territory. The only reason he had managed to escape before was because Hermes had located him and Ariadne and teleport them home—which was how he found himself in the Underworld, begrudgingly knocking on Hermes's door.

"Come in!" the god said in a muffled, singsong voice.

The merry tone only set Dionysus on edge, but he was right to be suspicious. As he pushed open the door, he found Hermes's ass in his face.

Well, not literally.

He wasn't naked, though he might as well have been. The leggings he wore were skintight and left very little to the imagination, and his crop top was basically just sleeves.

"What are you doing?" Dionysus asked.

"What does it look like?" Hermes asked, staring at him from between his legs.

Dionysus couldn't meet his gaze.

"Torture?" he ventured.

"A downward dog," Hermes said as he straightened and then bent over backward.

"As I said," Dionysus replied.

"You should try it."

"I'll pass," Dionysus said.

"You're just jealous I'm more flexible," said Hermes.

"I'm not sure jealous is the right word."

"Aroused, perhaps?" he suggested as he tried to get back on his feet but fell on his ass.

"Not in the least," Dionysus said.

Hermes frowned. "Well damn," he said, standing and brushing off his hands. "What do you want?"

"I need to locate a few pirates," said Dionysus.

Hermes narrowed his eyes. "Are you sure this isn't a sexual thing?"

"Has anyone ever told you how annoying you are?"

"Do you want my help or not?"

"I'm seriously reconsidering," said Dionysus.

"Well, that's just fine," said Hermes with a huff. "I don't have powers anyway. Why do you think I'm doing yoga?"

Dionysus glared. He knew Hermes didn't have magic, but he also knew that all gods had at least one magical article. Hermes was no exception.

"You have sandals," he said.

"You want my sandals?"

"I can't teleport to the ocean, Hermes."

"My sandals are relics! They belong in a museum, not on your feet!"

"If that's true, then where are they?"

"Like I would tell you!"

"You forgot about them, didn't you?"

"No!" he snapped, crossing his arms over his chest before letting them fall again. "If you want them, you'll have to take me to my house."

Dionysus cocked a brow. "Which one?"

Hermes hesitated. "We'll start with the one in Olympia."

"*Start*?" Dionysus repeated.

"It's been a long time since I've had to use them!" Hermes said defensively. "At this point, they're *symbolic*!"

"Fuck me," Dionysus grumbled, and before Hermes could open his mouth, he teleported, appearing outside Hermes's sprawling Olympia mansion, which had a steeply pitched roof and a stucco exterior.

Hermes approached the rounded entrance, which was grand and framed by a set of white columns.

Dionysus followed Hermes, who had started to pat his hips, his chest, even his ass.

"What are you doing?" Dionysus asked, already annoyed.

"I forgot my keys," said Hermes.

"Are you kidding me?"

"Don't judge me! I usually have *magic*!"

Dionysus sighed. "Move."

The God of Wine stepped forward and then shoved his foot against the doors. There was a cracking sound as they burst open with such force, they hit the interior walls, shaking the glass within.

When he turned toward Hermes, the god glared at him.

"You could have used magic," he said, sweeping past him into the house.

Dionysus followed and was immediately met by a massive double staircase.

"How do you decide which side to go up?" Dionysus asked.

Hermes opened his mouth and then closed it before answering. "I never gave it much thought," he said, his hands pressed to his head. "Fuck. How do I choose?"

Dionysus gave him an incredulous look. "*How* have you lived this long?"

"Hey!" Hermes said, pointing at himself. "*I'm* cunning!"

"Sure," said Dionysus, taking the staircase on the right. "And I drink water."

"You and Hades have issues," Hermes said as he followed.

Once they reached the top, he overtook Dionysus, taking the hall on the left. When Hermes switched on the lights, Dionysus was blinded by the color pink. It was everywhere—on the walls and the floor and the bed, even the chandelier—and all varying hues.

"Why is everything *pink*?" Dionysus asked, shielding his eyes.

"Because," said Hermes. "This is the pink room."

"The pink room?"

"Yeah, I have a gold room and a red room and a—" Hermes marked them off on each finger.

"Are they all bedrooms?"

"Yeah."

"*Why?*"

Hermes shrugged. "Why not?"

Because it's insane, Dionysus wanted to say but didn't.

"I never know what my mood will be," Hermes explained, shuffling over the pink carpet as he made his way into the adjoining pink bathroom. "Some nights, I'm a gold. Some nights, I'm a green."

Dionysus considered asking what that meant but decided against it. He was short on time, and he needed Hermes's sandals. The fewer distractions, the better.

Inside the bathroom was a safe door. It was also pink and framed by mirrors that reflected the light overhead. Dionysus imagined it was supposed to look glamorous, but it really just hurt his eyes even more.

Hermes approached the door and glanced back at Dionysus before cupping his hands over the safe's keypad.

Dionysus rolled his eyes. "I'm not going to steal whatever's in your closet, Hermes."

"If you could have stolen my winged sandals, wouldn't you?"

"To avoid you? Yes," said Dionysus.

"Rude," said Hermes as he turned the wheel, pulling open the door to reveal a massive closet with shelves upon shelves of shoes.

"Please tell me you only have one shoe closet," said Dionysus.

"Okay," said Hermes.

"Fuck me," Dionysus groaned.

"Don't judge me," said Hermes. "I have an obsession."

"Don't you mean addiction?"

"Tomato, potato," he said.

Dionysus's brows lowered. "Don't you mean to-mah-to?"

"No, I mean potato," Hermes said. "They are two different things entirely."

Dionysus rolled his eyes again. "Whatever you say."

Hermes smiled. "I knew you'd see it my way."

The God of Mischief sauntered into the closet to begin the search. Dionysus followed, eyes scanning Hermes's many and varied shoes. He picked up a pair of platform heels that were covered in gemstones.

"How do you wear these?" Dionysus asked.

"On your feet," said Hermes.

Dionysus shook his head. "Real funny," he said, putting them back on the shelf as Hermes snickered. "You know what I mean."

"I will admit it takes talent," he said.

"Don't you just fly everywhere when you wear them?" said Dionysus.

"That still takes talent," Hermes said.

"It isn't a talent," said Dionysus. "You are a god."

"We'll see about that," said Hermes. They continued to search the closet, but after a while, Hermes declared, "Well, they aren't here. We'll have to check the other closets."

"The closets in your other houses or the closets in this house?" Dionysus asked. It was an important distinction.

"The closets in this house," said Hermes. "If the shoes aren't here, then we'll have to check another house."

Dionysus rubbed his face in frustration. "Why do I put myself through this?" he groaned.

"Because you secretly love hanging out with me," said Hermes, sauntering past him. They left the pink room and entered a blue room, which was not among the colors Hermes had mentioned earlier and only made Dionysus far more worried. When the shoes were not there, they moved on to another. This one was purple and had more than just shoes in the closet but still no winged sandals.

As more hours passed, Dionysus began to wonder if Hermes still had them and started to consider other options for reaching the island of Thrinacia. He worried that by the time he managed to get the shoes and bury the ophiotaurus, it would be too late to rescue Medusa, but he did not have many options. He did not have a monster that could fly, and one that could swim would be just as dangerous as sailing given Poseidon's hatred of him.

Even with Hermes's sandals, there was a chance he'd be shot down from the sky by pirates, but at least his odds of landing closer to Medusa were better.

Those were the thoughts racing through his mind as he sank to the bed in the green room and nodded off.

He wasn't sure how long he was out when he heard Hermes exclaim, "Yes!"

Startled by the sound, Dionysus shot up from bed. Through bleary eyes, he saw Hermes exit the closet carrying a pair of leather sandals with feathery wings. They were surprisingly simple given the mischievous god's penchant for extravagant things.

"I found them!" he declared, but Dionysus recognized another problem.

"Why are they so small?" he asked.

"They aren't *small*," said Hermes, holding up the shoes.

"How big are your feet?"

"I don't know," said Hermes.

"How do you—" Dionysus stopped himself. He had asked that question too many times already, and it never got them anywhere. "How am I supposed to wear them if they don't fit?"

"They're basically soles with string, Dionysus," said Hermes. "Put them on."

Dionysus took one and tried to slip his foot inside, but the most he got was his first three toes.

"Why are your feet so huge?" Hermes asked. Then he met Dionysus's gaze and raised a brow. "Is it true what they say about shoe size and dick size?"

"I'm not sure what they say," said Dionysus. "But I'd really rather not talk about my dick with you."

"Fine," Hermes said, sniffing. "I was just curious."

"Well, I need these fucking shoes to fit," said Dionysus.

"Well, you have magic, idiot. *Make* them!"

"They are your gods-damned shoes. I can't change them!"

"You can add to them! Wrap vines around your fucking feet!" said Hermes. "Gods, and you think *I'm* stupid."

Dionysus felt his face flush, though he wasn't sure if it was from embarrassment or frustration.

He sat both shoes on the floor and stepped on the soles. Vines sprouted from them and wound together over his feet and calves.

"There! Now stand."

Dionysus did and was immediately thrown backward as the sandals flew out from under him. He hit his head on the bed as he went down. Luckily, it was soft, but now he was hanging upside down, the wings of the sandals strapped to his feet beating furiously.

"What the fuck, Hermes! Tell them to put me upright!"

"I can't," said Hermes.

"What do you mean you *can't*?" Dionysus snarled.

"They don't work like that. You have to learn how to balance, then you just glide. It's like skating."

"I don't have time to learn how to fucking skate!"

"I suppose you don't have to," said Hermes. "You can just fly all the way there like that."

Dionysus gritted his teeth.

"Come on, big boy. Just treat it like a sit-up. Once you are upright, your weight will help you land."

"Treat it like a sit-up," Dionysus mocked, yet he tried, tightening his abs and swinging up. The first time, he only made it halfway, the second a little farther. His third attempt had him doing a complete flip.

"Fuck!"

"You almost had it," said Hermes.

"I know I almost had it, Hermes! I don't need your commentary!"

He crossed his arms over his chest. "I'm just trying to be helpful."

"Well, don't."

"Fine. You *suck* at this."

Dionysus's frustration grew. For a moment, he just hung there and ground his teeth so hard his jaw hurt.

Then he took a deep breath.

"I'm sorry, Hermes."

There was a long beat of silence.

"You've got this, Dionysus."

The god nodded and tried again. He fisted his hands, tightened his core, and swung. Once he was upright, he held out his arms for balance. His legs felt wobbly, and his whole body seemed to vibrate with the beat of the winged sandals, but he was on his feet.

"Yes!" he hissed before he lost his balance and fell again. "Fuck. I am done!"

Dionysus used his magic to unlace himself from the sandals. When he did, he crashed to the ground, not realizing that he was no longer positioned over the bed.

"Stupid fucking sandals," he muttered as he got to his feet and snatched them from the air where they were still fluttering. "How do you make them stop...flying?"

As soon as the words were out of Dionysus's mouth, the wings stopped flapping.

"Just like that," said Hermes.

Dionysus glared. "You mean you can tell them to stop flying but you can't tell them to put me on my feet?"

"Yes," said Hermes.

"I hate you."

"Don't hate me. I'm just the messenger." Hermes paused and chuckled. "Get it? Because I am the Messenger of the Gods."

Dionysus glared.

Then he vanished, but not before Hermes shouted after him. "Wait! Take me back to the Underworld!"

———

Dionysus appeared on the coast of the Mediterranean Sea.

The sun was rising, casting rays of orange and yellow over the calm surface of the water. Always beautiful and mostly warm, it was hard to imagine the evils that took place on the water, but it was a lawless place ruled by a ruthless god.

Dionysus put the sandals on the sandy beach and stepped into them, bearing down as the vines twisted around his feet so they wouldn't fly out from under him again. When he was ready, he lifted his heels and stuck out his arms to steady himself as he rose into the air, the wings pumping hard and fast.

His heart beat hard in his chest, and sweat beaded across his forehead. Shakily, he lifted his hand to wipe it away before it dripped into his eyes. He would never admit it to Hermes—though he didn't need to, his struggle was obvious—but *fuck, this was hard.*

Hermes had always made it look so easy, gliding through the air in a flash of blinding gold light. Dionysus moved at the speed of a snail. At this rate, he'd make it to Thrinacia in a week, and Medusa would be long gone and likely dead.

Gathering his courage, he did as Hermes had instructed, tilting his body forward slightly. He could feel the wind pick up around him as he moved faster over the ocean, the colors blending together into a seamless shade of blue. The longer he moved at one speed, the easier it was to accelerate, and soon he felt as though he were sailing.

He started to laugh, filled with triumph, and then he lost his balance and tumbled into the sea, inhaling a mouthful of salty water that burned his throat as he surfaced. How was he supposed to get to his feet again? There were no rocks or islands for miles, and time was running out.

"Fuck!" he screamed as he wiped his eyes. "I fucking hate everything!"

He moved to float on his back and stuck his feet into the air. The wings on Hermes's scandals fluttered wildly and Dionysus found himself being carried through the air upside down with his head in the ocean.

He tried to get to his feet, but he struggled to breathe as salt water went up his nose and into his mouth. The drier the wings became, the higher he rose until he was finally out of the ocean, but by then, he was too tired to try getting upright, and he resigned himself to simply hanging there.

Until he noticed a high wave rushing his way.

"Gods fucking dammit," he said, his strength suddenly renewed, but when he found he could not right himself, he resorted to shouting. "I know you can fucking hear me!" he yelled at the shoes. "Fly higher, you idiots!"

But they did not listen.

The first wave hit, barreling into him with such force, it stole his breath. In the short reprieve before another came, he yelled again.

"You're useless! Just like your owner!"

The second wave was jarring, and he could not hold his breath through it, the water burning as it slipped down his throat and into his lungs. He coughed violently, unprepared for the next wave, and as the water surrounded him, he knew for certain that he was going to die. It did not matter that he was a god and could heal on his own. The sea was all-consuming, and he could not breathe in this dark and violent place, could not take the pain searing his chest and swelling in his throat—and then suddenly, a strange calm came over him, and he felt nothing.

For a few sweet moments, he was simply...*numb*.

But then he surfaced as Hermes's sandals carried

him above the fierce waves. Dionysus inhaled a painful breath, choking as he vomited water. He wanted to curse the shoes, but his throat hurt too bad to speak, so he just hung there as the ocean churned beneath his head, and he fell into unconsciousness.

―――――

It was a horrific smell that roused Dionysus. When he opened his eyes, he came face-to-face with the cockeyed gaze of a sheep.

"Baa!" the animal shrieked at the same time as Dionysus screamed. He clamped a hand over his mouth, both to shut himself up but also to keep from punching the sheep. Though the urge was still there.

Ariadne would be very disappointed if you punched a sheep, he reminded himself.

"Gods, why do you do that?" he demanded.

"Baa!" the sheep answered.

"*Shut up!*" he snapped as he rose into a sitting position, his head spinning for a brief moment.

He glanced at the sheep and then around, realizing that this place was familiar. He had come to the shore of Thrinacia.

Dionysus looked down, relieved to find that Hermes's sandals were still strapped to his feet, and then back at the sheep.

"What is that smell?" he asked.

The sheep replied with another loud cry, and while its breath was rancid, it did not compare to what permeated the island air.

This was something far, far worse. It was a smell that had memory, even after it had long since dissipated.

It was the smell of death.

Dread pooled low in Dionysus's stomach. It was possible the smell came from the decaying body of the ophiotaurus, but even he knew that was wishful thinking. Something else had happened here.

Something terrible.

He exchanged a look with the sheep, who still lingered nearby. The animal opened its mouth, bleating loudly before turning to lead him into the thick of the forest. Though he did not think he needed an escort to return to the cyclops's cave, following the creature provided some comfort as they navigated the dense terrain and rocky mountainside. All the while, the smell of rot grew worse and worse.

Dionysus had never thought long on the power of a smell, but this was like walking into a solid wall, and no matter how hard he pushed against it, it never moved. It just sat in the air, coating his clothes and stinging his nose.

By the time they made it to the mouth of the cyclops's cave, his eyes were watering, his nose was dripping, and he thought that at any moment, he would vomit, but he had found the source of the smell.

It was not just the ophiotaurus that lay within, rotting.

The cyclops was too.

Polyphemus.

His graying form lay like a mountain near the spring Dionysus had turned to wine. Hesitantly, he approached, one arm drawn over his nose, not that it could keep the smell at bay. Still, he wondered what had happened to the creature. He seemed to be in the same position as before, when he had passed out in his drunken state, except as Dionysus rounded the creature's shoulder, he found that his eye was stabbed through with a spear.

The cyclops had been murdered.

Dionysus peered into the darkness, wondering who had carried out the attack, though they seemed to be long gone by now. Perhaps the old man who had asked him to perform the execution had followed and finished the job. Whatever the case, he wondered what sort of curse would haunt the person who left him unburied.

Dionysus moved past the cyclops and made his way farther into the cave, suffocated by the scent of death, until he found Bully's remains.

He stood in mournful silence, thinking about how the creature had protected Ariadne. Though a monster with a serpent body and the head of a bull, he was a harmless creature who was more frightened than violent. Still, the Fates had assigned him a terrible destiny, but that was their nature: cruelty.

After a few seconds, he knelt and began to dig, using a sharp rock to make a trench beside Bully's body. When it was deep enough, he took the creature by the horns, hoping to pull his entire body into the pit, but he was so decomposed, only half of him made it, and Dionysus was forced to push what remained into the grave with his foot.

It was terrible, and the smell never lessened.

When he was finished, he covered the creature with a bed of soil. It was all he could manage before he raced from the mouth of the cave and vomited.

It was there as he bent with his hands on his knees that something struck him from behind, and he had the thought that his head was going to explode right before he lost consciousness. Again.

CHAPTER XXIX
PERSEPHONE

Persephone sat in her favorite chair in the library. A fire blazed in the hearth, and Cerberus, Typhon, and Orthrus slept nearby while she read—or tried to. Despite the peace of the evening, she could not shake the thought that something bad was happening. The feeling blossomed in her chest and grew into her throat, worsening as each quiet second ticked by.

Something wet splashed on her leg.

At first, she did not pay it any mind, thinking that perhaps she had imagined it, but then she felt a second drop.

She put her book down, expecting to see Orthrus standing near drooling on her, but he wasn't. All the dogs remained asleep before the fireplace.

Persephone frowned and then felt another splash, this time on her face. She wiped at the wetness, and as she pulled her hand back, she noticed her fingers were stained with crimson.

Strange, she thought.

When another drop fell, she looked up and went cold when she saw that the ceiling was saturated in red, and she knew it was blood. It pooled in places and then fell in heavy drops to the floor and glided down the walls.

Her heart started to race. Panic bubbled inside her.

She shot to her feet, only to wake and find that she was in bed beside Hades. There was no blood, just the cold silk of their bedding.

She took a breath and shoved the blankets aside, slipping from bed. Despite the fire in the hearth, the air was cool, and she shivered, her skin pebbling.

She crossed to Hades's bar and poured herself a glass of whiskey, but just as she brought it to her lips, his voice ignited in the dark.

"What are you doing?"

She whirled to find him standing close. Warmth radiated off his skin. She wanted it, leaned into it, as her eyes found his.

"Trying to chase away the darkness," she said.

"You will only feed it," he said, taking the glass.

She expected him to down it, but he didn't. He set it aside, never shifting his attention from her.

"Is that why you drink?" she asked.

He studied her for a few quiet seconds and then said, "I do not wish for you to be like me."

"Would you love me less?"

"Never," he said and then frowned. "That question was unkind."

Persephone dropped her gaze, and Hades inched closer, tipping her head back with his finger.

"Tell me," he said, his voice a deep rumble she could feel in her chest.

"There is nothing to tell," she said, looking at him. "It was only a nightmare."

Hades studied her, his eyes glittering like obsidian—a reflection of the desire burning with her.

"Do you wish to sleep?"

"No," she said. "No...I do not wish to sleep."

Hades's gaze fell to her lips.

"Then what is it you desire?"

His voice promised worship and made her blood simmer.

She slid out from between him and the bar, swiping a deck of cards from the mantle. "I desire a game," she said.

"A game?"

"A game with stakes."

Hades tilted his head to the side. "Tell me your terms, Goddess."

"Whatever you desire, so long as it brings me pleasure."

Hades's eyes darkened. "May I request the same from you?"

She tried not to smile. "You may," she said.

"And the game you wish to play?"

"Poker," she said.

Hades raised a brow.

It was the game he'd chosen the night they'd first slept together, and she chose it now because she wanted a distraction.

"Fine, Goddess," he said. "Do you wish to deal?"

"I'll let you have the honor," she said and sat, suddenly eye level with Hades's engorged cock.

She let her gaze drift to his.

"Hurry, my lord," she said in a breathy whisper.

She noticed Hades's fingers curl, and shadows danced in his eyes.

"As you wish, darling."

He sat opposite her and shuffled the cards before dealing two each.

Persephone did not move to look, and Hades raised a brow.

"Do you not wish to know your hand?" he asked.

She smirked, holding his gaze as she replied. "Darling, I win either way."

Hades tensed, and for a moment, she thought he might forgo the game and fuck her on the table that now divided them, but after a moment, he dealt five more cards face up—a jack, an eight, a king, a nine. and an ace.

Persephone turned her cards—a king and an ace.

Hades had a queen and a ten.

He had won.

She pressed her thighs together, suddenly overwhelmed by a hot wave of desire.

"Come," Hades said.

Persephone rose and lowered to her knees before him.

"Why do you kneel?"

"Forgive me," she said. "I assumed you would want my mouth."

Hades cupped her face, brushing his thumb across her lips.

"Do not take my question for rejection," he said. "I want your mouth, but I had something else in mind. On your feet."

She did as he asked, his hands smoothing over her ass,

and he pulled her close, remaining seated as he buried his face between her legs.

She sighed, sifting her fingers through his hair as she widened her stance.

"This was supposed to be about your pleasure," she said.

"This does please me," he said. His breath was warm against her, and the feel of him made her dizzy.

"What about this pleases you?" she asked.

He hummed against her flesh.

"Everything," he said as he spread her and licked her silken flesh, his fingers slowly inching into her liquid heat. It was hard to explain just how good he felt, and despite his attention between her legs, she could feel him all over.

"Hades," she gasped, fingers twisting into his hair.

She wanted to pull him closer and grind into his face.

She wanted to clench around him and come.

He slipped to the floor and guided her foot to rest against the chair. As he hooked his arms around her thighs, he sucked her clit into his mouth, gazing up at her before he released her.

"Pray to me, darling," he said. "And I may let you come."

"I do pray," she said, her fingers grazing his scalp as she gripped his hair. "I worship you."

She bore down against him, and he coaxed her to release.

"Fuck," she moaned, her limbs shaking. She bent forward, unable to remain upright as the tension inside her unraveled in long, slow waves. The move brought her breasts close to Hades's face, and he teased her nipples with his mouth, sucking and licking until she was able to straighten, though that did not stop him from brushing kisses across her skin.

"Shall we continue our game?" he asked, his voice deep and husky, his mouth glistening with her release.

She held his gaze, her hands on his shoulders. "Of course," she said, unsuccessfully trying to hide the fact that she was still breathless.

She started to move to her seat, but his grip tightened.

"No," he said, returning to his chair. "Sit."

Persephone raised a brow but did as he asked, letting him guide her into his lap, his cock nestled firmly against her ass. The feel of him made it hard to breathe, hard to focus on anything other than how empty she felt.

She preferred this—anything to distract from the nightmare that had preceded this.

"Are you certain you will be able to *perform*?" she asked.

Hades reached for the cards, and she moved with him.

"I thought we established I can multitask," he said, his lips and then his teeth brushing her ear. She shivered.

"I'm not sure I like when you multitask," she said.

"Do you find me lacking?" he asked, shuffling the cards in front of her.

"No," she said. "But perhaps it means that I am."

"You severely underestimate your power over me, darling. I am merely determined to do as you have bid."

She turned her head toward Hades's, hooking her hand behind his neck, her mouth opening for him, his tongue crashing against hers, and when they parted,

Persephone looked to find Hades's hands fisted, the cards smashed in his grip.

"You ruined them," she said.

"Fuck the cards, Persephone, and sit on my cock."

She smiled and lifted herself as Hades guided himself to her entrance. They both groaned as she slid down him. Hades's hands smoothed up her body, and he cupped her breasts, squeezing them while brushing kisses across her back. Then he spread her legs wide with his and gripped her waist, bouncing her up and down his length.

"Gods," she whispered, her head rolling back to settle against his shoulder. Hades gripped her jaw and brought their mouths together, kissing her as his hips continued to grind, and his hand moved between her thighs.

She gasped at the feel of him and breathed his name, her body bowing backward as the pleasure swelled, her shoulders pressing into his chest, her body tightening harder as she rose to the tip of his cock and slammed back down.

"Yes, darling. That's it. Come for me," Hades said, his face buried in the crook of her neck. "Fuck!"

She came in waves, each one shuddering through her as Hades's fingers teased her swollen and sensitive clit. She thought she might implode from the bliss.

When he was finished, he held her close, and as the silence descended, so did the darkness.

"I dreamed of bleeding walls," she said, and his jaw tightened. "What does it mean?"

His arms tightened around her as he answered. "It is a warning."

"A warning of what?"

"I don't know," he said and finally met her gaze.

Within his eyes, she saw his dread and felt it in her own heart.

———

When Persephone woke, she thought she saw a crimson haze from the corner of her eye and turned her head with a quick snap only to find the morning sun warming the windows. She took a shuddering breath and tried to calm her racing heart.

"Are you well?" Hades asked.

She turned to look at him, wondering if he noticed her fright. She shifted closer, melting into his warmth. If she could, she would stay here forever, but that was not possible for either of them.

Today, Aphrodite would announce the funeral games, and Persephone would return to work. She, Sybil, and Leuce had been working on a piece for *The Advocate* that would provide a detailed timeline of the atrocities committed by Triad and their Impious followers.

In the face of Theseus's accusations, they hoped it would demonstrate his hypocrisy and undermine his call to cease worshiping the gods.

As much as Persephone believed in this work, in the importance of exposing injustice, she feared retaliation, not against her but against everyone she loved.

Hades had the same fear early in their relationship and now, in the aftermath of Zofie's death and Sybil and Harmonia's kidnapping and torture, she understood his worry in a way she wished she never knew.

"It feels wrong," she said. "To…attempt this *normalcy* when so many are suffering."

Hades's thumb stroked across her upper arm. She

411

focused on the feel of his touch, distracting her from the static anxiety in her chest.

"If we do nothing, we cease to live," Hades said. "And if we cease to live, Theseus wins."

They were harsh words, but she knew they were true.

"Where will you be today?" Even as she asked the question, she wondered if he would tell her the truth or avoid answering altogether.

"I will visit Hephaestus," he said. "We have long planned for the need to arm our followers in battle."

Persephone stiffened at his words.

"What is it?" he asked.

"Nothing," she said, her voice a half whisper, but in truth, it was the first time he had talked about equipping their worshippers for battle. "I just…do not think I imagined that this fight would extend beyond us, beyond the gods."

"Theseus has riled the masses," said Hades. "When we clash, they will too."

"And what about the innocent?" she asked, pulling back to look at him. "The children? Where do they go during this war?"

Hades looked haunted. "I…do not know."

"We must know, Hades," she said. "How can we engage in this horror without a plan to keep them safe?"

He hesitated, and she knew the meaning of his silence. In all the battles he had seen, he had never considered it before. After a moment, he brushed a strand of hair from her face, a gentle move that contrasted starkly with their dark conversation.

"Then we will plan," he said. "And hope Theseus dies before we have to use it."

Persephone waited until Hades left to rise and shower. She could not shake the feeling that something bad was going to happen, which made sense given everything that had occurred in the last few weeks and knowing what they had planned for the funeral games.

Still, this felt different. *She* felt different.

In the time since Theseus had turned her world upside down, she had become someone else, a person she did not recognize—a person she did not know if she even liked.

This person, the one who wore her skin, was a murderer. It did not matter that she had not intended to kill her mother; it had happened, and she could not decide how to live with the shame of it. Even more unnerving though was the anger that burned beneath that despair, poisoning her blood with a need for vengeance, and she did not think she would rest until she bore witness to Theseus's suffering.

Perhaps this is how gods are truly made, she thought.

When she was dressed, she left her room and walked down the hall to the queen's suite to collect Sybil. She and Harmonia were still staying in the Underworld. Persephone did not wish for them to return home, not until everything with Theseus and Triad was settled.

She knocked and waited for Sybil to answer, not expecting that when she did, she would look so stricken.

Persephone's heart fell.

"Sybil, what's wrong?" she asked, taking a step forward. "Is Harmonia okay?"

"Oh, Persephone," Sybil said. Her eyes were red and teary.

"Sybil," Persephone said again. "What is it?"

The oracle turned her tablet around, and her eyes dropped to the screen. A loud ringing filled her ears as she stared at the words screaming back at her:

Goddess of Spring Accused of Matricide: Helios Tells All

CHAPTER XXX
HADES

When Hades arrived at the island of Lemnos, Aphrodite did not greet him as usual, though he was not surprised. She was likely organizing and preparing to announce the funeral games. As much as Hades understood Hephaestus's fear for her, he also felt that the games were the best way to lure Theseus into the open. If they succeeded in killing him there, it could easily be attributed to an accident despite the rules. Theseus might be a demigod, but he was slow to heal, and if he happened to be slain with a weapon of his own creation...well, Nemesis would call that karma.

Hades continued over the bridge that connected Hephaestus and Aphrodite's house to the craftsman's forge deep in the belly of a volcano. The last time Hades had visited, he and the God of Fire had discussed weapons. Specifically, Hades had wanted an arsenal of blades laced with venom from the Hydra and something that could cut through the inescapable nets Theseus had been using to trap and kill gods. He had not expected to find that weapon in the labyrinth in the form of the Nemean lion's claw, but he supposed he could count it as the only good thing to come out of that horrid place.

The problem was he only had one claw, and while there were more in Theseus's maze, they were not worth the terror of retrieving. They would all have to make do with the one.

The steady roar of the ocean brought Hades out of his thoughts. The last time he had been topside, everything had been frozen under layers of ice and snow. Now the sun was out, burning hotly against the bright blue sky. Hades could feel the scorch of Helios's rays. The God of the Sun did not like to be overshadowed or ignored, and the fact that Hades was the reason for the recent snowstorm likely made him even more angry.

Hades wondered if Helios was at all worried about Cronos. He was certain the all-seeing god had witnessed the murder of his mother, and given that he had sided with the Olympians during the Titanomachy, it was likely the God of the Sun was on his father's kill list, and Cronos, with his ability to manipulate and destroy with time, was not a god Helios would see coming.

Hades found reprieve from the heat as he entered Hephaestus's cavernous workshop. It was in its usual state of organized chaos, packed to the brim with inventions and weapons, leaving only the narrowest path through to his forge, which was at the base of a twisting set of stone steps.

As Hades descended, the air grew hotter, warming him from the inside out. When he finally entered the forge, he found Hephaestus standing before a table piled high with swords. He was holding one and polishing the blade, which had a black tint to the usually bright steel.

Hephaestus looked up when Hades entered.

"Have you forgiven me?" Hades asked.

"I will let you know after the games," said Hephaestus.

"Fair enough," said Hades as he approached the table, though as he had said before, they both knew Hephaestus would not let anything happen to Aphrodite.

"Weapons for your mortals," said the god, nodding toward the table and also to his right where there were piles of spears and arrows and buckets full of gleaming bullets.

"All laced with Hydra venom?" Hades asked.

"As you requested."

"As I requested," Hades repeated, though he could not help worrying over arming thousands of mortals with weapons that could wound and kill gods. "Am I making a mistake, Hephaestus?"

"If we cannot have better weapons, then they should at least be equal," said the god.

"Once they are in the world, there is no getting them back," said Hades.

"That is true of many things," said Hephaestus.

"Yes, but few things have such grave consequences," Hades replied.

In the past, he would not have thought long on the implications, but that was before Persephone. Now, all he could think was that the existence of these weapons was a threat to her safety, and he wanted to eliminate it, but he knew that was impossible. Even if they tried to take the weapons out of circulation, they would end up being sold on the black market. The same thing had happened after the Great War, and no matter how hard Hades worked, relics still slipped through his fingers.

"If we cannot take the weapons out of circulation, we will have to find another way to combat their effects," Hephaestus said.

"What do you suggest?"

"For now, I can forge healing arrows from the Golden Fleece," said Hephaestus, which would mean they could easily be used during battle if any of them were injured. "But it is a finite resource. Once it is gone, it is gone."

Finite, Hades thought. He wanted it to be infinite, but he knew that was not possible. The fleece had belonged to Chrysomallos, a winged ram born from the coupling between a mortal woman and Poseidon, and even if they were to attempt to recreate those circumstances—which he never would—it did not mean it would produce another golden ram.

"I have one more request," said Hades. Withdrawing the lion's claw from his pocket, he handed it to the god. "When I was in the labyrinth, I encountered the Nemean lion. Its claws happened to cut through Theseus's net. I was only able to come away with one, however. Can you forge a blade?"

"I can," Hephaestus said. "Perhaps two if I can split it."

"Whatever you can manage," said Hades.

Hephaestus set the claw aside. "Do you wish to see what I have made for your wife?"

"Of course," Hades said.

Hephaestus moved across the room toward a table that was covered with a heavy linen cloth. As he pulled it away, he revealed several weapons—bows and golden-tipped arrows, spears, and a trident—but it was the black armor and gold bident that drew Hades's attention.

The armor was in pieces—a breastplate and armored skirt, engraved with a flourish of gold details the god had likely done by hand. The bident looked as though it had been found in a garden, covered in vines and flowers. It was entirely ornamental.

"Hephaestus," Hades said, taking the bident in hand. It was light despite the added florals, which were mostly clustered at the base of its prongs. "This is…too beautiful to see battle."

"If the funeral games go as planned, then perhaps it never will."

They could only hope.

"Hephaestus!" Aphrodite called.

Her voice echoed with alarm in the cavernous forge, raising the hair on the back of Hades's neck. Her call was followed by a sharp yelp. They both teleported to her instantly, fearing the worst, finding that she had slipped and fallen coming down the steps.

"Hades," Aphrodite said as she tried to rise to her feet. "You must go—"

Her words were cut off by a cry of pain as she put pressure on her foot. She started to collapse, but Hephaestus caught her and lifted her into his arms.

"You must go to Persephone," she said as Hephaestus carried her out of the stairwell into his forge. "Everything is ruined. Our plan for the funeral games, it will not work now!"

"I do not understand," said Hades as Hephaestus set her on one of his tables. Now they could see that her ankle was swollen and bruised. Hephaestus wrapped his hand around it, and Aphrodite moaned as his magic healed.

When he was finished, she took a breath. "I hate being mortal."

"You were saying, Aphrodite?" Hades asked, growing impatient. *What about Persephone?*

"Helios is claiming he witnessed Persephone murder Demeter," said Aphrodite. "It is all anyone can talk about, which means not only will the announcement of the funeral games be overshadowed, but our purpose is meaningless. We can hardly point out that Theseus has murdered gods when Persephone has done the same."

"It is not the same," Hades snapped.

"Do you think the mortal world will care about details? A god killer is a god killer."

Hades did not care what the mortal world thought. He cared about Persephone and how this would affect her.

He glanced to his left where the weapons Hephaestus had made for them gleamed and picked up the trident.

"Hades, what are you going to do?" Aphrodite asked, an element of warning in her voice.

"Kill a god," he answered.

"Do you really think that is the best course of action given everything?"

"Are you really going to ask me that?"

"Do not make it any easier for the world to side with Theseus, Hades," said Aphrodite. "We still need followers. We still need worship."

"*You* need worship. I need nothing beyond the fear of death," he said.

420

"Do not be selfish, Hades. Think. What does killing Helios accomplish?"

"Vengeance," said Hades.

"And what does it accomplish for Persephone? Aside from confirming her guilt?"

Hades glared at her.

He hated that she was right almost as much as he hated Helios.

He pointed the trident at her. "Announce the games, Aphrodite. We will take down Theseus, and then I will make Helios pay for every moment my goddess is in distress."

Then he left in search of Persephone.

———

Hades found Persephone sitting among shoots of asphodel in the field just beyond the castle garden. She was crying, quiet tears streaking down her cheeks. He sat behind her, his chest to her back, his legs framing her body. He wrapped his arms around her and held her tightly, but his presence only seemed to make her cry harder.

He did not know what to do except wait, so that was what he did.

Finally, after some time, she grew quiet in his arms and spoke.

"It is not even fair that I should cry when I have taken a life," she said.

"You did not mean to hurt your mother, Persephone," said Hades.

"I did not *hurt* her," she said. "I *killed* her, and now the whole world knows what I truly am."

"And what is that?" Hades asked.

"A murderer," she said.

"We are all murderers, Persephone. Me, Hecate, Hermes, Apollo."

She did not speak.

"Would it ease you to know that her thread was cut?" he asked. "That the Fates decided it was time for her to go?"

"How do you know?"

Hades laced his fingers through hers and held her arms straight out.

"No threads mark your skin," he said.

She stared at her unmarred skin for a while, as if she expected something to appear any second and prove him wrong. Finally, she let her arms fall and rested her head against his chest.

"Why did they choose her?"

"I cannot speak for them," he said. "But I imagine it has something to do with her desperate attempts to destroy the destiny they have woven for you."

She was quiet for a few long moments, and then she turned to face him, sitting on her knees.

"I have ruined everything," Persephone said.

"You have ruined nothing," he said. "Helios cannot even prove his claim."

"I am not talking about Helios," she said. Her eyes were watering again. "Nothing is the same. Not even us."

Hades's brows lowered. "What do you mean?"

"I can usually lose myself in you," she said. "But I don't think even you can chase away this darkness."

"I'm not trying to chase it away," Hades said. "I just want to help you live with it."

"It has changed me. I am not the same, Hades."

"I do not expect you to be," he said. "But you are not so different that I do not recognize you."

"You say that now," she said. "But there are parts of me that I do not even know. Thoughts I think that are not even mine."

He studied her for a few moments and then brushed a strand of her hair from her face.

"Except they are yours...aren't they? They are just different and darker?"

She started to cry again. "I do not want to be angry," she whispered.

"You do not have to be angry forever," he said. "But it may serve you well right now."

Persephone leaned forward, resting her forehead against Hades's shoulder. He threaded his fingers into her hair and kissed her temple.

"I will love you through this," he whispered. "I will love you beyond this."

And he would murder everyone responsible for her pain.

CHAPTER XXXI
PERSEPHONE

The Stadium of Olympia was monumental. Crafted from marble, it was built between two steep hills, which gave the impression that it was sinking. The tiered seats of the arena were packed, brimming with mortals eager to see the gods and demigods clash. Between Theseus's accusations that a god had kidnapped his wife and child and Aphrodite's accusations that he and his followers were responsible for the deaths of Adonis, Tyche, and Hypnos, these games were no longer about the lives lost, though they never really had been, and Persephone mourned that, especially for Tyche, who deserved to be honored.

Aphrodite's announcement about the games and Helios's claims about Persephone had both drawn nonstop media attention, and the energy of the arena was palpable. Persephone was anxious to expose herself to thousands of people who now saw her as a murderer.

She inched closer to Hades. They were already pressed together, standing on the floor of his golden chariot, waiting in line with other Olympians for the signal to move and enter the arena. They were surrounded by both friends and enemies. Before her was the fiery helm of Ares, behind her the golden helm of Apollo.

She relaxed the moment Hades's palm came to rest low on her stomach and shivered when his lips brushed her ear.

"Do you think I would let anyone harm you?" he asked.

"No," she said, covering his hand with her own. "But I cannot help being afraid."

There was a hostility in the air she had never felt before, and she knew part of it was directed at her.

"You did not have to come," he said.

She turned her head to the side but didn't look at him, keeping her eyes on their surroundings. She could feel Hades's magic blazing around them, an invisible inferno warning away any potential threat, and while that might work on his fellow Olympians, she did not believe for a second it would scare away Theseus or his demigods.

If they were going to demonstrate the power of their weapons, they would do so today at the games, and what better way than to target her? The goddess who had murdered her mother?

"It would be worse if I didn't," she said.

"Worse for who exactly?"

"If I hide from the public, I look guilty," she said.

It did not matter that she *was*.

"Choosing safety is not hiding," Hades replied.

"You said I was safe," she pointed out.

His grip on her tightened. "That is not the point."

"I will not give Theseus the benefit of seeing me

run," she said, though she had to admit, she wasn't sure she was ready to see the demigod again. When she thought about it, her heart felt like it was going to jump out of her chest. "That is what he wants."

"Theseus wants everything," said Hades. "He does not care if you run or not. He can manipulate either choice you make."

Persephone's stomach knotted. "Those are not comforting words, Hades."

"I do not know that I can offer comfort where Theseus is concerned."

"Are you all right, Seph?"

Persephone turned her head to see that Apollo had approached Hades's chariot. He was dressed in a gold breastplate and leather ptergues. She had seen him clad similarly in the past when he trained at the palaestra with Ajax and other heroes.

"I am all right," she said and let her gaze shift past him. "Where is Ajax?"

"He is farther back in line," said Apollo. "He will enter with the other heroes after the demigods."

Persephone shuddered. "I hate that he must walk in the shadow of Theseus."

"I am not keen on the arrangement," he said. "But it is tradition."

Persephone wanted to roll her eyes, but she didn't.

"Will you join the games, Hades?" Apollo asked.

"No," Hades said. "Few wish to battle death."

"I think Theseus and his band of jackasses would like a go," said Apollo.

Persephone frowned. "Are you participating, Apollo?"

"I am," he said. "Single combat."

"As a mortal, right?"

"No," he said. His mouth was tight, as if the suggestion insulted him. "I am a god. I will fight as one."

"But, Apollo—"

"I will be fine, Persephone," said Apollo. "Despite having no powers, I still have my strength. It would be unfair to fight mere mortals."

A shrill whistle sounded, a signal for the gods to ready their chariots.

"Wish me luck?" he asked.

"You always have my luck," said Persephone, but she would also fear for him, not knowing what, if anything, Theseus and his men had planned.

Apollo grinned and sauntered off, returning to his chariot.

"I do not like this," Persephone said as Hades tugged on the reins, urging the chariot forward. "He has no power."

"Apollo does not rely on magic in battle," said Hades. "He will be fine."

She tried to take comfort in his words, but as they entered the vaulted corridor of the stadium, her anxiety only grew worse. The crowd already sounded like a storm, thundering all around them, and they were not even on the arena floor.

She kept her gaze on Ares as he left the shade of the tunnel, the sun glimmering off his golden armor, the plume of red feathers coming out of his helm like fire, spilling down his back. He lifted his spear into the air—the same one he had used to pin Hades to the ground.

As the God of War guided his chariot, he glanced back at her, a cynical smile on his face.

And suddenly it was their turn.

It was so bright, Persephone could barely keep her eyes open as they emerged from the shadow. It seemed to her that the sun was brighter and hotter in the aftermath of her mother's storm. Even now, she could feel its rays burning her skin. She blinked, eyes watering, as she brought her hand up to shield her face, emerging to a chorus of noise.

She could not distinguish the sounds—if they were cheers or jeers—but it did not really matter because she could feel the hostility in the air. Eventually, as her vision adjusted, she could see it in the angry, red-faced mortals shouting from the stands, their fingers curled into shaking fists, and while there were some who declared their love, the hate seemed far louder. Though as Hades followed the line of chariots to the footpath surrounding the dusty floor of the stadium, the crowd quieted.

Persephone glanced back at her husband. "What are you doing?" she asked.

"Putting the fear of death within them," he said.

"I do not want their devotion to be born out of fear," said Persephone.

Hades said nothing, but she did not need his words. Mostly she was just expressing her own fear—that she would never regain the trust of the mortal world.

Hades brought the chariot to a stop, and Persephone let her hands relax, realizing how hard she had been gripping its edge as she stretched her fingers. Hades took a step back, allowing her the space to turn and face him. He took her hands in his and kissed them, threads of healing warmth easing the ache.

She was not sure why she blushed. She was used to Hades performing far more lascivious acts, but there was something about the quiet brush of his lips she could feel deep in her gut.

He offered a small smile, as if he could sense the fire he had lit within her, and took a step down from the chariot.

"Let me help you," he said, looking up at her. His hands were already on her waist, his face level with her breasts, which he made sure to brush with his chin.

"You know I will not deny you," she said.

He lifted her, and when he set her down, he let her slide down his body. She felt every hard inch of him. She flushed again, holding his gaze.

"I know what you are doing," she said.

"And what is that?" he asked.

"You are hoping I will be aroused by your touch and ask to leave," she said.

"And are you?" he asked. "Aroused?"

She narrowed her eyes. "I am not leaving, Hades," she said.

"We do not have to leave," he said. "I can fuck you anywhere."

"You two are so gross," said Hermes as he sauntered by, dressed in gold armor and wearing a gold circlet with wings.

"What's wrong, Hermes?" said Hades. "Do you want me to fuck you too?"

The God of Trickery stumbled going up the steps and into the stands. Hades chuckled, but his amusement faded when his gaze returned to Persephone.

"That was unkind," she said.

"So were his words," said Hades.

"He was joking."

Hades snickered. "So was I."

She rolled her eyes and moved past him, following the gods into the stadium. Hades remained close, a physical shadow. They passed the first row of gods where Aphrodite and Hephaestus sat beside Apollo and Artemis. She had expected the goddess's disdain, as none of their previous interactions had gone well, and according to Aphrodite, Artemis had accepted Zeus's call to bring Persephone to him in chains, all for a title and shield, though it did not seem that she had attempted her mission. Persephone wondered if Apollo had something to do with that.

She held Artemis's gaze as she passed, sliding into the second row. With dread, Persephone realized she was seated in front of Hera, who sat in one of two throne-like seats, obviously intended for the King and Queen of the Gods, though the God of the Sky was noticeably absent.

Persephone wondered if all the gods knew what had befallen Zeus. Did they feel like the rest of them? Conflicted?

Hera was already seated, her shrewd gaze fixed on Persephone. She stared back and offered a single nod.

"You know this area is reserved for Olympians only," said Ares.

"How do you become an Olympian, Ares?" Persephone asked. "Is it when you defeat one in battle?"

Hermes put his hands to his mouth and shouted, "Burn!"

"She didn't burn me, you imbecile!" Ares snapped.

"I didn't mean literally," said Hermes. "Who's the imbecile now?"

Hades placed a hand on Persephone's shoulder and slid past her to sit on her left, between her and Ares. Thankfully, Hermes sat on her right. She leaned over, whispering, "How are Olympians chosen?"

She did not know, because since the gods had won the Titanomachy, the Olympians had never changed—never died.

"Well, first, one of us would have to die," he said. "And then I suppose Zeus would choose."

Persephone glanced over her shoulder to where Hera loomed behind her. "And if Zeus cannot?"

"Then the responsibility would fall to Hera," he said. "But that has never happened."

The way Hermes spoke, it almost sounded like he believed the twelve would never die, even Zeus who apparently hung in the sky, though as she glanced up, all she could see was a thick, bright haze.

Suddenly, the crowd's roar drew her attention back to the entrance where the demigods were now filing into the stadium. Persephone's heart felt like it was pounding throughout her whole body. She held her breath, waiting to catch sight of Theseus, hoping she would be able to control her reaction to the demigod who had stolen her peace, but she couldn't.

He led the group, flanked by a pair of demigods on either side. His eyes were bright, familiar even from a distance. He kept a wide smile on his face—charming, mortals would likely call it—and waved to the crowd.

Hermes leaned over. "He doesn't look too upset about his wife and baby."

Persephone's stomach knotted, and a flood of emotion racked her body—hatred so visceral, her eyes stung with tears, but there was also fear. It trembled within her, shaking her to her core. She squeezed her hands into fists to hide it.

Then Hades's hand covered hers, and slowly, the panic began to ebb.

Her gaze shifted to the others who marched beside-Theseus. She only recognized Sandros.

"Who are the others?" Persephone asked.

She watched Hades's face as he spoke, his hatred of them evident.

"The two on his left are Kai and Sandros. The two on his right are Damian and Machaon. He calls them high lords."

"High lords. That's the title given to leaders within the organization of Triad, right?" Persephone asked.

"Yes," said Hades. "It means nothing save that it provides us with a list of who to target first."

Persephone studied each one, able to identify their parentage from a distance. Kai looked like Theseus, which meant he was a descendant of Poseidon. Sandros had Zeus's striking eyes.

"Is...Machaon...Apollo's son?"

Hermes snorted. "Not a son but a grandson."

"And the one you called Damian?"

"He is the son of Thetis, a water goddess."

She continued to watch them, able to identify members of Triad by a triangle pin they wore that caught the light as they moved.

"Those are new," said Persephone, concerned. Before, members of Triad were far more discreet, which made sense, given that their agenda was mainly against the gods. Wearing such a symbol communicated an element of pride in their rebellion.

Hades said nothing, but his frown deepened.

Persephone sat up a little straighter when the heroes were announced and Ajax walked onto the field. He was hard to miss with his dark hair and large frame. She and Apollo both stood, twisting their hands in the air at the wrists—which was the sign for applause.

Ajax grinned and waved back.

Persephone recognized other heroes from the Panhellenic Games, including Hector, Anastasia, and Cynisca—all loyal to the gods because they had been chosen by the gods.

The heroes were followed by the mortal competitors, and once they were all positioned on the field, Aphrodite rose and approached a podium located a few feet away from where the gods had assembled.

She looked beautiful, dressed in white and pearls, though the sun beat down on her, igniting her like a flame. Her gaze seemed to linger on Hephaestus. Persephone glanced at him and saw that he was gripping the arms of his stone chair. It made the veins and muscles in his arms bulge.

"For centuries, our people have honored the dead through sport. Today, we carry on that tradition by celebrating the lives of Adonis, my favored, Tyche, the Goddess of Fortune, Hypnos, the God of Sleep, and the one hundred and thirty lives lost during the attack by Triad on Talaria Stadium."

A tense silence followed.

Aphrodite's commentary on the Talaria Stadium

attack was a painful reminder for many, including Persephone, who had not only witnessed the explosion that took so many lives but also fought to protect other innocent people. In the process, she had been shot, and while she had successfully healed herself, she would never forget the pain of the blast or the way Hades had reacted.

It was in those moments that she saw his true darkness.

But Triad could not deny the attack, because they had taken credit for it, defaulting to their usual argument: Where are your gods now? The argument was an excuse for violence and ignored the fact that the gods *had* been there, and they had fought—hard—but to no avail.

"Today we honor those whose lives were cut short by Triad, whose volatile actions only prove they have the freedom and free will they so often demand."

Her words were met with guttural boos and angry shouts.

"It is evident to me that fairness has escaped you," she continued, her voice rising above the noise. "For if such a thing existed, none who had a hand in these deaths would breathe the free air."

Persephone shivered, and Hades's hand squeezed hers.

Despite Aphrodite's words pointing out the hypocrisy of Triad, Persephone knew it was not enough to win back favor from mortals because the gods were no better. She was no better, though she had started her career pointing out similar hypocrisies; except then, no one had cared, not until Theseus had established himself as a viable leader.

And while Persephone could acknowledge that the

Olympians were not the best, they were the lesser of two evils.

"Let the games begin," Aphrodite said.

A horn sounded, marking the start of the games.

Aphrodite returned to her seat, and the competitors cleared the field.

"What is the first competition?" Persephone asked.

"Wrestling," said Hermes, rubbing his hands together.

She raised a brow. "Really?"

"What?" Hermes asked. "I like the outfits."

"They're naked, Hermes."

He grinned. "Exactly."

She was about to roll her eyes when someone shouted from the stands, "Death to all gods!"

It was not the first time Persephone had heard the chant, but it still made her blood run cold.

When no one joined, the heckler tried again.

"Death to all gods!"

Persephone's fists clenched. Hades rubbed his thumb over hers to ease her frustration, but it didn't work. She started to stand but was surprised when Hera rose to her feet and faced the mortal.

"Do you think you are funny, mortal?" she asked.

Her question was met with silence.

"I know you speak," she said.

Then the mortal began to scream, and so did those around him.

"She has turned his tongue into a snake!"

The screams of the man grew louder as he ran past the gods, tripping and falling to the ground. After that, he did not move. A man dressed in a vibrant vest ran to him and dragged him off the field.

435

"That was not well done, Hera," Hades commented without looking at the goddess.

"I'm not on your side, Hades," she replied.

The tension following Hera's words was unbearable. Persephone thought it might dissipate once the wrestling began and she could focus on naked men grappling in the dirt, but it remained heavy in the air.

She only noticed her leg bouncing when Hades reached over and squeezed her thigh.

She stopped and looked at him.

"I will keep you safe," he reminded her.

Beside her, Hermes's body seemed to convulse.

"What was that?" Persephone asked.

"It was a shiver, Persephone. *A shiver*," he said.

"Why?"

"You mean you don't shiver when Hades says things like that?"

As if to emphasize his point, he shuddered again.

She did, but she wasn't interested in saying that here.

"Why don't you date, Hermes?"

"I date," he said. "Just not…exclusively. I like a…a smattering of flavors."

Persephone scrunched her nose at his choice of words. "Flavors?"

"Yeah," he said. "Sometimes I like dick. Sometimes I just want tacos."

"Hermes," she said, a little confused. "Do you mean actual tacos or…"

"Of course I mean actual tacos. What other kinds of tacos are there?"

Persephone opened her mouth to answer, but then closed it and shook her head. "Never mind. I'm glad you like tacos."

She turned her attention back to the wrestling match. She was not surprised to see that Ajax and Hector were among the last on the field. The two were rivals, though Persephone was not certain if it stemmed from Apollo's attention or something else.

Whatever the case, the God of Music had made it worse with his indecisiveness, and though he had eventually chosen Ajax, the rivalry remained, as was evident by the way the two fought—brutally.

As Persephone watched, dread pooled low in her stomach. She looked at Apollo, who sat forward in his seat, eyes following their every move.

Suddenly, Hector rammed into Ajax and flipped him onto his back, slamming into him with such force, a crack echoed throughout the stadium.

When Hector got to his feet, Ajax did not move.

"No," Apollo said as he shot across the field, but Machaon had reached him first.

"What is he doing?" Persephone asked.

"Performing," said Hades as the demigod placed his hands on Ajax.

After a few seconds, the hero's eyes opened, and he was able to sit up.

The crowd roared with praise.

"A god could have done the same thing," said Persephone.

"They could," said Hades. "That is the point."

Persephone looked at Hades as understanding dawned. The demigods wanted to show that their powers were no different from those of the Olympians.

"I'm beginning to think giving Theseus any kind of platform was a mistake," said Persephone.

437

"I suppose we will find out."

Once Ajax was on his feet, Hector was declared the winner. They were led off the field, but Apollo did not return to his seat. He remained at Ajax's side, his anger apparent. She wondered if he would try to fight Hector. He had been eager for combat, and now he had a target.

The next game was announced: the footrace.

Persephone looked at Hermes. "Aren't you fast?"

"I can be," he said, and then he wiggled his brows. "But I can also go slow if you know what I mean."

"Do you have to be like this?" Persephone asked.

"I ask myself that question all the time," said Hades.

"Seriously?" said Hermes. "No one likes me for me!"

"My point is," Persephone said, refusing to go down that road, "I thought you loved wrestling and racing. Why aren't you competing? Are you afraid you'll get beaten by a demigod?"

Hermes sputtered. "Excuse you! I don't get beaten."

"Obviously not, because you don't compete."

Hermes's face flushed red. She wanted to laugh, but she also wanted him to take her seriously.

"You know what, Sephy? Fine. I'll show you."

He rose to his feet and cast off his robes. They landed over her head but slipped away, too silky to stay. She caught the God of Mischief running to the starting line in a pair of tiny shorts.

When she looked at Hades, she found that he was staring back, a brow raised.

"What?" she asked.

"Nothing," he said. "I'm just wondering what you are doing."

"We can't let the demigods win a second time, and

Hermes is the only god who can beat them in a footrace even without magic."

His lips twitched. "You do know the prizes for winning funeral games are boring?"

"It isn't about the prizes," she said. "It is about winning."

Hades chuckled, and she was so distracted, she jumped at the sound of the horn blaring, signaling the start of the race.

Persephone whirled and cupped her hands around her mouth.

"Go, Hermes! Go!"

But the god was *going*.

He made running look effortless. It was like he was soaring over the track, his feet barely touching as he remained one step ahead of the rest of the competitors.

As they came to the end of the first lap, Persephone looked at Hades.

"How many times do they have to go around?"

"Four," he said.

Four? Her chest hurt just thinking about it, but Hermes made it look *easy*.

It wasn't until the final lap that he even seemed to break a sweat, and as he neared the finish line, her excitement rose.

"Yes! Come on, Hermes!" she cheered, bouncing on her feet.

She had never seen the god so focused before. His brows were pinched, and his mouth was pressed thin. It would be an easy win. Only one came close to matching his stride, and that was Machaon.

Still, he could not—*would not*—overtake Hermes.

But then, the god stumbled, and as he struck the ground, the other runners surged past, leaving him in a trail of their dust.

Persephone's excitement burst, and a strange numbness spread throughout her body. She stared at Hermes and then at Hades, her mouth ajar.

Beside him, Ares laughed. "You should see your face, flower goddess. You would think they slaughtered a lamb, though I suppose Hermes is a close second."

She clenched her teeth, anger making her eyes water. "Machaon cheated!"

"Nobody cares," said Ares, resting his cheek on his closed fist as if he were bored. "These are funeral games. They are for no one but the dead."

"Shut up," she snapped.

It was a childish comeback, but she did not know what else to say. She turned her attention to Hermes, who now limped across the finish line. She started to go to him, but Hades held her firmly by the wrist.

"Do not go beyond my reach," he said.

She considered breaking free of him, but she had learned there was a reason for Hades's warnings, so she waited for Hermes to return to his seat. He did not look at her as he made his way up the steps, his ankle and elbow bruised and swollen. Guilt lanced through her chest.

"Hermes," she said, reaching for his hand, but he pulled away. "I am so sorry. I—"

"I don't want to talk about it, Persephone," he said, not meeting her gaze.

"At least…at least let me heal you."

"I don't need your help," he said.

Persephone took a juddering breath. She wanted to cry. She could feel it building in the back of her throat and tingling in her nose.

"Do you want to go?" Hades asked.

She didn't want to look at him, because she knew if she did, she would likely burst into tears, but she was saved from it when the next game was announced.

Single combat.

Apollo.

"Please," Persephone whispered.

Artemis scoffed and glanced back at Persephone. "You do not have to worry about my brother. No one is better than him, especially at single combat."

But this was not about the best, or Ajax and Hermes would have won.

As the competitors began, Persephone's stomach churned, though true to Artemis's words, Apollo shone. Despite not having his magic, his strength was evident. Each thrust of his spear landed with precision, and the power behind it had his opponents sliding back on their feet. His skill was evident, honed over thousands of years, and the only one who rivaled him was Theseus, who fought with a grace she had not seen among anyone but the Olympians.

She was not surprised when they stood opposite each other for the final fight, but she had never been so afraid. The churning in her stomach grew violent, the feeling rising into her throat. She held her breath until the first jab was thrown by Apollo, striking Theseus's shield. The second was made lower, a stab at his legs, but again, it glanced off his shield.

Persephone glanced at Artemis, who sat rigidly in

her seat, hands fisted. As much as she believed in her brother, this clearly made her anxious.

While Apollo fought fiercely, with skill and determination, Theseus fought with anger and hate. It fueled his strikes, and each one seemed to hit harder than the last until Apollo brought his shield down on Theseus's spear.

It shattered beneath the blow.

Hope rose, and Persephone sat straighter.

Then Theseus drew a sword.

Apollo cast his spear aside and drew his own blade.

"Why would he do that?" Persephone asked, frustrated.

"The sword is a better choice for this fight," said Hades.

She glanced at him, finding that he too had shifted forward in his seat, which did nothing to ease her worry. Nor did the ensuing battle, which was fought just as fiercely. Each clash of blade against blade, blade against shield, shield against shield, set Persephone more and more on edge.

"How can they be so equally matched?" Persephone asked.

"They aren't," Artemis snapped.

Persephone could not fault her for her frustration. She felt it too.

Her spirit rose when Apollo landed a blow to the front of Theseus's leather armor but quickly fell when the demigod was able to trap Apollo's arm, cutting him deeply.

"No," Persephone breathed. She was almost out of her chair, held there only because she did not think she could stand, she shook so badly at the sight of Apollo's blood spilling to the ground. He dropped his shield and tried to bring up his sword, but Theseus blocked the blow and brought his own blade down on Apollo's helm.

His blade shattered.

But then Theseus gripped Apollo's helm and dragged his head down, slamming his knee into his face. Apollo fell to his hands and knees, more blood dripping from his nose and mouth. Theseus shoved his foot into his side and pushed him onto his back.

Artemis rose to her feet.

"Don't let him win, Apollo!" she shouted, but her words were lost over the roar of the crowd.

"He's not moving," Persephone said. "Why isn't he moving?"

Then there was a flash of light as Theseus reached toward the sky, calling to Zeus's lightning bolt. But something was happening. The clouds had parted, and there in the sky hung Zeus for all to see.

Silence descended, and Theseus's gaze swept the crowd.

"Now look upon your gods," he said. "And know they are mortal."

Zeus's lightning bolt flashed as Theseus brought it down on Apollo. Persephone screamed, and so did Artemis. They shot from their seats, racing to the god—their friend and brother—as his body convulsed beneath the current.

At the same time, there were several loud booms—like a hundred explosions had just gone off—and at first the ground trembled, but then it seemed to roll beneath them, shaking violently.

Persephone teleported, and Artemis followed.

By the time they reached him, Theseus was gone, and Apollo lay on the ground, burned beyond recognition. Artemis fell to her knees, hands hovering over Apollo as if she were too afraid to touch him.

"Heal!" she screamed, the word drawn out and guttural. "Heal!"

Persephone felt dizzy, and just as she thought she would collapse, Hades's magic consumed them. Suddenly, they were in the Underworld, and someone was shouting for the Golden Fleece. It was a few moments before Persephone realized it was her.

"It's too late, Persephone," Hades said.

"It's not too late," she said, shoving him away. "Get the fleece!"

"Persephone," Hades said again, reaching for her.

"Why isn't anyone getting the fleece?" she screamed, whirling to find everyone—Aphrodite and Hephaestus, Hermes and Hecate, Sybil and Harmonia. Then her eyes dropped to Artemis, who had managed to lay Apollo's head in her lap, and it was then that she understood what Hades was saying.

She went to her knees.

Apollo was dead.

Part III

"For no god may undo what another god has done."
—OVID, *METAMORPHOSES*

CHAPTER XXXII
THESEUS

Theseus stood on the porch of his mother's home, the House of Aethra, which overlooked the entirety of New Athens.

Parts of the city were in ruin.

The Acropolis, once the tallest building in New Athens, an icon of the city, was no more, toppled by his father's earthquake. Its collapse was perhaps the greatest symbol of his triumph, but it was marred by the presence of Hades's abhorrent club. He had hoped it would fall during the earthquake like Alexandria Tower, but it had not even cracked.

Seeing it made him angry, and for a moment, he almost forgot that he should be celebrating today's success. Nevernight might be a stain on his city, but it would soon be eliminated.

Everything will come in time, he assured himself.

What was it mortals said? Sometimes things had to break to be rebuilt?

And he was just getting started.

Tomorrow, when morning came, he would purge the city. He would drag every priest and priestess from their temples and slaughter them in the streets. What was not destroyed by earthquake or flood—every business and building, every sacred garden and grove—would go up in flame.

He would destroy every holy place until no sign of the Olympians remained.

Until then, the city slept, oblivious to the horror that would befall them tomorrow—the horror that would begin tonight.

"All communications are down," said Helen. "How do you expect me to share your accomplishments beyond New Athens?"

"Do you not trust me to give you what you need, Helen?"

He looked at her, but she said nothing.

"From this day forward, you are responsible for how the world will see my creation. It will be you who shares the beauty and prosperity of New Athens under my rule. Your words will bring people from all over New Greece to witness the paradise I have created. It is you who will ensure I am worshipped."

"You have put a lot of faith in my words," she said.

"I have faith in them because they will not be yours," he said. "They will be mine."

Her mouth tightened. "Then you do not need me," she said.

"Every god needs a mouthpiece," he said.

He sensed that she stiffened, but he was not sure if it was from his comment or the fact that the dust had begun to stir, swirling until it took the form of a god. He was tall and broad, exceeding Theseus in size and height. He wore nothing save sheepskin around his waist. He had chosen to look neither young nor old, but he could not hide the depth of his ancient eyes, which carried a madness only present within those who had lived a long, terrible life.

"So you are the son of my son," said Cronos.

"Your grandson," said Theseus.

The Titan tilted his head, and there was a gleam in his eyes that Theseus had sometimes seen in his father's, a menacing amusement. "Do you think the blood of my blood means anything to me?"

"It was you who brought up my parentage," said Theseus.

It did not matter to him who Cronos was—grandfather or not, god or not. He only cared that he agreed to aid him in his battle to conquer the whole of New Greece.

A smile cracked across the god's face. "A wise one," he said. "You must take after your father."

"You did not know my mother," said Theseus.

Silence followed, a heavy and solid thing. Theseus had a feeling Cronos wanted him to shudder, to show some sign that his presence unnerved him, but he didn't.

Cronos's stare was steady.

"What do you want, blood of my blood?" he asked.

"An alliance," said Theseus. "Your power over time."

"And what would you do with my power over time?"

"I will end this world and begin again," he said.

Rebuild what was broken.

He would bring about his dream of a golden age,

and he would begin it in New Athens, and when word spread of its beauty and property and the fairness of its ruler, people would fall to their knees to worship him.

"If I destroy the world, you cease to be. Only gods endure."

"I am the blood of your blood," said Theseus. "I will endure."

The corner of Cronos's mouth tipped upward, but Theseus did not know if he was amused or impressed. What he didn't like was the doubt blooming in his chest.

"I do not need an alliance with you," said Cronos. "So what are you offering that might entice me?"

"I will give you worship," said Theseus.

"Mortals dread the passing of time like they dread the coming of death. I do not need worship."

Theseus had suspected as much. He tilted his head back just a little.

"A sacrifice then," he said, and from the dark doorway behind him, two of his men emerged with Hera.

"Release me at once!" she demanded, unable to hide the alarm in her voice. She might have fought, but she was draped in the thin veil of a net and had no ability to resist. They left her on her knees between him and Cronos.

"How dare—" she began, but her words were cut short when she looked up into Cronos's eyes. "Father," she whispered on a shuddering breath.

Theseus had never heard her take this tone before. It was almost meek. He found it revolting.

Cronos stared back, not a hint of feeling in his face.

"On your feet, Daughter. Are you not queen of

this world?" He reached for her and drew her up by her shoulders as if she were nothing more than a doll.

"Do not touch me!" she scowled. If she had the ability to move, Theseus imagined she would have jerked away from him. Instead, her eyes flashed with a familiar fury.

Cronos chuckled, a gravelly, unsettling sound. "A queen indeed," he said. "Demanding, even with no real power."

Theseus lifted the scythe he had been holding, letting the blade rest in his palm.

Cronos eyed it but did not take it.

"How dare you," Hera hissed, her eyes narrowed at Theseus in visceral hate. "You would be nothing without me!"

"Do not take this to mean I am ungrateful," said Theseus.

Cronos stared at Theseus. "You have given me a gift, blood of my blood," he said. "I will choose to see this as a favor and grant you one in return."

Theseus's jaw clenched. It was not an alliance like he wanted, but for now, it would suffice.

The Titan took the scythe and gazed at Hera.

The goddess, who was usually cloaked in a facade of cold grace, looked stricken, her eyes wide and haunted. "Father," she said again, her voice trembling.

Cronos's lip curled. "All things end, Daughter," he said, but instead of using his weapon, he took her by the throat and lifted her off her feet.

His hand spanned the entire circumference of her neck, and because she was draped in the net, she did not even fight. She just hung there, choking until she was silent. It was then he plunged the curved blade of his scythe into her.

Behind Theseus, Helen gasped, but Hera—she did not react.

She was already dead.

Cronos jerked the blade free and let her crumple to the ground before turning to Theseus.

"Until next time, blood of my blood," he said with a nod, his blade dripping with Hera's blood.

Then he vanished.

Theseus stared at the space where the Titan had been, his jaw tense. Their first interaction had not gone according to plan, but a favor was a favor. He would just have to ensure that by the time he collected it, Cronos had a reason to join his side.

Theseus caught movement from the corner of his eye, but when he turned, he found that it was only Hera's dark blood pooling on the stone.

His gaze shifted to the two waiting demigods. One was Damian, and the other was a new recruit named Markos.

"Have you recovered my son?" Theseus asked.

"He waits for you inside along with his mother," said Damian.

There was a pause.

"And Ariadne?" Her name felt thick on his tongue.

"She waits for you as well."

Theseus tried to control his reaction to the news, but a warm heat had already ignited low in his belly.

When his father's earthquake had ravaged New Athens and the resulting tsunami had cut it loose from the continent, Dionysus's tunnels had flooded too.

Flushing out the vermin, he'd thought. A much-needed cleanse of the world.

Though a few maenads had managed to escape drowning in the tunnels, they found themselves at the mercy of demigods who had been ordered to slaughter them on sight. He had only ordered that three mortals be left alive—his son, his wife, and her sister.

He let his gaze fall to Hera, whose skin looked gray in the moonlight.

"Cut her into pieces," Theseus ordered. "Tomorrow, we will feed her flesh to her followers."

They each gave a curt nod, and he moved past them into the house. As soon as he entered the doors, he could hear his son wailing from somewhere in the house. The sound was grating and made his skin crawl.

"Someone do something about that child," Theseus snapped.

"You could go to him," said Helen. "You have yet to meet him."

"I have other engagements," he said.

"You mean Ariadne?" Helen asked.

"Do not get jealous, Helen. It is not becoming."

"I am not jealous," she said. "I am disgusted that you would choose a woman over your son."

"Master," said one of his servants, sweeping down the hall to meet them. "May I take your coat?"

He said nothing, but he slipped out of his jacket and handed it to the old woman. Helen did the same.

"Do you require anything? Dinner? Perhaps some tea?"

Helen started to speak, but Theseus cut her off. "No."

The woman smiled. "Of course. Good night." She whirled and disappeared down the hall.

Helen turned to him. He thought that she intended to berate him, but the words never left her mouth as his hand closed around her neck. He pushed her into the wall, lifting her off her feet. Her fingers clawed at his hands and chest. She even tried to gouge his eyes, but he felt none of it.

"You live and breathe by my command," he said. "Remember that when you decide to have an opinion."

He released her, and she fell to the floor. As she gasped for breath, he straightened his collar and the cuffs of his sleeves and left for his chambers.

For the briefest moment, while he had held Helen's life in his hands, he had not been able to hear his son, but now, the sound of his wailing had returned. He thought that it was louder, or perhaps he was just nearing it. Either way, by the time he came to his chambers, every muscle in his body was on edge, wound tight with anger, and while he did not mind anger, it did nothing to encourage the swelling of his cock.

He took a few deep breaths and managed to ease the set of his jaw before he opened the doors to his room to find Ariadne.

She was seated in a chair, her arms and legs bound, her mouth gagged. Other than the restraints, she was in pristine condition. Not a single scratch or drop of blood marred her skin.

When her eyes lifted to his, they were full of hatred and fear, and he smiled, closing the door behind him.

"I have thought about this moment often," he said. "It is exactly as I imagined."

As he moved toward her, she slid her feet against the floor and her body into the back of the chair.

He chuckled at her attempted retreat.

When he was close, he withdrew a knife and cut the gag from her mouth, slicing her cheek, though to his disappointment, Ariadne did not react. Instead, she glared at him and spit in his face.

Still, he laughed—and he had every reason to. She had nowhere to go. She was his to control, his to punish.

He gripped her face, his fingers pressing into the bloody wound on her cheek. Her pained yelp sent a thrill straight to his cock.

He held her harder. "You know how I like a good fight."

"Where is my sister, you bastard?"

He studied her. It wasn't the name-calling that angered him but the worry over her sister.

"You should be far more concerned about what I have planned for you," he said.

"You think I'm afraid of you?" she asked.

"You will be," he said. "Until then, remember that you are afraid of what I can do to your sister."

He pressed his mouth to hers, his fingers digging so hard into her skin, he felt as though he were holding her skull, but then her teeth sank into his lip, and he pushed her away, her chair tilting back until she crashed to the floor.

"You keep fighting like you think it will deter me," he said, standing over her. "But really, it just makes me want to fuck you."

He bent and cut the ties that held her to the chair. Her arms and legs were still bound, but she managed to resist, thrashing about. Finally, he managed to throw her over his shoulder and carry her to his bed.

"No, please," she said, her voice rising with hysteria. The sound made him want to groan, his cock throbbing with pleasure.

"And now she begs," he said as he straddled her, forcing her hands over her head, hooking her bindings to an anchor in the wall.

"Don't," she breathed. "Don't."

He paused as she begged, his face inches from hers.

"You could have had a day to adjust," he said. "But you chose this."

His words made her fight harder. She jerked beneath him, trying to throw him off, but her efforts were useless. He shifted down until he came to her legs, keeping them bound until he had one secured and then restrained the other.

With her secured and spread before him, he cut away her clothes, and while she cried beneath him, he devoured her body.

———

When Theseus left Ariadne an hour later, he discovered his son was still crying. The sound had a visceral effect on his body, both because of its keen pitch but also because his wife had failed to subdue him.

All the tension he had managed to release on Ariadne suddenly came back. In a rush of anger, he made his way to Phaedra's quarters, which were down the hall from his own.

"Phaedra!" he shouted. "Shut him up. Do you hear me? Shut him up!"

When he reached the door, he found it was locked.

"Unlock the fucking door!"

He could feel his face burn as he yelled, and still his son cried.

"You bitch," he said as he stepped back, kicking in the door—and froze.

He had expected to find Phaedra attempting to console Acamas. Instead, he found her sitting slumped on the floor at the end of her four-poster bed, a sheet wrapped tightly around her neck.

She was dead.

CHAPTER XXXIII
DIONYSUS

Dionysus woke to a burn in his shoulder. He groaned, shifting to relieve the pain, and opened his eyes to see bright blue sky overhead. For a brief moment, he struggled to remember where he was, but the sound of a voice—though unfamiliar—reminded him.

"His highness awakes!" A rugged face appeared over him as he was hauled into a sitting position.

He was on a ship, his hands tied behind his back and his feet bound. Several strangers stared back at him, but they all had one thing in common—a tattoo of a dolphin on their forearm, branding them as Tyrrhenian pirates.

The pirate behind him grabbed a handful of his hair. "His head will fetch a pretty price!" he said. "Look! He wears gold in his braids!"

"There's nothing pretty about it," said another pirate.

Dionysus remained silent, assessing the crew. There were about fifteen on the deck, and there would be even more below deck. They carried a variety of weapons but mostly guns. The bullets could not wound him—unless of course they had somehow gotten their hands on Hydra venom.

He shuddered at the thought of feeling that kind of pain again.

When Dionysus looked to his left, he noticed that he was not alone. Another prisoner sat beside him, similarly restrained, though her mouth was gagged.

He knew who she was immediately, though he had never actually seen her before. Her beauty was enough to speak for itself.

Medusa.

"You should thank us," said another pirate. "She bites."

"Is that why she has a black eye?" Dionysus asked.

"Bitch deserved it," said one.

"I suppose that depends on why she decided to bite you," said Dionysus. "And given that she has been kidnapped, I imagine she had reason."

The pirate offered a humorless chuckle.

"You seem to know a lot, prince. Did you intend to be a hero? Because if so, I will warn you, it won't end well for you."

"Bold of you to think you can fight me."

"Well, you are the one in chains."

There was a beat of silence, and then one of the pirates nodded toward him.

"The man is a god."

A few of the men laughed. "What kind of god gets captured so easily?"

The kind that listened to their oracle.

Dionysus had not decided if he regretted that decision yet.

In truth, he could free himself from these bindings easily, but he had to think about Medusa before he made a move to escape. One of the challenges was that they were in the middle of the ocean. If they were going to run, he'd prefer to be within view of land.

"When we found him, he wore Hermes's sandals," the pirate explained. "What kind of mortal wears Hermes's sandals?"

"A favored one," said the pirate. He turned to look at Dionysus. "Are you favored, prince?"

"If I was favored, I would not be here," said Dionysus.

"See, Leo? Even the prince agrees."

Again, Dionysus glanced at Medusa. He had expected to see a thin and frail woman, someone whose traumas would make her meek and afraid, but instead she looked fierce and determined. He got the impression that if he had not arrived, she would have escaped on her own.

Dionysus waited until the pirates seemed distracted before turning to whisper to Medusa.

"Can you swim?" Dionysus asked.

She stared at him, her strange eyes assessing. They were like yellow starbursts—both beautiful and unnerving. She did not trust him, but he did not blame her.

Finally, she nodded.

"Good," he said.

He was quiet after that, waiting. He listened to the pirates' conversations and learned that they were crossing into the Aegean. Dionysus felt a little relief at that news, though he wondered why, and if they were heading to New Athens specifically to trade Medusa to Theseus. While it would be nice to have the pirates take him right to the shores of his home, facing him and his demigods would not.

As the sun set, Dionysus noticed clouds gathering on the horizon, and it wasn't long before it was dark, and the sky was filled with lightning.

Dread filled his stomach. This was not a normal storm.

"Those clouds came up quick," said one of the pirates, a note of fear in his voice. Normally, a seafarer would try to outrun a storm, but there were some—those that were divine in nature—that were impossible to outrun, and this one was supernatural. It meant they had caught the attention of some kind of sea deity. Dionysus just hoped it wasn't Poseidon.

When the ship began to rock and the waves grew tall, to the point that the water came up over the rails, he knew it was time to move.

A flood of crewmen were suddenly on deck, racing to bring the sails down, secure hatches, and stow loose goods.

Then it started to rain. It came down in a sheet, almost as though someone were dumping a continuous stream of water into the ocean. It was so thick, Dionysus could barely see. The only thing that helped was the lightning, which cracked across the sky, almost like frost on glass. It was beautiful but also terrifying.

"I told you!" Leo said. "I told you he was a god!"

"You're a fucking idiot, Leo!" another pirate called.

But Leo was the only one who wasn't an idiot.

"We are moving fast," one of the pirates cried. "It's almost like this storm is dragging us to the coastline!"

A few heads turned toward Dionysus, suspicious.

"Unless the water is wine, it's not me," he said, but he decided it was time to make their escape. As much as he wanted to be on land, he did not want to be on this ship when it crashed.

Normally, while he was in Poseidon's territory, he would not dare use his magic, because he did not wish to draw his attention, but if the storm was the work of the God of the Sea, then it was already too late. So he turned his bindings into vines, breaking them with ease. He did the same with the ones around his legs. When he looked at Medusa, he nodded to her wrists, and the ropes turned to vines. She tore them easily and then ripped the gag from her mouth.

"Stay down," he said. "Wait for my orders."

The pirates were so busy with the storm, they did not see him rise to his feet. Not that it would have done them any good. By the time they did notice, he had transformed into a jaguar and attacked his first victim.

He launched himself at the pirate, grabbing him by the nape of his neck before taking him down. He only had enough time to utter one scream before he was silent. It was enough of a disturbance to catch the attention of the rest of the crew and suddenly, Dionysus found himself under a spray of bullets. He was relieved to find they were not in possession of Hydra venom, and just as the bullets pierced his skin, they were quickly pushed out of his body as he healed.

Dionysus roared and turned, leaping toward his next victim, biting into his arm before tossing him off the ship. Two pirates raced forward with knives. Dionysus leapt on one while the other drove his blade into his side. The pain was sharp but more annoying than anything. He turned and tore into the man before throwing him across the ship, his body hitting the mast and sliding to the deck.

It was then Dionysus noticed that Medusa was gone.

"Fuck," he said as he returned to his human form.

"She went overboard."

Dionysus turned to see Leo, who had crouched behind a group of wooden boxes.

"You are certain?" he asked. His first thought was that one of the pirates had taken her below deck.

The mortal nodded.

Gods-fucking-dammit. Why didn't anyone ever listen to him?

Dionysus took a step toward him. He expected him to cower, but he didn't.

"You are smart, Leo," he said, and then he raced to the side of the ship.

Though the rain had ceased, everything was still dark, and the sea raged. The only time Dionysus could see was when lightning flashed in the sky. That was when he saw Medusa in the water. She was struggling to stay above water, but she was also surrounded by dolphins—the pirates.

"Fuckers," Dionysus muttered.

He jumped from the ship and shifted into the form of a shark as he made for the dolphins, biting down on one of their fins. They scattered quickly, but then he felt a sharp blow to his face. Medusa had punched him.

He shifted into his true form again as he surfaced, sputtering.

"It's me, for fuck's sake! I am trying to *help* you!" It was hard to hear over the noise of the storm.

"How can I trust you?" she asked.

It was the first time she had spoken, and her voice was just as beautiful as her ethereal face. It had a sensual, silky quality to it—like that of a siren.

"I don't expect you to," Dionysus said. "But if I leave you out here alone, you will find yourself back in Poseidon's hands."

At the mention of the god, her face changed, and fear flooded her strange eyes.

"Where are you taking me?"

"Land," said Dionysus. "And after that, we'll figure something out."

She was quiet, studying him—like they weren't floating in the middle of the Aegean Sea.

"Fine," she said.

"Yeah?" Dionysus asked. "You won't punch me again if I turn into a shark?"

"I think that's up to you," she said. "Don't do anything that will make me want to punch you."

"Let's hope swimming doesn't set you off," he said as he transformed again.

Medusa held on to him as he swam.

As it turned out, the pirates weren't wrong about how close they were to land. If Dionysus had not begun his attack when he did, they would have likely crashed within the hour. As he and Medusa made their way onto the sandy shore, he only wished he knew exactly where that was.

Dionysus squeezed the water from his braids.

"How did you know about Poseidon?" Medusa asked.

"He told me," Dionysus said.

Medusa's eyes widened, and she took a step back, immediately defensive. Dionysus realized that his comment made it seem like he was Poseidon's buddy.

"Not in a friend way!" Dionysus said quickly. "He told me in an enemy way!"

464

Medusa's brows lowered. "But you talk to Poseidon?"

"Because I was looking for you!"

"Why were you looking for me?"

"There is a bounty on your head."

She took another step back, her fist tightening.

"But that isn't why *I'm* looking for you," Dionysus said quickly. "You're not worth anything to me."

Medusa's fists faltered.

"That is to say I'm not interested in the money," he said. "I'm interested in your safety."

"You are really bad at this," said Medusa.

"Really fucking bad," said Dionysus. "I'm a little nervous you are going to punch me again."

"It isn't like it hurts," she said. "Aren't you a god?"

"Yeah, but I still don't like to be punched."

There was silence for a moment. "If you are a god, then promises are binding, right?"

Dionysus narrowed his eyes, suspicious. "Yes."

"Then can you promise me all you intend is to keep me safe?"

"Yes," he said without hesitation.

She seemed to relax a little. "And if I wish to leave, will you promise to let me?"

"No," said Dionysus.

What little headway they had made was gone.

"What about 'you aren't safe and there is a bounty on your head' don't you understand?"

"I understand it all perfectly well," she said. "I have *lived* it. I have also been held against my will. The freedom to come and go as I please is important to me."

Dionysus swallowed hard. "Fine," he said. "But will you promise me something?"

She stared.

"I won't stop you if you want to leave," he said. "I promise. Just…tell me when you do."

She was quiet for a moment, and finally, she nodded. She didn't speak the words, but he imagined that after being betrayed so often, promising anything was more trust than she could offer, and he didn't blame her.

"Now that that's out of the way," he said, gazing into the darkness. It was nearly impossible to see, but Dionysus thought he could make out a line of trees. "Let's build a fire or something. I hate being wet."

"You're not going to teleport?"

"Can't," he said. Picking a spot in the middle of the beach, he dug a small hole where he grew a few vines, letting them wither into nothing but dried remains.

"What do you mean you can't teleport?" Medusa asked.

"For someone who didn't want my help, you sure sound judgmental," he said, sparking a fire with a shock of energy that came from the palm of his hand.

"I didn't say I didn't want your help. I wanted you to promise me you meant it," she said.

Dionysus sighed. "I can't teleport because I have tried," he said and sat. "Which must mean we are still in Poseidon's territory. As much as I hate that, the only thing we can do now is wait for daylight."

Dionysus sat with his legs crossed, staring into the fire. It took Medusa a few seconds, but she finally sat opposite him.

"So who are you?" Medusa asked.

He glanced at her but returned his gaze to the fire. "My name is Dionysus," he said.

"Dionysus," she repeated.

"I'm sure you would have preferred an Olympian rescuer," he said. "Unfortunately, they are all busy trying to kill a sociopath."

"I didn't say that," she said. "I just asked your name."

"Oh," he said and then fell quiet.

"How much do you know about me?" she asked.

"Enough," he said. "I have been looking for you for a while."

"Why?"

"When I first heard about you, the rumor was you could turn men to stone with a single glance," he paused. Now that he had seen her, he understood where that rumor had come from. The thought made him uncomfortable.

"So you wanted me for this power you think I have?"

"Initially," he said. "But then everyone found out about you, and suddenly, you were in danger. I couldn't just…let you fall into the wrong hands."

"Because of my power, you mean."

Dionysus studied her. "I know you are resentful," he said. "But without the rumor of your power, I wouldn't have known about you, and I wouldn't be here now trying to save you."

She said nothing.

"Anyway, I had hoped to have you join my maenads."

"Maenads?"

"They're…mostly my friends," he said. "They're women who have fled from bad situations and need protection or a chance to start again."

"That almost sounds too good to be true," she said.

"They are," he said, and then he shook his head. "I'm not sure where I'd be without them."

Especially Naia and Lilaia, who had been with him the longest. They had shown him what it meant to be cared for. They had fed him and clothed him, but they had also listened and encouraged him. When he thought he was going to be taken under by madness, they were there to pull him out again. They had seen each other at their worst, which had only encouraged their best.

"I'm not sure how I got here," said Medusa.

"You mean on this island?"

"Here, at this point in my life," she explained. "I wanted to be a priestess."

"For which god?"

"Athena," she said. "I was studying at her temple in New Athens until I was taken."

"Taken?"

"I was walking home at night after leaving the temple when I was shoved into a car and bound. They took me to a hotel." She paused, her chest rising and falling fast.

"You don't have to tell me," Dionysus said.

It took her a moment to speak again.

"I thought…for some reason, I thought because I was a priestess, someone might find me. I prayed to Athena. I begged her. She never came."

"I'm sorry," Dionysus said.

She shrugged. "It was a hard lesson to learn, that nothing comes from devotion."

He hoped in time, she would learn otherwise, but he didn't say that aloud because he knew those words were useless here.

"Sleep," he said instead. "I will keep watch over you."

———

Dionysus woke when he inhaled sand.

Choking, he sat up and began to cough. His eyes watered, and his chest and throat burned. When he was mostly recovered, he looked across the dying fire at Medusa.

"You are lucky I can't sleep," she said.

He opened his mouth to speak, but she stood, brushing the sand from her clothes. "We're in Mycenae, by the way. Not Poseidon's territory."

"What?" he asked, confused.

"We're in Mycenae," she repeated.

"We can't be," he said. "I should be able to teleport."

"Well, he says otherwise." Medusa pointed to a man who was a few feet down the shore, pushing a cart of random goods.

Dionysus ran after him. "Sir! Sir!"

The man paused and turned to face Dionysus. He had wild hair and a large, wiry beard. "Ah, yes, sir! Can I interest you in a hat? Or a Mycenaean shell necklace? Made from the finest shells!"

"Mycenae?" Dionysus repeated, but even the hat was embroidered with the words Mycenaean Greek.

Dionysus tried to teleport to New Athens again, but nothing happened. Something was wrong. He should be able to teleport if this was New Greece.

"Do you want the hat or not?" the man asked, frustrated.

"Is there something happening in New Athens?" Dionysus asked.

"That depends," said the man. "How much money do you have?"

Dionysus summoned his thyrsus and pointed it at the man's neck. He dropped the hat and necklace as he put up his hands.

"Look, I don't want any trouble. I'm just trying to sell my shells."

"I'll tell you what," Dionysus said. "You tell me what's going on in New Athens, and you get to continue selling your shells."

"There's not much information coming out that way," said the man. "They're saying there was a huge earthquake, and the entire city just broke off into the ocean. At first, we all thought it was Poseidon, but now they're saying his son is responsible."

"Theseus?" Dionysus asked.

"Yeah! That's the one. Personally, haven't heard much about him, but if he can take over a whole city... fuck...he must be powerful."

Fuck indeed.

And if it was true, it meant the gods had failed to kill him during the funeral games.

"Thank you," said Dionysus. He pulled his thyrsus away and then bent to pick up the hat, shoving a handful of coins at the man's chest before turning to Medusa.

"Hey! You sure you don't want something else from the cart?" the man called.

Dionysus ignored him.

"Nice pinecone," Medusa said as he approached.

"Close your eyes," he said before releasing his magic in one sweeping blast. He teleported them to the border of Attica.

When they arrived, Medusa doubled over and vomited, but Dionysus was too distracted by the scene in front of him to ask if she was all right, because floating miles away from the jagged coastline was New Athens.

CHAPTER XXXIV
HADES

A strange, strained quiet settled between the gods, heavy with shock. It was a quiet Hades knew well, one he had often been responsible for but had rarely felt until Persephone. It was almost like she had taught him how to grieve—first for his mother and now for Apollo, who had come to mean more to him because of how much he meant to Persephone.

"We should prepare funeral rites," Hecate said.

Hades knew why she suggested it. The sooner she began, the faster Apollo would make it across the Styx, the sooner everyone would see him again.

Artemis's gaze snapped to Hecate's, her words slipping between clenched teeth. "If you touch him, I will kill you."

"There has been too much death already," said Hecate. "Do not threaten more."

The goddess dissolved into tears. It was strange to see her like this and harder to watch. When Artemis wasn't stoic, she was vengeful. There was no in-between—except for now.

"Please," she begged. "Do not take him away."

Hades stepped forward and knelt, his face level with hers.

"Without rites, he cannot rest," he said. "Let Hecate honor him so that you can meet him at the Styx."

"You will let me see him?" she asked.

"I swear it," he said.

She took a few more quivery breaths, looking down at Apollo's charred body. Hades did not know how she did it—how she held him so tightly when he looked nothing like he did in life.

"I'll see you soon," she told Apollo and bent to kiss his forehead.

When she released him, Hecate took him away.

"I don't understand," said Hermes. He sat at the bottom of the staircase, staring at nothing, his gaze unseeing. It was how everyone looked—completely lost. "I thought Theseus was vulnerable."

"Dionysus said he was slow to heal," said Hades.

"But even gods can be wounded," said Persephone. "Theseus's skin was like...*steel*."

"Then he has become invincible," said Hades.

"But...*how*?" Persephone asked.

"Hera," said Aphrodite. "She has a tree of golden apples that, with one taste, can make mortals immortal and the vulnerable invulnerable. It is obvious he has had a taste of the apple."

"It sounds like we all need to eat from that fucking tree," said Hermes.

"I suppose that depends on what you value

more—your immortality or invincibility," said Aphrodite. "The tree will take one to grant the other."

"Perhaps Theseus plans to eat another apple when all of this is done," said Artemis.

"We can only hope. It is rumored that partaking of the tree twice means death."

There was a beat of silence.

"So you mean he cannot be wounded at all?" asked Persephone.

"No," said Hades, and if they could not pierce his skin, they could not even poison him with Hydra venom.

"Even Achilles had a weakness," said Aphrodite.

"Theseus has many weaknesses," said Hades. "The question is, which one will kill him?"

————

As promised, Hades took Artemis to the Styx, though she was not alone in welcoming Apollo to the Underworld. Persephone and Hermes followed, and so did Aphrodite, Hephaestus, Harmonia, and Sybil. Thanatos arrived shortly after, followed by Tyche and Hypnos, who crossed his arms over his chest, eyeing the crowd of souls who waited with fragrant laurel and hyacinth and played sweet music on lyres.

"Where was all this when I died?" he demanded.

"Not to be rude, Hypnos, but you're not that popular," said Hermes.

"That *is* rude...ass!"

"Calling me an ass isn't exactly *nice* either," said Hermes.

"I wouldn't have called you an ass if you hadn't said I wasn't popular. I'm popular. Everyone likes to sleep!"

"No offense, but do you know how much I could accomplish if I didn't have to sleep?"

"I suppose we'll find out," said Hypnos, smiling with malice.

Hades rolled his eyes. "Fuck, they are exhausting," he muttered.

Persephone's soft laugh drew his attention. "I don't know. I think they are kind of cute."

"Try living with it for an eternity," he said.

"I hope I do," she replied.

Hades was surprised by her words, and he instantly felt guilty for his. It had been an insensitive thing to say given not only Apollo's death but also Tyche's and Hypnos's.

"You will," he said. "You have no choice."

She smiled at him, though there was no amusement in her eyes.

"You know that is not how Fate works," she said.

"I know what I will do if anything were to happen to you," he said. "The promise of that future alone should keep the Fates at bay."

He knew she was not convinced, and in some ways, he did not blame her. From where they stood right now, it was hard to envision a future.

Suddenly, there was a gleam on the horizon, and Charon's ferry came into view. From this distance, he could see Apollo standing at the front of the boat, the lantern on the bow swinging from the choppy waters of the Styx.

Hades wondered how the ferryman was handling the deaths of the Divine. In all his years ferrying souls, he had brought one god here, and that had been Pan, Hermes's son.

The souls cheered, and Persephone left his side to be nearer to the pier, though she was careful not to overtake Artemis, whose feet were barely on the dock. Hades worried she might fall in and be taken to the bottom of the river by the dead, but Apollo knocked her back, rocking Charon's boat as he launched himself at his sister and pulled her into a tight hug.

Charon docked his boat and came to Hades.

"There are hundreds of souls at the gates," he said. "What is happening up there?"

"Chaos," Hades answered. He had no other way to explain it.

He had expected Theseus to plan something during the funeral games but nothing on the scale he had managed today. Theseus had wielded the lightning bolt.

That alone was enough to convince the people of New Greece that his abilities exceeded those of the gods, but then he had murdered Apollo.

In that instant, Theseus had essentially replaced two gods.

And that had only been the start, because once Apollo had fallen and Zeus was revealed, Theseus called to his father, Poseidon, commanding him to make the earth tremble and the seas shift, bringing about a disaster Hades had only just begun to comprehend.

Suddenly, it was not just the gods who were under Theseus's threat but the whole of New Greece.

"If you do not do something soon, the entire world will reside here within your realm, and then you will have to worry about what Theseus has planned for you."

"I already do," said Hades.

His gaze shifted to the souls and gods gathered to welcome Apollo, and he wondered how he had come to care for so many people, but one look at Persephone and he knew—it was her.

She was the thread that bound them, the one who had brought them all together, and now he would do anything to protect them.

Except he was already failing, as was evident by Apollo's death.

"You are far too happy to be dead, Apollo!" Artemis said, but everyone knew what she really meant—*you are far too happy to leave me.*

His features softened. "Do not mourn for me, dear sister. I have wanted this for a long time."

"But why? Why would you want this?" she asked, stretching out her arms.

Apollo's gaze followed, shifting over the landscape of Hades's realm before he met her gaze again. "Because it is the only way to have peace."

Hades could feel Artemis's confusion. She did not understand the burdens on Apollo's soul. His regrets went deep. Hers did not.

When Apollo moved on to Persephone, she threw her arms around his neck and held him tight. Hades could feel her pain and longed to comfort her. But Apollo would not release her, seeming to convey all that their friendship had meant to him in a simple embrace. When she pulled away, he smiled.

"Don't cry, Seph," he said. "Nothing has to change. Not even our bargain."

And with that teasing statement, the energy around them lightened.

"Oh, fucking Fates," Hades grumbled. "How has that not *ended*?"

"Jealous, Hades? I was thinking that when things calm down, Seph and I could go on a picnic."

"Good luck," said Hades. "You have no magic to summon her."

"Then I guess I'll have to do it the mortal way and knock on your door."

"I will throw you in Tartarus," Hades shot back with a smirk, grateful for Apollo's levity and the relief it seemed to be bringing Persephone.

"That is a steep punishment for a knock. You should just be glad I offered. I tend to prefer just appearing where I'm not wanted."

"A picnic sounds nice, Apollo," Persephone said, wiping the tears from her face and beaming at the god.

He grinned. "Did you hear that, Hades? It's a date!"

Hades glared as Apollo moved on to greet Hermes, ruffing up his golden hair.

"Remind me to show Apollo a few spots for his upcoming picnic," said Hades as Persephone returned to his side.

"You will not send him into the Forest of Despair," she said sharply.

"What?" he asked. "It would be funny."

She leaned close, letting her hands slide up his chest. "You know what else is funny? Blue balls."

"No," he said. "That is cruel."

"And so is the forest."

He sighed. "Fine."

"I knew you'd see it my way," Persephone said.

She rose on the tips of her toes, and Hades bent to

kiss her when cheers suddenly erupted. They looked to see Apollo and Hyacinth surrounded by souls, locked in each other's arms, mouths pressed together in a passionate kiss.

Persephone took a breath. She pressed both hands to her heart.

"I did not think any good would come of this," she said.

Hades shifted uncomfortably, torn between telling her the truth and letting her believe a lie—except she didn't give him a choice between the two. She looked up at him, already suspicious of his silence.

"Hades?"

The way she said his name, half question, half pleading. It made his throat feel tight.

"Tell me he will not have to drink from the Lethe."

"No, he will not," he said. "But Hyacinth cannot stay."

Persephone blinked. "What do you mean he cannot stay?"

"It is time for his soul to reincarnate."

He realized it was terrible timing—not only because Apollo had just arrived in the Underworld but because the world was a terrible place—but there was nothing he could do.

The color drained from her face.

"Hades," Persephone whispered.

"I know what you would ask of me," he said. "But this is Hyacinth's choice to make."

She did not argue or beg, but she blinked away tears as she gazed at the two lovers.

"Perhaps he will change his mind now that Apollo has arrived."

But Hades knew not even she believed those words.

―――――

"We are still counting the dead," said Ilias. "But we are nearing a thousand with many unaccounted for."

After his conversation with Charon, Hades had sent the satyr to gather information on the state of New Athens.

There was no good news.

"We are no longer part of the mainland," he said. "It has become an island, surrounded by the Aegean, which technically makes it Poseidon's territory."

It was as Hades had feared, though he did find his brother's role in this suspicious. Poseidon had always wanted to rule, so it was strange that he would go to this extent to see someone else on the throne, even if it was his son.

"The separation destroyed mostly larger buildings. The Acropolis, the Parthenon, and Alexandria Tower have all fallen. There is also significant damage to the hospital though it is still operational unless its generator fails. The rest of New Athens is in total darkness."

Hades was quiet, considering.

The information Ilias had offered was good, but it was too general.

"If we are going to help those in need, we are going to have to have a better idea of what is happening on the ground," said Hades.

"I can summon a few contacts to Iniquity," said Ilias.

"It still stands?"

"For now, though I have a feeling Theseus is eager to destroy anything that reminds him of the gods, especially you."

"Flattered," said Hades. "But if that is the case, meeting there is not safe. I think you should summon them here."

"As you wish," said Ilias.

He did not wish it, but he had no choice because he knew where this was going. Theseus would target everyone who was loyal to the gods, and if they did not forsake them, he would execute them.

He wanted no worshippers left, save those who would bow to him, though Hades would challenge him to find one person who did not believe—or fear—death.

"Summon me when you return," Hades said and left his office for his chambers.

When he entered the room, he found Persephone lying on her side, her back to the door. He thought she might be asleep, but as he approached the bed, she rolled to face him.

He could not help staring. She was beautiful. Her skin was rosy and her hair mussed. She looked almost dreamy, as though she had just been roused from sleep.

"Did I wake you?" he asked.

"I don't know," she said. "I cannot remember sleeping."

Probably because she was so exhausted.

He sat on the edge of the bed and let his hand rest on her hip. She was warm beneath his hand, and he had to resist the urge to lie down beside her, because if he did, he would not get up again until morning.

"Where did you go?" she asked.

"Nowhere yet," he said. "I was speaking with Ilias. I have asked him to summon a few contacts. We need to get a sense of what is happening in the world, and the best way is through Iniquity."

Persephone sat up, letting her blankets fall away. She did not seem to care that she was completely naked, and while he appreciated the view, she made it very hard to concentrate on anything other than his growing erection.

"Can I come?" she asked.

Hades smirked. "I am usually inside you when you ask me that."

She shifted onto her knees. The position made her taller, and her breasts were level with his face.

"If you say no, then you may never come inside me again."

The humorous light in Hades's eyes died, and he lifted a brow, challenging her threat. "As if you could go a day without my pleasure."

"Do not underestimate me, my lord."

"As it is, neither of us will have to find out," he said, pulling her into his lap. He sucked one of her nipples into his mouth. She cried out, her hands gripping his face. He chuckled darkly as he released her. "I wasn't going to say no. Though I would prefer if you slept."

"You know I will not sleep," she said.

This time, her teeth and tongue grazed his ear. He shuddered, his hands tightening on her waist.

"No," he said and pulled away to meet her gaze. "And if I were to leave you, I would return to find all my whiskey gone."

"Someone has to drink it," she said, giving him a knowing tap on his nose.

He didn't think she had noticed, but of course, she was right. He had not had a drink since returning from the labyrinth, and he didn't know why. It was not as if he hadn't tried, but he hesitated each time he brought the glass to his lips.

He felt ridiculous.

It was not as if alcohol affected him, so why did he feel so haunted every time he picked up the glass?

Persephone slipped closer and kissed him.

"I am not laughing at you," she whispered.

"I know," he said, his fingers fanning out across her waist. "And I know I should celebrate my abstinence, but I fear what's coming next."

"What is coming?" she asked. Her voice was breathy but confused.

"I don't know," he said. "Something worse. Anger maybe."

It was always that way—when one thing ended, another took its place.

"Hades," she whispered. "Where is this coming from?"

"I always have found a way to deal with my pain," he said. "After the Titanomachy, I was isolated, and now I am numb. I coped with the first by being cruel, and now I drink. So what does it mean if I don't?"

She held his gaze and pressed her hand to his heart. "Do you feel numb now?"

"No," he said. "Not with you so near."

She curled her fingers into his shirt, her breath dancing over his lips.

"Then maybe you have already found another vice."

————

Hades manifested in the shadows of Nevernight with

Persephone, Ilias, and Hermes. He had no intention of announcing himself yet, curious to hear what would be said in his absence—likely something far more useful than what would be said if his presence was known.

He looked down at Persephone and pressed a finger to his lips before turning his attention to the members of Iniquity. Two sat at the bar, hunched over their drinks—an older man named Ptolemeos and a younger one named Jorn. A woman had made herself comfortable behind the bar. Her name was Stella. Three others sat nearby on a couch—Madelia Rella, Leonidas Nasso, and Damianos Vitalis.

"They say we've been completely cut off from the rest of the world. There aren't even ports or ships to get us out," Ptolemeos was saying.

"You expect us to believe you have no way off this island, Ptolemeos?" Damianos asked.

"I didn't say that, but it will cost more," he said.

Persephone stiffened beside Hades. He squeezed her hand, hoping it communicated what he wished—reassurance that he would not let that happen.

"The tunnels are flooded. The danger is higher."

Something heavy settled in Hades's stomach at that news. He had not considered that the tunnels would be flooded. Dionysus had measures in place for events like this. Had something gone wrong, and if so, where were he and the maenads?

"You intend to charge families to escape this fuckery?" Madelia Rella asked, her disdain evident.

"Commerce doesn't stop in war, Madelia. You know that best. Have these demigods not visited your establishments?"

Her mouth tightened. "If I could prevent it, I would.

They hurt my girls. When I banned them, they burned down one of my brothels."

Hades wondered when that had happened. Perhaps when he was in the labyrinth.

"They are certainly powerful," said Jorn. "Did you see Theseus with the lightning bolt and Zeus just hanging in the sky?" He paused to shake his head. "Are we foolish not to kneel to them?"

"That depends on whose wrath you wish to incur," said Madelia. "As for me, I'd rather have a pleasant afterlife."

"How do we know the Underworld hasn't been conquered too?"

A stark silence followed the question. Hades could feel Persephone rage beside him. Hermes too fisted his hands. Hades stuck out his arm to keep the god from revealing them. As much as he found disfavor with what was being discussed, he was also not surprised. And he wanted to know who was on his side.

Finally, Madelia spoke. "That is ridiculous."

"I appreciate the vote of confidence, Madelia," Hades said as he stepped out of the shadow, his gaze sweeping the room. "Since most of you have made it clear that you have no allegiance beyond what serves you, I shall give you a few seconds to choose the side you will take moving forward."

There was a pause, and then Ptolemeos straightened. "And what are the consequences for not choosing you?"

"There are none," Hades said. "Save what will befall you if your choice is wrong."

The old man scowled. "It is just like a god to speak in riddles."

Hades's mouth quirked. "Think of it as roulette, Ptolemeos. Are you willing to make the bet?"

"Not when I am staring death in the face," said the man.

"A wise choice," said Hades. "As you are all aware, Theseus, with the aid of his father, has taken over New Athens. It is true that he is responsible for the deaths of several gods. The only reason Zeus is still alive is because Theseus hopes to use him as a pawn to gain the favor of our father, Cronos. I do not know his plans beyond that, save that he has some delusional hope that he can rule the entirety of New Greece as its sole god, a feat he cannot accomplish while I still live."

Though New Athens was now under Poseidon's control because the landmass was so small, all that managed to do was prevent other gods from teleporting about the city. Hades, however, also had power over land, no matter its size.

"So what are you going to do?" asked Leonidas. "Free Zeus and hope he brings about peace?"

"Why does everyone keep suggesting that?" Hermes muttered.

"It has been a long time since Zeus has brought about peace," said Hades.

"So you do not mean to free him?" asked Jorn.

"At this moment, my brother is not my priority," said Hades.

"Then what is your priority?" asked Damianos. "So we are all clear."

"First, we find a way to give shelter to the innocent," he said. "But we cannot take people across the sea. Poseidon will sink your ships if you manage to get them on one."

"Many have fled to temples hoping for protection," said Ptolemeos. "But rumor has it that Theseus intends to raid them in the morning."

Hades exchanged a look with Persephone who asked, "Can we shelter here?"

"We could," said Ilias. "The challenge is getting them here safely, especially without the aid of Dionysus's tunnels."

"We are certain they are useless?" Hades asked.

There was a part of him that did not believe it.

"There is a chance a few have drained, but there willbe bodies," said Ptolemeos.

"And there are no survivors?" Persephone asked.

The old man shook his head. "None who have come forward, though I do not imagine they know where to go given the state of the city."

"Has anyone heard from Dionysus?" Hades asked. The god was just as involved as he was with the underground and well known among this crowd, but everyone shook their head except Hermes.

"He came to me a few nights ago and asked for my sandals," said Hermes, hesitating for a moment before he added, "He had some business on an island that belonged to Poseidon. I have not seen or heard from him since."

Hades suspected there was more to that story Hermes did not wish to share with the group. As much as he hated it, they were going to have to use the tunnels. Maybe along the way, they would find a few survivors.

"I think it is a risk we must take," said Hades grimly.

"Can we not…teleport them?" Persephone asked.

"If I do, I risk drawing the attention of my brother," said Hades. "And I do not want any more casualties if I can help it."

Someone chuckled, and Hades's looked up to meet Ptolemeos's gaze.

"What?" the mortal asked. "Does no one else find this ironic? The God of the Dead worrying over life?"

"If you knew him, you wouldn't find it ironic," Persephone snapped.

Madelia's lips twitched, and Hades's hand tightened on Persephone's waist.

"So we empty the temples and Theseus has no one to sacrifice tomorrow. What then?" asked Jorn.

"I say we blow them up just as the demigods head inside," said Leonidas.

"An explosion likely won't harm them," said Hermes. "For all we know, they are invincible like us."

"You don't seem to be all that invincible anymore," Damianos pointed out.

Hermes glared. "I'll show you invincible," he muttered, crossing his arms over his chest.

"The point isn't to harm them," Damianos continued. "It is to catch them off guard. Then you attack."

Hades didn't like the idea of more destruction, but he knew it was inevitable. It was the cost of battle among the Divine.

Then Leonidas stood. "You can work out among the gods who will target who, but as far as our involvement, that is what we can offer."

It was about what Hades expected, but it was enough. Between them, they should be able to empty the temples and get the mortals to safety.

"Fine," said Hades. "We start now."

And tomorrow, they would go to battle.

CHAPTER XXXV
PERSEPHONE

Hades departed with Ilias, Hermes, and Artemis to Dionysus's tunnels while Persephone summoned help to prepare for the arrival of mortals at Nevernight. While Mekonnen guarded the doors, Adrian and Ezio pushed the couches against the wall so Sybil could make pallets on the floor. Leuce set up water and snack stations while Harmonia gathered supplies for babies and games for children. Hecate organized a medical station, and Persephone tried not to think long on why it was necessary, though the goddess was reassuring.

"When mortals are involved, you cannot be too careful," she said. "They have all kinds of ailments."

"Can we not just heal them?" Persephone asked.

"If it is a usual ache and pain, we must let it run its course," Hecate said. "We are not miracle workers. You know our choice to heal can have grave consequences. That does not change, even in times of war."

Upstairs, Hephaestus and Aphrodite arrived with weapons and armor. They had divided each kind between the suites—spears, axes, bows. The last room had swords, and it was the one Persephone decided to enter, though all this felt a little surreal.

She approached the table and picked up one of the blades. The design was simple but still beautiful, as were all Hephaestus's creations.

The hilt was wrapped in leather, and the pommel and cross guard were smooth steel. She had never wielded a weapon before, so she was surprised by how light it was, though she supposed that made sense as they were usually carried in one hand.

"What do you think?"

Persephone jumped at the sound of Aphrodite's voice and turned as the goddess strolled into the room.

"I can't believe he managed to make so many," said Persephone.

She returned the sword to the pile.

"This is all he ever does," said Aphrodite. There was a note of disdain in her voice that Persephone decided to ignore. No one wanted Hephaestus to have to forge weapons like this.

"I hate that it was necessary," she said.

"Me too," Aphrodite said quietly.

"Are they to your liking?" Hephaestus asked.

Persephone was a little surprised by the sound of the god's voice. It was not often she heard it, but she found it was quiet and pleasant, like the warm embers of a crackling fire.

She and Aphrodite turned to look at him.

"I feel as though you are asking me a trick question, Hephaestus," Persephone said. "I am not sure what there is to like about war."

He gave a polite nod. "Fair, Lady Persephone."

"Am I right to assume that these are for...mortal soldiers?"

"Yes, Lady Persephone."

"And are they...poisoned with Hydra venom?"

Hephaestus offered a single nod. "Yes, my lady."

She let that sink in—the idea that thousands of mortals would be armed with weapons that could harm gods.

"Is that...a good idea?" she asked, though she imagined he and Hades had already had this discussion, weighed all the pros and cons. Still, it felt terribly frightening and horribly wrong.

"Theseus's followers will be armed with the same. Hydra venom deals a quick death to mortals. It would be a far more devastating fight for us without them."

She let that sink in before asking, "Where are our weapons?"

Hephaestus glanced at Aphrodite as he spoke, "I have entrusted your weapons to Hades for safekeeping."

"Of course," said Aphrodite. "Because obviously she is not capable and may impale herself."

As much as she understood Aphrodite's frustration, Persephone did not feel it was warranted here. She met Hephaestus's gaze and offered a small smile, and for a moment, she could see the exhaustion in his face.

Her heart hurt for him.

"The weapons are poisoned with Hydra venom," said Hephaestus. "I only wish to keep you safe."

"I understand," said Persephone quickly before they could spiral into a fight. "We have seen the damage Hydra venom can do. I have no wish to harm myself or others. In truth, I hope we never have to use them."

When Persephone left the suites, she felt like she was carrying the weight of the thousands of weapons piled into the rooms behind her. Each one was a person, a soul, and she felt responsible for them all.

As she emerged from the lounge, there was a quiet roar from downstairs. People had already begun to arrive.

"The air smells like fear," said Euryale, who stood guard at the doors of the lounge.

Persephone looked at the gorgon who was always dressed in white and blindfolded.

"New Athens is under siege," said Persephone. "We are all afraid."

"Even you, Lady Persephone?" Euryale asked.

"Can you not sense it?"

"Grief smells a lot like fear," she said.

"Perhaps I grieve too," said Persephone.

She walked to the top of the stairs to look out over the floor. It was strange to see Hades's club transform from something secretive and sinful to a sanctuary for survival. Normally, it was crowded with the young or the desperate, not families. Men, women, and children huddled together while others paced, unable to sit still. A few children zipped through the crowd with glee, blissfully unaware of why and where they were, though most did look afraid.

It was the first time Persephone had witnessed Theseus's impact on the mortal world, and these people were haunted. It occurred to her how this must feel to the Faithful—to the pious worshippers who said their prayers and made their sacrifices, who decorated altars and loved their gods. She had lost her friends, but they had lost their gods, and it felt like the very threads of their world were being torn apart.

Right now, they had no future.

A shriek brought her attention back to the floor below. More children had joined the game of chase, and another group arrived from the tunnels. This one was led by Hermes.

Persephone descended the stairs, making her way toward the god. As she did, one of the children who was running rammed into her. She placed a steadying hand on their shoulder.

"Oh," she said and then knelt before the child. He was about four, if she had to guess, with wide, brown eyes and curly hair. "Are you okay?"

"Do not touch him, Goddess of Death!" a woman bellowed, wrenching the child away.

Persephone blanched, shocked by the woman's reaction and words.

"You would do well to respect the Queen of the Dead within her home," said Hermes, helping Persephone to her feet.

"Cora, stop!" A man joined the fray.

"Do not act as if you do not know," the woman said. "As if you *all* do not know that this goddess has killed the Great Mother!"

The woman looked about wildly as if she might find support here, within Persephone's territory.

But no one spoke. They all just stared.

"Cora," her husband said, placing a commanding hand on her shoulder, but it was Persephone's turn to speak. She took a step forward. The man and woman cowered, but the child held her gaze.

"Mortal woman, I will grant you more mercy than I showed my mother," said Persephone. "But if you insult me again—with a simple thought or a spoken word—one day, you will beg for death, and she will never find you."

"She will never speak ill upon your name again," said the man. "I swear it."

Persephone's eyes shifted to his, and she saw within him a virtue his wife did not possess. As much as he would try to honor her, his wife would not. She was surprised by the thought, though she felt deeply that it was true and wondered if this was how Hades felt when he looked at souls.

"I will not hold you to a promise she should make," said Persephone, and then her eyes fell to the little boy. "You are welcome to play. I only wished to know that you were okay."

"We are grateful, my lady," said the man as he pulled his wife and child away.

Persephone stared after them. She did not mean to, but she could not look away.

She would not say that she could see their souls, but she understood them—the man was hardworking and honest, but his wife carried hatred in her heart, and it had made her angry and bitter. Inherently, she was not bad, but she sought someone to blame for her pain.

In the end, she would curse her name.

"Are you all right, Sephy?" Hermes asked as he approached.

"Yes," she lied, but that was easier than the truth, which felt complicated and confused, swirling inside her like a terrible storm. "Did you come through the tunnels?"

"I did," he said, and Persephone knew by his expression that it was as they feared. "It's not good, Sephy."

Her stomach twisted violently. "You don't think... they aren't all dead?"

"I don't know. Hades is still investigating," said Hermes, and he paused for a moment. "Dionysus will be devastated."

She did not know the god very well, but she had learned more about him since meeting Ariadne. She knew that he had spent a lot of his years helping women escape horrible situations only to now have them die a terrible death at the hands of Theseus.

"I hate him, Hermes," Persephone said.

"So do I, Sephy," he said. "So do I."

Ilias was the last to arrive with only a handful of people.

"Is this everyone?" Persephone asked, only confused because every other group had been far larger.

"No," he said. "Quite a few refused to leave."

"Refused?" Persephone repeated.

"I told them what would happen tomorrow, what Theseus was planning," said Ilias. "But they did not wish to abandon Athena."

"It's her *temple*, not the goddess herself," said Persephone, immediately frustrated.

"I won't pretend to understand it," said the satyr. "But it complicates things for tomorrow."

"Fuck."

Battle should serve a purpose beyond bloodshed, Athena had said the last time Persephone had seen her outside Thebes. That was before the Olympians had battled, and neither she nor Hestia had participated. Persephone wondered now if the goddess would change her mind, especially if it meant her followers would face needless and violent deaths.

"What do we do?" Persephone asked.

"We'll talk to Hades when he returns," said Ilias. "Perhaps if the other temples are destroyed, it will be enough of a distraction to keep Athena's safe."

Persephone frowned but agreed, her anxiety returning as she was once again reminded how long Hades had been gone.

She distracted herself with tasks, passing out water and replenishing snacks. Eventually she found herself sitting at the base of the steps, growing wildflowers to make crowns for the children who sat around her, entertained by her magic. Harmonia joined her, and Persephone could tell by the feel of her magic, warm and radiant, that she was using it to maintain peace within the crowded space.

Eventually, everything got quieter as the mortals settled in. One by one, the children left to sleep, and Persephone rose to her feet with Harmonia.

"Are you all right, Persephone?" the goddess asked.

"No," she said, meeting her soft gaze. "If I don't distract myself, I think I might break."

"It's okay to break," said Harmonia. "Do it now before tomorrow comes."

She almost did. The tears were already burning her eyes, but then she felt a rush of Hades's magic, and her heart rose in her chest only to fall into the bottom of her stomach when he manifested in the middle of the floor with an unconscious woman in his arms.

Persephone ran to him.

"Hecate!" he snapped, lowering the woman to the ground.

"What happened?" the goddess asked, appearing beside him in an instant.

"I don't know. I found her in the tunnels," Hades said. "Her name is Naia."

Naia.

Persephone recognized her from her short visit to Dionysus's tunnels, though she barely resembled that person now, her face pale and her lips blue. She was nearly drained of life.

Hecate placed a hand to Naia's forehead and then over her chest. After a few seconds, a trickle of water came out of her mouth but nothing substantial.

"Bring her," said Hecate, rising to her feet.

Hades glanced at Persephone as he followed, disappearing behind the curtained area Hecate had designated as the infirmary. He placed Naia on one of the pallets while Hecate worked to concoct some kind of bitter medicine.

"Is she the only one who survived?" Persephone asked.

"There are more parts of the tunnel I have not checked," said Hades. "I will return with help. Hopefully we can cover more ground and find more survivors."

"Is there no chance others escaped?"

She thought of Ariadne, Phaedra, and the baby. *Please say it is possible*, she begged.

"It is possible," he said. "We can try to broadcast within the underground and see if anyone responds, but with communications down, it will be far more difficult."

Persephone's gaze fell to the woman. When she

looked at her, it seemed that her soul was almost under-water, like her body had been in the tunnels. She understood what it meant though—that she was in limbo.

Naia had not decided whether to stay or go.

"I will treat what I am able," said Hecate. "The rest is up to her."

Persephone stepped out of the curtained room, and Hades followed.

"Are you well?" he asked. Slipping a hand around her waist, he drew her close.

"That has a complicated answer," she said.

"I am sorry to leave you again," he said.

"I could help," she offered.

He shook his head. "It isn't that I do not want your help or need it," he said. "But I do not wish for you to see what I have seen."

She understood, trusting the horror in his eyes.

"I love you," she said, closing her eyes against the feel of his lips on her forehead.

"I love you," he replied. "Rest, darling. There will be none after tonight."

When he released her, she felt like she might collapse, but she managed to remain on her feet as she watched him cross the room to Ilias, Hermes, and Artemis. When they left, she made her way upstairs to Hades's office, slumped against the doors, and broke.

————

Persephone was roused by a gentle shake. When she opened her eyes, she found Hades sitting beside her. She had fallen asleep on the couch in his office.

"Hades," she said, her voice thick with sleep.

"Come," he said. "Let us spend the rest of the night in our own bed."

It took Persephone a few moments to rise, but when she did, she felt more awake.

"Did you find any more survivors?" she asked.

"Only two," he said. "Though I do not have much hope for their survival."

Persephone's eyes instantly watered, and Hades's fingers danced along the height of her cheekbone. Her face felt tender.

"You have been crying."

"I tried not to," she said. "But I could not contain it."

"You do not have to," he said. Rising and gathering her into his arms, he teleported to the Underworld.

The familiar smell and warmth of their room eased the tension in her chest.

Hades placed her on her feet and slid his hand into her hair.

"I know I have not been able to make you forget," he said. "But I would still make love to you tonight."

Her eyes watered even as he kissed her, his hands dipping beneath the collar of her dress. As it slipped from her shoulders to her feet, she wrapped her arms around his neck, and he drew her legs around his waist, carrying her to bed.

When he laid her down, he kissed her long and slow, and as his fingers danced over her skin, she grew warm, and a different ache overtook the one that had burdened her all day, one so deep and desperate she had no desire to wait for him any longer. She reached for him and guided him to her heat, and when she was full of him, all the air left her lungs. It was blissful—a death like no other.

Hades kissed her, one hand cradling her head, the

other hooked beneath her knee, and for some reason—maybe it was the way he looked at her or the heat—she was reminded of when she had dreamed of him. For a moment, she feared this wasn't real and that soon she would wake to find all this had been a dream.

Her fingers bit into his skin, desperate to keep him.

"Where are you?" he asked, brushing damp strands of her hair from her face. She held his gaze, and he bent to kiss her, whispering against her lips. "Live in this moment with me."

"Don't say that," she said. Her chest *ached*. "It is what you said when you weren't real."

"I am real now," he said. "I am here now."

She wept. "I'm not worried about now," she whispered. "I am worried about after."

Hades cupped her face, brushing away her tears. "I will be here," he promised. "So do not leave me now."

He pressed his mouth to hers, and it unlocked something frenzied in each of them. Hades took her by the wrists and held them over her head, pressing them into the bed. His thrusts went harder and deeper. Persephone wrapped her legs around him, her heels digging into his ass. She wanted to move with him, but all she could do was hold on as he thrust. His pace set a dizzying rhythm that had her body twisting and tightening. A moan welled in her throat.

"Yes," she whispered over and over, and all the while, Hades's eyes never left her face.

When she came, he kissed her with his tongue and teeth, his hips grinding hard into hers as he followed her over the edge.

He settled against her, his head resting on her chest, and she held him tight.

He did not disappear, and she refused to cry.

CHAPTER XXXVI
PERSEPHONE

A knock woke Persephone from sleep.

Hades was on his feet before she had even opened her eyes, making his way across the room, his magic cloaking him in robes as he went.

"Hades!"

It was Ilias. The sound of his frantic voice made Persephone's heart race.

The doors opened, and the satyr rushed in, his eyes wide with panic.

"Theseus has struck. Artemis sent word. He is raiding Athena's temple as we speak!"

Persephone rose from bed.

"He wasn't supposed to act until morning," Persephone said, using her glamour to dress.

"He must have gotten word that we emptied the temples," said Ilias.

Or someone had betrayed them. Either way, the battle was happening sooner than any of them had anticipated.

Hades turned to Persephone. There was a haunted look in his gaze, and she knew that he did not want her to come, that he did not want her to be part of this battle.

"I have just as much need to watch him die as you do, Hades," she said.

He held out his hand, and she thought that he meant for her to take it, but instead, a ribbon of shadow came from his palm and wound around her body, turning into leather-like armor.

"Come," he said, and this time, she took his hand.

They teleported together.

Persephone did not know what to expect when they arrived, but she certainly did not think it would be so *bright*. It was supposed to be *night*.

"Helios," Hades growled.

Persephone blinked, eyes watering, and as her vision adjusted, the true horror of what was about to unfold became clear.

Hades had appeared beside Artemis, Hephaestus, and Hecate. Opposite them were four familiar demigods. Each one held a blade to the throat of a priestess. The women had their eyes closed, their mouths moving in silent prayer. In the distance, she could hear screams from inside the temple where the other mortals were locked inside.

"It's good that you could join us," said Theseus.

"Why are you doing this?" Persephone demanded. "None of these people have harmed you."

"If I am to make a new world, there can be no one left who believes in the old gods."

"We are not old gods yet," said Hades.

"But you have old weaknesses," said Theseus. He glanced up at the sky. "How is the sun treating you, Hecate?"

Persephone looked at the goddess, who offered a small smile. "It is kind of you to ask, Theseus, but I am well."

She did not understand the exchange. Did the sun weaken Hecate's magic?

"I am nothing but concerned for your well-being," replied the demigod.

It was then Persephone's gaze caught on something in the distance—the gleam of steel. It was an army of foot soldiers—of hundreds of mortals.

It was also a distraction. A series of low gasps sounded, and Persephone's and Hecate's magic flared to life, freezing the demigods' hands, but it was too late. Their blades had landed, and blood was already spilled.

A strange sound followed, like the air was being sucked out of the world, and the demigods broke the hold Persephone and Hecate had on them, dropping the priestesses to the ground.

The air flooded with magic, thick and heavy—a dizzying mix of all the gods. Debris began to rise. Persephone couldn't tell who was responsible. Maybe they all were— their power collectively reacting to the horror before them.

The demigods drew their weapons, Hades summoned his bident, Hephaestus his fiery whip, and Artemis her bow. Persephone and Hecate remained weaponless. As she eyed the sharp tips of the demigods' blades, anxiety swirled in her chest.

Magic did not matter if that poisoned end met her flesh.

She started to consider her first move, glancing to her left and right. She was flanked by Hecate and Hades—Hades, who looked magnificent, towering in black armor. In some ways, she wished she was as battle honed as he was, but she would not be a liability.

Then Hecate vanished.

Persephone's heart raced, and the demigods raised their weapons.

Theseus chuckled.

"It appears your Titaness has abandoned you. Perhaps you should get used to the feeling."

But Persephone knew that wasn't true. She could still taste the metallic tang of Hecate's magic on the back of her tongue.

Then Theseus looked down, scraping his shoe against the pavement.

"Oh, now isn't that unfortunate?" he said. "There is blood on my shoes."

Persephone gritted her teeth, and her nails bit into her palms. Her magic raged inside her. She knew Theseus had said it to provoke, that he liked jabbing an already-raw wound, and as much as she wanted to attack, she didn't make the first move. Artemis did.

The Goddess of the Hunt gave an angry cry as she darted toward Theseus, grief fueling her rage, and as their blades clashed, the demigods who had murdered the priestesses attacked.

Persephone had expected Sandros to challenge her first, given that she had buried him under a pile of adamant outside the labyrinth, but she was surprised when Kai appeared before her. Looking at him was like looking into the face of Poseidon and Theseus, his eyes the same sparkling aqua.

She had come to despise them.

He had a spear, and he jabbed at her throat. Persephone summoned a wall of thick thorns that shattered beneath the power of his thrust. She managed to dodge the blow but was hit by a blast of power straight to her chest. She felt the impact of the ground as she was thrown back, the earth exploding around her.

Despite the strength of the blow, she rose quickly, rising from the fissure her landing had made. As she did, she realized she had come within a few feet of the mortal army. Their cries of hatred were accompanied by the sound of their swords clashing against their shields, the whir of arrows, and the explosion of bullets—one of which grazed her shoulder. The burn shocked her and instantly made her nauseous.

She summoned a wall of thorns to block their approach, though she knew it was only a matter of time before the mortals managed to scale them or hack their way through, but then they went up in ethereal flames. The magic belonged to Hephaestus, and while the fire would not burn her thorns, it would incinerate any mortal who touched it, preventing the army from advancing.

Before she could move, she was slammed with another blast of energy. It felt like being hit by a powerful wave and stole her breath like she was drowning. It sent her to her knees, and as she worked to fill her lungs with air, she looked up to see Kai approaching, a horrible grin across his face.

He lifted his spear parallel with the ground and aimed,

only to be thrown back and pinned to the ground by the impact of Hades's bident in his chest. Then suddenly, Hades was in front of her, helping her to her feet, his hands framing her face, eyes searching and a little frantic.

"I'm okay," she said.

He said nothing, but he kissed her hard on the mouth, and she thought she might burst into tears, but the hair on her arms rose, and she knew that something else was coming. They tore away from each other just as lightning struck Athena's temple. The blow came from Theseus and was directed at the only part that would burn, its wooden doors.

"No," Persephone breathed.

"Go," Hades said.

He moved past her, breaking into a run as he plucked his bident from Kai's chest and charged after Theseus.

Persephone teleported to the porch of the temple where Theseus's divine fire raged. The flames put off heat and smoke, but they were not destroying the wood—it was like Hephaestus's fire. From the other side, she hear desperate screams. Panic rose inside her as she thought about how many people might be trapped within.

Before she could decide how to tackle the fire, she felt a surge of electricity behind her and whirled, coming face-to-face with Sandros, his eyes aglow. He gave a menacing smile.

"Remember me?"

"How could I forget?" she asked. "You are as ugly as your father."

His lip curled, eyes sparking with rage. His hand crackled with lightning as he sent a blast barreling toward her. She jumped out of the way, thinking that the impact might cause the doors to burst open, but it only made the fire worse.

Fuck!

Persephone sent spikes of black thorns barreling toward the god. They slammed through him, each one forcing him back step after step, his body jerking violently. Despite this, he managed to blast her with another bolt, and she went flying. Smashing through a marble column, she landed hard on her back.

The demigod followed, launching himself at her, only to be impaled on a thicket of black spires that she had summoned around her. Blood dripped from his body onto hers. She was too frantic to be disgusted, even as she dismissed the spikes and his body fell on top of hers.

She threw him from her, and he fell off the side of the porch.

As she rose to her feet, there was a flare of light in the sky. Persephone looked on both in shock and awe as she followed the path of the sun as it fell from the sky. When it crashed to the ground, there was another flash, and the earth shook the same way it had when New Athens had been severed from the rest of New Greece.

Darkness flooded the world, and the only light was that of Selene's moon, which bathed everything in silver.

It was then that Persephone understood where Hecate had gone. She had torn Helios from the sky.

Persephone did not have long to think about what that actually meant. For now, she had to save the mortals in the temple.

Regrouping, she scrambled to the door. At first, she did not know what to do, but then she noticed that the flames had an energy that felt a lot like *life*, and if something had life, it could also *die*. She focused on the feel of the fire. Its wild heat was almost like a pulse. She could feel it in the palm of her hand, and once she had captured its beat, she closed her fingers around it, crushing it, suffocating it until there was no sign of it left.

Without thinking, she touched the handle of the door and instantly felt the burn of hot metal melt her skin. She screamed, her pain feeding her magic, which caused vines to burst from the ground. They tore into the crevices of the door, slowly rotting away the wood until she could kick them open.

But no one ran from the temple, and as the smoke cleared, she saw why. Beyond the threshold, there were only bodies.

Everyone was dead. She was too late.

Something struck her from behind. The blow was hard and instantly made her sick. She staggered but didn't fall, whirling to find that Sandros had returned, healed but bloody from being skewered by her magic. In his hands, he held a piece of marble, and something inside her snapped.

She screamed, and her magic turned to shadows, peeling off her body and barreling toward the demigod. They raced through him, and he dropped the bloodied piece of marble as he stumbled back until he came to the edge of the steps and fell.

Persephone followed, swiping the marble from the ground. She pounced, slamming it into his head over and over until she noticed thin black shadows wrapping around her wrists and slithering up her arms. She dropped the bloodied rock and rose to her feet, watching as the tendrils of the demigod's soul seeped into her skin. She realized what she had just done.

She had taken a life thread that had not been cut.

Her heart hammered in her ears as she frantically scanned the battlefield. Would the Fates take someone as retribution? Or would they give birth to something far worse? She knew the price of taking life—*a soul for a soul*.

Then her eyes found Hades, and everything around her seemed to slow. He was on his back, motionless.

"No," she breathed as she stumbled toward him. Then she screamed. "No!"

She fell to her knees beside him and brushed his hair from his face.

"Hades," she whispered.

His eyes were half-open, and there was blood on his lips. For one strange moment, she felt like she had been here before, that she had seen this before.

Hades lifted his hand, brushing a finger along her cheek.

"I thought…I thought I'd never see you again." He spoke quietly, more blood spilling from the corners of his mouth.

"We have to get you to the Underworld," she said, gripping his shoulders, as if by some miracle, she might be able to lift him. "The Golden Fleece—"

"I can't, Persephone," he said.

"What do you mean you can't?" she said, hysteria rising inside her. "Hades, *please*."

He took her hand and squeezed. When she looked down, she saw the black threads of the demigod's soul marring her skin.

"A soul for a soul, Persephone."

"No," she said. She refused to believe it, not only because she did not wish for it to be true but because she knew it *wasn't*. The Fates would only trade Hades's life for that of another god.

She *knew* that.

"It's over, Persephone."

"No," she repeated, her hands shaking. She didn't know what was happening, but she knew this wasn't real. "No! Hecate! Hecate!"

She searched for the goddess, but all she could see was ruin and fire. There was nothing else.

"Persephone," Hades said.

She couldn't look at him, because she knew if she did, he would drag her back in. He would convince her this was real. *He would say goodbye.*

"Persephone, look at me," Hades begged.

"I can't," she said. A guttural sob erupted from her throat.

"I love you," Hades whispered, and then he fell silent, and though she knew she shouldn't look, she couldn't help it. She had to know.

Her gaze fell to his face. He was still.

"Hades?" she whispered, frantic to hear his voice again. She shook him, but he did not move. "Hades, please!"

She placed her hands on his face. His skin was growing cool.

"Hades!"

She screamed, and a pain more acute than anything she had ever felt ripped through her. She felt like she was being torn to shreds, and then a wave of magic barreled over her, and Hades's body began to break apart, and the landscape around her seemed to burn away and melt, revealing a different world beneath.

The real world.

What she had sensed was true—the vision she had seen of Hades's dead body was not real. Instead of kneeling before him, she was kneeling on the ground before Athena's temple. Sandros lay beside her, blood pooling on the ground around him.

Confused, she looked into the sky and saw two gods fighting.

One she recognized as Cronos, and the other was Prometheus, the Titan God of Fire, and suddenly she understood that the reality the God of Time had crafted to torture her had been broken by Prometheus, and now they battled in the sky.

Hades manifested before her, and she rose to her feet, flinging her arms around him, a sob escaping her mouth.

"I'm here," he said, and then they vanished.

CHAPTER XXXVII
THESEUS

Theseus watched as Cronos and Prometheus battled in the sky. The appearance of the Titan God of Fire was a surprise, enough for Cronos to lose control over the illusion he was using to entrap the gods.

A wave of anger twisted through Theseus, and he summoned his lightning bolt. Its powerful heat wafted over him. If he was not invincible, it would have melted his skin from his bones. He turned in the direction of Hades, who had just manifested before Persephone, but as he took aim, they vanished.

Another surge of fury tore through Theseus. He pivoted to see Damian locked in a vicious battle with Hephaestus. Theseus lifted the lightning bolt and aimed for the god, but Hephaestus must have sensed the attack, because he raised his hand, and the bolt was swallowed by a stream of fire that shot from his palm. Fortunately, his magic was quickly extinguished when Damian impaled him with his spear.

Hephaestus gave no pained cry. He only grunted and fell to his golden knee. Damian tore the weapon free and reared back, preparing to stab him again, when Hecate appeared, blasting the demigod with a ray of black fire.

Theseus summoned his lightning bolt again, but the Goddess of Witchcraft, whose eyes glowed with an ethereal light, met his gaze. The blazing magic in his hand flickered and then faded, and a strange cold enveloped him. He tried to summon the bolt again, but all he could manage was sparks.

He gave a frustrated cry and drew his sword.

"What did you do, witch?" he demanded.

"Do you not know?" she asked. "If Zeus dies, so does his magic."

Theseus lowered his brows, at first confused by the goddess's words, but then the reality of what she was saying hit. He ground his teeth so hard, he thought they might break.

"I will murder you, witch."

She smirked. "Then murder me," she said. "But know that I will cling to you, even in death. You will never know peace, not in your waking hours or in sleep."

As she spoke, he could feel something overcome him, a deep and terrible madness. He buried his face in his hands, nails biting into his flesh. "Do not offer me your prophecy, witch. I am already destined to win."

"I am not giving prophecy, you idiot," she said. "I am cursing your ass."

Then she was gone, taking Hephaestus with her.

The only ones left battling were Cronos and Prometheus, whose magic shook the earth with each deafening strike, but even that came to an abrupt end when the Titan God of Fire vanished.

For a few seconds, Theseus and Cronos stared at the spot where he had been, a shared anger thickening the air between them. Prometheus was a traitor, to both Cronos and Zeus. He had loyalty to no one, save mortals. Theseus had not known that the Titan had escaped the Underworld. He had been in another part of Tartarus entirely, chained to a rock while an eagle feasted on his liver.

Cronos met Theseus's gaze from the sky.

"I will have vengeance against the other Titans as I will have vengeance against my sons," said Cronos. "Consider our alliance formed."

Theseus would have liked to celebrate, but he was too angry. He turned his gaze to the sky, catching sight of Zeus. He had left him suspended there as a reminder to the mortal world of his power. Now, he teleported to the god and saw that there was a gaping hole where his heart once beat.

Theseus's rage boiled over, and he lifted his blade, hacking at the God of the Sky, carving pieces of his flesh from his body and letting them fall to the earth.

It wasn't until he was finished that he saw how many had gathered to look up at him from below, not only Impious but Faithful mortals who had yet to seek refuge within Hades's obsidian tower.

As he lowered to the ground, splattered with the blood of Zeus, he declared, "The King of the Gods is dead."

His words were followed by deafening cheers and a chant that dissolved his doubt.

"All hail Theseus, King of the Gods."

———

Theseus's body crawled with the threat of Hecate's words, and he was eager to shed their weight. She might have murdered Zeus, but that did not diminish the prophecy of the ophiotaurus, and now he was assured of Cronos's alliance. He would win this war and would reign supreme over a world of his creation. Everything he'd planned for had come to fruition.

When he returned to the House of Aethra, passing the high wall surrounding his mother's residence, his servants waited on the porch, bowing as soon as he appeared. They would not meet his gaze, and he knew it was because they had witnessed him cutting Zeus to pieces.

If Ariadne were standing here, she would hold my gaze, he thought. *And she would refuse to bow.*

It wasn't that thought that brought him pleasure, it was what he would do to punish her for her defiance. He would force her to her knees and shove his cock so far down her throat that she choked around him.

The thought of how she would feel sent a thrill through him.

Suddenly, he was eager to go to Ariadne again, to see how she had changed in the hours since he'd left. Would she fight him again?

He entered the house and made his way to his bedroom, pausing when the noticed the door ajar. Instantly suspicious, he approached with caution, peering through the opening to see Helen leaning over Ariadne. A blade gleamed in her hand as she cut through the bindings on her wrists.

515

"Why are you helping me?" Ariadne asked. She spoke in a whisper.

"I have to," Helen said. "I can't…live knowing what he's doing to you."

Theseus doubted Helen even realized the irony of her words—though perhaps she soon would.

Theseus continued to watch, curious to hear what would be said.

Once Ariadne was free, Helen slid a backpack off and pulled out a bundle of clothes. She had come prepared.

"Hurry and dress," she instructed. "We don't have much time."

"Where is he?" Ariadne asked.

Theseus found the fear in her voice amusing.

"The gods are fighting downtown," said Helen. "But I don't know how long he will be away. Theseus does not fight his own battles."

Theseus's teeth clenched at her words.

Ariadne said nothing as she pulled on the clothes. Helen drew a sheathed knife from her bag, tossing it on the bed.

Ariadne took it. "Where will we go?"

"They're saying Hades has made Nevernight into a refuge. I will take you there."

"What about you?"

"I betrayed his wife and queen," said Helen. "I will not be welcome there."

Theseus waited until Ariadne was finished dressing, until her eyes met Helen's.

Then he appeared behind Helen, gripping her chin and the back of her head.

"You will regret that I chose to fight this battle," he

said, jerking her head to the side. The bones in her neck snapped.

He was close to tearing her head from her body, but Ariadne bolted for the door.

He released Helen and lunged for Ariadne, his fingers closing in the fabric of her shirt.

"No!" she screamed. She whirled to stab him, but his skin was impenetrable. Her hand slipped, and she cried out as the blade cut her palm. She dropped the knife, and it fell to the floor, along with fat drops of her blood.

Theseus grabbed her by the wrists and hauled her toward the bed, but Ariadne dug in her feet. The blood made her slick, and she slipped from his grasp. She seemed just as surprised as he was as she stumbled back and fell on her ass. He charged after her, and she scrambled to her feet. She reached the door and threw it open, racing down the hall.

He let her run, let her scream. He was keeping count of her transgressions, and later, he would decide how she was to be punished. For now, she was about to learn the consequences of leaving his room, because at the end of the hall was Phaedra's room, and the door was open, broken and splintered.

He knew when Ariadne caught sight of her sister, still dangling at the end of the bed, because she froze and a different kind of wailing came from her open mouth.

Slowly, she made her way to the floor, unable to stand.

"What did you do?" she moaned. "What did you do?"

"I did nothing," he answered. "Your sister chose this. She abandoned you. She abandoned her son."

"She would never!" Ariadne seethed with a deep and

guttural anger. She glared at him, and he felt the full force of her hate.

He could not help it, he chuckled and said, "Then you do not know her at all."

Ariadne launched herself at him with a shriek. He could feel her nails scrape down his face, but he felt nothing. For a few seconds, he let her rage, but he soon grew bored and snatched her by the wrists, dragging her into Phaedra's room.

He threw her on the bed, his hand around her throat.

"Fight this, and I will murder my son in front of you."

"You wouldn't," she wheezed, her eyes watering. "He is your blood."

"Try me," he said. "I can have many sons." He let his gaze fall to her stomach before he met her gaze again. "Perhaps there is already a replacement on the way."

He smiled at the look in her eyes, a mix of devastation and disgust, but she did not fight him as he pushed her knees apart and took her on the bed from which her sister still hung.

CHAPTER XXXVIII
HADES

Hades appeared in his office at Nevernight.

Only one thing had gone to plan during the entire battle, and that had been their exit.

"What was that?" Persephone whispered.

He knew what she was asking based on the raw rasp of her voice. She was still trembling from the horror of Cronos's magic, and he could not blame her. He was too.

"Cronos can make our greatest fears reality," he said. "Where do you think I got the ability?"

He hated sharing anything with his father, but what he hated most was that he had used that power on Persephone once before.

They were not alone long when the doors to his office opened and Harmonia, Sybil, and Aphrodite raced into the room.

"I thought I sensed your return," said Harmonia. "Thank the Fates!"

They do not deserve your thanks, Hades thought as Harmonia crossed the room to embrace Persephone, followed by Sybil.

Aphrodite lingered behind, her eyes wide. He knew by her expression that something was wrong.

"My powers are back," she said.

It was something she should be excited about or at the very least relieved, except that Hades felt like he understood her shock because in this instance, it meant that Zeus was dead.

Hecate's magic filled the room, signaling her return. She appeared with Artemis and Hephaestus, though the God of Fire was clearly injured. He was on his knees. One hand was flat on the ground, the other clutching his chest and covered in blood.

Aphrodite paled and ran to him. Kneeling at his side, she placed her hand over his as if she could somehow stop the bleeding.

"I'm fine," said the god, rising to his feet. He summoned a golden arrow and, without a second of hesitation, shoved it into his chest.

"What are you doing?" Aphrodite demanded, but then the arrow vanished and so did his wound.

Aphrodite looked on in wonder, her fingers brushing over his skin.

"I asked Hephaestus to turn the Golden Fleece into something we could use on the battlefield," said Hades. "Arrows seemed like the best option. If we are wounded by Theseus's weapons, we can be healed from a distance."

"Woo-hoo!" Hermes said, appearing suddenly. "My powers are back!"

His enthusiasm seemed to dim as he realized exactly what that meant. He looked at Aphrodite.

"Our powers are back," he said, quieter this time. He looked at Hades. "So...Zeus is dead?"

Hades hesitated. He was just as much in the dark as everyone else, but then Hecate spoke.

"I killed Zeus," she said.

They all looked at her. Even Hades was a little stunned.

"You only ever mentioned saving him," she said, half shrugging. "But the death of Zeus is the death of his magic. Theseus has no lightning bolt. Aphrodite and Hermes have their powers back...and I have a new heart."

Hades supposed that was fair enough, though he genuinely had not expected Hecate to make the decision.

"Did you just say you have a new heart?" Hades asked.

"I did," she said, a small smile on her face, adding, "Everyone knows not to kill a god before harvesting their organs."

There was a beat of silence, and then Hermes spoke. "Everyone, keep Hecate away from my dead body."

"Don't worry, Hermes. I would never think of it," she said.

"Well, that's comforting—"

"I only harvest quality organs."

"Hey!" Hermes put his hands on his hips. "I'm quality!"

The Goddess of Witchcraft looked him up and down and then shrugged. "Eh."

"Don't 'eh' me! You just called Zeus's heart quality!"

Hades was about to teleport to the Underworld to

escape the two when he felt Athena's magic. It pressed on his own—a request to teleport into his territory, one he granted.

When the Goddess of Wisdom appeared, she was dressed in gold robes. He had not seen her since she'd refused to fight outside Thebes. *Battle*, she had said, *should serve a purpose beyond bloodshed*, and though he would have welcomed her help, he could not blame her for refusing. He knew the cost of war, and it was a high price to pay if the fight meant nothing to you.

"Hades," she said.

"Athena," he said.

She raised her head, proud.

"My priestesses were slaughtered this morning. They begged for me, and I could not save them. I would join your side and fight against the evil that prevented me from protecting my own."

"It would be foolish of me to refuse," Hades said.

Athena seemed to relax, head lowering and shoulders falling. Then she took a step forward.

"You must tell me everything about this enemy," she said.

Hades glanced at Hecate, Artemis, and Hephaestus. While there was an element of urgency, they were also exhausted.

"We will rest," he said, looking down at Persephone. "Then reconvene."

"Are you really going to rest?" Hermes asked, suspicious. "Or are you just saying that so you can sneak away and fuck?"

"Do you ever just...*not* say exactly what you are thinking?" Persephone asked.

"Curious minds want to know," the god argued.

"I think you mean depraved," said Artemis.

"You say that like it's a bad thing."

Hades did not wait to say goodbye. He drew Persephone near and teleported to the baths. He wanted to be alone with her, to purge the horror they had witnessed on the battlefield.

Her back was to him, and he touched her shoulder. The shadows of her armor peeled away from her body, leaving her bare, and he bent to press a kiss to the hollow of her neck. She shivered and then turned to face him. Then she slipped her arms around his waist and held him tight, her head resting against his chest.

"I heard your heart stop beating," she said.

He held her tighter.

"So long as you live, it will never cease," he said.

"You cannot know that," she said. "Do not promise it."

"I would like to believe it all the same," he said.

Hades was content to hold her, given the horror he had witnessed in his own vision. In it, Persephone had been torn to pieces before him. Just as she had thought she would never hear his heart beat again, he had thought he would never hold her again.

"It was strange. The entire time, I had the sense that I had seen it all before...when you trained me...yet it was still different," she said.

Guilt blossomed in his chest from the memory of that day. He had manifested her greatest fear, which turned out to be his death, but he had not prepared her.

That was cruel, she had said, and she had been right. As much as he had wanted to prepare her for the cruelty of gods, it was not fair to her.

"But that was how I knew it wasn't real."

She pulled away, and their eyes met. She pressed her hand to his chest, and his armor turned to shadows and fled from the light, leaving him naked.

Her eyes fell to his cock. He wanted her to touch him, but she didn't.

"Is this selfish?" she asked.

"Does it feel selfish?"

"Yes."

He studied her and touched her cheek. "Then you are not aroused enough," he said, and as their mouths came together, their bodies did too.

———

When Hades woke, he was alone.

He rose and went in search of Persephone. He found her standing outside the palace with Cerberus by her side. He was still three-headed and dwarfed Persephone with his size. Hades approached her and slipped his arms around her waist. She relaxed against him, her hands folding over his.

"Can your monsters rise from the dead?" Persephone asked.

"Cerberus is not dead, but yes," Hades said. "Now that the sun is no longer in the sky."

He felt her freeze for a moment. "That was not a dream? Has Helios truly fallen?"

"Yes."

She turned to face him. "Then...I truly killed that demigod?"

Hades studied her for a moment and then took her hand. As he did, a single black thread surfaced.

524

"What will the Fates do?"

"It is hard to say in times of battle," said Hades. "It depends on who they favor."

"How do we know if they favor us?"

"We will know if we win."

They were not comforting words, but they were true.

"Come," he said. "We will meet with the gods."

They returned to his office at Nevernight, and Hades was surprised to find Ares waiting with the other gods. Beside him, he felt Persephone reach for her magic.

He could not blame her. The God of War's presence was immediately suspicious.

Hades's gaze slid to Aphrodite, who stood beside Ares.

"Aphrodite," Hades said. "Give me one good reason for Ares's presence within my realm."

"I have come to join your fight, Rich One."

Hermes laughed. "It's because he wants to be on the winning side."

Ares glared at the God of Mischief, though if not for Aphrodite, Ares would have likely waited until he was certain his choice would win.

"It sounds to me like you are asking for a favor, Ares," said Hades. "And if that is the case, I will require one in return."

The god straightened. "A favor in exchange for my battle prowess?"

"Do you mean your bloodlust?" asked Athena.

"Need I remind you that no one asked for you at all?" said Hades.

Hermes inhaled between his teeth. "Oh, you must be in pain after that burn."

"I will show you pain, Hermes," Ares threatened.

"Is that a promise, battle daddy?"

Hades sighed. "I am surrounded by idiots."

"Like attracts like," said Hecate.

"You take the offer, Ares, or you do not fight on the side of the gods," said Hades. "That is the deal."

There was a moment of silence, and then Ares crossed his arms over his chest. "Fine."

Now that that was done, Hades's gaze shifted to the rest of the gods.

"We cannot allow ourselves to be taken by surprise again," said Hades.

"Then we should attack first," said Aphrodite. "Take Theseus by surprise."

"Surprise is not as important as terrain," said Athena. "And Theseus has the advantage. He has the higher ground, and he is behind a wall."

"Then we take down the wall," said Hermes.

"And how do you propose we do that?" Aphrodite asked.

"I don't know, explosives?" he said.

"Sure," said Athena. "If you manage to battle your way through the army Theseus puts in front of it, then you can use explosives."

"Well, if you're so smart," said Hermes, "what should we do then?"

Athena shrugged a shoulder. "I would offer them something they cannot refuse—a weapon so deadly, they cannot help but open the gate."

"And what would that be?" Aphrodite asked. "Theseus already has weapons that can kill the gods."

"It sounds like you are talking about the Trojan

Horse," said Hermes. "You do know that's been done, right? They'll see it coming from a mile away. Literally!"

"Not the Trojan Horse. *A* Trojan horse," said Athena.

"I don't get it," said Hermes. "You said the same thing."

"She is saying we need a diversion, Hermes," said Hades.

"I have Zeus's balls in a jar," said Hecate.

Everyone looked at the goddess.

"Okay, that is definitely distracting," said Hermes, adding under this breath, "and disturbing."

"They can be a powerful weapon," Hecate said. "It just depends on what is born from them."

"I think we're all aware," said Hermes. "Do we really want to play chance with Zeus's balls? I mean, what if we get another Ares?" His mouth twisted in disgust.

"Fuck you, Hermes," said Ares.

"It's a valid concern!"

"I think if we are going to offer something to entice Theseus to open his gates, we should know what it is," said Athena.

Hades had an idea, but no one was going to like it.

"What about surrender?"

"You cannot be serious," said Aphrodite.

"As the dead," he replied.

"You keep using that joke, and it's not even funny," said Hermes.

Hades ignored him. "Theseus would open the gates if he thought I was surrendering."

"No," said Persephone. "He would kill you the moment you stepped over his threshold."

"He will want to gloat before he does that," said

Hades. "It is a valid plan. I will go tonight and offer an alliance. By the time you arrive at his gates, I will have them open."

"And if you don't?" Persephone asked. He could feel her fear and her fury. "What do we do then?"

"You fight until they open," he said.

"That all sounds well and good," said Hephaestus. "But what about Cronos? The Titan can manipulate our world, make us see things that are not there."

"He will have to be distracted so he cannot use his power again," said Hecate.

"I can manage that," said Ares.

"You cannot," said Hephaestus.

Hermes snickered.

"Are you trying to challenge me, metal leg?" asked Ares.

"Shut up, Ares," Aphrodite snapped.

"I am warning you," Hephaestus said. "You do not know Cronos's capabilities because you were not there today."

There was a beat of silence, and then Persephone spoke. "What about Prometheus?"

"He would certainly distract Cronos," said Hades. "There is no love between the two."

"Will he join our side?"

"He will not exactly join our side," said Hecate. "But he will help if mortals are under threat. We will not have to ask him for that. He will just appear as he did today."

Prometheus was the creator of man, and he had sacrificed a lot to see them thrive—namely his quality of life.

"I hope you aren't wrong," said Ares.

"I am never wrong, Ares," she said.

"Hmm, debatable," Hermes said.

Hecate elbowed him in the ribs.

"Ouch!" he cried. "Motherfucker!"

With their plans set, the gods dispersed. Hephaestus, Aphrodite, and Ares left to arm the mortals who had agreed to fight tomorrow. Hades had hoped Persephone would stay behind so they could talk about his decision to surrender to Theseus, but she left his office with Hermes in tow.

He knew she was upset but also scared. With Cronos's reality fresh on her mind, all she could think about was the possibility of his death, and he could not blame her. It was the same for him.

"Are you well, Hades?" Hecate asked.

She had yet to return to her duties—whatever they were. Harvesting organs, apparently.

He took a breath and then stood. "I think I need fresh air," he said.

"I will join you," she said.

Together they made their way to the floor of Nevernight and stepped just outside the entrance.

Hades stared up at the sky.

"I have never known you to stargaze," said Hecate.

"I am not," said Hades. "I am looking at what isn't there. The ophiotaurus has not returned to the sky."

Hecate looked. "Hmm. You are right. Pity."

Hades's gaze fell to her. "I know that voice."

"Of course you do," she said. "It is mine."

"I mean, I can tell you are disappointed," he said. "What did I do? What did I miss?"

"I am not disappointed," she said. "But your creativity is lacking."

"I admit I am only creative in one area of my life," he said.

She snorted. "That is because nothing else interests you."

"You are not wrong."

"Tell me the prophecy, Hades."

He had thought of it so often over the last month, he knew it by heart.

"If a person slays the ophiotaurus and burns its entrails, then victory is assured against the gods."

"Victory," she said. "What is victory, Hades?"

"Victory is winning," he said.

"Very good," she said, and though Hades glared, she continued. "And what can you win?"

"A battle," Hades said. "A war."

It was the obvious first choice.

"You are almost there," she said.

He stared at her for a moment and then answered, "A game."

"And there it is," she said.

"You are saying I can fulfill the prophecy by losing a game to Theseus?"

"I am saying that he has won a lot of battles against the gods, and still the ophiotaurus remains absent. Is it not worth a try?"

Hades supposed anything was worth a try.

"I do not just want to sabotage his future," Hades said. "I want him dead."

"Ah yes. Too bad he is invincible."

"You know you are not helping."

She shrugged. "Aphrodite was right. Even Achilles had a weakness. You already know Theseus's."

He did, although it was obvious for anyone to see. The demigod was arrogant.

It is not hubris if it is true, he had told Hades, though his comment was just another example of his excessive pride.

Hades was determined that it would be his downfall.

There was silence for a moment, and in the quiet, Hades thought he could hear the shuffling of feet. He turned to look down the street, and his heart seized when he met Dionysus's gaze. The God of the Vine had returned. He looked exhausted, angry, and devastated. Beside him was a woman Hades did not recognize, but he guessed she must be Medusa.

"Dionysus," Hades said, turning to face the god.

"My maenads," Dionysus said and stopped.

"I know," Hades said. "Come."

He led Dionysus and Medusa inside to Hecate's infirmary. When he pulled the curtain back, he was surprised to see Naia awake, propped up with pillows. She looked pale, and there was a cloudiness to her gaze that Hades attributed to her grief.

When she saw Dionysus, she burst into tears. He went to her and knelt beside her, taking her into his arms.

"He has Ariadne, Dionysus," she wailed. "He took her and her sister and the baby. There was nothing we could do."

"Shh," Dionysus soothed. "You did everything you could, Naia. Everything."

Hecate took Medusa away, and Hades left the two to reunite and grieve together.

Hades was surprised when he found Persephone standing with Artemis, though as he approached, the Goddess of the Hunt departed. Hades watched her go before turning his attention to his wife.

"What was that?" he asked.

"A truce," she said. "Did I hear correctly? Dionysus has returned?"

He nodded. "Naia is also awake. She says Ariadne, her sister, and the baby were taken by Theseus and the other demigods, which means they are likely behind the wall of Theseus's fortress."

Persephone paled. It was evident that breeching the wall would be an important element to winning this war, but now it was necessary to rescue the three.

"I know you are angry with me," he said.

"I am not angry," she said. "But it is hard to think of you walking into Theseus's territory. It is like the labyrinth all over again."

"If I felt there was another way, I would take it," he said.

"I know," she said.

There was a quiet pause, and then Hades spoke. "I wish to show you something, but I do not know if you are ready to return to the arsenal."

She shivered as she took a deep breath. "I suppose that depends on what you wish to show me," she answered. "Is it a memory that will overshadow what happened there before?"

"I'm not sure anything can do that," said Hades. He pressed his forehead to hers. "There is no wrong answer here, Persephone."

"I will go," she said. "If I cannot face what I have done, do I really deserve to heal?"

Hades tilted her head back. "Everyone deserves to heal, if not in life, then in death. It is the only way the world evolves when souls are reborn." He paused. "If it is too much, you will tell me?"

She nodded, and then he cradled her in his magic and took her to the Underworld.

He did not appear inside the arsenal, hoping that entering it from the hallway would prove to be far less overwhelming. He pressed his hand to the pad beside the door, and it opened.

"You repaired it," said Persephone, standing at the threshold.

"Yes," he said. He had done so when he had brought Hephaestus's weapons to the Underworld.

He watched her as her eyes scanned the room, halting when she spotted the armor at the center. Without a word, she left his side and went to it. He had displayed it beside his own, a smaller version of what he wore on the battlefield—layers of black metal, embellished with gold. Elaborate details decorated the breastplate. She traced the design with her fingertips.

"It is beautiful," she said and then met his gaze. "Thank you."

"I have something else for you," he said and produced the bident Hephaestus had made for her.

It had been his weapon for centuries, a symbol of his rule over the Underworld, and now she would have one too.

"Hades," Persephone whispered, wrapping her

fingers around the handle. "I…but I don't know how to use it."

"I will teach you," he said. "It is not for this battle."

She met his gaze. "Not for this battle but for others?"

"If we have lifetimes ahead of us," he said, "there is sure to be another."

"When I think of our future, I do not want to think of war," she said.

"What do you want to think of then?" he asked, tilting her head back.

"I would like to think of all the things we will celebrate with our people and our friends," she said. "Endless ascensions, the opening of Halcyon, your first birthday."

"My first birthday?" he asked.

"Yes," she said. "You've never celebrated, have you?"

"I don't exactly know when I was born," he said. "Even if I did, it isn't a day I would wish to celebrate."

"That is why I have chosen a new day of birth for you," she said.

"Oh? And what day is that?"

"November first," she said.

He stared down at her, curious. "What made you think of this?"

"Other than you, it was the only good thing that came out of the labyrinth."

CHAPTER XXXIX
HADES

Hades chose to dress in his usual black, tailored suit.

When he appeared before the gate of the House of Aethra, he did not want to do so in armor. He was not going to fight; he was going to make a deal—perhaps the greatest bargain of his life.

"Are you ready?" Persephone asked.

He turned to look at her, dressed in Hephaestus's fine armor. She was beautiful, a warrior in her own right.

"Are you?" he asked. He touched her chin, his thumb brushing over her bottom lip.

"I am ready for it to be over," she said. "So we can start our life."

He gave her a small smile and then kissed her, his hand slipping into her hair. He held her close and tight, tasting her until she was the only thing that filled his senses.

When they parted, Persephone touched the pocket of his jacket, and there, a red polyanthus flowered.

Her eyes lifted to his. "I will look for you at the gates," she said.

He took that as a promise, and with a final kiss, he left.

Hades was not surprised to hear the groan of several bows nocking when he appeared before the gate of Theseus's house. He stared up at the mortals who aimed at him, the tips of their arrows gleaming beneath Selene's moon.

He said nothing as he waited. He was not often anxious, but today the feeling burned his chest and churned in his stomach. Despite believing this was the right course of action, he knew it would be difficult. He did not like the idea of surrendering to a man he hated, even if it was only to gain entrance and proximity to his target.

He hoped he could maintain the act.

As he expected, Theseus kept him waiting under the threat of his archers. When he finally appeared, it was on the wall at the very center of the gates.

He looked down at Hades, eyes glittering with amusement.

"What a surprise," Theseus said. "To what do we owe the honor of your presence, Lord Hades?"

The demigod was already testing his patience. Hades worked not to show his frustration—or his hatred.

"I have considered much and consulted many," said Hades. "I hoped we might speak."

Hades wanted the demigod to be intrigued by the vagueness of his statements and let his imagination run wild with possibilities of what had brought Hades to his gates in the middle of the night, but if that was the case, Theseus did not let it show. Instead, he tilted his head to the side and offered a single word. "Speak."

"I have convened with the Fates and borne witness to your future," said Hades, though it was a lie. "The promise is great."

"You have told me nothing I do not already know," said Theseus.

"No," said Hades. "You have always been certain of your destiny."

"It is hard to argue with prophecy," said Theseus.

That was not true, but Hades would not disagree.

"So you have come to what?" Theseus asked. "Do not dance about, Hades. Neither one of us has time for that."

"I have come to surrender," said Hades. "To offer my allegiance to your side."

He was not prepared for how horrible those words would taste. He wanted to spit the moment they left his mouth.

There was a pause, and then Theseus chuckled. The mortals surrounding him followed until great peals of laughter filled the night. When it ebbed, Theseus spoke.

"That must have been so hard for you to say."

"It certainly took practice," said Hades.

"A waste for sure," said Theseus. "You see, I cannot accept your allegiance when I have accepted your father's. It would be...unbecoming since you two are enemies."

Hades stared at Theseus for a few long moments before he said, "If you are going to refuse me, then we should at least make it fun."

"Oh, I am having a blast," said Theseus. "But do proceed."

"A game of your choosing," said Hades. "If I win, you accept my offer."

"So eager to join the winning side," said Theseus. He looked to his left and then to his right. "What do we think? Shall we accept the god's offer?"

His army cheered, although Hades did not know if it was meant to encourage or dissuade. Though if Hades had to guess, Theseus had already made his decision. He merely enjoyed performing. His intention here was to humiliate—and it was working.

"Well, Hades," he said. "It looks like you have a deal."

Despite his acceptance, Hades did not feel any relief. In fact, he only became more anxious as the gates creaked open. He did not immediately cross the threshold.

"What's wrong, Hades?" asked Theseus. "Are you afraid?"

"You never gave me your terms," said Hades.

"My terms do not matter," said Theseus. "Because if I win, you will not live to take your next breath."

"You expect I will go down without a fight?"

"I hope not," said the demigod. "That would be very disappointing."

"Quite," said Hades, and then he moved forward, through the gates, and into Theseus's territory. Inside the gates, there were more mortal soldiers.

"I assume your brethren are still on the way?" said Theseus.

"They will fight until the bitter end," said Hades.

"Bitter indeed," said Theseus. "Come. Let us play this game."

The demigod turned, and Hades followed him across the stone courtyard and up the steps, but as he came to the top, he faltered.

"Hera?" Hades whispered.

It was not her, of course, but her soul. She stood trembling, her eyes wide with fear. She muttered things, though Hades could not hear the words.

Theseus stopped too. "Does she linger here?" he asked.

Hades looked at the demigod. "She will until she is laid to rest."

Not all souls needed funeral rites, but there were some who could not move on until they were performed.

"Oh, well, that will never happen," said Theseus. "I am afraid she is being fed to her followers at this very moment. Cronos is quite vengeful when it comes to the Olympians."

Hades could not hide his disgust.

"I would have thought you would consider it a fitting end for her, given your history," said Theseus.

"I would not wish such an end for anyone," said Hades. "Not even you."

"How noble of you," said Theseus as he made his way inside.

Hades's eyes lingered on Hera a moment longer before he followed the demigod into the house. He had half expected to hear Ariadne screaming from somewhere in the home, but the only noise was the sound of a child crying, which did not seem to bother Theseus as he led him to an office.

It was a dark room, open to the outside. The only light came from the fireplace and two large braziers blazing on the porch where there was a table and two chairs. It almost seemed as though Theseus had been prepared for him, but then Hades noticed the area looked out over the battlefield beyond the wall.

"Expecting someone?" Hades asked.

Theseus grinned. "Just preparing to enjoy the view. Have I ever told you I am not a card person?" Theseus asked as he crossed to the fireplace, though he knew the answer. They had never had any conversations beyond challenging each other.

"What do you prefer?" Hades asked, eyeing Theseus.

"Dominos," said Theseus, picking up a black box. He turned, lifting it. "I hope you don't mind."

"I did say it was your choice," Hades replied.

"You did," said Theseus, and Hades was unnerved by the amusement glittering in his eyes. The demigod gestured to the porch. "Please."

Hades exited the room and took the seat on the right. He felt as though he had walked out on a stage. He knew Theseus's men watched from the wall and the courtyard below.

Theseus followed. "Do you know how to play?"

"I am familiar," said Hades.

"Good," Theseus said. "Then you know the game moves fast and is won when there are no tiles left. What do you say to four rounds? Best out of four?"

"As you wish," said Hades.

Theseus turned the box over, spilling the ivory pieces onto the table. As Theseus turned over the tiles, a servant appeared with a silver tray. She set two glasses down.

"Drink?" Theseus asked.

"I have my own," said Hades. "If you don't mind."

"Be my guest," said Theseus.

Hades took out a black flask from his jacket pocket and poured a small amount of whiskey into the glass. He was not eager to drink, but he thought that perhaps the smell would offer comfort.

While he filled his glass, Theseus mixed the tiles on the table. When he was finished, they each chose seven. Hades looked at his hand, recalling that the player with the highest double laid down the first tile, which appeared to be Theseus, who laid down a double six.

"I heard congratulations are in order for more than just your recent victories," said Hades as he laid down a six-two.

"You are referring to the birth of my son," said Theseus, who laid down his next tile. The game did move quickly. "Yes, I suppose that is an accomplishment. Progeny are so important. Critical to carrying on a legacy. Oh, apologies. Am I right that you cannot have children?"

As Theseus spoke, he laid down his final tile, winning the first round.

Hades was still. His eyes rose to Theseus's face, seeing his lips curled in amusement. He clearly thought his comment was funny. Hades considered asking how the demigod knew something so personal, but he remembered that Poseidon had been present when Zeus's oracle had spouted her prophecy about his marriage to Persephone. He had been forced to reveal that the Fates had taken his ability to have children.

They transitioned into a new game, mixing tiles once more and choosing their pieces as they spoke.

"It is unfortunate that those who do not appreciate

children are able to have them while those who desire them cannot," said Hades.

The jab did not affect Theseus. "But you did not always desire them. You traded your ability to have them to give divinity to a mortal woman. Why was that?"

Theseus was not wrong. Hades had given a mortal woman divinity. In fact, it had been Dionysus's mother, Semele, who had died after she demanded to see Zeus in his true glory—a form that no mortal could look upon without perishing. Though she had only done so because Hera had tricked her.

After her death, Zeus took Dionysus, still only a fetus, and sewed him into his thigh so he could be born again. It was how the God of the Vine had come to be called the twice-born.

Later, Dionysus came to Hades, and when he could not rescue his mother from the Underworld on his own, he had begged for her release.

"I wanted to extract a favor," said Hades. He had seen potential in utilizing Dionysus's ability to inspire madness whenever he pleased.

Theseus chuckled and slid his final tile into place, winning this second round. "We are not so different, Hades."

"We are worlds apart, Theseus," said Hades as they moved seamlessly into the third round of the game.

"Perhaps we are now," the demigod said. "I like to think that I am what you could have been if you had not grown soft."

Hades slid a tile in place, the sound grinding against the wooden table.

"Are you saying my love for Persephone makes me weak?"

"Is she not the reason you found yourself locked in the labyrinth?"

"If Persephone is a weakness, what does that make Ariadne to you?"

It was the first time Hades noticed Theseus hesitate.

"Nothing at all," said Theseus.

"Nothing at all," Hades repeated. "Yet you flooded all of New Athens just to flush her out of Dionysus's tunnels."

"If you think I flooded New Athens for a woman, you are a fool."

"Did you not marry her sister to maintain control over her?"

"I married her sister because she *could be* controlled. Ariadne is untamable."

"Yet you keep trying," said Hades.

Theseus slammed a tile down on the table, jarring the dominos. Hades met his gaze and slid a final tile into place. He'd won this round, and Theseus seethed. It was the first time Hades noticed madness gleaming in Theseus's eyes.

"I don't have to *try* to tame Ariadne anymore," the demigod snarled.

Hades's stomach twisted as he considered what that could mean for Ariadne. They moved on to the final round of the game. Though Hades was not trying to win, he worried over losing. Theseus was often quick to dispense justice. Would he do the same here?

"What does Phaedra think of your obsession with her sister?"

"It does not matter. Even if she were still alive, I would not allow her the option of having an opinion."

The news that Phaedra was dead caught Hades by surprise.

"How is it that you do not know she is dead when you are the God of the Underworld?"

"I have been a little distracted with your invasion of my city," said Hades.

"Your city?" Theseus asked, chuckling humorlessly. "Since when has New Athens been your city?"

"It has always been mine, Theseus. Why do you think it is me you are fighting in this war?"

A horn sounded, and Hades looked to see steel gleaming on the horizon like stars.

"Oh look," said Theseus. "Your army has arrived."

There were shouts as orders were given. The gates opened, and soldiers marched out, but there was an unhurried air to their movements. It was almost as if none of this was serious, like they thought it would all be over before it really began.

As Hades looked out, he searched for Persephone. It was hard not to watch the approach of his queen, clad in shadow and battle ready, and though he knew she could do this and his friends would protect her, he still felt as though he should be there.

"Hephaestus is quite the craftsman," Theseus commented. "Impressive that he has managed to arm the gods and your mortal army with a copy of my creation."

"I believe you once called it an opportunity, did you not?"

"Do not become distracted, Hades," said Theseus. "Or you will miss witnessing your defeat."

Hades's gaze moved back to the tiles as Theseus slid

his last in place. He was not sure what he had expected once Theseus won, but it was not what followed. The demigod dropped his hands from the table and leaned back, staring with a darkness in his gaze Hades had never seen before.

After what seemed like an eternity, Theseus spoke.

"I know you let me win, Hades. You could not have tried harder to lose. You were not even counting the tiles."

Hades did not speak.

Theseus continued to stare as if he were considering what he was going to do. His jaw ticked, and he rapped his knuckles on the table, offering a small laugh. "I knew when you declined to choose the game you had come with a plan. No one who desires control as you do would relinquish it. The question is why?"

Hades shrugged. "Now you have defeated a god," he said.

There was a beat of silence, and then Theseus began to laugh. At first, it was quiet, and then it deepened. He laughed so long and so loud, he started to cough. He swiped Hades's glass from the table and downed the contents. When he was finished, he slammed it on the table.

Before he spoke, he chuckled again. "I have to give you credit for creativity, Hades," he said. "But it was a stupid plan. I have already fulfilled the prophecy, and now you have lost to me."

Theseus summoned a blade. The end was dark with Hydra venom.

"You understand, don't you?" he asked. "A bargain is a bargain."

Hades held Theseus's gaze and watched as his eyes

filled with pain. His face almost seemed to crumple—an expression of his agony.

He dropped the knife, and his hands went to his stomach as he doubled over and vomited blood at Hades's feet.

When he met his gaze, his eyes were red and watery.

"What did you do?" he screamed.

Hades just stared as Theseus fell to his knees, his breathing ragged.

"I learned a funny thing," said Hades. "Did you know that the rumors about Hera's apple tree are actually true; you cannot eat a golden apple twice?" He bent and took up Theseus's knife, which was covered in blood. "The second time will kill you."

More blood came from Theseus's mouth, and his face was turning a reddish purple. Hades rose to his feet then, the knife in hand.

"Everyone has a weakness, Theseus," said Hades, positioning the blade over Theseus's heart. "Mine might be Persephone, but yours...yours is hubris."

He held Theseus's gaze as he drove the knife deep, and as the life drained from his eyes, he gripped his head to keep him upright as he spoke.

"I'll meet you at the gates," he said and then let him fall to the floor, dead.

CHAPTER XL
PERSEPHONE

Persephone stood with Hecate on her left and Hermes on her right. Farther down, Aphrodite and Hephaestus were flanked by Athena and Ares, both wielding their spears and shields. Then there was Artemis, who had been entrusted to use the golden arrows during battle and heal those who had been wounded.

Directly behind them were the most experienced soldiers among their Faithful army. They had large shields that they locked in place to create a barrier so they could advance on the Impious army opposite them.

Leading the Impious were Kai, Damian, Machaon, and an additional demigod Persephone had not seen before.

"The one on the right is new," said Artemis, her eyes narrowing.

"His name is Perseus," said Dionysus. "And he is mine."

"Damn," said Hermes. "You picked the hot one."

Persephone and Hecate both looked at the god.

"What?" he asked. "I'm just being honest."

"That's your half brother, isn't it?" Persephone asked.

"Your point?"

"I don't know. I think it's kind of weird that you think your brother is hot."

"*Half*," said Hermes. "And why is it weird? It isn't like I want to fuck him."

A strained silence followed Hermes's words.

"Why do I get the feeling that none of you believe me?"

"Because we don't," said Hecate.

"I bet you've fucked your brother," said Ares.

"You wish, Ares!"

If Hades were here, he would have started this battle just to shut them up, Persephone thought.

She eyed the wall that surrounded Theseus's fortress. It was tall and tiered, and hundreds of archers stood ready with their bows, armor gleaming in the firelight.

"The gates are still closed," Persephone said.

"Give him time," said Hecate.

She would because she had no choice, but Persephone worried. She had hated Hades's plan from the moment he had suggested it. It felt like allowing him to return to the labyrinth, and with the horror of Cronos's reality still plaguing her, all she feared was that he would not return this time.

"So many mortals," Persephone said quietly.

So many souls, she thought.

"All willing to die for a demigod who has no control over their afterlife," said Hecate.

"Already considering how you will punish them?" Persephone asked, looking at Hecate.

"Aren't you?" Hecate returned.

"I don't see why we have to wait until they are dead," said Persephone.

In the next second, the ground between them opened, and Cerberus climbed from the depths of the Underworld. He was fearsome to behold, his eyes red and glowing with rage, teeth bared, his deep and guttural growls echoing in the quiet.

It was the first time Persephone saw movement from the Impious, the first time she sensed fear.

"I knew I trained you well," said Hecate with a smug smile that Persephone returned.

She placed a hand on Cerberus's side. As she did, there was the distinct sound of a bowstring loosening. She caught sight of an arrow whizzing toward Cerberus, but it was cut down by Artemis, whose own white arrow shattered it into pieces. Briefly, Persephone met the goddess's gaze, offering a nod of thanks before she stepped beyond their lines.

"How dare you try to hurt my dog," she said as power gathered in her hands. The ground trembled beneath her and opened, splitting the ranks of the Impious. Some were swallowed by the earth while others managed to race away. As they broke formation, the mortals began to yell and raced toward them, weapons in hand, and a volley of arrows came down on them.

Persephone summoned her magic, and vines grew up the sides of the walls, knocking rows of soldiers from their places.

The demigods vanished, and Persephone barked an order.

"Cerberus, snack!"

Her three-headed monster gave a low growl, his massive paws clawing at the earth, sending it flying in all directionsas he charged at the enemy army.

Then the demigods were before them, and all around, the sound of weapons clashing was thunderous. It shook Persephone to her core, but soon her attention was directed to the demigod before her—a woman she did not recognize, but her eyes were Poseidon's.

She cut her blade toward Persephone with an angry cry, but Persephone blocked the blow with a thicket of thorns and then blasted her with shadow magic. She staggered back and blasted her again.

Then Persephone felt a shock of pain at her back, and she arched against it, gasping. When it released her, she whirled to find no one.

She waited, her magic creating a barrier, knowing another attack would come. Within moments, she felt the disturbance and whirled, a series of black spikes bursting from her palm. They hit her target, who, as she had suspected, was invisible and wearing Hades's helm.

She called to her magic and turned the earth beneath his feet into mud. As he went to attack, he slipped and fell, and before he could react again, Hermes appeared and drove the sharp end of his caduceus into his back. Persephone pulled the helm from the demigod's head.

It was Damian, the son of Thetis, and he was dead.

"One down," said Hermes.

Persephone handed him the helm.

"Get this to Dionysus," said Persephone.

"You got it, Your Majesty," he said, scooping up the helm and vanishing in a blur of golden light.

As adrenaline coursed from her system, Persephone

remembered that she was injured. She felt like she was drowning, as if her lungs were full of blood. She pressed a hand to her chest, and it came away bloody.

She turned toward the sky, searching for Artemis, but she only managed to catch sight of Ares's brutal attack on Macheon before she felt the approach of another. As she turned, Kai raced toward her. The earth gave way beneath his feet, but he didn't stumble, navigating the ground with ease, weapon raised. Persephone staggered back, but she was not quick enough, the edge of his sword cutting into her chest, though she could barely feel the pain, too distracted by her wet breathing.

Then she watched through blurry vision as Kai lifted his blade, preparing to deliver the killing blow when he was stopped by two sharp prongs exploding through the front of his body—the tips of Hades's bident.

The demigod fell to his knees and then on his face.

"Hades," Persephone said, but her words were slurred. She knew the Hydra's poisonous venom was racing through her veins.

"Artemis!" Hades's command sounded far away, but she could feel the vibration of it in her chest. "Now!"

Something sharp pierced her chest, and then a blissful warmth spread, and suddenly she could breathe again. When her vision cleared and she could see Hades's face she threw her arms around his neck.

"Hades!"

"Are you well, darling?" he asked as he held her tight.

"I am now," she said.

He helped her to her feet just as the ground began to tremble.

"What is that?" Persephone asked. She looked at

Hades and then at Hecate, who appeared beside her. It was different from before when New Athens shook during the funeral games. It wasn't one continuous vibration. Instead, it was an interrupted shudder that reminded her of...footsteps.

Then Persephone saw it—a creature she only knew from history, a son of Gaia, a serpent-like monster. He walked on all fours, his body like that of a reptile, armored with scales and a long, lethal tail, but it was his head that terrified her the most. It was made up of hundreds of snakes. He was huge, and she knew that if he rose onto his back legs, his head would brush the stars.

"Typhon," Hecate whispered.

A terrible cry escaped from the creature, though it sounded unlike anything Persephone had ever heard, a high-pitched roar with a strange hiss. As it bellowed, poisonous venom rained down on the land and their army, melting them where they stood.

Those who were not hit by the venom were crushed beneath his feet and thrown with a swipe of his great tail.

"Cerberus!" Hades said, his voice a command, and the monster launched himself at the giant, the teeth of all three heads sinking into different parts of the creature— his hind leg, his back, and his neck. Typhon bellowed, and the snakes that made up his head hissed violently, spewing more venom. Cerberus yelped as the spray stung him, burning him to the bone.

"Cerberus!" Persephone cried as he retreated and came near so she could lay her healing hands upon him. The wounds from the venom healed, but Typhon had turned his attention to them, his many serpent heads shrieking.

But then there was a flash of light as Hermes ran past, swinging his caduceus, decapitating several of the snake's heads. Hephaestus did the same with his whip, and then Aphrodite with her sword. Athena lodged her spear into the creature, striking Typhon's back repeatedly.

Persephone summoned vines from the ground and Hades his shadows. They wrapped around the monster's legs and waist. Typhon roared as he buckled beneath their pull. With him restrained, he was suddenly surrounded, both by gods and mortals, stabbing him in every part of his body.

"Well, this," Hermes said, jabbing his blade into the creature's belly, "was far easier than when Zeus did it!"

Typhon roared. Hades's shadows quivered and Persephone's vines snapped as the monster managed to rise to his feet.

"Why did you have to open your fucking mouth?" Aphrodite snapped at Hermes over Typhon's bellow of anger. He took a great step, and the ground shook and split. Hundreds of mortals were crushed or drowned as huge drops of his blood fell to the ground.

"Hear me out," said Hermes. "We trip him and try that again."

"It didn't work the first time, Hermes. Why would it work a second?" Persephone pointed out

"You can't argue that he isn't weaker now," said Artemis.

It was true and evident by how much blood covered the giant's scaly body. If they failed to kill him, it was likely the Hydra venom would, but it was impossible to say how long that would take in a body so large. By then, he might destroy the entire world.

"Now might be a really great time to use those balls you have been going on about, Hecate," Hermes said.

But they all knew it was a dangerous option. They did not know what Zeus's organ would create—worse, how much more destruction it might cause.

Before Hecate could consider it, Hephaestus appeared in the sky and shot molten spears into Typhon from his palm. The giant staggered but did not fall. Again he screamed, but this time, something shot out of the dark wreathed in fire.

Prometheus, Persephone realized as he slammed into Typhon with such force, he went straight through the monster.

The giant groaned and swayed on his feet before falling to the ground again. His impact was so great, the earth buckled beneath him, moving like waves beneath the gods' feet. While the gods were able to rise into the air and avoid falling, it sent both armies to the ground.

Prometheus hovered in the air, dripping with the giant's blood.

"Fuck yes!" Hermes shouted.

But the victory was short-lived as Cronos appeared behind the Titan God of Fire, taking his head between his hands and twisting it free. Prometheus's body fell from the sky, landing like a fiery meteor.

"Fucking Fates," said Hades.

It had all happened so fast. Persephone shook with fury and terror as she watched Cronos toss the Titan's head to the side as if it were nothing.

Beside her, Hecate vanished and appeared to surround Cronos in her triple form, black fire in her hands that she released on the god in a flaming stream.

Cronos vanished, but then so did Hecate. When they appeared again, they slammed into each other, and the sound was like thunder. As much as Persephone wanted to look away—to focus on the war raging around her—she couldn't tear her eyes from the sky.

She watched in horror as Cronos snatched Hecate and slammed her over his knee. She seemed to break in half.

Persephone did not recognize the sound that came out of her mouth. She wailed. She thought she would be sick, and then she was. She bent over and vomited.

"No, no, no!"

Each word was uttered louder and louder until she was screaming at the top of her lungs.

She fell to her knees, her arms spread wide.

Instead of power flowing from her, it flowed to her.

It coursed through her blood, feeling like lightning in her veins, gathering in her hands, and as the power came to her, the world around her changed. The horror that Cronos had painted disintegrated, and suddenly the god was standing before her, his horrible face contorted into a scowl.

He reared back, his scythe in hand, and aimed for Persephone's head.

She screamed, her hands coming together, and in them she held Cronos's power. Her body vibrated with it, a power she'd never experienced before, and with it, she wove a world for the Titan that was filled with his greatest fears.

As she did, she used her own power to call to the earth. From it, roots sprouted, and they wrapped around the God of Time until he was completely consumed within the trunk of a tree, its branches reaching toward the sky before blooming in a waterfall of pink blossoms.

It was magnificent.

When it was done, Persephone felt as though all the life had been drained from her body.

She swayed and Hades's arms came around her. She knew it was safe to rest.

"You did it, darling," he said. "It is done."

CHAPTER XLI
DIONYSUS

Dionysus battled to get to the gates.

He had one goal, and that was to rescue Ariadne. Even killing Perseus was an afterthought.

Then he felt something slam down on his head, but it was not a weapon—it was a helmet. He placed his hand to the cold metal as Hermes appeared in front of him.

"It's the Helm of Darkness," he said. "Go get your girl."

Hermes gave him a little push, but Dionysus did not need it. He cut through the ranks of the Impious, wishing instead that he were incorporeal so that he might race through to the gates, but he was anxious to find Ariadne, worried he would be too late.

Those thoughts made him angry, and he pushed harder through the onslaught of metal-clad bodies, slamming his thyrsus into anyone who stood in his path. If he could not be a ghost, the helm provided the next best thing—surprise.

When he made it through the gates and was within sight of Theseus's fortress, he felt the greatest sense of relief. He was almost there.

Ari, I am almost there.

He took the steps two at a time but stopped short at the top as Perseus approached.

Dionysus had wondered where the demigod had gone, but like the coward he was, he'd retreated behind the wall.

"I know you are there, Dionysus," Perseus said. "Why don't you come out and play?"

Dionysus clenched his jaw and gripped the helm. "You mean the same way you did when you attacked my home?"

"It was only fair," the demigod said. "You stole what belonged to Theseus." Perseus laughed. "Does that make you mad? Or is it just the thought of Ariadne belonging to Theseus that pisses you off?"

"What is it with all you fuckers talking about people like you own them? Like they are fucking currency?"

"People are currency," said Perseus. "You should know that best considering the price you paid for Phaedra."

It was hard for Dionysus to think about his maenads without feeling the storming of madness. When he had finally made it to the tunnels, he'd discovered hundreds of bodies all resting in a line, covered with sheets. He would learn later that Hades, Hermes, Ilias, and Artemis had gathered his dead. Hecate had begun funeral rites, but they hadn't wanted to bury anyone until he'd had a chance to say goodbye.

"I hope she was worth it," said Perseus. "That's

why you did it, isn't it? So Ariadne would let you fuck her?"

Dionysus just stared, his hatred for the demigod burning deep. He knew Perseus was trying to antagonize him enough so that he would make the first move, and it was that piece of knowledge that kept him from boiling over—that and the fact that Ariadne had just emerged from inside Theseus's house. She was covered in blood, but he did not think it was hers, given that the blade in her hand was dripping. Her eyes were dark and angry, full of an anguish he had seen often in the eyes of his maenads.

It made him sick, and it made him angry.

He held Perseus's gaze as Ariadne approached from behind and answered him. "No," he said. "I fucked her before that."

Then Ariadne's blade burst through Perseus's chest, and as his body arched, Dionysus jabbed his thyrsus through the demigod's neck. They both withdrew their weapons at the same time, and when Perseus fell, they were left to face each other.

"Ari," he breathed her name.

It was then he noticed she was wearing some kind of wrap. He realized Acamus was nestled inside it.

He looked at the baby and then at Ariadne. "Where is Phaedra?"

Her mouth quivered. "She didn't make it," Ariadne said, dissolving into tears.

She fell into him, and he caught her, holding her against him. Fuck, he wished he wasn't wearing armor right now so she had something soft to rest her face against.

"I've got you," he said, threading his fingers into her hair. "Both of you."

CHAPTER XLII
PERSEPHONE

When Persephone woke, she felt like she could have slept for an eternity. Even now, it was a challenge to open her heavy eyes, so she didn't. She lay still and quiet, but she was so hot, and she didn't know why. It was what had woken her, the feeling of her skin burning.

She struggled to remember how she had gotten here—wherever here was—and all she could recall was the feel of fire-hot power coursing through her veins. Her body hummed with the memory of it. She shivered, hating it.

It was not hers. It belonged to Cronos.

Cronos. She remembered. She had trapped him in a tree with his greatest fears, and Hades had killed Theseus.

Hades.

The last thing she remembered was the feel of his arms around her and his voice.

You did it, darling. It is done.

This time, she had no trouble opening her eyes, and

when she did, she found she was plastered against Hades. Beneath her, his body felt like an inferno. She peeled herself away, expecting to find him awake, but she found that he slumbered.

She relaxed a little, watching him. It was so rare to see him like this—unaware and serene. His forehead was smooth, and there were no lines between his brows.

There was a part of her that did not believe this was real, that feared she was still trapped within the labyrinth.

She touched his lips, full and slightly parted, and then bent to kiss him. It was real. *He* was real.

And they *had* won.

Hades inhaled, and his hands came down on her, his tongue slipping into her mouth as he deepened the kiss, his arousal growing hard between them.

"I did not mean to wake you," Persephone said when they parted.

"I do not mind," he said. "Especially when you do it like this."

He gripped her ass and ground his hips into hers. She took a deep breath, and he slid his tongue into her mouth again. They were content to kiss for a while, but eventually Persephone pulled away and whispered against his lips, "I want to taste you."

He grinned.

"Darling, you can have me anytime."

She loved his smile and the promise in his words, and she kissed him again before moving down his body, lips brushing over his chest and stomach. She let her nipples, peaked and hard, trail over his skin and his length, which lay heavily against the bottom of his stomach.

As she sat back on her knees and took him into

her hand, Hades adjusted his pillow and braced a hand behind his head. He looked languid and content, but she wanted to make him writhe. She felt more alive than she had in months, unburdened by fear and the dread that came with the possibility of never seeing him again.

She was hungry for him, and she wanted him to be voracious for her.

She pumped her hand up and down his cock, bending to lick the come that beaded at the tip. As she did, her hair fell, curtaining her face. Hades gathered it into his hands and swept it to the side.

"I do not wish to miss a single part of this," he said.

She met his gaze, and then she licked him, teasing one of the veins that had risen to the surface of his soft skin. She let her tongue swirl over the top of him and took him into her mouth.

Hades groaned, and the sound vibrated in her chest, down to her very core. She tensed, her thighs squeezing together.

"I love when you take me deep," he said.

His fingers were in her hair again, and she let him hit the back of her throat, keeping him there for only a moment before she released him to breathe. Suddenly, he was gone, and she felt his fingers slide between her legs and tease her damp heat. She realized he had teleported behind her.

"That's not fair," she moaned.

"Nothing is fair, darling," he said, slipping one finger inside. "Fuck," he said, planting a kiss on her ass before removing his finger and pressing his mouth to her slick skin.

"Yes," she moaned. "Yes."

She pulled away from him and then turned, dragging his mouth to hers. She kissed him hard before she lay on her back and spread her legs again. Hades's eyes glittered, dancing over every part of her body.

"I fucking love every part of you," he said.

Then his mouth was on her again, and his fingers dove into her flesh. Everything inside her started to feel tight, wound by Hades's hand, and then, as if a thread snapped, she was unleashed, body seizing as wave after wave of pleasure shuddered through her. She had never felt something this intense, but it was like everything she had kept inside her for weeks—all the pain and the guilt and the fear—was suddenly released. Now she had room for hope.

She had room for dreams.

As if he knew, Hades stretched out, resting his body against hers and the head of his cock between her legs. She brought her knees up, framing his body, ready and desperate for him to be inside.

"Are you well?" he asked. He brushed his fingers along her brow.

"I am," she replied. "More than."

Then he kissed her, and Persephone opened her mouth against his, taking a breath as he filled her.

"I love you," she said.

Hades grinned again, and a breathless laugh escaped him.

She lifted her legs, wrapping them around his waist. "Why do you laugh?"

"It is merely disbelief," he said, his words punctuated with a breath as he moved inside her. "You have become my past, my present, and my future."

Her eyes watered, but for once, it wasn't because she was afraid. It was because she was happy—ridiculously happy.

And so very much in love.

Hades lowered his forehead to rest against hers, and then they kissed once more before there was nothing more they could say with words.

———

Later, Persephone lay draped over Hades. They were both naked, bodies spent from their lovemaking, but it was in this quiet that the darkness crept in. Persephone could feel it like a cool blanket settling over her, and she shivered.

Hades felt it, and his warm hands eased her prickly flesh.

"What are you thinking about?" he whispered. He sounded drowsy, and she liked that. It said a lot, that he felt comfortable enough to rest.

She was quiet. At first, she had a hard time tracking her thoughts. They seemed to move rapidly through her mind, jumping from one concern to the next. She thought about all the work they had to do to rebuild New Athens, and while that would be a grand undertaking, nothing was more daunting than earning the trust of mortals again. They had to prove they were worthy of worship, and that would require building a different kind of pantheon, one where mortals were not punished for the shortcomings of the gods.

But what had brought about the chill were the thoughts she'd had about herself.

"I am only trying to decide who I am now that the war is over," she said.

"You are Persephone," he said. "You are my wife and my queen. You are everything to me."

She traced a circle on his chest but did not look at him. "But even you know I am not the same as before."

"If you weren't, you could not live in this world," he said. "I am not afraid. Why should you be?"

"I don't know," she said. "I think I worry that if I live long enough, I will cease to care for the world. I already feel it, this urge to be selfish, to not go beyond our borders."

"It is not selfish to have a desire to be where you are loved, Persephone," Hades said. As he spoke, his warm hand continued to move soothingly over her back. "Doubt and suspicion are not the same as losing your humanity. If anything, they will protect you better than even your magic."

They were quiet, and then Persephone spoke. "What are you thinking about?"

"I am not sure you wish to know," he said.

She lifted her head and looked at him. "I always want to know your thoughts."

Hades smiled, his eyes glittering. "They are not so complicated," he said, but then he paused before saying, "I am thinking about how many times we have come close to never having a moment like this again."

Persephone was quiet after his confession. In some ways, it was comforting, knowing his thoughts were similar to her own.

"Do you think those thoughts will ever go away?" she asked.

"Eventually," he said.

"What do we do? Until then?" she asked.

"Whatever it takes," he said. "But we should make a promise that if either of us has those thoughts, we will tell the other."

She raised a brow at his suggestion. It was ironic, given that he had not wanted to tell her his thoughts earlier. "You realize if you make a promise, it is binding?"

He smiled. "I do," he said, brushing her hair behind her ear. "But I will do anything to keep you from suffering alone with your thoughts."

She held his gaze for a few moments and traced his bottom lip.

"I love you," she said, and she wanted him to feel just how much. She kissed him, softly at first, then harder, shifting so that her knees were on either side of his body, highly aware of his arousal and the heat it stirred inside her.

She sat back, sliding over his cock.

"Care to share your thoughts now?" she asked as his hands closed over her breasts. He squeezed them as she ground against him.

He grinned. "There are too many to count."

"I did not ask you to count them," she said.

"Hmm. I am thinking about how beautiful you are and how much I fucking love your breasts and that I want to suck them until you scream. I'm thinking about how long I'll let you ride my cock before I fuck you into oblivion."

"All those things sound like promises," she said.

"They are," he replied.

She smiled, almost delirious, and slid down Hades's length. They both groaned, and then the doors burst open.

"Wakey wakey, eggs and…" Hermes paused when he saw them on the bed and then grinned. "Sexy!"

Persephone groaned again and then collapsed against Hades's chest. The high she'd been riding crashed hard. "Hermes, what are you doing here?"

"I'm here to collect your plaything," he said. "Sorry if he's in use, but this is nonnegotiable."

"*Everything* is negotiable," Persephone said.

"I'm afraid this isn't," said Hecate, sweeping into the room.

"Hecate!" Persephone said, pushing against Hades's chest. She had every intention of running to the goddess and pulling her into a tight hug, but the sudden movement reminded her that she was both naked and currently impaled by Hades's cock. It occurred to her that she should be more embarrassed, but with friends like Hermes and Hecate and a lover like Hades, it was pointless.

They had no boundaries, and Hades was willing to fuck her anywhere. Though she did cover herself with a blanket.

Hecate smiled. "Hello, my dear," she said.

"Am I the only one who finds this really fucking annoying?" Hades asked.

"With the way Sephy keeps moving, I imagine you find it quite unbearable," said Hermes.

"Considering you are aware of today's schedule, you have only yourself to blame," said Hecate.

"What schedule?" Persephone asked, and then she looked down at Hades. "What's going on?"

"It is a surprise," he said.

"A surprise that has a deadline," Hecate reminded, clapping her hands. "So come on! Up, Persephone."

"I'm not sure that is the command you wish to give," said Hades.

Hecate lifted a brow, and then she narrowed her eyes. "I am going to step out those doors and count to ten," she said. "And if you both are not out of bed and *reasonably* clothed, I will curse your sex life for the next week." Hecate turned. "Hermes!"

"What? I am here for accountability!" he said.

"I'll curse you too, Hermes. Do not try me!"

"Fine," he whined and stomped toward the door. "No one ever lets me have *any* fun."

When the door was closed, Persephone looked down at Hades.

Outside, she heard Hecate yell, "One!"

"I am trying to decide how long it would take to make you come," Persephone said.

Hades laughed. "I think it depends on whether Hecate decides to actually count to ten," said Hades.

"Nine!"

"And there is your answer," Hades said.

Persephone scrambled off him and summoned a robe while Hades sat up in bed, dragging a sheet over his erection, and when that didn't work, he grabbed a pillow.

"Ten!"

Hecate threw open the doors.

"You skipped, like, seven numbers!" Hermes complained.

Hecate entered the room like a storm, her expression determined, though Persephone was used to this version of the Goddess of Witchcraft, especially when she was involved in organizing something. She took pride in the work and wanted everything to go smoothly.

568

Now that she was dressed, Persephone went to her. "I am so glad to see you, Hecate," she whispered as her arms slid around her waist.

The goddess held her close and spoke against her hair. "And I you, my dear."

Persephone pulled away, but Hecate held her hand.

"Come. We must get you ready for tonight!"

Persephone looked over her shoulder at Hades. "Remember, you made a promise," she called as Hecate dragged her out of the room and down the hall to the queen's suite.

Inside, the lampades waited near the mirrored vanity. Persephone smiled at the silvery nymphs who had come to be an integral part of her glamorous routine.

"I am so glad to see you," said Persephone. "It has been too long."

"Lucky for you," said Hecate. "You will need them for quite a few things this month."

Persephone wondered which things, but mostly she was curious about tonight. She did not think it was time for the ascension ball, though it was fast approaching.

She sat down, though it took her some time to face herself in the mirror. When she finally lifted her head and met her gaze, she did not see what she had expected.

She'd thought she would see a stranger, a shell of the person she had been in her previous life.

Instead, she saw strength.

She saw pride.

She saw a woman who was *queen*.

She let her gaze rise to Hecate, who watched her in the reflection.

"Now you see yourself clearly," the goddess said.

The lampades worked, smoothing her hair into perfect waves, which complimented the simple but glamorous makeup they had chosen—winged eyeliner and a bold red lip. The look made even more sense once Hecate dressed her. The goddess had chosen a black gown with a narrow waist, a flared skirt, and a high slit.

Hades will like that, Persephone thought.

The bodice was almost a corset, and while the fabric over her ribs was sheer, the fabric over her breasts was velvet and embellished with shimmering black beads.

It was just simple enough, and Persephone loved it.

"It is beautiful, Hecate," she said, meeting her gaze in the mirror. "But what's the occasion?"

The goddess smiled. "You will know soon enough."

"You can't blame me for trying," Persephone said.

There was a pause, and once again, in that quiet, darkness seeped in, and Persephone spoke.

"I saw you die," she said. "I will never forget it. Cronos *broke* you." She could not look at Hecate, but she could feel her gaze. "I love Hades. I will not live without him," she said. "But I cannot live without you either, Hecate."

"Oh, my dear," she said, her voice thick with tears. "You will never have to."

When Persephone looked up, she saw that Hecate's eyes were watering, but the tears never fell. Instead, she drew Persephone into a hug, and when she pulled away, she touched her chin.

"I do not have children of my own," Hecate said. "But you, I consider a daughter."

This time, Persephone burst into tears, and suddenly, the lampades were fluttering around her, fanning her face and touching up her makeup. Before they could risk any more heart-to-hearts, there was a knock at the door.

"It looks like it's time," Hecate said.

As soon as Persephone stepped outside the room, she was met with cheers. She halted, startled by the sudden sound but also the appearance of so many souls. They lined both sides of the hallway, creating a path for her to follow.

"Oh, Hecate," Persephone whispered. Her hand came to rest over her racing heart.

"This is only the start," said the goddess, and she offered her arm.

Persephone took it, and together they walked down the path of souls as it curved into the foyer, past the library and dining room. The journey took a while because she paused to hold hands and pull others in for hugs. Everyone was here, crammed into the palace—even the children, who raced to her and wrapped their arms around her legs.

It wasn't until she saw Yuri that she really began to cry, and she wondered why she had bothered with makeup at all. The young soul approached and threw her arms around Persephone's neck, and while they hugged, she caught sight of Lexa and then Apollo. With each friend, each embrace, she felt like her heart was going to burst from happiness.

"Apollo," she whispered, holding him tight, her head resting against his hard chest. He had no heartbeat, but he was warm.

"You look beautiful, Seph," he said.

"I miss you," she said.

He chuckled. "You won't for long."

She pulled away. "Don't say that."

He shrugged. "Call it self-awareness," he said. "I'm a needy motherfucker."

She laughed, and Apollo smiled, then he turned his head, nodding in the direction of the throne room.

Persephone looked, and it felt like her heart had stopped and all the air had been sucked from her lungs.

Through the open doors, she could see Hades on the dais before his throne, his eyes burning brightly, the deep sapphire blue of his Divine form. His hair was down, falling thickly past his shoulders, and his horns were on display, making him look even larger. Beside him stood Hermes, who was dressed in a gold himation, the fabric moving almost like water. He was also in his Divine form, his white wings spread wide.

Cerberus, Typhon, and Orthrus waited too, no longer in their monstrous form. They sat stoically on Hades's right, though Persephone could see Orthrus's body wiggling. It was taking everything in his power to remain where he was.

"Hecate," Persephone asked. "What is this?"

"Your coronation," the goddess said. "You are Queen of the Underworld, but you have not been crowned."

Persephone's lips parted in surprise, and she met Hades's gaze again.

Hecate tugged on her arm, guiding her forward. Yuri, Lexa, and Apollo followed behind her. She looked at Hecate, confused.

"They're your handmaidens," said the goddess. "It's tradition."

Persephone felt like she was in a daze as she made her way into the packed throne room, her eyes never leaving Hades's. She had never felt so nervous. It was like marrying Hades all over again, except that this time, she was basically marrying his entire realm.

Hecate led her right to the bottom of the steps.

"Your Highness," she said, nodding to Hades. Then she turned to Persephone. "I love you, my dear."

Persephone's mouth quivered. "I love you too," she whispered.

The goddess smiled before leaving her side, making her way up the steps to stand on the other side of her ivory throne.

Persephone's gaze slid to Hades.

"My darling," he said, his voice quiet but warm.

"My love," she replied.

"Sephy," said Hermes.

Hades glared at the god, but Persephone laughed.

"Bestie," she said.

Hermes grinned. "See, Hades, we're besties."

"Curse, Hermes!" Hecate snapped.

"Fine," he said, crossing his arms over his chest, pouting.

There was a beat of silence as Persephone's attention returned to Hades, though it had never truly left. She was always aware of him, even when she wasn't looking at him. She could feel him, an anchor to this world.

"Darling," he tried again. "I have chosen you as my wife and queen. Do you accept—"

"Yes," she said.

Everyone laughed, including Hades, his eyes glinting. "Ever eager."

She felt the rasp of his voice in the bottom of her

stomach. There was a pause, and this time when he spoke, she did not interrupt.

"Do you accept responsibility for the people of this realm and all who will pass through its gates?"

"I do," she said.

She had, but then they all already knew that. They had watched her fight for them, and she would do so over and over again.

"And you promise to uphold the laws of my court?"

Persephone lifted her head, her answer a little more hesitant. "Yes?"

Hades chuckled. "Fair enough."

Hermes approached Hades and handed him a crown. It was made up of black spires, identical to the one Hades wore now. With it in hand, he approached. He was already tall, but now he was elevated by the steps, which forced her to tilt her head back to hold his gaze.

"Then it is my pleasure, my greatest honor, to offer you this crown as a symbol of your dedication and love for my people and this realm."

She lowered her head, staring at Hades's chest as he placed the crown upon her head. She was surprised by how heavy it was, but it also felt as familiar as the weight of her horns.

Hades offered his hand and helped her up the steps, kissing her deeply before they sat on their thrones.

Only then did the dogs move. All three shot forward, crowding Persephone, desperate for pets and head scratches. She was all too happy to oblige, but then Hades whistled sharply, and the three sat immediately.

"Oh, Hades," she said. "They are fine."

"With the way they act, you would think they never get any attention."

She arched a brow. "If I didn't know any better, I'd think you were talking about yourself."

Hermes snorted.

Then Hecate spoke, her voice resonating in the crowded room. "All hail our King and Queen. May they reign forever."

The crowd cheered, and Persephone looked at Hades.

"Forever," she said.

"Forever will never be enough," he said. "Not when I have lived half my life without you."

She considered commenting that he might say otherwise when he had lived half his life with her, but she knew he would disagree.

"Perhaps I can make you forget you were ever alone," she said.

"I accept," he said.

"Did you take that as a challenge?"

"No," he said and grinned. "A promise."

Author's Note

When I started *A Touch of Chaos*, I don't think I had any idea how complicated this book would become. I knew it would be difficult. I was closing out a series that ended up being far bigger than I ever imagined, spanning seven books. Since 2019, this cast of characters just grew and grew, and I felt the pressure of bringing it to the perfect conclusion.

For a long time, I would tell people, I know two things about this book: I must get Hades out of the labyrinth, and there has to be another Titanomachy, but I knew nothing else. I kept thinking I was going to need more *things* to make it a grand conclusion, when in reality, the book is literally those two things, and it is enough—more than enough.

It is the perfect conclusion to this series, and I am so proud of this book, so grateful for how it came together, and none of it would have happened without my readers.

Thank you all so much for your dedication to Hades

and Persephone. You have challenged me in ways you will never know and made me a better author. This series—this *book*—would be nothing without your encouragement, without your demand to see Hades's side of this entire world. It would be nothing without your love, and I will love *you* endlessly for it.

Now, as you are likely used to, I'm going to go into a lot of what inspired *Chaos*. I always appreciate those of you who stick around to read this entire thing, because the research aspect of my books is one of my favorite things, and this one has a lot.

As mentioned before, I always knew I'd have to have a second Titanomachy. I spoke about this at the end of *A Touch of Malice* and the way the gods tend to repeat cycles—the primordials were overthrown by the Titans (technically, it's Cronos overthrowing his father, Uranus), and then the Titans were overthrown by the Olympians, each one beginning with castration, which we saw in *Malice* when Hecate decides to punish Zeus.

I like this as a start to Zeus's downfall because it also marks a change in how the cycle repeats. Instead of having a god who is vying for the throne perform the procedure, it is Hecate. It is likely one of the reasons Zeus doesn't think twice about it marking the end of his reign and also because he has managed to avoid any prophecy predicting his downfall, which is another cycle that repeats throughout myth.

When Zeus learned his first wife, Metis, would bear two children, one of whom would overthrow him, he tricked her into turning into a fly and swallowed her. Zeus decided to marry Thetis, a nymph and goddess of water, to Peleus once it was predicted that she would have a son greater than his father (this was the case whether she bore a son to him or Poseidon).

I started to feel like at some point, this prophecy was gunning for the King of the Gods, and there would come a time when he would not be able to avoid it, which meant that the fate that befell his father and his grandfather would come for him and inevitably lead to another Titanomachy.

Most of what we know about the battle between the Titans and the Olympians comes from *Theogony*, a work by Hesiod that is essentially a creation myth and includes basically the beginning and end of the Titanomachy. Because the actual ten-year battle between the Titans and the Olympians is not described in detail, I drew inspiration from another ten-year battle, the Trojan War.

The Trojan War

During the Trojan War, Zeus was mostly neutral, believing that the battle would help depopulate the earth. He takes a similar stance throughout this series, preferring not to intervene even when the other gods call him to do so. Hera was invested, especially because she felt slighted by the Trojans, but Zeus forbade the gods from intervening, so Hera decided to seduce him with the help of Hypnos, which freed the gods to disobey his orders.

Hera enacts the same plan in *Chaos*, and the only exception is that when he is finally asleep, she orders that Zeus is to be hung in the sky, which she sees as revenge for when he had done the same to her after she attempted to overthrow him previously.

Another element I added to *Chaos* was the funeral games for Adonis, which were common across many cultures. These were a particular reference to the games held for Patroclus during the Trojan War. At the start, there is usually chariot racing, but since I already had a scene in *Malice* with a chariot race, I decided to reference this by having the gods arrive to the event on chariots.

The raid of the temples and killing of the priests and priestesses is a reference to when Achilles raided a city and captured a priestess of Apollo, who begged the god to free her. Apollo retaliated against Achilles and his men by shooting a plague arrow into animals, men, women, and children. In *Chaos*, I have Artemis shoot the first arrow to start the first battle after the priestesses are killed.

The Labors of Heracles

There are a few references to the Labors of Heracles in the labyrinth. They include the slaying of the Nemean lion, the Erymanthian boar, and the Cretan bull. Of the three, the Cretan bull was actually killed by Theseus in myth. I felt like including these challenges in the labyrinth connected nicely to *A Game of Retribution*, and their appearance further entwined Hera's involvement with Theseus. Hera hated Heracles and drove him mad, causing him to murder his wife and children, which eventually led to the labors.

There are details about the Nemean lion from myth, like its sword-like claws and its rancid breath. The way Hades kills the lion is also how the lion was killed by Heracles. Heracles also skinned the lion using its own sharp claws.

Hermes appearing as a baby in the labyrinth is just a reference to a few myths that include baby Hermes (like one where he steals Apollo's cattle).

Jason and the Argonauts

The entire saga of the Golden Fleece was a reference to the challenges Jason faced while retrieving the fleece.

When the Argonauts arrived on Ares's island, they were chased by birds with arrow-like feathers. They are said to be similar to the Stymphalian birds, but I preferred to make them a smaller version of that since I also used them earlier in the book during the labyrinth scene. Additionally, the Argonauts chased them away with noise by beating on their shields with their weapons, so I thought having Hermes scream would be both relevant and hilarious.

The one element I did not use from Jason and the Argonauts is the fire-breathing bulls of Hephaestus. I mention this because the Cretan bull in the labyrinth is wearing bronze armor. This is a reference to Hephaestus's bronze bulls, but they are not the same.

Smaller References

When Hades was in the labyrinth, Theseus challenged him to rebuild the labyrinth walls. This is a reference to *The Aeneid*. When Aeneas flees Troy to found Rome, he stops in Carthage and helps build the walls around the city that Rome will later destroy.

Galanthis was a servant or friend (given the myth) of Alcmene, Heracles's mother. She is basically how Heracles was able to be born despite Hera's wishes, and because of this, she was punished by being turned into a cat or a weasel. In *Chaos*, I made her into a eudaimon, which is just a guiding spirit much like Charon. Eudaimons are good spirits and are said to sometimes be deified heroes. There isn't really any specific explanation of what they looked like, but some were depicted as serpents, so I felt like it was valid that one might took like a cat.

Hermes tells Hades and Persephone that Ares owes him a favor from ancient times. Hermes is referencing a time when he saved Ares from being trapped in a bronze jar by two giants.

There are many more, but I think I'll stop there.

For those of you who are sad that this saga is over, I am a firm believer that all good things come to an end, but don't worry. I'll be back with Aphrodite and Hephaestus.

Much love,
Scarlett